THE DEAD OF AUTUMN

THE DEAD OF AUTUMN

A PIPER BLACKWELL MYSTERY

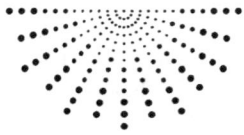

JEAN RABE

Boone Street Press

The Dead of Autumn
A Piper Blackwell Mystery
Jean Rabe

Boone Street Press

Boone Street Press
Illinois

Cover design by Juan Villar Padron

Interior design by John G. Hartness

Editing by Christine Verstraete and Janet Deaver-Pack

Boone Street Press

First Boone Street Press Edition: May 2022

Name: Rabe, Jean, author

Title: The Dead of Autumn, a Piper Blackwell Mystery / Jean Rabe

Description: First Edition. Boone Street Press

Identifiers: ISBN 13: 978-1-7325267-4-7

Printed in the United States of America

Praise for *The Dead of Winter*

Mystery just got a little less cozy in THE DEAD OF WINTER.
 — *New York Times* and *USA Today* bestselling author Steven Savile

Jean Rabe delivers a suspenseful morsel that not only celebrates the Yuletide season, but also keeps you up at night with a well-crafted mystery. THE DEAD OF WINTER is chilling indeed!
 — Raymond Benson, *New York Times* bestselling author

THE DEAD OF WINTER was a blast—lots of fun to read! Jean Rabe's characters come to life through the written word, and it takes a real writing talent to accomplish this feat.
 — Denise Dietz, *USA Today* bestselling author

Praise for *The Dead of Night*

Jean Rabe always manages to surprise and never fails to deliver the goods! THE DEAD OF NIGHT has plenty of twists and turns. Highly recommended!

— Jonathan Maberry, *New York Times* bestselling author

Jean Rabe writes the perfect mystery! I was kept guessing about *everything* to the very last word. Great characters. The girl can write!

— *New York Times* bestselling author Faith Hunter, writing as Gwen Hunter

In THE DEAD OF NIGHT, Jean Rabe gives us another compelling Piper Blackwell mystery. After a clandestine meeting with a grizzled WWII veteran "Mark the Shark," also known as "Mr. Conspiracy," Piper stumbles, literally, over the bones of a child. Rabe weaves Piper's investigations of this long-cold case and the high-tech theft of an old man's earnings into a thoroughly satisfying and complex novel with deeply realized characters and beautifully vivid writing.

— Jaden Terrell, Shamus Award nominee and internationally published author of the Jared McKean Mysteries

Praise for *The Dead of Summer*

Just when you think you've read the best from author Jean Rabe, she throws the thrill ride of a lifetime into her latest mystery. THE DEAD OF SUMMER starts with a bang, a scrunch, a twist, and screams... lots and lots of screams. The book hooks you from the start.

— Mary Cunningham, author of the Andi Anna Jones Mysteries

Jean Rabe immerses you in the sights, sounds, and smells of summer in rural Indiana, as she subtly weaves characters, clues, and high-speed action into a satisfying criminal confection worthy of a blue ribbon as Best Summer Mystery. Not quite a cozy, but a helluva whodunnit.

— Donald J. Bingle, author of the Dick Thornby Spy Thriller series

Sheriff Piper Blackwell's third outing has her getting on the wrong side of some very bad dudes in a murder investigation. The best thing about Rabe's series is not only her ability to spin a good yarn, but to write such believable and interesting characters that her books are like visiting old friends. They're all back in this newest one, and it'll keep you turning the pages far past your bedtime. Don't miss it.

— Michael A. Black, author of *Blood Trails*, *Legends of the West*, and *Dying Art* and *Stealth Assassins* in the Executioner series (as Don Pendleton)

Praise for *The Dead of Jerusalem Ridge*

Piper Blackwell is a smart and capable small-town sheriff, a thoroughly modern woman who leads a colorful cast of characters in this entertaining read. Well-crafted and suspenseful, THE DEAD OF JERUSALEM RIDGE adroitly threads the needle between Cozy, Procedural, and Action-Thriller. Jean Rabe's fans——both old and new ——won't want to miss this one.

—— Baron R. Birtcher, multi-award winner, and LA Times Best-selling author

Rabe once again mixes the most colorful parts of a cozy mystery with the grittiness of suspense in THE DEAD OF JERUSALEM RIDGE, launching Piper Blackwell into the most personal, and potentially heartbreaking, intrigue of her career. Don't start this story if you need to be up early the next morning!

——Janet Walden-West, GRW Maggie winner and author of The South Beach series

THE DEAD OF JERUSALEM RIDGE had me hooked from page 1. The characters were so real it felt like they could walk right off the page. Warning, once you start it's next to impossible to stop reading until you reach the perfectly-crafted ending.

——Angela Crook, author of *Fat Chance* and *Chasing Navah*

This one's for
Steve Rouse, Greg Schwartz, Carol Clarkson,
Warren Langlois, Janet Deaver-Pack, Jerry Wayne,
Thomas Harrison, Sue Paul, Jeremy Vosberg, Paul Baughman, and
Brenda Arbogast
who donated to my Hudson's Halfway Home birthday fundraiser.
Thank you.

Hudson's Halfway Home, a special-needs dog rescue,
was founded by the most marvelous Jeni Hudson of Decatur, IL.
Missy the Bossy Terrier, Hunny the Pug, and Jolly the Pembroke Welsh Corgi
are Hudson alumni who share my office and my heart.

Piper and I are especially fond of dogs.

CHAPTER ONE

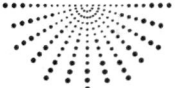

5:30 P.M. SATURDAY, OCT 31ST

Teal organza wings embellished with silvery clock gears shimmered strangely beautiful in the setting sun. They were attached to the shoulders of a woman lying face-down in a ditch, a quarrel protruding from her neck, the blood that had streamed from the wound still wet. Another quarrel was lodged in the middle of her back. Sheriff Piper Blackwell guessed the woman was roughly her height, a little over five feet.

The breeze gusted, ruffling the wings just enough that Piper could see the deceased wore skimpy short-shorts covered in green sequins matching the lone sequined tennis shoe on her right foot. The left foot was bare and tangled in coarse fescue.

A Halloween costume, obviously. Piper had spotted several children trick-or-treating on her drive here and had stopped to lecture a pint-sized Superman who'd darted in front of her Explorer.

The farmhouses on this county road sat a half-mile to a mile apart. The woman might have been going to one of them, attending a party perhaps; Piper would check on that in a little while. She wanted to ease the victim over, get a look at her face, find some identification, but she wouldn't disturb the body until after the coroner arrived.

"Dr. Neufeld said she'd be about twenty minutes," said Detective

Basil Meredith. He had a deep, rich voice. At six-feet-tall with espresso brown skin, Basil didn't go unnoticed in mostly white Spencer County. "Said she didn't appreciate being pulled from her cocktail hour."

Piper edged into the ditch and turned on her body cam. Basil did the same. He clicked away with the department's camera, a recently purchased Canon Rebel XT that would yield high quality digital photos.

She picked a path around the woman, carefully bending the tall grass, looking for a purse or cell phone. Nothing. Maybe they were under the body. Piper took her time, mindful of the slope, as she was a little off-balance with her left arm still in a sling. She'd badly broken the arm in September on Jerusalem Ridge, and pins and a titanium rod now held it together. Another few weeks or so, the doctor said, before it would be fully healed. Until then she had restricted duty: no pushing, pulling, or lifting.

"Seen a lot of death," Basil observed.

Piper knew he referred to his years with the Chicago Police Department's Gang and Narcotics Division. She'd seen a lot of death, too, from her tours in the Middle East.

"But I've never seen a fairy killed by arrows, Sheriff Blackwell. A first for me."

"For me too," Piper returned. "But they're quarrels, bolts from a crossbow. I used to hunt with my dad. There's a difference."

"Who the hell would shoot Tinker Bell?" Basil mused.

The victim's skin appeared smooth and tanned, the arms toned. Thin, delicate fingers sported gaudy rings. Her coppery-red hair was fashioned in an up-do, a diminutive ivory bedazzled top hat perched on the side with pheasant feathers attached to it. Piper really wanted to turn her over and get a better look.

"Let's talk to the man who found her." Piper started out of the ditch, and the detective extended a hand to help her. She whispered, "Not how I'd planned to spend Halloween, Basil."

"I take it you had a bowl of candy ready by the front door."

"Oh yeah," she replied. "More than necessary probably. Nang's stuck with treat duty."

Piper had grabbed only the good stuff for her first Halloween in Hatfield—full-sized Milky Way bars, packets of cookies, and boxes of crayons. The entire population of her dinkburg was eight hundred, so not all that many kids were likely to come by. Still, those who did would skip away happy. She was disappointed she wouldn't be there to see them.

"Esme's taking our kids through the neighborhood. Promised to email me pictures." Basil glanced at his watch. "Probably leaving in a half-hour. Shaya picked a Ruth Bader Ginsberg costume from Walmart across the river. She doesn't know who Ginsberg was, but she liked the black robes and lace collar. Jelani is SpongeBob. I hate that cartoon. He looked cute, though."

"Nice weather for trick-or-treating," Piper said.

It was seventy, a few degrees above normal for the end of October in southern Indiana. She pointed across the road to a man in knee-length shorts and a Colts t-shirt, sweat stains evident around his neck and armpits. His eggshell white bicycle with BIANCHI in bold type on the frame leaned against the side of her Explorer. The man seemed intent on his cell phone, head down like he was praying to it. Piper took another look at the girl in the ditch and then headed toward him, her feet crunching against the gravel.

He looked up. "I could tell she was dead, Sheriff, didn't touch her or anything. I watch CSI—the old reruns, not the new version. I know not to touch anything. But I called 9-1-1 right away." He thumbed a button on his cell phone and put it in a side pocket. "I'll admit I took a picture of her." A pause. "To show my wife. Otherwise, Ginny'll never believe I found a body on a ride. A real dead body. It being Halloween, I first thought maybe someone stuck a mannequin in the ditch ... to scare folks. Wouldn't spook many, though. Not much traffic out here. Not many houses. A waste of a good scare, you know. Besides, when I took a good look, I could tell it wasn't a mannequin. In fact—"

Piper cut him off, figuring he'd keep babbling out of nervousness. Or maybe he was just a talker. She swiveled so her back was to the

Explorer and the man had to turn to face her. That way she could keep an eye on the ditch with the body and he wouldn't be looking at it. "And you are—"

"Rodney. Rodney Rhimer. I live down the road, the gray farmhouse. I'm not a farmer. I lease my land to the Duncans for that. They plant soybeans. Well, this past year it was soybeans. I run a used car lot in Rockport."

"Rhimer's Reasonable Autos," Basil put in. "That lot?"

"Sure. That's my lot. And if you're ever looking for a—"

"About the body, Mr. Rhimer."

"Just Rodney, Sheriff. My dad's still living. He's over in Henderson. He's Mr. Rhimer. Just call me Rodney."

"Rodney," Piper said. She put him around forty, midway between chunky and muscular. His hair was brown and curly, cut short on the top and sides, a mullet in the back. Hints of gray along his temples, his face ruddy. There was stubble on his chin, not like he was trying to grow a beard, more like he just hadn't bothered to shave today.

"You were riding along the road," Basil interjected. "Going east when you saw her."

"Yeah. I do a circuit. Ten miles total, every other day or so. I need the exercise. I don't know what made me look into the ditch over there. I usually keep my eyes on the road in front of me. But for whatever reason I saw something flapping, all shiny. I got close and saw those wings fluttering. Like a fairy princess. Maybe God told me to look in the ditch. Maybe God wanted her found before the coyotes could get her." He sucked in a deep breath. "Looks like somebody shot her with arrows. Who'd go and do that? Arrows, damn."

Piper did not correct him.

"I don't know who she is … was. You were going to ask me that, right?"

Basil nodded.

"Well, from the back she doesn't look familiar. If you flip her over so I can see her face, she might look familiar then. Small county, a lot of folks know a lot of folks. But from the back, can't say that I—"

"Mr. Rhimer," Basil began.

"Rodney. Call me Rodney."

"Rodney," Basil said. "Did you notice people out during your ride?"

"Don't get trick-or-treaters on this road. Never have, and I've lived here twelve years. Houses are too far apart."

"What about cars?" Basil asked. "Did you see many cars on your ride?"

"Cars? Yeah. Saw some cars, more than usual, actually. Like it was rush hour. Typically, not much traffic on this old road."

Piper hadn't seen a car drive by since they'd arrived.

"The cars," Basil pressed. "Tell us about the cars you saw."

"I know cars. Saw four. And four's a lot in a stretch around here. The best was a Rambler, probably early 1960s. I'd guess 1962. Sweet cherry of a piece. Robin's egg blue. A jeep, recent model looked to me, pumpkin orange. Damn ugly color. Something in that color would sit on my lot a long time unless it was cheap. There was a silver Hyundai Sonata, and that was likely eight to ten years old by the body, most likely ten. Sonata's a reliable car, you can keep them for a ton of miles before too many things start to go wrong. And a big, boxy Explorer like you folks drive. That wasn't a Sheriff's Department Explorer, though. At least I don't think it was. Maroon, rust on the side panels, dent in the front bumper, a crimp in the grille, easily twenty years old. You don't drive 'em that old, do you? No logos on the side."

Basil shook his head *no*. "You didn't see any people out, walking along the road? No hunters?"

"Nope. Only person is that dead girl over there." He shifted his weight from one foot to the other. "Are you going to flip her over?"

"In a while," Piper said.

"Your neighbors," Basil pressed. "Any of them having a Halloween party?"

"Not that I know of," Rodney said. "And we're all pretty far apart to be called neighbors. In any event, me and Ginny, we didn't get invited to a party. Halloween's a stupid thing to have a party about, don't you think? Just an excuse to dress silly and get drunk. Or if you're a kid to beg for candy that'll rot your teeth. An unhealthy holiday for every-one. No. No parties around here that I know of."

5

Basil edged closer. "You have a good eye for cars, Rodney. Remember any of the license plates?"

Rodney shook his head. "Just paid attention to the cars. I have a Rambler on my lot, from 1969, last year they made 'em. It was one of the end cars to roll off the assembly line in Kenosha, Wisconsin. Satin black paint, redone interior. Classic collector car. I want thirty-nine for her. I'm probably asking a little too much, but she's pretty special. I can afford to keep her in the showroom until the right buyer comes along."

Piper pulled a business card out of her pocket. "Please call us if you remember anything else, Rodney. We'll contact you later if we have more questions."

"Fine. And I'd sure like to know who that is ... was. And why'd somebody shoot her? I know its deer season for bows right now, and for turkeys until tomorrow. I used to hunt turkeys with my brother. I can't see somebody mistaking her for a turkey or a deer. She looks like a fairy, like—"

"Thank you, Rodney," Piper said. "We'll be in touch."

"Guess that means you'd like me to leave," he said.

"Public road," Basil said. "You can stay, but don't get in the way."

Rodney shrugged. "I better head home. Ginny'll wonder why I'm off my time." He put his helmet on, got on the bike, peered across into the ditch, and pedaled away.

***

D r. Annie Neufeld arrived minutes later in a red Toyota Camry driven by her wife, who had painted her face green and sported a black hat. They parked behind Sheriff Blackwell's Explorer.

Neufeld's gray-brown hair was in pigtails tied with blue gingham ribbon that matched her flared-skirt jumper. Beneath that was a short-sleeved white blouse.

"Dorothy," she said, pointing to her outfit. "From the Wizard of Oz. Bebe's the Wicked Witch of the West."

Piper thought the witch ensemble appropriate, as her run-ins with the defense attorney had not been pleasant. She was thankful Bebe didn't get out of the car.

"I'll go home and change, get my kit and van, after I see the body." Neufeld scowled, let out a huffing breath, and added: "Damn inconvenient death. I was having a good time, Piper. Really. I haven't been to a party in months."

Piper almost apologized, but kept the words in.

Neufeld pointed to the camera in Basil's hand. "That looks new."

"It is," he said.

She walked past him, her ruby red slippers crunching the gravel, whistling when she gazed at the body. "Not something you see every day. I think those are quarrels. Like from a crossbow."

"They are," Piper said, joining her.

"Yep. Definitely not something you see every day. It is hunting season," Neufeld said as she stepped into the ditch.

"For turkey and deer," Piper replied.

Basil added, "Not for fairies."

After a few minutes, Neufeld crossed her arms and stared at Piper. "Tink is fresh. Dead an hour, if that. Less than two since there's no trace of rigor. I'll take some temps when I come back with the van, but my estimate here will stand."

"I want to turn her over, Dr. Neufeld, get a look at her face. We need to—"

"I don't want her on her back, Sheriff. Don't want to move the quarrels, keep them in place until the autopsy. I don't want the entry wounds distorted. But I can ease her on her side—carefully—so Basil can get some pictures. You need the face, right, to—"

"That would be helpful," Piper cut in. "We need to identify her as soon as possible, contact relatives, and—"

"—and start your investigation so you can find out which one of Captain Hook's sick son of a bitch pirates slew Tinker Bell," Neufeld finished. The coroner knelt on one side of the body and gently levered it up. "Click quick and get your fingerprints. You can print the quarrels and anything else you want later."

Basil took a series of photos, including several close-ups of the face.

Piper saw no cell phone, purse, or wallet underneath the body.

"Less than two hours, you say," Piper said.

"I don't need my tools to tell me that," Neufeld returned. "And, really, I'm still guessing closer to one hour. Figuring the time it took for you to get here, call me, and then me showing up—"

"—the guy on the bike found her right after it happened." Basil pulled out the fingerprint kit. He stared at Piper. "I wasn't quite right, Sheriff, calling her Tinker Bell."

"Steampunkerbell," Piper said.

"Yeah, that's about it," Basil returned.

Piper studied the front of the costume before the coroner eased the body back onto its stomach.

The getup was impressively ornate—a green satin bustier embroidered with shiny black thread. Myriad gold beads were woven into clock gear images, and little lengths of silver chain looped along the bodice. Skull-shaped buttons stretched from an armpit to her hip, and where the bustier met the green sequined shorts a twist of gold chain bedecked with dangling keys served as a belt. A lot of work had gone into the outfit. It had probably been expensive.

Her makeup was precise and whimsical, with thick curled lashes and teal eyeshadow, mint-green lipstick, sparkling rouge, and sequins glued on her eyebrows. Clock gears were big hoop earrings, and a pocket watch hung from a black velvet choker necklace.

"Young," Piper said. "The makeup, costume, make it difficult to guess an exact age. But I'd say a teenager."

"Twelve going on twenty," Basil said softly.

Piper knew that for all her remaining years, she would see the teen's face. She had been going to a Halloween party; no one puts that much effort into her appearance without a special destination in mind. She was going to have fun, maybe dance, flirt with the boys … her risqué take on the fairy definitely suggested the latter. It was supposed to be a singular night, magical.

"A teenager," Piper repeated.

"Who didn't get enough years on the planet," Neufeld pronounced, rising. "Leave her be. I'm going for my van, and then I'll take her away."

"Sun's almost down. We're losing light," Basil said. He turned on a flashlight and aimed the beam at the ground.

They walked along the road past where Steampunkerbell had been killed.

A white Chevy Impala rumbled past, the driver slowing to take a look. It had been the only car they'd noted since arriving on the scene. A few minutes later a blue Ford F-150 drove in the opposite direction, the driver waving and continuing on a little too fast for the posted limit.

"No visible tracks," Basil noted. "At least not here. Tink might have come this way and we can't see it because the grass is so thick. Maybe we need to get the dog." The detective paused and looked back toward where they'd found the body. "But judging by how she landed in the ditch, she had to have come from this direction." A pause. "Or maybe she was thrown out of a car."

Piper shuddered. "Maybe one of the cars Mr. Rhimer saw." They'd be doing a vehicle search for the four cars he'd mentioned, pulling up license numbers and owners of those makes and models, narrow it down; it would take a while.

"Maybe." Basil kept going with the flashlight.

She wondered if it had been fast, the death. Piper would ask Dr. Neufeld about it later. More, Piper wondered why someone would kill the teen. And with quarrels? An unusual murder weapon. It couldn't have been a hunter's accident, could it? The girl had been dressed too flashy to be mistaken for a deer, too tall to be mistaken for a turkey.

"What the hell, Basil?" Piper said, stopping.

"Yeah, exactly. What the hell." The beam of his flashlight held on a green-sequined tennis shoe in the tall grass. The light played around it, circling out, stopping on a tread mark where the edge of the gravel road gave way to a strip of dirt too narrow to be considered a shoulder. It had rained this morning, leaving the ground soft enough to hold the image.

"And there's a print from a tennis shoe." Piper pointed. "And another." The prints were in the dirt leading away from the tire mark. The prints stopped when the thick grass claimed the ditch. Piper could see where clumps of grass had been disturbed near the discarded glimmering shoe.

"Looks like a vehicle swerved off the road, left a trace, then returned to the road. Too near the shoe to be coincidence," Basil said. He took pictures of the shoe, the few prints, and the tread mark. "Did she jump out of the car? Get tossed out? Either case, she was alive here. Lost her shoe there, and then my guess ran. Got shot somewhere between this tread mark and where she landed. Shot by someone in a field? An accident? Shot by someone in a vehicle she got out of? Deliberate?" He swept the light around. "I'd say deliberate. Hell of a thing."

Piper fixed her gaze on the shoe. What was it Rodney Rhimer had called Halloween?

An unhealthy holiday.

"Yeah, a hell of a thing," she agreed.

CHAPTER TWO

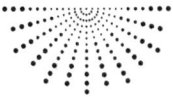

6:30 P.M.

Millie stared at the body face-down in the middle of the yard. A dagger protruded from between its shoulder blades, a vivid red stain stark against the white hoodie. The tips of its mud-caked boots rested on the edge of a concrete sidewalk that curved from the driveway to a front door festooned with cornstalks and orange ribbons. Three large jack-o-lanterns glowed on the stoop.

All of it eerily illuminated by a spotlight perched near the street and aimed this way.

Millie had almost called the coroner when she pulled up to the Fulda residence. Fortunately, she took a closer look before keying the radio. She figured if she had summoned Dr. Neufeld that would have made her the butt of endless jokes in the Spencer County Sheriff's Department, where she'd been working as a deputy for the past six months.

The body had straw protruding from slits in the blue jeans.

Across the street a half-dozen children skittered along the curb, bulging sacks in hand. Millie noted Raggedy Ann, a cowboy, Shrek, an impressive-looking Mandalorian, the Flash, and Cinderella. A few houses down a boy dressed as a pickle waddled with an adult, and just beyond them Princess Leia strolled with an astronaut. Millie remembered wearing a Princess Leia outfit when she was five-years-old. She was heading toward twenty-five now.

The block glowed with front porch lights. It was festive and spooky at the same time. The costumed kids chattered, giggled, and Cinderella pointed at Millie and waved, but they stayed on the other side of the street.

Sent here by the dispatcher, Millie had parked her Explorer in the driveway. The 9-1-1 call had come from a hysterical passing motorist.

From the street the body looked realistic; she understood why someone called.

Millie took a picture of the display with her cell phone and was halfway up the walk when the door opened.

"You're scaring the kids away," grumbled a wizard who came out onto the stoop, box of candy in his left hand, the fingers of his right wrapped around a tall, gnarled staff that was heavily lacquered.

She'd seen all the *Lord of the Rings* movies, and knew this was Gandalf, the gray version, complete with torso-length white beard and long white hair. Hard to tell how old the man actually was given the makeup. The dispatcher had said the homeowner's name was Harrold Walthrop, but provided no other information about him.

"Got a call about the body in your yard, Mr. Walthrop," Millie said.

Across the street a trio of scary-looking clowns reminiscent of Stephen King's "It" laughed and gestured her way. One of them held a large red helium-filled balloon.

"It's been out there since Tuesday," Gandalf replied. "Not a real knife. Just a decoration."

"I see that," Millie said.

Gandalf growled at her. "It's a dummy, straw. A dummy. I add some fresh stuffing and put it out every year. Ain't had the police come before. It's just a dummy."

Millie did not correct him that she was with the sheriff's department. Only two cities in Spencer County were large enough to have their own police departments—Rockport and Santa Claus.

"It looks pretty real from the street."

Gandalf's chest puffed out. "I hope so. That's the point."

There was nothing criminal to charge him with. Perhaps the village had some covenant that might apply, but that would be civil in nature, not her problem. Millie stood there another few minutes, looking over her shoulder at the creepy clown trio. The tallest set down his treat bag, raised his hands, clawed at the air, and screeched.

Millie let out a long sigh. Her grandfather was the chief deputy, and he was on vacation. He'd told her before he and his wife left for Pigeon Forge, Tennessee, that Halloween was "weird to work," and that he usually took time off then to avoid the odd calls. She intended to email him a picture of the body in Gandalf's front yard.

"Sometimes I move it around," Gandalf said. He leaned on his staff and ambled down the few steps, closing the distance to her. He smelled strongly of sweet-spicy aftershave, like he'd upended the bottle over his wizard robes. "Tuesday it was closer to the street. I sit out on my stoop with coffee after breakfast, dinner, watch the reactions from the passersby, the dog walkers, people in their cars, you know. Wednesday, I moved it close to the driveway. Young guy stomped on the brakes. I heard 'em squeal. He jumped out of his car and ran up, was going to give it mouth-to-mouth or something. Then he saw me sitting up there on the stoop, realized it was a dummy, and gave me one of them air high-fives. Thursday, I moved him in front of the evergreen. Tonight, I put him right in the middle and shined the light on him."

Millie was thinking maybe she could come up with a public nuisance citing. She was taking online law courses, with the intent of being a lawyer "down the road." No, she couldn't even think of an applicable nuisance charge. She had to admit it was a well-done Halloween decoration, and didn't think he should catch grief for it.

"Quite a few people stop and gape," he continued. "Takes 'em a little looksee to figure out it's a dummy. Sometimes I change the shirt on him. Once they realize it's not real … well, it's just hilarious. The kids … the kids know. They always know, pay it no never mind."

Millie rocked forward on the balls of her feet.

"I'm going to take him in tomorrow morning," Gandalf said. "Clean him up. Get him ready."

"Ready for what?"

"For Christmas! I dress him as Santa for Christmas. Let him sit in that chair on the stoop. Sometimes I let him be the Easter Bunny." He held out his box of candy. "Take a piece or two, and then get out of my driveway. You're scaring the kids, I say. I bought a lot of candy and I aim to pass it out. I'm diabetic, can't keep the stuff in the house. I need to give it all away so I won't be tempted."

Millie selected two bite-size Butterfingers.

"There you go," Gandalf concluded. "You have a happy Halloween."

Millie retreated to her Explorer, where the dispatcher gave her directions to the next call-out.

Across the street a big red balloon bobbed in the dead tree branches.

CHAPTER THREE

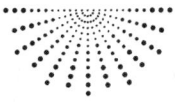

7 P.M.

Dead.

Too damn pretty and way too young to be dead, Teegan thought as she looked at the photo Sheriff Piper Blackwell had emailed her. The makeup, hair, sequins, so well decorated for the night. Teegan wondered if the coroner could conduct the autopsy without ruining all the sparkles. The girl had gone to a lot of effort to look like that.

Too much work to be washed away on a stainless-steel table in the basement of a hospital. She should be buried in all her glittery glory.

"You would've won all the costume contests for certain."

Teegan had taken Rodney Rhimer's 9-1-1 call. "Somebody's dead, in a ditch," he'd said. "It's horrible. Come quick."

She'd hoped it had been a prank. Teegan answered a lot of prank calls on Halloween, and most of them had a fun element.

Way too young.

Creepy.

Evil.

Teegan shivered and glanced away from the screen. She'd heard the sheriff call the girl Steampunkerbell. Teegan liked steampunk styles, almost as much as goth. Teegan would have loved a Halloween costume like that in her earlier, skinnier years.

"I'm supposed to help find out who you are ... were ... pretty girl."

No active missing person reports in the county fit. But the girl probably hadn't been missing long enough for someone to have noticed. She wouldn't go unidentified long, Teegan knew. A girl like that had people, friends and relatives, and they would be looking for her when the night ended and she didn't come home.

But Piper wanted her identified ASAP and had tasked Teegan with checking high school yearbooks and online sources trying to put a name to the face, as no ID was found at the scene.

No hits on fingerprints so far. The girl looked too innocent to have gotten in trouble with the law, too young for the military.

Teegan guessed the girl was fourteen, fifteen ... somewhere in there.

She could use some help.

"It's an odd night." Teegan called Zeke, the first-shift dispatcher. "Peculiar stuff. Weird 9-1-1s. Always strange calls on Halloween, which is why I like to work it. And—" she paused for dramatic effect. "Tonight, we have a murder."

"Murder? You sure it's a murder?"

"Well, I heard them mention it might be a hunting accident, but it sounds like Sheriff Blackwell thinks it's a murder."

"Who got killed?"

Zeke sounded out of breath, and Teegan was curious why. "I don't know. We don't know. You busy, Zeke? Got company? Did I interrupt something? Sounds like you're—"

"I'm on my bike, riding home. I was at Nang's garage working on my car."

"How about you detour over to the department? I'll order Chinese from the delivery service. My treat. I could use an extra pair of eyes on this maybe-a-hunting-accident-but-more-likely-a-murder-thing. High school yearbooks."

"Yearbooks? Someone young?"

"Yeah, Zeke. Too young."

"I'm on my way."

The Spencer County Sheriff's Department had fourteen deputies and one detective—Basil. They worked in three shifts of four days on, two off, rotating schedules so no one was stuck on the night shift forever. With the chief deputy on vacation, Millie and Diego responding to calls, and Piper and Basil working this murder, only one deputy was in the office. That was Rocco, and he was busy with reports and keeping an eye on a trio of drunks that had just been booked. Besides, Teegan wasn't especially fond of Rocco's been-here-too-many-years-should-go-do-something-else attitude.

Teegan figured Zeke wouldn't mind helping, as he'd made it clear that when he hit the magical age of twenty-one in less than two years, he intended to make deputy.

"I want sweet and sour chicken and an egg roll," Zeke replied. "No, make that three egg rolls."

Sure, a big order since I'm buying. "Pedal fast," Teegan said, "and you should get here about the same time as dinner."

She fielded another 9-1-1 call, handed it off to Rockport Police, and went for the first stack of yearbooks. She preferred paper and would leave the computer search to Zeke the Geek.

"Teegan, wow. What did you do?" It was more of an exclamation than a question. Zeke stood open-mouthed in front of Teegan's desk. Wearing knee-length faded jean shorts and a long-sleeve LA Rams t-shirt, grease smudges attested to his story of working in Nang's garage. He brought his bicycle in and leaned it against the wall and ran a hand over the top of his head, hair cut in a severe military style. "What. Did. You. Do?"

Teegan pointed to the breakroom, where she'd set up a spare laptop.

"What did I do, Zeke? I was on vacation last week."

"Yeah, I know," Zeke said. "I caught a couple of double shifts because of it. Not complaining. I always need money. But what—"

17

"What did I do? A hairdo. That's what I did. I had my hair done."

"Yeah, I guess. Double wow."

Teegan didn't know if that was a compliment. She was forty-five and usually dressed like a teenager, previously resembling Morticia Addams because of her pale complexion, long black hair, and heavy eyeliner. Except she'd ditched the black hair during her days off.

It felt weird, Zeke staring at her like that. Rocco had stared too. Good thing the chief deputy was on vacation, he was quick with disparaging comments about her piercings and tattoos and overall appearance. He'd say something worse than: "What did you do?"

"I needed a change," she said, again pointing to the laptop visible through the doorway to the breakroom. "I went to the salon inside Walmart across the river. This guy put color remover in my hair ... cost me seventy bucks and two hours on my rump in an uncomfortable chair. Then I picked out this shade after he cut off a few inches. The shade was another fifty."

"A lot of inches cut," Zeke said, still staring.

"Life's short, Zeke, as our murder victim points out."

"And so's your hair."

Teegan's new hairstyle: a layered bob that ended at her jawline and nape of her neck. The inky black had been replaced by—

"The stylist called it spiced plum."

"I like it." Zeke grinned. "Has Oren—"

"He hasn't seen it. He's on vacation as of today. And I like it too." Teegan's neck tattoos were more visible with the short style, and it easily showed all the ear piercings. The hair color matched the purple flowers in a vine tattoo that ran from her right shoulder to her wrist.

"Teegan, this murder victim—"

The delivery man appeared with a large sack. The scents of oyster sauce, garlic, green onion, and ginger filled the department. Teegan breathed deep and handed over a nice tip.

"Cool costume," the delivery man told her on his way out.

Teegan frowned. She wasn't wearing a costume. She had on a short-sleeve black blouse, with a V neck that showed off three necklaces of varying lengths, a simple silver chain with a skull charm on it, a string of polished turquoise chips, and a wire-wrapped chunk of glass she'd fused in her kiln and that dangled from a braided leather cord. She'd completed her look with a small hoop in her nose, a brass ball stud beneath her lip that matched the one in her tongue, and a little barbell in her left eyebrow.

"The victim's picture is on the screen. You wanna check the online yearbook photos?"

"Sure." Zeke grabbed his share of the Chinese and retreated to the breakroom.

Teegan fielded another call. "9-1-1, what is the—"

"It's dreadful, ridiculous," the caller replied. "It's disrespectful, and something must be done."

Teegan smiled, took a breath, and reached for some chopsticks. It was another odd call; she'd happily listen. Maybe there was an emergency attached. But it sounded more like it would be amusing.

"There are a dozen crosses and tombstones in my neighbor's front yard. More than a dozen probably. He put them out this afternoon. Draped fake webs from his trees. When it got dark, he put a spotlight on everything. He's having a Halloween party over there. The music is loud. 'Monster Mash,' 'Thriller,' 'Werewolves of London,' an endless loop."

Teegan checked the caller's location—Grandview—definitely a Spencer County Sheriff call. She waited, listening to the woman's rant, and watched the switchboard, sampled her shrimp fried rice and found it delicious. No other incoming calls at the moment.

"I can have a deputy swing by and tell them to turn the music down," Teegan said. She figured that would mollify the woman.

"It's not the music that's the problem," the caller continued. "I don't mind the music. It's a good sound system. I kind of like the music."

"Then the problem is—"

"The tombstones! I just went over and took a closer look at his makeshift cemetery. He's got names on the stones. On all of them. One says, 'Here lies Miz Karen Blue, a fat grumpy old shrew.'" There was a sputtering sound. "Well, my name is Karen Blue, and I don't think it is an appropriate Halloween decoration. It's insulting.

19

Demeaning. 'A deep dirt nap for George Dunlap.' George lives next door, and he isn't dead. All the tombstones are offensive. I'm going over there with a baseball bat if you don't—"

Teegan immediately dispatched Diego to her address.

"A deputy will arrive in a few minutes, Ms. Blue." Teegan let the savory shrimp sauce linger on her tongue and wondered which homeowner was going to get arrested for disorderly conduct.

Another call, and this time Teegan pegged Millie to deal with it.

"Gotta love Halloween," Teegan said as she stepped away from her desk, taking her shrimp fried rice with her. She stood in the doorway of the breakroom, deftly eating with chopsticks. She was close enough to her desk that she could dart back if—when—another 9-1-1 call came in. "I like working Halloween, Zeke. Made sure the last day of my vacation was yesterday so I could take this shift. Working dispatch on Halloween is more entertaining than any party."

"It doesn't usually include murder, does it?" Zeke was intent on the laptop, drumming the fingers of his right hand on the mouse and eating an eggroll with his left. "This is awesome Chinese, by the way. You usually order pizza."

"Swore off pizza during my vacation."

"A lot of changes in your week off."

Teegan feasted on half the fried rice before answering. "Biggest change, Zeke ... I bought a house. I put in an offer middle of last month, and they finally accepted. It had been on the market a while. Closed on it the first of the week and finished moving in yesterday."

"A house?" Zeke looked up from the screen, and then stuffed the rest of the eggroll in his mouth, gesturing for her to explain.

"A big house on Little Church Road. Near Santa Claus. Technically *in* Santa Claus, I guess."

Zeke grabbed another eggroll. "I'm off tomorrow. I'd like to see it."

"I'm *not* off tomorrow. I come in at three. So how about you stop by at noon. I'll order sub sandwiches and strawberry cupcakes. You can bring one or two of those big bags of ice for my cooler. I go through them pretty fast. I don't have a refrigerator yet, and I'd like to chill some Diet Dr. Pepper."

"Sure. Ice. Bring ice." Zeke devoured the eggroll and kept talking.

"Didn't catch what you said, Zeke. Didn't your mom tell you not to talk with your mouth full—"

He swallowed. "I said, don't need to skim the yearbooks. I know the girl. The dead girl."

Teegan nearly dropped her fried rice carton.

"A friend of yours, Zeke? I'm so—"

"I wouldn't call Billie a friend. Just someone I knew in high school. She was a freshman when I was a senior. So that would put her a sophomore now. Maybe fifteen, probably sixteen. She looked a little familiar right away, but I had to think about it because of all the makeup. Billie's blonde, so maybe she's got a wig or colored her hair for Halloween."

"I need to call Piper." Teegan stepped to her desk. "Billie … what?"

"Billie Glempse," Zeke returned. "I knew her through the computer club I ran. She was bright, but easily distracted … like that cartoon dog that would go after tennis balls. She didn't make all the meetings. She was also on the JV cheer squad. I'll pull up her home address for you."

Teegan sat at her desk. She'd been hungry when she ordered the Chinese, selecting the fried rice, a half order of General Tso's, and Crab Rangoon. Having a name to go with that pretty face made her lose her appetite.

Sixteen. A high school sophomore. Too damn young to die. She activated the radio.

"Sheriff Blackwell," Teegan began, "we have a positive ID on Steampunkerbell."

CHAPTER FOUR

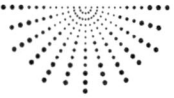

7:30 P.M.

The burly man wore oil-stained overalls and a hockey mask. He carried a chainsaw, a yellow wiffle bat, and to Millie looked wholly unimpressive as a costumed villain. The cardboard chainsaw, covered in peeling aluminum foil, wobbled, and so did he.

He was stumbling on a sidewalk outside the Red Baron tavern in Dale—the bartender had called the department out of concern that the man not drive and had taken his car keys. The drunk had tipped over a few chairs and a beer bottle, but caused no real damage.

"I'm sorry," he said to Millie when she pulled up. "I'm sorry I spilled the Bud."

Millie gave him a ride home rather than arrest him.

Drunk, check.

Disorderly, not terribly.

He was polite and thanked Millie for not taking him to jail, and he waited until he got out of her car before throwing up.

"I'm sorry," he repeated before staggering up the sidewalk to the front door where his stern-faced significant other waited in a ratty bathrobe. He dropped the wiffle bat, waggled his fingers at Millie, and went inside.

The peeping Tom turned out to be two kids dressed as zombies pestering their older neighbor, who didn't have his porch light on. No light meant no goodies were being passed out at a residence, and so kids were supposed to leave those homeowners alone.

Millie gave the walking dead a stern warning, confiscated their as-yet unused cans of spray paint, and went onto the next call.

She'd heard that Piper and Basil had caught a murder case, and she wondered how the investigation was going, who'd been killed ... how and why. There was little radio chatter about it—typical in the early stages, especially if relatives hadn't been notified. Millie had been briefly excited when she'd taken the call to Gandalf's house, thinking she had a murder, too.

Not that she wanted someone to be killed, but if there was going to be a murder case, it would be fine if she got a piece of it. Millie had degrees in criminal justice and communications, a good combination for her transition into law school. Oren, her grandfather, had helped pay her way through the university in Evansville, and maybe that's why she decided to take law courses part-time online, so she could work in the sheriff's department with him and do something to pay him back. Law enforcement seemed to be in the family blood. Her great-grandfather had been both a sheriff's deputy and a police officer. Her parents? Another story; they were more than three thousand miles apart, and she was barely in touch with either of them.

She would have liked to text her grandfather that she was working a murder case, something significant, not the nutjob call-outs of Halloween.

But maybe this next one might have more meat to it.

A short drive to Gentryville, and she pulled out her cell phone to take more pictures to send her grandfather.

It was impressive and awful. Millie wondered if there was some sort of contest in the county to see who could come up with a lawn display that would irk the most neighbors.

Bodies were strewn across the front and side lawns, some impaled on various objects. She got a good shot of a body dangling off the roof, and another of a wheelbarrow filled with body parts. Fake blood dripped everywhere.

Costumed kids skipped by, venturing up to the house, collecting candy, then scampering on to the next. A boy in mummy wrap flipped Millie the finger as he shuffled past.

Millie motioned to the man on the doorstep. He was dressed in cut-off blue jeans, fake blood—she was quick to determine—spattered on his white t-shirt.

"Haven't seen you before," he said. Holding a pail of bite-size candy bars in one hand, he stuck out the other hand for her to shake. "Last year deputies stopped by three times to make sure nothing was real. But you're new, right?"

"My first Halloween with the department," Millie said. "Amelia Isaakovitch. I go by Millie."

"Ethan Pendleton. My second Halloween in Spencer County. Used to live in Dallas," he replied. "East Dallas, actually. My displays were more elaborate there. I didn't bring everything with me when I moved. I used to do flying ghosts and fog machines, oversized snowmen at Christmas. Now I have to get spooky creative with mannequins and forty gallons of fake blood."

He stepped away from her for a moment to pass out candy to several knights and superheroes. Then he handed her a peanut butter cup. "These are the best. I'll eat all the leftovers of these." He nodded toward the wheelbarrow. "The neighbors know this is all fake. Must have been someone driving by who called you. Someone who doesn't appreciate Halloween."

"Must have been." Millie took another look around, unwrapped the candy and ate it. "Nice job, your yard. Looks disgusting." She didn't know what else to say. *Could maybe charge him with disturbing the peace, but no reason to be hard-assed about things on Halloween if no one was getting hurt,* she thought. "You're taking this down tomorrow, right?"

He laughed. It was a good, rich laugh, and she noticed that the smile reached his green eyes. "I'll *start* to take it down tomorrow. Have a deadline to make, that comes first. In fact, if I hadn't been under deadline pressure, I would have had even more decorations, maybe hosted a block party."

She cocked her head, curious. "Deadline?"

"I'm a greeting card designer. Promised to deliver a series for a new line by November first."

Millie's curiosity grew. "An artist? And you moved from East Dallas to Spencer County?"

He laughed again and gestured toward his house. The large Victorian had a sweeping front porch. Millie had driven by it during the day and remembered thinking someone should fix the shutters.

"This was my uncle's house and he willed it to me. A free house in Spencer County beat what I was paying to rent an apartment and art studio in Texas. I live upstairs, and my studio is down. I've found the temperatures more agreeable here. I don't melt in the summer."

"You have a nice night, Mr. Pendleton." She accepted another peanut butter cup and turned to go back to her Explorer. Maybe she could catch an update on the murder.

"Hey, Ms. Isaakovitch, would you be interested in lunch sometime?"

She looked over her shoulder. "Maybe."

"Ever been to Nang's Quick Stop in Fulda? I know it's a gas station, but—"

"Love the place," she returned. "Nang's a great chef."

"I'll call you," he said, as he passed out candy to Kermit, Miss Piggy, and Dracula. "I can get you through the sheriff's department, right?"

She nodded.

Her radio crackled; Basil was asking for her help with the murder investigation.

It was turning out to be an interesting night.

CHAPTER FIVE

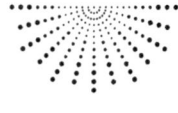

8 P.M.

The Glempse house on the north side of Rockport was a two-story Craftsman with an attached garage. Looked immaculate, as much as Piper could tell in the glow of front porch and window lights. Oblong plastic pumpkins lined the sidewalk. A life-sized scarecrow in a Garth Brooks t-shirt hung from the lamppost in the middle of the yard.

Piper stood at the curb where she'd parked her Explorer and watched a ghostbusting trio run up the front steps hollering "trick-or-treat trick-or-treat treat treat treat!" The voices echoed happily in the canyon of homes.

It really was a lovely night, still warm, toads chirping and sounding birdlike, children laughing. She wished the circumstances different, instead sharing Halloween with Nang.

"Trick-or-treat treat treat treat!" One of the ghostbusters did a little dance.

The door opened, and a man shouted: "Who you gonna call?"

"Ghostbusters!" the dancer answered.

"Treats for all the ghostbusters!" He had a tray with a mounded assortment of goodies on it. From this distance she couldn't make out the selections, but there certainly was plenty to pick from.

The kids said "thank you" in unison and hurried to the next house.

Piper remembered that her mom talked about getting taffy apples at Halloween when she was a kid ... in the long-ago days before everything had to be individually wrapped and sealed for safety. No razorblades in gentler times.

Trick-or-treating ran from 6 to 9 p.m. throughout the county. One hour left. She wondered how Nang had managed with the kids in Hatfield. How many had come to her door? She would have enjoyed passing out treats with him. They'd planned to watch a spooky movie afterward, eat gourmet popcorn, and drink a bottle of Bird Dog Blues, a semi-sweet berry wine they'd picked up from Pepper's Ridge Winery. All of that would have been preferable to this.

She really wished the circumstances were different.

Behind her she heard more cries of "trick-or-treat treat treat treat." From somewhere down the block music played, an oldies rock song she couldn't quite remember the name of. Something by Chicago, it had that vibe.

The wine and popcorn would keep. Tomorrow night maybe, though she suspected that an optimistic notion. Murder cases played hell with personal plans.

Snow White, Robin Hood, and a football player dashed up the Glempse walk, chattering about what they'd already scored and would Robin Hood trade Snow White a Snickers for a pack of gum. A woman had been walking with them, and she stopped next to Piper.

"Trouble in the neighborhood?" she asked, glancing down at Piper's arm. "You're with the sheriff's department, right?"

"I am."

"Trouble?" the woman repeated.

Piper shook her head.

"Nice night for this," the woman continued. "I worried it was going to rain. It rained this morning. Supposed to again later, around midnight, I think. So cloudy now you can't see the stars. My Ellie, she's Snow White, was afraid she wouldn't be able to go trick-or-treating if it rained. She's growing so fast, a weed, this costume will only be good for the one year. If she hadn't been able to go out tonight, it would have gone to Goodwill unworn."

"She's cute," Piper said.

"The love of my life." The woman waved to the kids, who said a "thank you" in unison to the man at the door, then skipped to the next house. The woman followed a dozen paces behind.

The man stayed on his front porch, noticing Piper.

Piper took a deep breath and picked up the scent of something deliciously charred; one of the neighbors had barbecued.

"Let's do this," she whispered as she walked toward him. She'd thought about bringing another deputy with her, most likely Basil, as he'd ask questions pertinent to the investigation. But Basil said he could talk to the parents tomorrow, intent on scouring the road where Steampunkerbell died, while everything was still fresh and the forecasted rain didn't wash away anything important. She turned on her body cam so Basil could replay her meeting with the parents later if he wanted.

"Mr. Glempse?"

"Yes." He was a sturdy-looking man wearing creased blue jeans and a short-sleeve pale green shirt unbuttoned at the top, showing a leather cord with a polished wood cross dangling from it. Salt and pepper hair, ruddy complexion, heavy eyebrows, and a nose that seemed a little too long for his face. Glasses protruded from his front pocket. She figured him for late forties, maybe fifty. His hands looked smooth, not a laborer. "You're the sheriff, aren't you?"

"Sheriff Blackwell," Piper said.

He went pale in that instant.

"Billie. You're here about Billie, aren't you? Is she in trouble? It's that boy, isn't it?" His face gained a livid cast. "It's that damn boy. I never should have—"

"Can we go inside? Sit down and talk?"

He looked past her to a woman pulling a wagon with two toddlers in it made up to look like garden gnomes. The wagon had a bent wheel and it clattered along the sidewalk. He waved them away and turned off his front porch light.

"Come inside? Sure. It's about Billie, isn't it? My Billie."

Piper nodded. "Yes, it's about your daughter."

His glare softened and his fingers worked. "Oh, dear God. What did she do? Did you arrest her? Drunk? Did that boy do something to her? Rape? She was going to a party with that boy. She's underage, shouldn't have alcohol. Is she—"

"Let's sit down, Mr. Glempse."

"Robert," he said. He gestured to the couch beyond the entryway, his hand nervously twitching. She heard his breath catch. "Can I offer you something to drink? Water? Soda?"

The living room melded into the dining room, an "open concept" design. Family photographs perched on pieces of furniture, a smiling Billie Glempse from a toddler on up. Tasteful and varied paintings hung from the walls. A house worthy of a *Better Homes & Gardens* photo shoot.

"I think we have some lemonade, too. Orange juice?"

She shook her head and sat on one end of the couch. It was tan leather, comfortable, pricey. He picked a wing-back chair nearby, put his hands on his knees, all of him trembling a little, anticipating bad news.

"You have a lovely home," Piper said. "Is your wife here?"

"Lovely? Oh, my wife is responsible for the décor. She's the artful eye. Lovely. It is, thanks."

"Your wife, is she here?"

"You look so young," he said. "I didn't vote in the election last year, but I read in an article that you're twenty-three. I remember reading that."

"Twenty-four now," Piper replied. He was deflecting, talking about something other than his daughter, putting off whatever awful thing Piper was going to say. She wondered if Mrs. Glempse was around. She should be sharing the tragedy with both parents. "Robert, is your wife—"

"Not here." He pointed to the front door. "She's out on the block. Your arm, is it broken?"

"Mending," Piper said.

"What's this about, Sheriff? What about Billie?"

Piper had watched a lot of *Law & Order* reruns, a fairly accurate police procedural. They usually asked questions about the deceased first, gained information before revealing the death. Maybe Basil would have taken that approach, too, just like Lennie Briscoe.

"Robert—"

"Bob, actually. Everyone calls me Bob." He sucked in a breath. "So, you're only twenty-four. That's young for a sheriff. But I remember the articles, you were in the Army, right? Something like that? Saw action overseas."

"Two tours in the Middle East," she said. "I had MP training at Fort Campbell. Army four years."

"I'd say 'thank you for your service,' but that's pretty cliché sounding, don't you think? I know your dad was the sheriff before you. Long-time sheriff. Keeping it in the family, right?"

"Something like that."

"You ran because he died, didn't you? That's what a news article said, that you wanted to take his place. Cancer is awful. I had a brother who—"

"My father had cancer," she said. "Twice. But he made it through all the treatments. He's the police chief of Santa Claus now."

"Oh, good to hear. Glad he's okay. Cancer sucks. My older sister died of bone cancer."

"I'd really like to have your wife here for this, Mr. Glempse, Robert. But we'll go ahead. I'm going to show you a photograph, and I need you to confirm whether this is your daughter, Billie." She pulled out her cell phone and keyed up an image, a close-up of the girl's face. It looked like she might have been sleeping in the grass, her eyebrows glittery like miniature stars.

"Oh, dear God."

"Mr. Glempse—"

"Yes, that's Billie." He dug his fingers into his knees and rocked forward. "She's sixteen. Turned sixteen the end of September. Sixteen. Drunk? Tell me she's only drunk, passed out, and you arrested—"

"I am so very sorry. She's dead, Mr. Glempse." Piper took the

30

phone away and told him more, but not much, not that she thought it was murder, not about the quarrels, not about the face-down in the ditch part. Those were all ugly things that could wait a while. "Will Mrs. Glempse be back soon or—"

He shook his head. He started crying, choking sobs, shook his head harder. "Trick-or-treating. She took Grant and Wendy out through the neighborhood. Said they'd be back by nine." He glanced up at a polished walnut grandfather clock. "Back soon. Yes. They'll be back soon." When he controlled his breath again, he asked:

Was it a car accident?

Someone run her off the road?

Fall and hit her head at the party?

Did she have a brain aneurism?

Roughhousing, a fight, maybe. Some mean girl went at her?

Had she been drinking at the party, too much alcohol like in a sorority hazing?

How did it—

"We're investigating," Piper cut him off. "She was found about three hours ago." It was her turn to have trouble breathing. "Accident, maybe. We don't know yet. We're investigating. I will tell you more as we learn more." And she would. Maybe it was a hunting accident; that would be preferable to murder.

But the girl was wearing a lot of sparkles, difficult to mistake her for a deer.

Maybe a hunting accident, but not likely.

Murder, Piper was still thinking. She couldn't tell Billie's father that, though, not until all doubt was dissolved. *Don't tell him it was murder until you know for certain.*

"Can I see her?"

Piper hadn't anticipated that question. "I think so, but Dr. Neufeld will have to—"

"She's the coroner. Oh, God. She's going to cut up my baby." His shoulders shook and he folded in on himself.

And in that instant the front door swung open and girl of perhaps two or three dressed as a ballerina pirouetted in. *That must be Wendy,*

31

Piper thought. She was followed by a fireman—Grant, who was probably a few years older. Behind them came a woman—Sandra Glempse, her husband quickly introduced—wearing bleached jeans, blue Gucci sneakers, and a long-sleeve t-shirt with Van Gogh's "Starry Night" set with rhinestones on the front. Piper was getting to be a pretty good judge of age; the woman looked to be roughly thirty, a noticeable age gap with her husband.

The children were ushered upstairs, the treat bags set on the kitchen counter, and Sandra returned, her husband and Piper explaining about Billie. Sandra appeared horrified and reached in her pocket for a tissue. She swayed and grabbed a chair back for support.

"It's my fault, isn't it? I bought that outfit for her, on Etsy," Sandra said, tears starting. "Bob thought it was too risqué, but she really wanted it, didn't have enough money for it. I bought it. She was a target because of that little costume. This is my fault, and—"

"Not your fault, Sandra," Robert said.

Piper sat back and listened to them for the next half hour. Crying, mostly, shooting blame back and forth.

In the lengthy exchange she learned that Sandra was Bob's third wife, and so Billie was her step-daughter. Made sense, Sandra looked too young to be Billie's natural mom. Was Billie from wife number one or number two? *Didn't really matter at the moment, did it,* she thought. But the ballerina and fireman were from this marriage; those children clearly favored Sandra and shared her blonde hair and blue eyes.

Eventually, the pair calmed down and Piper edged forward.

"I need to ask a few questions," she began. "You mentioned Billie was going to a party."

"Some party in the country," Sandra said, crying so hard her shoulders jumped. "A big barn party." She fiddled with an earring, an emerald as shiny and bright as the girl's costume had been, twisting it so much Piper expected the ear to bleed. Grief was ugly and painful.

"I didn't ask her where the party was," Robert added. "She was all huffy about it because I told her the outfit was too skimpy. We argued before she left. I shouldn't have argued. I should have told her I loved her. Why didn't I tell her I loved her?"

"I shouldn't have bought her that outfit," Sandra said again. "My fault. She looked so pretty and glittery. She seemed so happy. But there wasn't much to that costume. What the hell did I do, buying that expensive skimpy thing?"

"You mentioned a boyfriend," Piper continued.

Sandra nodded, gulping air and trying to stop crying. "That would be Maurice. Maurice—" she held the word for a moment, clearly thinking. "Langston. Maurice Langston. A couple years older than her." A pause: "What's age, right? Just numbers. My life, work, is all wrapped around numbers. Just numbers, age differences. I let Billie take my car so she could come home when she wanted, so she wouldn't have to rely on Maurice, wouldn't feel trapped if she wanted to leave. That was smart, right? The one thing I did right, let her take my car. I didn't ask her where the party was. Billie didn't like it when I asked too many questions."

Piper noticed Sandra was pregnant, the overlarge t-shirt helping to cover the bump.

"Ask too many questions?" Robert growled from deep in his chest. "Sandra, you never asked questions, never paid enough attention to Billie. Hardly talked to her about school, dreams. Talked about clothes, you two. Hair. Those things, the things that didn't really matter."

"She's *your* daughter, Bob. She's my bonus kid." Sandra took in another big gulp of air. "I paid enough attention to buy her the outfit she asked for. And I let her take my car so she could leave the party when she wanted, wouldn't feel trapped. I cared about her, Bob. Don't you dare say I didn't care."

"About the car, Mrs. Glempse. What kind—"

"Pumpkin," Sandra, said. "It's pumpkin orange, Jeep Renegade."

"She bought it this past summer," Robert said.

"Replaced my Mustang," Sandra said. She started talking fast, nerves and sorrow taking control, practically babbling. "That was a convertible, and I miss it, but it had bent rims and a cracked axel from an argument with a curb. It would've needed repairs. Pretty blue metallic, leather. The backseat was too small, with a baby on the way, and I picked the Renegade because everyone could fit. Didn't like the pumpkin orange. Really, who would make a SUV in that color? But it was roomier for all these kids and I got a great price because it was pumpkin. The color grew on me after a while. I figured I'd replace it anyway in a year or two." She touched her stomach and eased into the other wing-back chair. Her shoulders rounded and she put her head down. "That damn costume. Why the hell did I buy the costume for her?"

Piper felt awkward, wanting to offer comfort and yet wanting to be clinical and gain more information about Billie. What would Lennie Briscoe do? It didn't matter what Lennie would do, it mattered what she would do.

"Mrs. Glempse," Piper said, "What party did she go to? Where was it?"

"Don't know," Sandra replied. "Yes, I should have asked."

"*I* should have asked," Robert added.

"You should have asked," Sandra cut in. "You should have. I should have."

Robert sobbed louder and came up for air. "Dear, God, why didn't I ask her? Why didn't I know where my daughter was? I just … Sheriff, she's a good girl."

"*Was*," Sandra said. "Was a good girl."

"When did she leave for the party?"

"Early," Sandra said. "Billie left early because they were going out to dinner first, meeting some friends for sandwiches before the party. She left here about four." She raised her head and stared at Piper. "Billie—Wilhelmina—wasn't my child, but I was always good to her. Gave her money when she asked, let her borrow my car after she got her license. Bought her that damn barely-there Halloween costume. Steampunk Tinker Bell it was called. Handmade from an Etsy shop, tailored to her measurements. She said it had to be Steampunk."

"Whatever the hell Steampunk is," Robert muttered.

Piper wished she would have brought a deputy with her. This was uncomfortable and heart-rending, taking a lot longer than she had expected. She'd ask Basil's advice later about how she could have handled it better. Oren, he might have done this differently, but he'd taken the week off. Said he didn't like working Halloween. She wasn't liking working Halloween either.

Pumpkin orange, the jeep. Piper wondered where it was. The bicyclist had mentioned a pumpkin orange Jeep Renegade. Obviously, someone other than Billie had been driving it. She doubted there were many pumpkin orange jeeps in the county.

"Mom! Mommommom!" Grant had edged halfway down the stairs, in pajamas and holding the fireman's helmet he'd worn with his costume. "Can I have another piece of candy? Mom! Please."

"It's past his bedtime." Sandra gave Piper a half-smile, wiped at her tears, and eased out of the chair. She reached into a treat bag and pulled out a miniature Butterfinger, went to the staircase, took hold of the boy's hand, and continued up to the second floor. "One more piece," she said. "Then brush your teeth again."

"Billie's mother, birth mother. I'll need to contact her." Piper would have to establish legal custody of the girl.

"You won't be able to do that, Sheriff. My first wife, Willow. She died of a brain aneurism about a week after Billie was born. Wilhelmina was the name of Willow's grandmother—Billie's great-grandmother, and we used that. Too old fashioned, I know. But we called her Billie. Everybody called her Billie. Wilhelmina's still alive, a hundred and one. I'll call her at the care center in Owensboro in the morning to tell her about Billie. Maybe I should go over and break the news. This will crush her. Billie's uncle, Wes, is in Owensboro, too. Tell both of them with one trip. Tell them all." He waited a beat. "My second wife, Emma, I'll let her know, too. We were only married about two years, just didn't work out. She was Canadian, thought she'd like the States, but then changed her mind. Maybe she just didn't like little Spencer County ... or me enough." He rubbed at his eyes. "A lot of things in life don't work out."

Piper wanted to say "I'm sorry," but kept the words in.

"When can I see her? Billie? When do you think the coroner will be finished?" Robert pressed. "When will you know how she died, what happened?"

"We've just started looking into this," Piper said. "An investigation takes a while."

He shook his head. "I should have asked where the party was. Shouldn't I? You'd think I would have asked where my sixteen-year-old daughter in a skimpy green costume was going with her older boyfriend."

Piper didn't answer that; it wasn't her place to judge. "Did she carry a cell phone?"

"Sure. What sixteen-year-old isn't glued to a cell phone? Always has it on her. Always." He let out a great huffing breath. "September, first of September, I put the MamaBear App on it. She was getting her driver's license at the end of the month and I ... I dunno ... I wanted to know where she was when she borrowed one of our cars. Said it would let me track how fast she's driving, look at her social media messaging. You know, I never did that, poke into her social media. I thought it intrusive. I just wanted to make sure that when she took the car she wasn't speeding." He gave a laugh. "Problem was the opposite. She was a nervous driver, always always always drove below the speed limit. Got stopped once because she was going too slow and slogging up traffic. What little traffic there was downtown. Didn't get a ticket, just a written warning from a Rockport cop. She was always slow and careful, probably was afraid of putting a scratch on Sandra's Renegade. New, you know, that jeep."

He shook his head again. "When can I go get the jeep? I work full time, a shift manager at the power plant. Sandra's going to need the jeep to go to work Monday. She's a financial advisor, works part-time, three days a week. I think we'll both be able to get some days off for this, and—"

"Mr. Glempse, we haven't seen the jeep." Piper took the honest route. "You daughter was found alone in the county. But we'll be looking for the jeep."

"Dear God," he said. He sobbed again, hollow and dry like all the tears had been used up.

Piper waited.

"Sheriff, was my daughter killed because of the car? A carjacking? We paid twenty-five thousand for it. A big chunk of money, but really not all that much for a new SUV with some bells and whistles. And it's an odd color. Was my daughter killed because someone wanted the ugly car? It wasn't an accident, was it? Car theft. My beautiful daughter is dead. What am I going to do?" He fixed her with a stare and repeated, "It wasn't an accident, was it?"

Piper waited.

"Sheriff—"

"Mr. Glempse. Robert. We're investigating—"

"Sheriff—"

What would Lennie Briscoe do? What would Basil or Oren or anyone else in the department who had more than her ten months of experience do? What would she do?

"No, I don't think it was an accident." There. The words she had told herself not to speak tonight. But Piper figured Lennie would have been forthright, too. "I don't know that for certain. Like I said, we're investigating. But I think it looks deliberate." How many times had she told him, "We're investigating"? She kept going. "We didn't find a cell phone on her. Would you please use that MamaBear App and get a location on her phone? That would help." She'd get a search warrant if he declined. She'd get a search warrant anyway to be safe.

They could chase Billie's phone through other channels if the girl had left it turned on, but this would be faster with his permission. She watched him pull out his cell phone and fiddle with the keys. His hands shook. She'd get the jeep's license plate number through DMV records.

"And what can you tell me about Maurice Langston?"

Robert kept working on the phone. His voice quivered. "Maurice? Wild. A wild boy. But he looked clean-cut. Polite, strangely. I saw his wild streak on the football field when we went to a few games last year. We'd go to watch Billie cheerlead. That was a skimpy costume, too."

"Maurice?"

"Maurice played running back, college potential. Pros eventually, so fast. He had something to do with Billie's death, didn't he? Older, wild boy. From the wrong side of the tracks, they used to call it. Maurice and Billie started dating in July, after the big party in the park on the Fourth. I should have told her 'no,' but she was smitten. Thought she was in love. Teenagers don't know spit about love. I'm going to call his parents and—"

"Mr. Glempse, don't do that. Not yet."

"You call them, then. They live somewhere near Dale, out in the sticks." He passed over the phone. "The screen. That shows where her phone is pinging. Maurice's number is in my directory. Any boy that dated my daughter, and there were only a few, I put the number in my directory."

Piper keyed his phone to transfer the information to hers, and she sent it to the office as a backup. She downloaded Maurice Langston's phone number and would get his address when she got back to her Explorer.

"You call them," Robert repeated. "Or I will. I won't be polite about it. And download whatever you want from the App. You call them."

Piper transferred what she could. Then she punched in the numbers for Maurice and stood, walking to the door. "I'm calling him," she said. She put Robert's phone down on a decorative table by the door, next to the tray with all the candy. "And I will call you later. I need the names of Billie's closest friends if—"

"Do you think one of them killed her?"

"Robert, I just want to talk to them."

"I'll get you a list. Tomorrow."

Piper met his sorrowful gaze. "Again, I am so sorry about Billie."

The call to Maurice went to voicemail, but Piper didn't leave a message. She was fast down the steps and to her Explorer, radioing Teegan.

"Teegan," Piper said. "I'm just leaving and heading to—"

"Sheriff." It was Zeke, not Teegan who answered. "Listen, Sheriff Blackwell. I'm in helping tonight. And I figured out where Billie Glempse was going."

"Tell me."

"I should have realized it right away when I saw her costume. A party, I was invited, too. But I didn't have a date. Didn't want to go solo. The party's called Hot and Steamy Hallows' Eve, a steampunk theme. They have a different theme every year. Last Halloween it was creepy clowns and—"

"Where's the party, Zeke?" Piper showed her impatience.

"Carlson's Dutch Knuckle." He rattled off a vague address, halfway down this county road, turn right at the old grain silo. "It's high school and college kids, supposed to be soda, wine, beer, and dancing. Costumes are required. It's invitation only because they want to limit the crowd. I went last year, and it was good. Just didn't want to go alone this time. They're always careful, card for beer, Roger Carlson does. He throws the party because so many of the kids detassel corn for him in the summer, hire on for seasonal work. It's a thank you sort of thing."

Teegan came on. "I sent Basil the address a little while ago ... with better directions than Zeke spit at you. Didn't want to interrupt you and your death notification because—"

"I need something else," Piper cut in. "I need an address on Maurice Langston."

"Maurice?" Zeke shot back. "I know Maurice. He graduated with me, Sheriff."

She started her Explorer and fed in the GPS of Billie's cell phone. "Tell me about Maurice."

"Nice, but not too bright. Barely graduated. Skated by. Teachers looked the other way because he was so good at sports. I think he's in college somewhere on an athletic scholarship."

"Maybe he's in college somewhere," Piper returned. "But tonight he was supposedly with Billie Glempse."

"Holy shit," Zeke said. "Do you think he did something to her? Killed her? Holy—"

"Radio Basil to look for Maurice Langston at the party; he's a person of interest. Look for a pumpkin orange jeep in the lot. And give Diego this GPS signal I'm tracking. Have him meet me at the ping, and bring Thresher with him." The dog might be useful.

She needed more people, and maybe she'd call in some off-duty deputies, depending on what turned up when she found Billie's phone. Maurice Langston's address was only a few miles beyond the cell phone signal. That would be her second stop. If Maurice wasn't at the party, maybe he was home.

"Millie's with Basil. So put Rocco out in a car to deal with the crazy calls," Piper radioed.

Not that this entire night wasn't crazy.

And horribly unfortunate for Billie Glempse.

CHAPTER SIX

9 P.M.

The music had a back beat with heavy bass. Basil felt the ripples skitter across the ground and rise through his feet. It sounded like a mix of industrial and synth-pop, with some new age sprinkled in. At first odd, driving, interesting, neither pleasant nor unpleasant. After a few minutes, it became just a jumble of unexpected syncopated noise.

A big barn in the middle of nowhere, he figured they'd be playing hillbilly tunes, like he'd heard at the county fair. A lot of things about Spencer County had been unexpected ... that he'd like the job and find the rural setting tolerable; that he wouldn't mind working for a sheriff who was only twenty-four, eight years his junior; and that he was mostly okay with being the only black person in the department. He was displeased that the county overall lacked diversity—and that had made him almost pass on the job, but his children didn't seem to care. They loved the place, and were recently delighted by the Fun Fest at Lincoln State Park, Fall Heritage Day at the Pioneer Village, and the Haunted Barn at the Farm Market ... and now trick-or-treating around their white subdivision without him.

He had photos on his cell phone of wide-grinning Ruth Bader

Ginsberg and SpongeBob with their bags of treats; his wife had sent the pics to him with a note: "Wish you were costuming with us."

It would have been nice to go around the neighborhood with them. But RBG and SpongeBob were young, and there would be other Halloweens when he could join them. Certainly, there wouldn't be a murder at the end of every October.

Basil stood next to his Explorer. He listened, looking out over a field-turned-parking lot that must have close to one hundred cars and pickups in it—a massive turnout in a rustic county outside this big barn.

"If it's this loud out here, I'm not looking forward to going inside," Millie said. She'd helped him search along the road where Billie Glempse had been found, and talked to some of the homeowners in the area. They'd come up with nothing useful.

"Dutch Knuckle, Zeke called this."

"A style of barn," Millie explained. "Big city detective like you, I suspect you don't know a lot about barns."

"I know most of them are red. And this one looks like it could stand some fresh paint. But Dutch Knuckle?"

"Barns are probably red because of tradition. Hundreds of years ago farmers would seal their barns with orange-colored linseed oil. Stir in some rust, good for killing the moss that grew on wood, and it turned red."

"And you know this because—"

"American farm history class I took for the hell of it in Evansville," she replied. "As for the Dutch Knuckle, it's called that because of the roof."

The barn was roughly three stories high, probably sixty-feet wide and more than one hundred deep. Basil guessed it covered close to five thousand square feet.

"A gambrel roof," she continued, "the rounded shape, a symmetrical top with two slopes on each side, looks a little like a knuckle. Common for dairy farms, which I think this was once upon a time."

"And you learned all of that from your history course?"

She shook her head. "No. On the way here I googled 'Dutch

Knuckle' because I was curious. My history course was good for the red paint."

The music shifted as they walked toward the open door. It still had a synth-pop vibe, but now the tune was mixed with ragtime and sounded like an orchestra backed it. The singers had the feel of a boy-band, and the words were foreign, probably German.

"I don't like the music," Millie said. "Maybe I'm too old for it."

Basil laughed. "You're twenty-five, right? I hardly think that makes you too old."

"Okay, how about my musical taste runs toward songs that don't offend my eardrums? Music that sounds like music."

"Or that doesn't sound like angry rush-hour Chicago traffic?" He gestured inside, where a pulsing strobe illuminated dancers. "Apparently our murder victim was on her way here, but died about two hours before the party was scheduled to start."

Millie turned on her body cam. "Did Zeke say it was supposed to kick off at seven?"

"Yeah, and he had an invite, but no date. He took a pass and is keeping Teegan company."

They entered. The wall of sound merged with a wall of scents—sweat, perfume, food. Large disco balls hung from rafters and scattered flashes of color across everything. It overloaded Basil's senses, and he concentrated to take it all in and turned on his body cam.

Probably two hundred teenagers and young adults, half of them dancing, the rest lining the walls and stalls and sitting in the hayloft drinking, eating, and chattering, their voices lost in the cacophony. Everyone was in costume.

Many were in Victorian garb, but there were others, including Red Riding Hood in a skimpy red-sequined piece that might have paired well with Billie's Steampunkerbell, and assorted characters from *The Wizard of Oz*, *Star Wars*, and *Game of Thrones*.

He felt his radio thrum and put it to his ear. After a moment, he turned to Millie.

"Look in the lot for an orange Jeep Renegade." He rattled off the license plate number and hoped she heard him. He suspected there weren't many recent-model jeeps in that color. He reached for his phone and pulled up a high school yearbook photo Zeke had sent of Maurice Langston. Maurice might be difficult to spot in a Halloween costume amid the revelers.

Millie eyed the photo, turned, and appeared grateful to leave the barn. Basil edged in deeper.

He threaded his way through a pair of Dr. Frank N. Furters, a nun, Bullwinkle, a female Elvis Presley, and a male Marilyn Monroe. Around him young people in ornate Victorian garb danced wildly and bounced into him. The scent of alcohol added to the miasma of odors. He put their ages between fourteen and twenty-four, and all of them appeared to be having a good time. If the hosts of the party were in the mass, he couldn't pick them out.

He passed Betty Boop, who wide-eyed pointed at him and jostled Freddie Krueger, who reeked of whiskey. Freddie didn't look old enough to drink.

"The sheriff," Betty Boop squealed. "Look, it's the sheriff!" Basil barely heard her.

The Statue of Liberty and a Roman Centurion gave him a wide berth and nudged several people. The Centurion pointed at Basil, and said: "Po-po."

"That's not a costume," he heard a heavily-made up Victorian gentleman say. "The black dude is some sort of real cop."

"Great costume," a punked-out Mary Poppins told him. "Dance with me."

Most of the costumes were impressive and all of them had elements in common—gears, keys, vests, top hats, goggles, corsets, canes, parasols, pocket watches, and an assortment of odd-looking handheld inventions.

Basil recognized the trappings of steampunk, having watched movies like *Mortal Engines*, *Hugo*, Downey's *Sherlock Holmes*, and other genre films. Steampunkerbell—Billie Glempse—would have fit in well with the other partygoers.

A steampunk Zorro tapped him on the shoulder and pointed toward the back of the barn. Zorro had some age to him, natural gray in his hair and beard, lines on his tanned face. He said something to Basil, but the words were lost in the music.

Basil followed him past tables filled with chips and pans of pulled pork, a station with beer kegs and a soda fountain, to a spot under the hayloft where George Washington and Han Solo worked a DJ N-Wave Pack with a beat machine and amplifiers.

"Turn it down!" Basil shouted and pointed at George. "Not off, just down! Way down!"

The president and Han Solo complied as a susurrus of boos and hisses came in response from the dancers.

Basil fixed Zorro with a stare. "Are you running this?"

Zorro nodded and thrust out a hand. Basil did not shake it.

"You're Roger Carlson?"

Zorro nodded. "I have a permit for the beer," he said. "I stamp the kids' hands if they're old enough to drink. No stamp, no beer. Been doing this every year for the past seven or eight. Police have never come by before. Never had trouble, not close enough to anyone's house for the noise to—"

"Invitation only, right?" Basil had gotten that message from Zeke.

"Have to, otherwise kids from nearby counties and into Kentucky would show up. Don't have the space for that sort of crowd. This is my limit."

"Hey! Turn it up!" someone shouted from the hayloft. "More music!"

"Girl named Billie Glempse on your invite list?"

Zorro shrugged. "Don't ask me to remember all the names." He nodded toward George Washington. "My son can help with—"

"What about Maurice Langston?"

Zorro nodded aggressively. "Sure. Sure. Great kid. Maurice has detasseled for me four or five summers, does odd jobs. This past summer and into September he—"

Basil waved an arm out toward the crowd. "Is Maurice here?"

Zorro stroked his beard. Basil noticed that the man's bandolier was decorated with gears and faceless pocket watches. "Maurice was

45

invited. Hell, he's usually here every weekend. He's like a second son. He hasn't shown yet, but he will."

Basil spotted Millie working her way through the dancers.

"George Washington," Basil directed. "Close the doors. No one is leaving." He swung back to Zorro. "Mr. Carlson, it is not my intent to make arrests, despite an underage Freddie Krueger being drunk on his ass, and a nun who's tottering and certainly doesn't look twenty-one."

Zorro blanched in the strobing light; the colors scattered from the disco ball painting his face like a jittering kaleidoscope.

"Deputy Isaakovitch and I are going to talk to everyone here. A few questions and we'll be on our way." He made a show of calling on his radio for backup, not letting Zorro see that he hadn't punched the button. He honestly would have appreciated backup, but the department was already stretched thin tonight and he didn't want to divert resources from somewhere else, as the partiers did not appear threatening.

He closed on Zorro until he could smell the man's breath—not beer, definitely pulled pork. He picked up other scents. "Is that oregano I smell burning up in your hayloft? Smells a lot like marijuana to me. But I'm going to trust that it's oregano and incense, so I won't go up. Have them come down. I will talk to everyone here."

Millie held up a clipboard she must have retrieved from her car. "No orange jeep."

"We're taking names and statements," Basil continued. "As for the beer and whatever kind of alcohol Han Solo just stashed under that table…I'll watch you pour it out. I don't want to spend my time filling out a stack of paperwork with charges. Drunk underage kids will be released to their parents. I won't test every juvenile and I won't charge the adults with contributing." He gave a dramatic pause. "This time. Not *this* time. Anyone intoxicated will have their keys confiscated and be given a ride home, where they can explain their short night to mom and dad rather than getting a county judge and a jail cell involved. If you're magnanimous, they can sober up at your place gratis. Understand?"

Zorro sadly nodded.

"Let's do this as quickly as possible," he said to Millie. "I don't want to be here until midnight." He tapped her clipboard. "Walk with me. We get the names, pictures, phone numbers, and addresses of everyone. We find out what they know about Billie Glempse and Maurice Langston. We keep our cams on and can play it all back later."

"Aren't we going to arrest—"

"No." Basil's eyes were like stone. He stood close and spoke into her ear. "There's too many of them. We are way the hell outnumbered —one hundred to one—and affecting any kind of arrest here could be difficult. I don't see pitchforks and shovels lining the walls, so that's a plus. But we can't tell if anyone's carrying. We don't provoke and turn this into a mob scene. We control it friendly, but stern, and get what we want with cheesecake rather than a whip. Our priority is a homicide investigation and we shouldn't be distracted with minor offenses of pot and underage drinking. We could take Mr. Carlson in for contributing to the delinquency of minors. Or we could look the other way *tonight* and work our case."

"Got it," Millie said.

"And we make sure Mr. Carlson doesn't host a Halloween party next year."

CHAPTER SEVEN

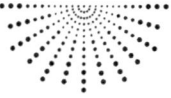

10:30 P.M.

Piper would have passed it by. The sky overcast, no homes in the immediate area, everything was inky dark, and silent save for the sound of her wheels rolling over the graded earth road. Her headlights sliced through the black, but they couldn't part the tall weeds growing on either side.

She would have missed the jeep if she didn't have the ping courtesy of MamaBear.

Piper pulled to the side, put on her flashers, radioed Teegan and Diego, and grabbed the high-powered flashlight out of the back. She focused on the weeds, and noticed a spot where some had been tamped down by a car driven off the road.

The pumpkin orange Jeep Renegade sat nose-down in a section of ditch so deep it had swallowed the vehicle from view of the road. The front bumper had crumpled from the impact, and the hood had buckled. Piper figured the jeep must have been going pretty fast considering the damage. The hatchback had popped open a half-dozen inches, which might or might not have been a result of the crash.

She panned the beam, turned on her body cam, and put on a pair of gloves. The margins of the ditch were steep, and she gingerly slid down, still unbalanced with one arm in a sling, and feeling burrs grab at her skin and poke like tiny needles through her clothes. The weeds smelled sour and faintly of pineapple, and she felt the sap of something smearing against her forearm.

She heard Diego pull up.

"Sheriff?"

"Down here," she hollered. "Gloves, body cam."

"Gloves, body cam, flashlight, and Thresher. Got it."

The driver's side door open, Piper looked in and saw that the airbag had activated and then deflated. No sign of occupants. She leaned in, smelling perfume or cologne mingling with the scent of the thigh-high weeds. Aiming the beam, she noticed the glovebox also open and the items spilled out. From the accident? She spotted a small black sling bag with a gold chain strap on the passenger side floorboard. The purse flap was raised and the contents strewn around ... wallet, cell phone, compact, lipstick, breath mints. Had they scattered in the accident or been dumped out?

"Dumped," she decided. Someone had been through the jeep looking for something. Did they find whatever it was?

With only one hand to work with, she laid the flashlight on the driver's side and angled the beam. A few green sequins glittered on the passenger seat. She stretched and grabbed the cell phone; it was on and she confirmed it was Billie's. The wallet was Billie's too, and while it contained her driver's license, it had no money.

Robbery? Why not just grab the whole wallet or purse rather than take the time to pull out the cash? Nothing under the seat except a few roadmaps and an ice scraper. Some lint, but basically clean and tidy.

Billie might have left her house driving the jeep, but she hadn't been driving when it went in the ditch—she'd already been killed. The sequins hinted she'd been a passenger at one point. Plus, the driver's seat, pushed far back, indicated someone tall had been at the wheel. The girl wouldn't have been able to reach the gas pedal. Piper bagged the purse and contents, which she'd fingerprint and look through at the office where she could study them easier. She bagged what she believed came from the glovebox separately. A third bag for the maps and ice scraper.

49

In the backseat she found an empty vinyl backpack that had been slit with something sharp. Was this also Billie's? And what had it contained?

"All of this needs to be dusted for fingerprints," she said, emerging to see Diego and Thresher in the ditch with her. The deputy had the leash in one hand, a large flashlight in the other. They'd moved so quietly she hadn't heard them approach. "But not here. We'll put it in our garage, go at it there. I'll call Teegan."

She edged around to the back and looked inside—three twelve-packs of soda: Coke, Diet Pepsi, A&W Root Beer, a receipt taped to the root beer showed it was purchased yesterday ... perhaps by Mrs. Glempse, who had not gotten around to taking them into the house.

"Dreadful color," Diego said. "Bet it's even uglier in sunlight."

Piper's beam focused on the ground; she was looking for some trace of tracks—the person who'd been driving, the person who'd searched the vehicle. The weeds were tight and had been disturbed by her walking around the jeep. Nothing else was obvious.

Diego whistled. "Butt ugly. A pumpkin on wheels and no Cinderella to ride in it. I would not drive that thing."

"Nobody's going to be driving it out of here," she returned. "Gonna take a tow truck." She remembered Mr. Glempse saying they got a good price probably because it was pumpkin orange. He'd also said Mrs. Glempse would need it to get to work. This vehicle wouldn't be driving anywhere without some significant repairs.

The dog whined, interested in the jeep, anxious to be given a task.

A beautiful dog, expertly trained, the Belgian Malinois was two-feet-tall at the shoulder, muscular, sleek, and looked to be carved from a piece of polished mahogany. The black ears and muzzle were the only color deviations, its eyes too dark to discern the pupils. The dog had been paid for by a bequest from Mark Thresher, the same man who'd gifted Piper her house, and vintage vehicles and motorcycles. They'd named the dog Thresher in his honor.

"He's keying on the jeep, and he's picking up a scent," Diego said. "Probably lots of scents. He likes working in fields." The deputy had spent the most time with the dog and had gone through part of the training with him. "Something has his attention. See?"

The dog whined louder and looked up the far side of the ditch.

"He can see something we can't," Diego continued. "Or more likely smell it."

"Go. Find out what he's interested in. I'll catch up. We can have him check out the jeep later." On her radio to Teegan: "Hurry on the tow truck and pull Rocco off the odd calls. Get him out here." She wanted someone watching the vehicle while she and Diego traipsed through the field following Thresher. Next, she radioed Basil, who said he'd come out as soon as he "wrapped up the party."

"Sheriff," Diego called from the field beyond. "A patch of blood. We're tracking."

Piper stared at the opposite side of the ditch, sweeping the flashlight and finding a place which looked easier to climb. A few more weeks and she could abandon the sling.

Breathing deep, taking in the cooling air, she noted a sweet, pungent zing ... the sharp, fresh aroma of ozone signaling that it would rain soon, just like the forecasters predicted. Piper wanted the jeep towed before the sky opened up. She radioed Teegan again.

"That tow truck? When I said hurry, I really meant hurry."

"Should be there in ten, fifteen," Teegan replied, then paused. "More likely twenty, twenty-five. You're pretty far out in the sticks."

"I need a bay cleared in our garage. If Zeke is still there, ask him to move something out. This jeep needs to get towed in before it gets drenched."

"Yeah, Sheriff, Zeke is still—"

"I'll get him some overtime." Piper clicked off and took it slow up the slope. The ground that stretched in front of her was scrubby and had been planted in rows marked by the remnants of dried vines dotted with rotten pumpkins and squash that hadn't been good enough for the market. They were typically the last vegetables harvested in this area. Her flashlight beam didn't reach all the way to the edges, like the field went on forever. She didn't see Diego and Thresher, but she heard the dog bark, saw the faint glow of a flashlight, and headed in that direction, jogging in a relatively flat gap between rows.

Her radio crackled as she went, chatter between Rocco and Teegan. Her deputy was on the county road and would be here in minutes. She didn't want the jeep left unsupervised and wondered if she should have stayed with it, at least print parts of it with the kit in her car. But she continued to hurry, focusing on Diego's light. Piper cut to the east across harvested rows and hurdled the remains of a giant smashed pumpkin. Her beam bounced along, aimed at the ground so she wouldn't trip over something that would send her sprawling.

Faster, and then she stopped, light aimed at the row directly to her right.

Diego was talking to her, but not quite loud enough for her to catch it. She fixated on the dirt ... a tire track. Recent? Had to be. It had rained this morning, and the track was clear, hadn't been washed out by the earlier shower. She panned the beam to rows on either side, no other tracks. Just the one.

A motorcycle, dirt bike maybe, thick tire.

"What the hell? Who was out here?"

She took a picture of the track with her cell phone, leaning close. "A knobbie," she said. Wider and deeper than a standard motorcycle tire, intended for off-road.

"Sheriff!" This time Diego's voice cut through her concentration. "A body, Sheriff!"

"And two is four," Piper said. Careful not to walk in the row where the motorcycle had been, she sprinted toward Diego.

Thresher stood at attention.

"I've not seen anything like this, Sheriff," Diego said as she closed. "Guy was going to a Halloween party, had to have been the way he's dressed. So why is he out in the middle of Thompson's pumpkin field dead?"

"Murdered," Piper said. "Maurice Langston. The Halloween date of Billie Glempse."

"You knew him?"

"Not personally. But I know who he is. Was."

Three quarrels protruded from the body ... stomach, left shoulder, and what looked to be the center of the heart.

On his back, hands up as if he'd raised them in defense, mouth open wide as if he'd been trying to speak or perhaps scream.

"Steampunkerbell's Captain Hook," Piper said. There was a wallet on the ground next to him, but she didn't have to open it to confirm it was Maurice. He looked enough like the yearbook photo Zeke had emailed her, though he was heavily made up. Long black, curly wig, mustache and goatee that may or may not be real, white poofy-sleeved shirt, red and gold brocade vest decorated with gears, three pocket watches hanging from a wide leather belt, black billowy pirate breeches. He had a leather tube around his left arm and hand festooned with gears, odd symbols, ending in an impressive curved hook. A few feet away lay a tricorn hat emblazoned with a skull and crossbones and a red sash.

He'd been a handsome young man, clearly fit, broad-shouldered. His blue eyes appeared to stare right at her. Looked like he could have posed for the cover of a romance paperback, or more likely a steam-punk work.

Diego knelt next to the body, but didn't touch it. "Sheriff, looks like he was shot in the back, too. There's a broken quarrel behind this shoulder. I'm thinking he got shot, ran, dripped the blood Thresher found, kept going as long as he could. Turned to face whoever chased him. Got shot again."

"And again and again." She gestured to her right. "I saw a tire track. Motorcycle, dirt bike. Might be connected. Might not. But I'm guessing that whoever shot him was on the bike, chasing him. I want detailed pictures of the track, just in case, and I want it traced as far as you can ... where the bike entered the field, where it left. I know it's tough because it's dark and in a friggin' pumpkin patch, but we have to work this fast."

"Because rain's coming. I can smell it."

Smell it? This night, these deaths, all of it smells rotten, she thought.

"Those really are crossbow bolts, quarrels," Diego said. "Open field like this, maybe some weird hunting accident. But I don't think so. I think you're right about the shooter on a bike. Chasing him."

"No accident," Piper agreed. "No way in hell are these hunting accidents. The shooter had it in for Peter Pan's supporting characters. We have to find out why and who is going medieval with murder. Get moving on the tracks, get close-ups with a good camera, see if Thresher keys on anything else. I'll keep Maurice company until Dorothy in her ruby slippers arrives."

She radioed Teegan.

"The tow is close. Rocco's on site, Sheriff, a garage bay is open, and—"

"Call Dr. Neufeld," Piper interrupted. "Give her directions to this location and ask her to get here before the rain. Diego or Rocco will escort her to the body."

"Another body, Sheriff?"

"Tell her ASAP."

Piper ticked off her to-do list … stop by Maurice's parents and give them the bad news and confirm the ID; go into the office and start sifting through things; have the jeep examined, though that might not happen until the morning or the day after because she'd want to get a search warrant; and call Nang to tell him she's not coming home tonight.

Piper tipped her head back, took in a deep lungful scented with earth and decayed pumpkins, her sweat, and the sweet hint of approaching rain.

For just a moment, she turned off the flashlight and let the darkness cocoon her.

CHAPTER EIGHT

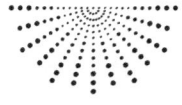

MIDNIGHT

Florence Henderson of *The Brady Bunch* was born here; Abraham Lincoln was raised on a nearby farm, his mother's grave on the site; and the inventor of the reflection seismograph once called this home; as did legendary basketball coach Del Harris. Humble beginnings for accomplished people, Piper mused.

The place used to be named Elizabeth, back when it was laid out in 1843. Soon after that it got a post office—still running—and the name of the town changed to Dale in honor of Robert Dale Owen, who was a congressman at the time. Piper had been delving into Spencer County history ever since she was elected in November of the previous year. To her, the congressman was one of the more interesting bits about this area.

Owen, born in Scotland, was her age when he immigrated to the United States and became active in politics, first with the Indiana House of Representatives, then as a member of Congress. A Democrat, he pushed the bill that established the Smithsonian Institution and served on its first board of regents. Widely published, he edited the *New-Harmony Gazette*, advocated women's property and divorce rights, opposed slavery, supported free public schools, and endorsed birth control to keep the population in check. Piper had read his autobiography, which was in her basement library.

She wondered how many residents of Dale—there were roughly fifteen hundred of them, making this one of the larger dinkburgs in the county—knew how impressive Robert Dale Owen had been. Let alone that their community was named for him. Most people knew about Florence Henderson.

Piper followed Buffaloville Road on the edge of Dale and slowed shortly before it turned into 350 E. The homes were spaced about a hundred feet apart on large lots, the ones in this area older, likely built in the forties or fifties.

The Langston ranch resembled a shoebox, simple design, low roof, exterior gray shingle siding. She pulled into the driveway that had two cars in it, an old Plymouth and something smaller ahead of it she couldn't make out. Her headlights showed a yard overdue for mowing, a flowerbox filled with weeds. The trim and shutters had so much paint peeling it was as if dried fish scales had adhered to the wood. The windows dark. The immediate neighbors' houses were also dark, not a single porch light on along this strip.

When she turned off her headlights, everything went inky like a setting in a horror movie—maybe similar to the one Nang had picked to watch with her tonight. She almost grabbed her flashlight. But there was a light on a pole across the street and down a few houses, and when she let her eyes adjust to the gloom, it was just enough.

She'd rather wait on this until the morning, not have to wake up Maurice's parents to tell them their son was dead. But the news wouldn't be any more palatable after they'd gotten a night's sleep.

Radioing her position and confirming the jeep had been tucked away in a garage bay, Piper got out of her Explorer and stood on a driveway made of chipped landscaping rocks. Was this going to be as difficult as her visit to the Glempse house?

"Get it over with. Over with. Over." She heard a quick staccato burst of dog barks coming from somewhere across the road. Faintly came a rumble of thunder. "Get it over with." She felt a drop of rain, then another.

Piper approached, pushed the doorbell, didn't hear it ring, pushed it once more and then knocked. She waited, listening to the dog bark again, more thunder—this time louder. There was a metal awning over the front stoop, and she heard rain gently patter against it.

She knocked louder.

And waited.

The rain came a little faster, she knocked once more, and finally the front porch light came on. Someone grumbled behind the door, fumbled with the knob, then opened it.

"Dammit, Maurice, I told you to take the house key—" The speaker was backlit, but Piper saw that he was young, naked, had obviously been sound asleep, his hair a tangled mess. "You're not Maurice. Just a moment." He slammed the door, and Piper waited again.

The rain was thrumming down steadily when it opened again minutes later. The man now wore a pair of faded red sweatpants, unlaced tennis shoes. He stood nearly six-feet, lanky but with muscular arms. He had a square jaw, long nose, sunken-appearing eyes, and thin eyebrows, his hair long and tied back. She noticed faint stubble on his face, and that he smelled like he'd just liberally applied some aftershave or cologne.

"You a cop or something?" He yawned.

"Sheriff Piper Blackwell," she returned.

"Maurice in trouble? Hell, of course Maurice is in trouble or you wouldn't be here. I told him not to hang with that fancy girl."

"Maurice isn't in trouble. Maurice is—" Piper shifted from one foot to the other. "Look, can I come in and talk? Are your parents home?"

He laughed and gestured her inside. "One of them is."

"And you are—"

"Wally. I'm Maurice's brother. Older."

The small living room had worn, plain furniture: a two-person couch, rocking chair, coffee table cluttered with magazines and soda cans, an old television—the tube kind, and a four-tier shelf filled with trophies and framed photographs. Several other trophies covered the fireplace mantle. Through an open hallway she saw the kitchen, which looked like something out of the 1960s. Piper thought the place vintage and dated. It had a musty smell, not unclean, just old, needed airing out. And it smelled like he'd burned something for dinner.

He pointed to the rocking chair and she took it, noting the beige couch had bare spots on the arms from age and use. A well-used crocheted afghan in a riot of fall colors draped across the back.

"Your parents—" she started.

"That's mom, Darcy Louis Smith Langston," Wally said, nodding to the fireplace. "Never made it past thirty-seven."

Piper saw that one of the trophies was actually an urn.

"Dad's in Florida. Took off when she died five years ago. Left me and Maurice the house and one beat-to-shit car. Dad took the Bronco 'cause it could pull a little U-Haul trailer." He eased onto the sofa and set his hands on his thighs.

She listened to the rain.

"So, Maurice was fourteen when your mother passed," Piper said.

"Yeah, and I'd just turned seventeen, I guess that was close enough to eighteen that nobody was bothered by us staying here. Maybe nobody noticed. Or maybe nobody realized Dad took off—we didn't tell anyone. Anyway, we didn't want to move."

"Didn't the neighbors—"

"Don't really have anything to do with our neighbors. Never did, though Maurice would mow the Williams' place across the street when he was in grade school for five bucks a whack. They're all old farts right around here and probably still don't know Dad's gone."

"But you could have—"

"Didn't have any relatives to move in with. Didn't need anybody else. Me and Maurice get on just fine."

She started to ask a question, but he barreled ahead.

"We pay all the bills, work steady at the power plant, and Maurice does summer weekends at some big farm in the county, two nights a week at Splashin' Safari in Santa Claus when it's open. We're not making a fortune, but making enough. Just bought us a second car, that little Honda. We're good. 'Cept the girl is trouble. Too good to be true. Told him not to date someone in high school. I got nothing to do with that girl. What's Maurice accused of Sheriff, rape? Statutory rape 'cause she's sixteen? If they're fooling around, I guarantee you it's consensual. That's why you came by, right? If she's claiming—"

"I came out here because your brother is dead, Wally. I'm sorry."

He didn't say anything for the next half hour, never asked how it happened or where Maurice was found, none of the uncomfortable questions Mr. Glempse had posed. He sat looking at his shoes, rubbing his thumbs on his legs as if he was trying to absorb the bad news. Piper sat quiet, watching him, thinking about Billie Glempse, crossbow bolts, and county roads.

Finally, Wally got up and walked to the fireplace, took down a trophy and returned to the couch, dropped into a cushion and focused on the brass plaque beneath the figure of a football player.

"Maurice ... I called him Maury when we were little, but he hated it. He always corrected everyone. 'Maurice,' he'd say, 'that was the name my father gave me. I'm Maurice Tyler Langston.' After he graduated last May he had a chance go to Southern Miss on a football scholarship, but he didn't take it. He should have taken it and got the hell out of this pathetic county. I tried to talk him into it. But Maurice never had much ambition, said he'd never make it in the pros, said why bother wasting four years at a university to not get drafted into the NFL at the end of it. Funny, a couple of weeks ago he signed up for Ivy Tech, the Tell City branch near here. Was supposed to start in January, going to study some machine tool program and cut back to part-time at the power plant. I guess he'd picked up a little motivation over the summer."

"I'll need to contact your father, give him the news."

"Good luck with that. Like I said, he's in Florida ... or I think he is. I got a postcard from him three or four years back from Tampa Bay. Never gave us an address or a phone number. Just left. Name's Wallace Tyler. Wallace Tyler Langston. I was named after him. If you find him, tell him I said 'hi'."

He sat quiet again, fixated on the trophy.

Piper ordered the questions she intended to ask and focused on the sound of the rain hitting the roof. It had turned into quite a downpour.

She guessed she'd been here nearly an hour when he spoke again.

"Maurice started dating that cheerleader this past summer, meeting up at the big party in the park on the bluff. I was with him. I told him to stay away from her. But she'd come on to him. Fifteen, she was then, all pretty. Turned sixteen after summer was done. I know that 'cause for her birthday Maurice bought her a tennis bracelet he spent too much on. He told me they clicked over dead mothers. Mom died of a brain tumor. Maurice said her mom died to a brain aneurism. Dead brains, dead mothers, an awful thing to have in common, don't you think? But he was smitten. I figure she's why he enrolled in Ivy Tech, said he needed a better job with better pay because he was looking at forever with her. Maybe there's money in machine tools, you think? I told him he didn't need to worry about that. Girl, the way she dressed, had enough money for both of them. Still, machine tools, he was fixated on that. Do you think a machinist pulls in bucks?"

"I don't know. But I suppose a machinist can do well with the right company," Piper said. "He was going with Billie to a party tonight, right?"

Wally bobbed his head, eyes still on the trophy. "Maurice dressed up in some weird-shit outfit. She was dressed pretty skimpy when she came by to pick him up."

"When was that?"

"A little after four. Said she had errands first and wanted to stop for a sandwich in case she didn't like the snacks at the party."

"Do you know where they went before the party?"

"Nah. Errands, wherever the hell that took them. She came here in an ugly jeep and asked Maurice to drive it. She said they weren't going to show up at the party barn in Maurice's beat-to-shit Sundance. Classic car, though, ninety-three. He was gonna fix it up nice some-day." He paused. "Maybe I'll fix it up."

Piper continued with her questions, and Wally answered glumly.

"Enemies? Not any that I knew of ... unless the cheerleader had another suitor who was mad at Maurice for taking his girl. Maurice was a friendly guy, liked to read comic books and graphic novels, play video games, and hang out with the girl. Everybody liked him."

No problems at work—at the power plant, farm, or Splashin' Safari. "At least no problems he ever mentioned to me."

"Shouldn't have dated a wild teenager. He'd still be alive if he'd left her alone, went after someone his own age."

"No debt, but not all that many assets. This house? It's ours, free and clear, but the deed is still in Dad's name. We pay the utilities, property taxes."

"Drank sometimes. Who doesn't drink? Did you want something to drink, Sheriff? I should have asked you earlier. Pardon my manners."

"No thank you," Piper said.

"Like I said, he enjoyed video games, and bought a new one last week for his Xbox. But between work and the cheerleader he didn't have much spare time to play. It's still in the shrink wrap, the game."

Maurice had an iPad, which Wally retrieved and passed over freely.

Piper toured Maurice's bedroom, finding nothing especially interesting, and would meet with Basil tomorrow and share the information she picked up. Maybe she'd come back with search warrants to make it all proper, for the cars, too. But maybe they weren't necessary.

"Can I ask you a question, Sheriff?" Wally slowly lifted his eyes from the trophy.

Piper nodded. "Sure. I'll answer what I can."

"Was it a car accident? Did he get drunk at the party and run off the road? Did the cheerleader die, too?"

"Billie died too," Piper replied. "It wasn't a car accident."

"Was he wearing his costume?"

Piper nodded.

"I thought it was damn silly, the getup. But I was a little impressed. I told him he looked stupid, and I wished I hadn't said that. He'd made that costume. Picked up some clothes at Goodwill and added buttons and wires and pocket watches. Tooled a hunk of leather and turned it into a fake arm. Said he was Captain Hook and Billie was Tinker Bell. I saw the movie, you know, the original. Tinker Bell dies of old age and Captain Hook, I think he escapes. Damn. I wish I hadn't told him he looked stupid. It was a good costume, actually." He sucked in a deep breath. "Someone should tell Billie's folks."

"They know," Piper said.

She got up and walked to the door, turned off her body cam; she'd come back later or send a deputy to check on him.

Wally didn't budge from the couch.

"What am I going to do, Sheriff?" He looked at the trophy again, rubbing a thumb across the name plaque. "I don't have anybody now. I don't have anybody."

CHAPTER NINE

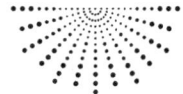

2 A.M. SUNDAY, NOVEMBER 1ST

Her silvery-blonde braid reached to the middle of her back, not a strand out of place. Her makeup was muted except for overlong eyelashes that would put country singers to shame. Piper wondered if the woman had trouble seeing because of them.

"Hey boss," Candace greeted as Piper walked past the dispatch desk. "What the hell are you doing here this time of the morning? I know there's a murder, but shouldn't you get some sleep?"

Two murders actually, Piper thought. And, yes, she should get some sleep.

"I want to go through a few things," she replied. "I'm not going to stay long."

"Coffee's fresh, if you want some." Candace Dennison was thirty-one, thin, stately, and had gray eyes that glimmered through the tinted lenses in her wire-framed glasses. She was the new eleven to seven a.m. dispatcher, and this was her third day on the job. Piper was happy to have her. Candace had been dispatching part-time for the Rockport Police Department, and when the Spencer County Sheriff's Department had a full-time opening, she'd been fast to apply.

Candace had told Piper she loved working for the police, but she wanted full-time, insurance, and she didn't care what hours she worked because her husband was in the Marines and had just been given a twelve-month assignment at the base in Okinawa, Japan, a long way from the recruiting station across the river in Owensboro that he'd been manning. Piper figured when the year was up and her husband came back Candace would either want a different shift or would go somewhere else.

"Zeke cut out of here with Teegan hours ago," Candace continued. "He left you this." She wagged a sheet of paper, and as Piper took it, she noticed that the dispatcher's manicured fingers had sparkly silver polish.

Piper had found Candace to be efficient, well-versed on Indiana law, a whiz at handling dispatcher duties, and a bit of a fashion plate. Today she wore navy linen pants and a crisp ivory blouse. A navy blazer was draped over the back of her chair. Piper had told her casual attire was fine, especially for the third shift, but Candace said she considered it important to "dress for the success you hope to be."

"I brought these in for you," Candace said, stretching behind her desk and retrieving a big canvas tote filled with magazines. "I'm done with these, should have thrown them out after my wedding. Good thing I didn't, eh? You might find some ideas or a dress you're dying to have. Toss them when you're done."

Piper took her evidence bags into the breakroom and came back for the tote. "Thanks, Candace."

"Have you set a date yet?" the dispatcher wondered. "I just love weddings."

"We're still mulling it over," Piper replied. "It will have to be after the first of the year so I can get some vacation time."

Candace's smiled wide, revealing perfect bright white teeth. "Ooooh, honeymoon. You need time off for a proper honeymoon. We went to Holland. You?"

"We're mulling that over too." Piper carried the tote into the breakroom to escape Candace's chatter. She eyed the coffeemaker. Craving coffee, dark roast. But that might keep her up even later.

Piper had almost gone home after the Langston visit; she was that tired and depressed. But at the same time, she was too anxious for sleep. Two dead teenagers and an unknown killer with a crossbow—a dozen shades of weird and wrong.

No motive stood out yet.

Basil must have come in after the jeep was towed. He'd started a murder board in the breakroom, pictures of Billie Glempse as Steampunkerbell and Maurice Langston from a high school football game at the top.

Down the side were some names she didn't recognize, but guessed they were from the party; Basil and Millie had reported that the neighbors along the county road had been no help. He'd texted her that he would be in at ten, right after early church services with his family. He would print the jeep then, treating it as part of a crime scene. He wouldn't be able to lift anything from the quarrels until after the autopsies.

"Definitely *no* on the coffee." She spread a sheet of butcher paper on the table, and went to work. Careful, methodical, she printed everything she'd taken from the pumpkin orange jeep, logged the evidence, and downloaded the fingerprints into the database for a search. Any DNA samples would be checked with the Combined DNA Index System, a national database used by law enforcement. Maybe they'd get some hits that would lead to the killer.

Next, she went through her messages.

Nang had sent her several, friendly mushy missives that included a report on the trick-or-treaters who were apparently "beyond happy" with full-sized candy bars and boxes of crayons. "Not much left." There was an unfortunate message, too:

"Night manager said kids egged my Quick Stop. Going over now to help clean it up. Will catch a few hours of sleep at the trailer before work tomorrow. Come for lunch? Something new on the menu."

"Lunch. Sure," she texted. She had to eat sometime.

There was a text from Dr. Neufeld: "Tink's autopsy first thing Monday, pulling all the strings to slip Captain Hook in after that."

Finally, she stared at the long note Zeke had left:

I remember Billie from the computer club. She shouldn't have joined, not as a freshman anyway. Smart, but distracted, didn't make many meetings. She only seemed to show up when she wanted help with something. For a novice, Billie was good with computers. Told me once she wanted to pursue fashion. I helped her with software, set her up with Adobe Illustrator for Fashion Design. I think she would've been good at it.

Easily noticed at school. She was pretty, hung out with the popular girls. Was voted freshman rep to the homecoming court last fall, nominated again this year, just missed out.

I poked around on her Facebook page, lots of cheerleading pictures, some pics of her and Maurice, lots of quotes about 'being your best self' and 'march to your own drum' stuff. Some pics of kittens. A lot of fashion shots and some video clips of runway models. Says her favorite shows are Say Yes to the Dress, Project Runway, Making the Cut, and Queer Eye for the Straight Guy.

This hits hard, two people I know dead. Sucks.

Let me know if I can help. I'll be home in the morning, then at Teegan's for lunch to check out her new house. I'll have my cell with me, so just holler if you need another hand.

This really sucks swamp water.

It does indeed suck swamp water, Piper thought.

She yawned, thought about going home, getting a few hours of sleep, feeding the dogs and the cat, and coming back in.

Piper pulled out the wedding magazines and spread them out like playing cards, thinking they might take her mind away from the dead teenagers.

She wouldn't have bought a single issue of any wedding magazine, though she'd watched a couple of episodes on television of *Say Yes to the Dress*—one of Billie's favorite shows. She had looked through some online sites that offered "barely used" dresses at discount prices. It had been a fun distraction and she'd imagined herself in a few of them.

A church wedding and a beautiful dress … dreamy and ridiculous at the same time, right? she mused. A one-day event that was an expensive big deal. A wedding at the courthouse was just as legal and certainly more practical. The courthouse route would be more sensible, and that's what she should suggest to Nang.

But the dresses on the covers were striking.

She'd wear such a dress once.

Once.

It wasn't practical to buy something fancy and frilly, and most certainly costly, for a one-day experience. A decorated Army veteran and a sheriff, lacy and delicate shouldn't suit her. Wasn't her style.

Shouldn't be her style?

Could it be?

She thumbed through the magazines: *Premier Bride, Wedding Style, Get Married, Brides, Town & Country Weddings, Martha Stewart Weddings, Bridal Guide, The Knot, Southern Bride, Weddings With Style, Modern Bride*.

Dresses shown ranged from several hundred dollars to a Vera Wang for $3,600 and an Oscar De La Renta "celestial gown" for almost $15,000.

Piper guessed Candace had put a lot of thought into her wedding … or just liked bridal magazines.

The courthouse would be easier.

The headlines were in bold bright type: 700 + Ways to Wow; Gorgeous Gowns for Your Budget and Style; Find the Perfect Dress; New Way to Wear Your Hair; Dream Dresses; and Cakes You'll Love.

"And two is four." Piper put the magazines back in the tote and would look through them at her leisure from her couch.

Maybe she would find the perfect dress in one of them. Because even though it wasn't practical or her style, she wanted a fancy dress with lace and sequins. It would cost too much, and it would be worn only once, and she'd stand next to Nang and look beautiful—hair and makeup flawless, nails silvery.

She'd look like a princess and let her dad walk her down the aisle.

A princess.

A wedding dress was just a costume, a garment that would take her out of the ordinary so she could appear as something else, someone else, for a day.

Billie Glempse's green-sequined costume was spattered with blood. Again, the teenager's face loomed in the back of her mind. Billie would never get to say yes to the dress.

"You leaving, Sheriff?" Candace fluttered her manicured fingers as Piper left the breakroom, carrying the tote.

"I'll be back by eight," Piper replied. "Thanks for these magazines."

"Hope you find a dress in there you like."

Piper hoped so, too. "With sequins," she said. "Lots of white sequins."

CHAPTER TEN

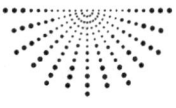

8 A.M.

Piper started with Betty Boop. That's the costume Victoria "Vic" Halliday wore to the steampunk party on Halloween. Piper glanced at her laptop, the costumed Vic on one side of the screen, her high school yearbook photo on the other; the dimpled chin and blue eyes the only features connecting the two images to the girl across from her.

Vic sat in the chair nearest Piper's desk.

"I didn't know Billie Glempse," Vic said. "Never heard of her." She had a lilting voice, and Piper thought she could do well in theater. A sophomore majoring in zoology at Kentucky Wesleyan College in Owensboro, Vic lived in Rockport, sharing an apartment with her older sister, Danica. At best only a half-hour drive, Wesleyan was a private school, tuition pushing $30,000 a year before books and other expenses. Maybe Vic had a scholarship.

"Never met her that I know of. She was that girl killed last night, right?" Vic looked around the sheriff's office before meeting Piper's gaze. "Heard Maurice was dating a high school cheerleader. Was that Billie Glempse?"

Piper nodded.

"Were they killed in a car accident or something? Maurice was supposed to be at the party last night. I was looking forward to catching up. We'd dated a few times my senior year."

Basil had put Victoria Halliday on his list of partygoers who had some connection to the murder victims. When he'd recorded the names, he hadn't known Maurice was dead.

"You didn't know Billie Glempse?"

"Didn't know her. Said that already. Did not know her."

"You knew Maurice Langston, dated him."

"Yeah, aren't you listening to me? I knew him. A few times, we went out, me and Maurice. I knew him sort of intimately," Vic continued. "The first time we went out, I was a junior, actually, and he'd just made the varsity football team … even though he was only a sophomore. I'd hang with his brother sometimes at the games, and we'd cheer him on. Maurice's brother—Langy, I called him—swore Maurice was going to get a college scholarship and turn pro. Langy had dreams of him getting drafted by the Rams so the two of them could move to California. I bet Langy is broken."

Piper had put Basil in charge of the investigation, but she was staying involved. And she was trying to build a picture of Maurice and Billie, getting to know them from their friends' perspectives. If she could paint a good enough picture, it could help lead to their killer.

"You hung out with Maurice *and* his brother." Piper regarded the girl. Pretty, just a touch of makeup, blonde hair tied back in a braid that stretched to her waist. It must have been difficult to tuck it up under her black Betty Boop wig. She wore tight blue jeans and an oversized purple sweater, a small tattoo of a butterfly on the back of her left hand.

"Yeah, I did. That's what I told you. Yeah, I knew Maurice *and* Langy. Do I need to repeat that again? But I didn't date Langy, just Maurice."

Piper didn't reply.

"When I was in high school, I'd hang out with both of them. Even went out with Maurice a couple of times early this summer. Everybody liked him. Not terribly bright, but he was fun, sociable, and maybe we all thought it'd be awesome to look back in a few years when he made it in the NFL and say 'I know him. He was a friend.' Jay Cutler was an NFL quarterback, and he's from Rockport. No, Santa Claus. He's from Santa Claus." She crossed her arms, obscuring the butterfly. "Langy asked me to tutor Maurice in biology. He didn't pay much, but it was only a few hours a week. I helped him pass the class —barely. Tutored him in chemistry, but that didn't take and he dropped the course. But he managed to graduate."

Vic leaned forward and put her elbows on the edge of the desk, the butterfly showing again; it was a Viceroy. "It wasn't a car accident, was it? Double-suicide? Something like that? You wouldn't call us in here for a car accident."

"We're investigating," Piper said. "I can't really comment right now. But is there anything else you can tell me about Maurice? Did anyone *not* like him? Any arguments or fights that you recall?"

Vic shook her head. "Nah. Like I said, everybody liked Maurice. And I never knew him to be depressed. So, it wasn't suicide either, was it? Maybe I'll call Langy and see if he'll tell me something. Hey, do you need me much longer? I have a test tomorrow, comparative verte-brate anatomy, and I need to study."

Piper made a note that Victoria might be prime for a second inter-view, and brought in the next one on the list.

Arthur Wilson had dressed as Dr. Frank N. Furter from *The Rocky Horror Picture Show*, his photo from the party showing a bustier bedecked with gears and keys. He was tall and athletic looking, wearing a Kansas City Chiefs sweatshirt and khaki jeans. According to the yearbook he was a junior, a wide receiver on the varsity football squad, and a member of FFA, Future Farmers of America.

"I only knew Maurice through football. I was on the JV team when he was a senior, and sometimes we'd all practice together, do the drills. Helluva runner. Oh, excuse me. You're recording this. Didn't mean to curse. He was gifted. I figured he'd take the scholarship and go to Mississippi, go pro after that. Everyone figured he'd take the scholarship."

Piper asked a string of questions, not finding much illuminating.

"He got along with pretty much everyone at school. Never hung with him besides football. But the quarterback last year wasn't too keen on him, thought Maurice was stealing the spotlight, making it more difficult for him to get noticed by the universities. Hell. Oh, excuse me. Heck, the quarterback was nothing special. It was Maurice who made him look good on pass-plays. Maurice helped his stats. He should have been grateful, not pissy about it."

"Never heard the two of them argue, exactly. Hell. Oh, excuse me. Language. Only once did he and Maurice really get into it, and that was after a game last year, September, when Maurice was supposed to get a lot more touches, but the quarterback went off script and we lost big time. Neither one of them ended up in college. But Maurice should have. He had the offer. He shouldn't have stuck around here. Hey, he'd be alive, right, if he'd went to Mississippi?"

Piper wrote down Reginald Willingham, who had been Maurice's quarterback during his junior and senior years.

"Nope. Reggie wasn't at the steampunk bash. Reggie never detasseled for Mr. Carlson. Reggie only worked for his dad, who runs the hardware store in Rockport. I think Reggie's still working there. I mean, what else is he gonna do?"

"Billie Glempse? Sure, if you went to any of the JV games you knew her. Well, knew who she was. Prettiest cheerleader. I knew Maurice was going out with her. Folks at the party were talking about it, figured Maurice would be showing up with her in tow. Maurice lucked out." A pause. "Except he didn't luck out. He ended up dead. Was it a car accident?"

The next interviewee was a little more interesting to Piper because she presented a better look into Billie's life.

"My BFF, you know. That means best friend forever. We were on the JV cheer squad together." Sally Lopez was short, broad-shouldered, and sported a jet-black pixie cut that looked like an acorn cap. She'd been a steampunk Statue of Liberty at the party, her torch a pipe that had copper wires and miniature tools affixed to it. According to Millie's notes, the torch lit up with a strobing effect.

Sally said she was ecstatic to get an invite to Hot and Steamy since this past summer had been her first for detasseling at Roger Carlson's farm.

"I didn't drink, nothing alcoholic. My dad always smells my breath every time I go out to make sure I don't drink or smoke. We're Catholic. Strict. I was lucky he let me go to the party with Jennifer. She's my neighbor, has detasseled two summers. Anyway, I stuck to the apple cider, which was amazing. They had pulled pork sandwiches, too. They were amazing. The music was amazing. I think everything was amazing that night." Each time she drew out the word so it sounded like a-maaaaaaaa-zing. "Amazing until the police showed up and asked all these questions, made them pour out the liquor. The party folded after that. I didn't dance much. I should have picked a better costume for dancing, all the fabric tangled around my legs. I was looking forward to seeing Billie's costume. She ordered it on Etsy, said her step-mom bought it for her, expensive. She was always trying to get her step-mom to buy her stuff."

The girl chattered on about the party and her friends' costumes. Piper listened, hoping to pick up some gems.

"You said Billie was your BFF. Tell me about her."

Sally went into another long stretch, with Piper waiting until something beyond cheer practice came through.

"She was sweet, always wanting to help people. Help with homework, sometimes just help by listening to your problems. Very sympathetic. She helped at all the cheer fundraisers, the bake shop, taffy sale. If you needed something, she'd try to get it for you. She'd be your shoulder to cry on if you were having a rough time. I told her she'd make a great nun. She laughed at that, said she wasn't Catholic. But it was true, she would've killed it as a nun. I figured after high school she'd go into social work, maybe go to a big city. She wanted to go to a big city for sure, New York. Told me over the summer that she wanted to enroll in Parsons School of Design right after high school. Hella expensive. She said it was about two thousand a credit. But she would've nailed some sort of scholarship or got her folks to cover it. She was amazing at fashion design. Wanted to audition for *Project Runway* when she hit eighteen. Have to be eighteen." Sally took a breath and kept going. "She didn't need to buy the Tinker Bell costume on Etsy, she could have made it. I just think she was so busy with classes and cheering and spending time with her boyfriend—Maurice Langston, who she swore she was in love with—that buying the costume was easier. She emailed me a picture of it. I sure would have liked to see her in it."

Sally started crying then, folding in on herself and shaking. Piper let her be and glanced out the window.

Piper was tired, had stayed up into the early-morning hours, nabbed only three hours of sleep and a shower before coming back in. Hungry, and definitely craving coffee. When this interview was over, she'd get a big mug.

"Everyone liked her," Sally said when she came up for air. "She was my best friend. Giving, kind. Honestly, she would have been an amazing nun."

Sally hadn't asked how Billie had died. Maybe she'd heard through Spencer County's notorious grapevine. Maybe the how of it wasn't important to Sally, just that she'd lost her friend.

Several minutes later, mug of steaming coffee in front of her, Piper called in the last one on her list this morning.

Glenda Smith: senior, glee club member, varsity cheerleader, occasional corn detassel worker, and Little Red Riding Hood. The picture from the party showed her outfit was skimpy, scarlet-sequined with a big gear over each breast, and might have been a good companion piece to Billie's Steampunkerbell.

"Couldn't stand her," Glenda said. "Little Miss Pretty Perfect who had the boys following her around the halls. I'm sure Billie thought she was hot shit." A few more questions and Glenda admitted to dating Maurice during her junior year. "Didn't go out with him in the summer, too much going on. Found out he'd hooked up with Billie at the Fourth picnic in the park. Dropped me for her. And now they're both dead. Pity. He might still be breathing if he'd not hooked up with her."

It certainly didn't sound like Glenda was sad, but she wasn't a suspect. Glenda was home with her parents until her date picked her up at 6:30 for Hot and Steamy.

Zeke poked his head in after Glenda left. "Hey, Sheriff, need a refill? I'm going to the breakroom for a Dew."

Piper nodded and passed over her mug.

She intended to drink a lot of coffee today.

CHAPTER ELEVEN

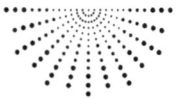

11 A.M.

Nothing from Diego and Rocco this morning," Piper said. She and Basil had been discussing the evidence and her brief interviews with Billie's friends. They sat with coffee and herbal tea respectively in the breakroom. The whiteboard was cluttered with photographs and names.

"That rain we had late, I didn't expect Thresher to get more hits in the pumpkin field after," Basil said. "And he didn't. But in the jeep, the dog keyed in on that backpack and floorboards right away. The backpack had something in it at one time. Floorboards in the front had something, too. Getting some samples sent to the lab first thing tomorrow morning. I'm guessing drugs, but we'll see what the lab tells us. What kind of drugs."

The detective stared at the surface of his tea. "Printed the jeep, matches Maurice, Billie, and there are five other sets. The others could be the Glempses, kids and parents. Could be someone else, but no one on record." He pushed back from the table and went to the board.

He pointed at Roger Carlson's name. "Seemed to mean well, hosting a party for young people who'd done work for him. But I don't like him. Served under-age kids alcohol. I know there was some pot. And he knew there was pot."

"As for Trenton Carlson, the son, George Washington here cooperated, but had an attitude. And he has one arrest on file. Twenty-one now, but last summer he got pulled over for a DUI and leaving the scene of property damage. He'd taken out a couple of mailboxes and a flower planter on his way home from a friend's house. Under the legal age for drinking at the time."

Next, Marc Tolbert. "Han Solo was the buddy who supplied Trenton the alcohol last summer. Friendly kid, turned twenty-two a few days ago. Scared to death I was going to arrest him for something."

Basil underlined three names. "These girls are cheerleaders, friends of Billie Glempse. Had nothing but good things to say about her, how amazingly talented, witty, and stylish she was." One of them was Sally, the girl with the acorn cap hair. He underlined three more. "These girls couldn't stand her, considered her a 'mean girl' who body shamed pudgy students. Typical high school stuff." One of those girls was Glenda.

He pointed to the rest. "These all knew Maurice, and spoke good and bad. Called him friendly and helpful, but unambitious. One labeled him a loser, another said he was a big disappointment. Most thought he had a great football record at high school and that he should have pursued it in college on a scholarship. Diego is chatting up some of the other partiers this afternoon."

Basil returned to the table and finished his tea. "None of the kids I talked to last night knew Billie and Maurice were dead at that time, just figured the two were in trouble since I was asking about them. In fact, I didn't know Maurice was dead until I got a radio call as I was leaving the barn. I don't consider any of the kids suspects. But we might be able to get some more information from them, something useful that'll point us to an actual suspect. What you got this morning was insightful." He paused. "Millie was good help yesterday, by the way."

"Something useful. Like why someone wanted Billie and Maurice dead," Piper said. "I didn't pick up a motive from my chats this morning. But there was some jealousy."

"Jealous boyfriend? Jealous girlfriend? Neither one of our victims had a juvenile record, or an adult record in Maurice's case." Basil tapped his fingers on the table like he was playing a tune on a piano. "Were both targeted? Or just one? And if that, which one?" He tapped faster. "Was the other killed as collateral? To silence a witness to the first killing?"

He looked up to the board with the column of names. "Like I said, I don't think any of the kids at that party—and I have pictures, names, addresses, phone numbers of all of them—directly had anything to do with the killings. Still, maybe one of them knows something, about an enemy, debt, something that could help us."

"But isn't talking enough," Piper said.

"Isn't talking enough *yet*." He leaned back in the chair. "I'm going to sort through them all today, decide if there are more to add to our interview list, who likely *really* knew Maurice and Billie. Roger Carlson again, certainly. Maurice worked for him. See if something shakes out about who in the county might have had it in for one or both of them. I figure on stopping at the high school tomorrow after the autopsies, talk to the teachers."

"You're very good at all of this," Piper said.

"That's why you hired me." Basil grinned.

Piper ran a thumb around the rim of her coffee cup and lowered her face to inhale the dark roast scent. "I stopped by the Glempse house earlier, and they turned me away, so I came back here. Said the family was going to service church and that I should come over tomorrow."

"Have to respect that," Basil said. "Might want to wait anyway until after the autopsies before you go back."

Piper nodded. A good idea. She could give the Glempses more information and might come up with additional questions. Wallace Langston, too. She'd revisit him after his brother's autopsy and to make sure he was handling the situation. Rocco and Diego had stopped there this morning and reported that a couple of friends from his work were there trying to console him.

"I haven't been able to locate Maurice Langston's father," she said. "I've put out feelers to sheriff and police departments in Florida. I searched records on voter information in the state. With few exceptions, once filed, a voter's name, address, phone number, email, all of that is public. I found zip."

"Maybe Maurice's father doesn't vote."

"Crossbows don't make much noise," Piper said, abruptly shifting the topic. "Not like a gun. But they strike me as an unusual weapon, unless you're a bow hunter."

"Yeah, I've been stuck on that, too," Basil admitted. "I searched on archery shops in the area that also sell crossbows. The closest one is in Ferdinand, a little over a half-hour drive."

"It's not open on Sunday. I searched, too," she said. "But there's a sporting goods place way over in Corydon that's open today. I called. The owner says he'll be happy to talk to me about crossbows. I'll head over after lunch. I promised Nang I'd come by for—"

"I'm going to Nang's for lunch, too," Basil cut in. "I'm meeting Tug there at one. Why don't you join us? I can introduce you."

"Is he your friend who just bought the Fulda tavern?" The detective had mentioned a few days ago that a former partner from Gangs and Narcotics decided to try the rural life and move here, following Basil's lead.

"Tug always talked about buying a bar downtown," Basil returned. "This is way the hell miles from that. The culture shock and whiteness of this county hasn't wholly registered on him. But the price of the tavern was a steal, and it came with a furnished upstairs apartment."

The tavern in Fulda had been owned by a retired school teacher. But she, her brother, and two other individuals had been charged with killing a man in September. She'd put the tavern up for sale to help cover her legal fees.

"I'm glad the place is going to stay open," Piper said. But she wasn't sure she was being honest. Depending on what Basil's friend did with the place, it might compete with Nang's Quick Stop for dining options, and that kind of competition in a bitty-burg could be unfortunate. She tried to banish that thought. Nang was an excellent chef and would be difficult to challenge; he could weather any competition.

"Yeah, I'll bet both you and Nang are glad," Basil returned skeptically. "Just tons of glad. So, join us?"

"Sure."

"Don't worry, the business isn't going to last all that long. Tug was born in Chicago, don't think he ever lived any place else. He won't be able to handle Spencer County. I give it six months before the ruralness sends him packing."

"Maybe he'll surprise you."

Basil's eyes narrowed. "Never liked surprises, Sheriff. Rarely are they good."

CHAPTER TWELVE

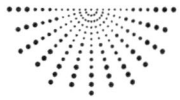

12:20 P.M.

B FH," Zeke declared. "Big Effin' House."

Teegan's place was on St. Peter's Church Road as far east as you could get and still be in Santa Claus' limits. The next house over was considered in the county's jurisdiction.

It was huge, compared to what he'd expected. A rustic run-down castle. Teegan lived alone, why the hell would she need something this honking big? It had to be at least sixty feet across. White—but in need of paint or new siding; two stories—though technically three with those turret things on the corners; an enclosed front porch—some screens needed replacing—that stretched the length and wrapped around one side; and a detached garage behind the house that could hold three cars or a seriously nice workshop. A massive oak tree shaded the entire front lawn.

He walked his bike up the gravel drive, balancing two bags of ice on his shoulders. Paul Blackwell's car was parked next to Teegan's.

Teegan came out a side door. "You're late." She wagged a finger.

"Not by much," Zeke returned.

"Late is late."

"I have impressive leg muscles," Zeke said. He leaned the bike against the side of her house.

"I don't give a crap about your leg muscles." Teegan took the bags of ice. "I care that the ice looks melty. I would have drove to the gas station and got ice myself if I'd known you were going to ride your bike and let it melt."

"Serilda's still in the shop," Zeke said. "And it's not all that melty. My goosebumps have goosebumps from carrying it."

Serilda, a Teutonic name meaning "a maiden in battle armor," was a 1974 Chevy Nova he'd acquired in May for the princely amount of $300. It would likely remain at Nang's for another two weeks for the current restoration project, and then would return to the garage in the spring for more repairs. He had saved up and bought the parts. Nang had volunteered to do most of the work in his spare time, provided Zeke pitched in and followed directions. Rear-wheel drive, three-speed manual gearbox, metallic blue, nearly three hundred thousand miles, a supplanted V8 engine that Zeke intended to eventually replace with a standard ss six-cylinder she would have come with, bench seats, and a huge "three body trunk." It would likely take more than a year to wholly restore her.

It was one of those win-win things for Zeke; his ride was slowly getting turned into a showpiece, and he was getting in better shape. He'd lost eight pounds, not that he really needed to. But he'd increased his stamina from riding his bicycle everywhere. He'd been riding so much that he was considering entering one of the long-distance races scheduled in Indianapolis toward the end of the month. If he won, he'd use the prize money for more parts for Serilda.

He followed Teegan up cracked cement steps into an outdated kitchen. The walls were a faded mustard yellow, the curtains a gaudy sunflower print, and the floor was brown checkered linoleum worn and scuffed in places. No appliances, but there were empty spaces for them. An oval table with a gray-veined Formica top and four card table chairs sat in the middle.

Paul Blackwell, the chief of police of Santa Claus and the former Spencer County Sheriff, was already seated. Sub sandwiches, a dozen small bags of chips, and a box of cupcakes took up the center of the table.

Zeke watched as Teegan dumped the ice into a chest that held cans of Diet Dr. Pepper, Mountain Dew, and Budweiser.

"Loved the tour," Paul said. He reached for one of the sandwiches and unwrapped it. To Zeke: "Maybe she'll show you around her new house after lunch."

"New? My new house isn't so new. It was built in 1860," she said, joining them. Teegan poked through the sandwiches and found one labeled SALAMI AND PROVOLONE. "Three thousand, eight hundred square feet, seven bedrooms, two bathrooms—though that'll change. Got two window air conditioners, and it's a good thing we're in the fall because two window units are not enough for our summers." She paused. "It has good bones, but it needs a little work, this place."

"A fixer-upper," Paul said. He started in on his turkey deluxe.

"Why'd you pick this? I mean, it's beat up, Teegan. And it's friggin' huge. It's going to cost a lot to turn this—" Zeke realized he'd misspoken when he saw the flash of irritation on her face.

"*You* invited yourself over," Teegan bit back. "*You* wanted to see the place. And *I* think it's fine and dandy. Good bones, I said. It cost me thirty-thousand dollars. They wanted more, originally asking fifty, which also would have been a steal. But for whatever reason it sat on the market for about two years, so they took my offer. I paid cash. Some cars cost as much as this house, Zeke. And, yeah, it is a little worn. Okay, a lot worn. I've got a contractor lined up to start next Wednesday. Blow-in insulation, new drywall, paint, update the plumbing. New furnace and central air—two HVACs, he said I should have. You don't need to insult my—"

"Sorry. Sorry. I'm sorry," Zeke said. He really was. "I didn't mean to insult you or your house. I'm envious, actually. I live in a third-floor crappy little apartment and you've got three entire floors all to yourself."

"Two," she cut back. "The turrets don't really count. They're just roundish rooms and I'm going to put a telescope in one and a big beanbag chair in the other to make it a reading nook. I've picked out some wallpaper and—"

"I like your purple hair," Paul said. "Good sandwich."

"The stylist called it spiced plum." She let out a long breath. "I like the new color and cut. And I like my house, too."

"It's a fine house," Paul said. "You'll be happy owning one and—"

"I don't know if I'll ever have enough money for a house. Well, not anytime soon," Zeke groused.

"Serilda costing you too much?" This from Teegan.

"Costing me some, but it's the online classes I started taking last month that's drinking most of my money."

"Didn't think college was in your plans," Teegan said.

Zeke shrugged. "I'm going for a bachelor's in Information Security. It's good for police work. I'm focusing on project management, getting certified as a business analyst. It's through Western Governor's University, a customized IT program with cyber security, information assurance, network operations, and stuff like that. All online, self-paced. Even working full time, I'll get a four-year degree in three because I'm fast with the computer part of it."

"Nice," Paul said. "And good on you. That'll make you valuable for law enforcement."

"Hey, Paul, did you hear we had two murders last night? Teenagers? I knew them. I knew both of them." Zeke was fixated on the cases, hadn't slept much last night thinking about them. "Makes you realize how short life is. That you can die at any time. Be killed. Crossbow bolts, like all medieval or Dungeons & Dragons or Warcraft or—"

Paul sat his sandwich down and reached for a bag of Sun Chips. "Piper says they don't have much on either case, just a bunch of questions. Santa Claus was quiet in comparison yesterday. Worst call we had was a neighbor complaining about a Christmas-themed Halloween party where the elves were having a contest to see who could ho-ho-ho the loudest."

"I caught the first murder call," Teegan said. "Tinker Bell—Steampunkerbell, actually—in a ditch. Lord, she was pretty."

The conversation drifted back to Teegan's house as the sandwiches and chips disappeared. Zeke delighted in the thick allotment of peppers and onions on the beef that put some zing in his mouth. The sauce was wonderful, too, and he held it on his tongue.

"This place came furnished," she continued. "Included trash, old stuff in the attic, and tacky drapes. Oh, and a riding lawnmower that works. The real estate guy said someone had broken in and swiped the appliances out of the kitchen, and the washer and dryer from the basement. They left the ratty old furniture that I'm having removed."

"I'll check if he filed a police report," Paul volunteered. He stretched over and lifted the lid of the cooler, plucked out a Mountain Dew and handed it to Zeke. He passed Teegan a Diet Dr. Pepper, and retrieved the same for himself. Then he grabbed two cupcakes. "If he filed a police report, you might be able to claim something through insurance."

Teegan fluttered her fingers. "Not worried about it. I ordered new everything, stainless for the kitchen, they come in Thursday. The day after I'm having new kitchen cabinets installed with quartz counter-tops. I have a table on order, too. I'm gonna relegate this one to the garage. I'm getting a stackable washer and dryer and turning one of the upstairs bedrooms into a laundry room and walk-in closet to make one of those master suites like you see on the home reno shows. Not going to traipse up and down rickety basement stairs to get clean clothes. Adding a bathroom, too, with one of those fancy rainfall showers. Converting another bedroom for that. I do not need seven bedrooms. And one of them will be an awesome craft room." She grinned wide. "See, the house is paying to furnish itself. I don't have to slay the rest of my savings. In fact, that's exactly why I bought this as-is fixer-upper. The real estate agent didn't realize the gem he had."

"Huh?" Zeke took another big bite of the roast beef and chewed quick. "I'm lost. The house is paying for itself?"

"I found some goodies in the music room. The piano in there is in rough shape and I'm going to junk it. The violin is broken, the clarinet is missing all the pads, which is fixable. The console stereo is clunky. But the albums. Jackpot. The albums are at the root of my grabbing this house. I probably would have paid forty thousand, maybe fifty. Just because of the records."

"I didn't know you were into music," Zeke said.

"Jazz, blues. And there was a big assortment—still is, I only sold half. See, I know the blues, and the real estate agent didn't. I sold quite a few on eBay to a music collector." She cocked her head and tapped her thumbs against the Formica, as if trying to recall the specifics. "*The Freewheelin' Bob Dylan*, mono version with four extra cuts, I got fifteen grand for it. John Coltrane's *Blue Train*, Hank Mobley, Roland Kirk's *Triple Threat*, and a dozen and a half other rares, basically mint condition. All totaled bringing in twice as much as what I shelled out for my rundown palace. They're furnishing my house and paying for some of the renovations. And I still have more albums to put up."

Paul whistled. "You find any other treasures?"

"There's a bunch of stuff in the attic, and I've poked through it only a little. I need to get back to digging. Seems to be mostly cobwebs and Christmas decorations. I can probably deck my halls to my heart's content."

"Sweet," Zeke said. "After I get my degree, I'm going to start saving up to buy a house, too. If I get Serilda all shiny, I can sell her to help." He downed the Mountain Dew and let the bubbles tease his throat. He finished the roast beef and eyed the cupcakes. "You going to give me a tour?"

"I've got to be in the office by three," she said. "So, yeah, I've got time for a tour."

"I have to get home to Wrinkles. My pug doesn't like it when I leave him alone too long. Separation anxiety." Paul rose and stretched, worked a kink out of his neck, and looked around. "Waste basket?"

"Just leave everything on the table, and I'll clean up," Teegan said. "The house came with a lot of trash, and no wastebaskets. I need to add them to my shopping list." She sighed. "Trash? I almost forgot to tell you. I found one hundred pizza boxes—all empty except for crumbs and mouse turds—spread out between the kitchen and dining room. Like the previous owner wasn't willing to part with them. Ah, the pain of buying a hoarder's haven."

"So that's why you've sworn off pizza," Zeke said.

"I'll never order a pizza delivered to this place," Teegan returned. "Now, for that tour."

Zeke had watched a few of those HGTV remodeling shows late at night; he liked the one where a husband and wife gave a facelift to a little town in Alabama. As Teegan took him through the rooms, he imagined what they'd look like modernized. Some wainscotting here, dropped light fixtures there, polish on the hardwoods.

"What made you decide to buy? I mean, you were looking, right? Before you saw Bob Dylan?" Zeke *really* wanted his own place. He needed a hefty bank account for the down payment. No way would he be able to find an "as is" place with a treasure-trove of antique jazz albums.

"A rocking chair," Teegan said flatly, as she took him up to the second floor.

"You wanted a front porch where you could have a rocking chair? You're not that old."

She laughed. It was a nice laugh. He didn't think she laughed often enough.

"My apartment in Rockport? And by the by, I was hoping for a house *in* Rockport so I'd have a shorter drive to work ...until I found Bob Dylan and Hank Mobley here. My apartment was on the first floor, and a guy named Craig was on the second right above me. I'd come home from work, crash, and be woken up about three every morning with this funky creepy creaking sound. I went upstairs and banged on his door, trying to get him to cool it."

"And—"

"I found out Craig and his wife recently had a baby and he'd get up and rock it around three every morning to get it to settle down."

"In a rocking chair."

"Yeah, a big old rocking chair that was starting to fall apart and was crooked. It made this loud eerie sound each time he went back and forth. I stopped up there a few mornings in a row, asking him to shut it down, which he ignored. I finally volunteered to buy him a new rocking chair that would be quiet."

"And—"

"He got pissed, said this old rocker was from his grandfather and it had sentimental value. Then he went and complained to the apartment manager about me." She snarled at the memory as she led him through the second-floor rooms. "The apartment manager—who never liked me because he said I looked like a cross between Morticia Addams and a biker chick—told me I was going to have to move to another apartment. He had an efficiency on the other side of the building." She paused. "A *little* efficiency."

"So, you started house hunting."

"Yep, and this is the eighth house I looked at. I found the turrets, Bob Dylan and friends, and figured this was the place." She stretched up, pulled a cord, and a ladder extended down from the ceiling. "The attic. You must come up and take a look at my nightmare. Be careful. You have to walk on the rafters. I don't want you falling through the ceiling. Though you might as well do that before the drywallers come."

Zeke almost didn't follow her. A fusty miasma wafted down and he saw dust motes dancing when she turned on a light. But curiosity tugged him. The ladder felt a little rickety, but he'd lost eight pounds. Svelte, he was hopeful it would support him.

He poked his head up and took in a maze of boxes, most of them with labels. "There's gotta be a hundred."

"More than that, I'm thinking. And none of them are pizza boxes," Teegan returned. "Come on. I'll give you a hand."

Zeke balanced on the rafters. It was hot, stuffy, the scent of old things pummeling him and threatening to push him downstairs. Teegan edged away, walking effortlessly like she performed a balance beam routine. She held up a small carton.

"Barbie in a box. She looks to be one of the older models, might be worth selling."

Zeke noted a lot of Halloween costumes in their original packaging: Sylvester, Tweety Bird, Mickey and Minnie, Raggedy Ann and Andy. Everything taped.

"Hey, Teegan, do you ever watch *American Pickers*? Those kids' costumes have some value."

"Yeah, I was thinking that. I'd like a deck off the back of the house. Maybe I can find enough stuff up here to pay for one."

The bulk of the boxes looked to be Christmas decorations, including three large artificial trees, one of them the old aluminum kind with the color wheel. Vintage stuff, Zeke figured, trashy assets.

"Some luggage, bowling ball bags without the balls, all sorts of odds and ends," Teegan said. "I really need to pick through this carefully. Care— oh, look, a Care Bear in a plastic bag. And here's a My Little Pony. Boxes and boxes of ornaments. And there are a few sea chests that have old costumes in them. See?" She opened one and Zeke slid toward her, coughing on the dust cloud she raised. "I don't think they're Halloween costumes. Way the hell too elaborate for that. Fancy material. A lot of velvet. More like something you'd wear in a play at the theater. 'Cept I don't know if there was ever a theater around here."

Zeke thought the Steampunkerbell costume had been elaborate. Some folks went all out for Halloween.

"And there's a box with a wedding dress and another labeled wedding pictures," Zeke said. "And more Christmas. Most of these are marked, Teegan. Garland, Christmas cards, manger one, manger two, manger three, manger six, tested outdoor light strings, tested indoor light strings," he continued to read. "Rudolph, Prancer, Mrs. Claus, styro candy canes."

"Skeleton in a chest," Teegan observed, raising another lid. "Shit. Shit. Shit."

Zeke nearly toppled off the rafters when he peered through the disturbed dust motes and saw what Teegan gestured at. He held onto a stack of Christmas light boxes for balance as he shuffled over.

"That really is a skeleton," Zeke said.

"A real skeleton," Teegan said. "Shit. Shit. Shit."

"I wonder if it's someone who used to live here." Zeke stared, not enough room for it to be laid out straight in the chest, it was sort of scrunched up and would have been uncomfortable if the man or woman had been living when put in there.

"I'm going to be late for work today," Teegan said.

"Yep." Zeke continued to stare. "Nifty as-is house you bought, Teegan. Bob Dylan, Hank Mobley, and … this. Hey, you did say the place had good bones." He backed away, inching toward the ladder. "I'm going to call Paul to come back. You're in Santa Claus. It's his jurisdiction."

He heard her say "Shit. Shit. Shit." once more before he stopped on the second-floor landing and reached for his cell phone.

CHAPTER THIRTEEN

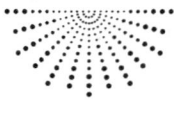

1 P.M.

Piper pulled into Phan's Quick Stop in Fulda. There were four pumps under an aluminum canopy. Two offered regular and premium; the others were diesel with nozzles set higher to accommodate farm vehicles. She filled up her Explorer, parked, and went inside to join Basil and his friend.

The interior was immaculate—it always was—with four tight aisles of snacks, bread, cereal, and canned fruits and vegetables. One wall consisted of glass-doored refrigerators that held beverages, dairy, eggs, and sliced meats. A smaller section was a freezer stocked with ice cream and popsicles. A limited assortment with fair prices that offered Fulda residents an alternative to driving to Rockport for groceries.

All traces of the once copious Halloween decorations were gone. A small rack of greeting cards had Thanksgiving choices, and she spotted a few Christmas cards. She wondered how early Nang would put up decorations for Christmas; the whole county tended to be early with that.

An area roughly a dozen feet square beyond the restroom doors had three round tables with four chairs each, and through a doorway behind the counter she spied the tiny kitchen. A middle-aged man busily worked there; one of Nang's recent hires.

Altogether, the gas station/grocery/restaurant fit in roughly three-thousand square feet, and it had a full-service garage attached. Nang had created this little empire with the winnings from a lottery ticket coupled with a lot of hard work.

She'd met him on her first stop to this Quick Mart in January, the second day of her job as the new sheriff of Spencer County. He'd intrigued her immediately, though she had no clue then that it might turn into forever. She caught him grinning at her now from behind his register.

"Over here!" Basil waved from the farthest table.

She joined him, Nang following with a pad to write their orders.

"I'll take the Crab Meat Sui Mai and Dan Dan Noodles Chen," Piper said, as she sat. "I know you put something new on the menu, but I really want the Sui Mai." A pause: "And coffee, black. A big cup."

Basil ordered next. "Spicy mung bean noodle soup, extra-large, and decaf tea."

The man across from Basil studied the menu. "Really wanted a hot dog." He was built like a linebacker, muscles evident under his gray mesh tank, head shaved, a gold cross dangling from his left ear, the soul patch the only bit of hair she noticed. His skin was the shade of polished chestnut, and she saw one tattoo on his upper right arm: an eagle and anchor with U.S.N. printed under it. "I had my heart set on a couple of hot dogs with sauerkraut and mustard."

"They are bad for you, hot dogs," Nang said. "My food is very good."

The man scowled. "How about an order of pork dumplings in chili oil, and a cup of that noodle soup that Sherlock's having. And a giant Diet Coke, cherry if you have it. Not a lot of ice, I don't like it watered down."

Nang hurried into the kitchen.

"Hot dogs," Basil growled. "Really, Tug? Everything here is excellent."

"So you've told me." Tug swiveled to face Piper. "And you're Sherlock's boss."

"Piper." She extended her hand.

"Sheriff Piper Blackwell," Basil said.

"Heard a lot about you, Sheriff Blackwell." Tug shook her hand. She felt a grip iron, his fingers calloused. "Most of it good. Told me all about your shattered arm and your shoot-out in Kentucky. Impressive. And as for hot dogs, I don't care if they're bad for you. Life's short, right? We're all temporary. Eat what makes you happy."

Again, she thought of the teenagers.

"Too short sometimes," she replied. "And I like hot dogs too."

"I miss the hot dogs on the corner outside the station." Tug leaned back in the chair. "Hell, I miss the corner and the station. I miss the city and I've only been away for two and a half weeks. The quiet around here is monotonous."

Piper glanced down at the cardstock placemat with a November calendar on one half and a picture of an impressive pagoda-style temple ringed by orange and yellow flowers on the other. She listened to Basil and Tug talk about the Gangs and Narcotics Division, their conversation drifting to the back while she thought about the murders. A crossbow. Why kill someone with that? Quiet? Certainly, when compared to a gun. But not as lethal unless you were a good shot ... which the killer appeared to be. At neither scene did they find extra quarrels that had missed the mark. Was the weapon used solely because it was quiet and could kill at a distance? Was the killer into unusual weapons?

"Here you go." Nang sat a tray on the table, and then took off a plate brimming with crabmeat and noodles and placed it in front of Piper before serving Basil and Tug. She knew if the Quick Stop was busy, he wouldn't be waiting on them and they'd instead get one of his employees ... or maybe he would wait on them anyway because she was here.

He arranged the silverware and chopsticks and retreated, coming back with drinks. "Coffee, Dark Italian," Nang said. To Basil: "This is organic Vietnamese cinnamon herb tea that I recently started carrying. I have boxes of thirty-six bags for eight dollars if you're interested. I also have my usual green tea, but I thought you should try this." To Tug: "Diet Cherry Coke, light on the ice. Nice to meet you. I understand you have purchased the tavern down the road."

"The one that belonged to the murdering retired school teacher." Tug nodded. "I did, indeed. One of those impulse things."

"Piper is also impulsive. I hope you will like Fulda, Mr. Tug," Nang said. "Lovely small community. And except for the two murders this past year, it is peaceful." He retreated to the cash register to ring up a farmer buying gas and scratch-off lottery tickets.

"I'm curious," Piper directed to Tug. She knew Basil answered her detective posting because he wanted to stay in law enforcement and get away from Chicago. Too much gun violence, he'd said, thinking about his children's safety. She'd heard on the news this morning that sixty-eight people were shot in Chicago during the past two days, one of them a four-year-old boy who was getting a haircut in an apartment. But what had lured Basil's friend and former partner? "What brings you to Spencer County? Basil's rave reviews?"

Tug half-snorted his soda. "Ha! I suppose that's one way to look at it. Honestly, I do not like specks on the map. Give me a big, sprawling, noisy, wonderful city with baseball and music fests. And Chicago is the best. But ...." He swiped at his forehead, as if wiping out a memory. "Hope you're not the gossipy sort, Sheriff. My seventeen-year-old daughter got caught up with the wrong people. I had to choose between the city and my job ... and her."

Piper was intrigued, but he hadn't yet wholly answered her question. She dug into her lunch, letting the flavors float on her tongue, watching Basil and Tug enjoy Nang's cooking.

Finally Tug surfaced again. "This is good." He pointed to his plate. "I could get used to this."

"Told you Nang's an exceptional chef." Basil pushed his empty soup bowl away. "There are sixty gangs in Chicago, Sheriff Blackwell."

"Fifty-nine," Tug corrected. "A lot of them have splintered to neighborhood and block alliances. About a hundred thousand members in the metropolitan area, I'd wager most of them active.

Cops deal with them all the time. You can stop one operation, but there's always something else out there. Arrest a bunch of gang-bangers, and more replace them. Nature of Chicago. Nature of big cities."

"It's fascinating, awful, and exciting police work," Basil said. He picked up his tea.

"Until it hits home. My daughter, Angel, got hooked up with a high-ranking Vice Lord. It's a gang that goes back to 1958, thousands of members throughout the country, the biggest knot of them in Chicago and the Great Lakes region. Once upon a time, I think maybe in the sixties, they got involved in community development to pick up a more positive image. But that didn't last. Today, there are several factions of them, and they're linked with the People Nation, Black Gangster Disciples, and Latin Kings. Me and Angel lived on the South Side, Morgan Park, and she fell in with some of them. When I worked nights, I couldn't keep track of her all the time."

"You did what you could, Tug," Basil said.

He shrugged, the gold cross glimmering in the fluorescent lights. "Sure. But it wasn't enough. She's pregnant, due in mid-December, and the daddy Vice Lord says she and the baby are moving in with him. Told her that if she didn't, he'd kill her, wasn't going to let the baby grow up under another man's roof, or without a father. Here's the thing—I know damn well he doesn't have any serious interest in Angel or the baby. What's that racist crack the white patrolmen spew ... what's the most confusing day in Chicago?" He paused and fixed Piper with a stare. "Father's Day in the Projects. Baby-daddy is just interested in laying claim to the daughter and grandchild of a deco-rated Chicago detective. I'm taking the threat as real. We packed up and left early one morning."

He stopped his story to finish the meal and chase it down with a slug of soda. "No way I can protect her in Chicago ... no matter where I would move in the city. But Green Acres? I am pretty damn sure the gangbangers will not follow her to Hooterville. It's what I'm betting on. And though there are a lot of sleepy boring little burgs across the country, this one has Sherlock. Best damn detective, best damn partner I ever worked with. I trust him to have my back if I get a whiff of the Vice Lords calling. Just safer being in his neighborhood."

"The tavern is in my name," Basil said. "Mine and Esme's. Tug and Angel can't be tracked that way."

"I paid for it, though," Tug said. "Cheap. I suspect because it's in Hooterville and a murderer owned it." He chuckled. "I tell you, Sheriff, I always wanted to own a bar. Figured it would be in the Loop, a cop bar, friendly, rowdy, something to do when I retired."

"You're forty, Tug," Basil said. "You don't have your twenty in yet with the department."

"Everybody retires someday. I'm just getting my bar earlier than planned, farther from the Loop than I ever dreamed. Hey, it comes with a big apartment upstairs. Three bedrooms, two baths, nice kitchen with a six-burner stove." He downed the rest of the soda. "But this isn't going to turn into forever. Hooterville doesn't suit my style, and this county is way the hell whiter than Sherlock implied. I figure two years ought to be enough time for Angel's baby-daddy to forget about her and me. Maybe it won't take that long, we'll see. My plan is to wait it out, get Angel in a good spot, high school diploma, some plan for her future. Then I'll look about moving back to Chicago, pick up where I left off on the road to retirement and a pension. Or maybe Baltimore, something big on the east coast if I can carry my time over."

Basil put in: "You won't have trouble rejoining a police department with your record and commendations. You know, the little departments around here, Santa Claus, Rockport, have openings once in a while."

Tug frowned. "Easier to find me if I take a public job, you know that. Besides, tiny town crime doesn't interest me. Bartending will be more entertaining."

Piper thought her small county's crimes too exciting sometimes.

"He's renamed the tavern The Thirsty Turtle," Basil added.

"Angel picked it. She's pissed about the whole moving thing, leaving the neighborhood and her friends and the gangbanger she swears she's in love with. She said we're like turtles, hiding in a shell, pulling our heads in so we won't get noticed. The Thirsty Turtle."

Nang rang up another gasoline and lottery ticket sale and returned to refill their drinks.

"This tavern," Nang approached.

"The Thirsty Turtle," Piper said.

"Will you be serving food?"

"Gotta serve food at a tavern," Tug answered quickly. "Have to give the drinkers something to help soak up the alcohol. Pizza, burgers, and hot dogs, stuff I can fix. Oh, and fries and onion rings for Sherlock in case he's still not eating meat. I damn well am going to serve hot dogs and sauerkraut. Keep it simple, easy, heavy on the grease. Bar food." He paused. "I won't be competing with you, if that's what you're worried about."

"I am not at all worried about competition," Nang said with a smile. "I am happy to welcome you and The Thirsty Turtle to Hooterville."

CHAPTER FOURTEEN

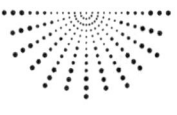

2 P.M.

I close my eyes and see Billie's face. And then, when I think about it, I see the faces of the others. Hemi, Mark Thresher, Conrad Delaney, all of them gone."

Nang sat in the passenger seat and listened. He'd talked her into letting him ride along to the archery shop in Corydon. An hour and a half on the road each way presented an opportunity to spend some quiet time together. His recent hires for the Quick Stop meant he didn't have to be there all the time, could leave on a whim, like now. He still needed to pick up a full-time mechanic, as that part of his business was increasing. He would put an ad online and in the little local paper tomorrow.

"Tink ... Billie Glempse ... bothers me the most. Young, her face just hangs there like a green sequined ornament on an ugly dead tree." Piper let out a long breath and shifted the position of her right hand on the wheel. "She didn't get a chance to really do something, you know. To do anything. Still in high school. I left for the Army right after high school."

He glanced away and looked out the window, watching the yellows and oranges of the trees blur. This far south in Indiana, the fall colors peaked the final two weeks of October, and he suspected they would remain for many more days. The windows were down and he smelled the harvest scents, and he imagined cinnamon. It was Nang's favorite time, the weather cooling, the brightness coming out before winter iced it all over into a drab sameness. Never a fan of winter, he sometimes wondered if heaven was autumn all the time; he hoped so. Piper had told him she liked summer best.

"Don't tell me I need a therapist, Nang, though I've thought about it," Piper continued. "I don't really dwell on death, except when I'm on a case ... or remembering lost friends. Then that seems to be all I think about. Faces floating in the back of my mind. I guess maybe I do dwell on it."

"You do not need a therapist," Nang replied. He turned his head to study her, beautiful face in profile, jaw set, eyes on the road. "You would need a therapist if you stopped seeing them and if it ceased to bother you."

"I love you."

He almost said "I love you more," but that was a movie cliché. "Hope so. I hope you'll be with me for life."

The radio crackled softly, chatter between the dispatcher and a deputy answering a "car in the ditch" call.

"Life can be short, you know," she said. "Sixteen for Billie. Nineteen for Maurice. Not long enough."

"So, let's not wait," Nang returned quickly. "I know we were talking a spring wedding, but let's not—"

"—wait that long," Piper finished, eyes still fixed on the road. "Okay." She paused. "But when? I have no vacation days yet and I want us to go somewhere. It's important to me. I don't know why a honeymoon is important. Tradition, maybe it's a tradition I want to hug. Maybe I just want to get away. Maybe—"

"You walked into my store the second of January." Nang touched her shoulder. "How about then?"

"A winter wedding?" Her voice was soft and he worried she didn't like the idea.

Worse, he wondered if she would change her mind altogether about getting married. She'd said "yes" when he proposed in September, and "okay" just now to moving it up. Impulsive. They'd known each other only ten months. He'd asked her out within days of meeting her and something had clicked between them. Before Piper, he hadn't considered the notion of marriage or a family; he was content with his store and being alone. The more weeks passed, the more inseparable they'd become. Nang had tried, at first, not to get so attached. Piper had been shot, stabbed, nearly died a few times in those ten months. She led a dangerous life. He'd told himself to 'keep it casual' because he wouldn't know if she'd be coming home.

They passed casual at the beginning of summer and now he couldn't imagine being without her. But could she imagine being without him? She'd told him more than once that she'd intended to re-up in the Army after her term as sheriff was done, that she'd run in the first place for something to do while she shepherded her father through cancer treatments. She'd been going to see the world and rise through the ranks, probably collect more medals and do amazing things.

"We could do that," Piper said.

He noted her lip turn up slightly in a half-smile, as if the idea had appeal.

"January second. Yeah. I think I'd like that." She sucked in a breath. "We'll have to work fast. Two months away. Only two months. A winter wedding."

"With a beautiful dress the color of the snow," Nang put in. "And I will have a tux. Suits, yes, I have a few. But I have to get a tux. Never wore a tux before. Black?"

She grinned wide. "I don't think the color is important." A pause: "But I do want that beautiful dress. With sequins."

"You shine." Nang gently squeezed her shoulder. "I want to bake the cake." He considered himself a chef, not a baker, though he'd won several baking contests at the Spencer County Fair and had the ribbons hanging on the Quick Stop wall behind the register. "Something big. I've watched *Cake Boss* reruns, *Ace of Cakes*, *Buddy vs Duff*. I can do that."

"I think you can do most anything you set out to."

"Big and fancy like you'd see on one of those baking shows or in a magazine," he added. "I will practice in Louisville."

She raised an eyebrow.

"Thanksgiving weekend, in Louisville, there is the Holiday Cake Bake. It will be filmed and shown on television sometime before Christmas."

"It sounds great, but why is that practicing? It sounds like a big competition."

"Practice for an even bigger competition. The Holiday Cake Bake in Louisville is part of the Best American Baker series, and the winners from the various Cake Bakes will compete nationally in the spring, televised just like *Cake Boss*. Anyway, I filled out the forms, sent pictures, did a Zoom presentation. I hadn't told you because I wanted it to be a surprise if I get in." He huffed. "And I won't know until next week if I get picked. I think I might have a good chance, because I had a second Zoom interview last week. The producer says I have a great backstory ... the Quick Stop owner and auto mechanic with a Vietnamese food catering business on the side who got into baking to enter the events at the county fair. If I get in, it will be because they find me interesting. Different."

"I find you wonderful," Piper said. "I hope they pick you."

Nang held up crossed fingers. He really did want to win a major cooking or baking competition, especially if it entailed appearing on one of his favorite shows. Maybe it would be validation that he was good, or maybe it would just be fun. As an added bonus, the prize money was substantial.

"Come January second, I hope you'll bake our cake. Lemon, red velvet, doesn't matter. Surprise me. And I want sequins." She laughed lightly. "Not on the cake, on my dress. When did this get to be me?"

It was his turn to quirk an eyebrow.

"I was all guns and combat boots, then guns and a sheriff's hat. And here what I dream about is lace and music, dancing, flowers, cake, and coming home to you every night. When did I turn into this woman?" Her face grew serious. "And what right do I have to think all these pretty thoughts and be happy when I've two murders to solve, when Basil and I have to find justice for two kids? Doesn't seem right, but I'm going to take it."

Nang hadn't thought she'd turned into anyone different; she was just letting her softer side show. He knew she was never likely to abandon the guns, sheriff's hat, and crime-solving. He didn't want her to.

The radio crackled with a report of a fender-bender in the parking lot of the monastery, and then her cell phone rang.

"Odd," Piper said, pointing at the Bluetooth connection as she touched the button. "From Teegan, but not coming from the department."

"Hey, Sheriff," Teegan said.

Nang turned to look out the passenger window, distancing himself from Piper's work, not wanting to intrude. But he listened, always curious about her cases.

"I'm not coming into work, at least not this afternoon. Sylvia's got my shift. Your dad's here, at my house. My new place." She made a humming noise. "My new place is an old place. I found a skeleton in the attic. A real skeleton. Dead. Well, a dead body with just the bones left, so I don't know if it was a man or a woman. Your dad says that it is his jurisdiction, that technically I'm in Santa Claus town limits. He's got the coroner coming to collect the bones and whatever other evidence there is. He says he needs to talk to me and the guy I bought the house through, and some of the neighbors. He's treating it as a murder, Sheriff. Shit. Shit. Shit. My new-old house was the site of a murder. Anyway, I have to stick around here until your dad's done."

"Wow," Piper said. "A serious cold case."

"Too bad I didn't find a house out in the county, eh?" Teegan said. "Too bad Basil isn't investigating the skeleton." A pause. "Omigod. Sorry, Sheriff. I didn't mean your dad can't investigate. I worked for him a bunch of years. He's great. He's—"

"—not a big city decorated detective whose nickname is apparently Sherlock," Piper said. "I'll call you after dinner and you can tell me more." She disconnected.

Nang didn't say anything, just listened to the radio crackle.

"A skeleton in Teegan's attic. A murder. That's awful and interesting and Dad better tell me everything when I see him."

"Sounds like a true-crime show."

"A honeymoon," Piper said after a few minutes. "We need one, to get away."

"Germany?" Nang remembered Piper had hoped for a post in Germany. "Someplace tropical? Costa Rica? Hawaii? Bahamas?"

"I love summer, but we don't have to go all beachy. Where do *you* want to go?"

"I've never been to Germany. Actually, outside of a trip to Vietnam I've never been out of the middle of the US."

"Yeah, I thought I'd like to go to Germany, but that was for a posting. Doesn't seem to appeal right now. Seriously, what about you? Got any ideas? Distract me from Teegan's skeleton and my two dead teenagers."

Nang had been thinking about a honeymoon ever since he'd proposed, but it wasn't tropical or romantic. "My idea isn't grand enough," he said.

"Try me."

"What about a road trip?"

"You thinking Route 66?"

Nang nodded.

"Chicago to Santa Monica," Piper said. "I always wanted to drive that."

Nang saw a smile reached her eyes.

"I'd say that's an awfully grand idea."

"Rent a car," Nang said. "It would take about two weeks to drive, figuring in the stops for the diners and giant balls of twine and everything. Fly back."

"The world's largest catsup bottle, Henry's Rabbit Ranch, Lincoln's Watermelon Monument. I'm all in."

"With sequins," Nang said.

Corydon sat north of the Ohio River in Harrison County, with a little more than three thousand people, a few wineries, several antique shops, a rare bookstore, and an archery shop. Piper pulled into the parking lot.

"I'm glad you came with me," she said to Nang. "I'm going to ask the owner a few questions, shouldn't take long. Then we'll turn around and go back."

"Mind if I come in?"

Piper stared at the shop's front door.

"I'll not be in the way."

"Of course, you can come in," she said.

The building was small and the goods inside tightly packed. Compound and recurved bows mostly, though she noted some cross-bows among them, gear, vests, books, and in the long display counter a significant assortment of hunting knives. Nang focused on the knives, reminding himself he needed to order some new high-end ones for the Quick Stop's little restaurant, and a personal set he could take to cooking contests.

"Sheriff Blackwell." The owner waved her to the back.

"Ed Mayweather?" Piper asked.

"Yep. Yep. Been expecting you."

Nang listened to her discuss a little bit about the deaths.

"I have pictures of the quarrels," Piper said. Nang guessed she must be showing him something from her cell phone.

"Any idea who might have—"

"No, we're at the beginning of our investigation. It's an unusual weapon," Piper said.

"Unless you're a bow hunter," Ed returned. "Chance it was a hunting accident?"

"Might have been a hunter, but I don't believe it was an accident."

"You're thinking murder. The guy might have had to use a bow or crossbow to kill from a distance. Convicted felons are not allowed to own or possess firearms."

"*Legally* own or possess," Piper said.

"A crossbow or a bow is not considered a firearm, and I don't need a criminal background check to sell them." The man drummed his fingers against the counter. "You thinking the fellow bought the weapon here? I've owned this shop eleven years. The quarrels in your picture are pretty standard. I carry them. But you can buy them—"

"I don't know where he—or she—bought them," Piper said. "I hunted with a crossbow once, when I was a kid, out with my dad. But I was a lousy shot." Softer, she added: "On purpose. I really didn't want to kill anything." Louder: "I stopped by here for a little education."

Nang suspected Piper had probably already dug through the internet about crossbows. She'd told him more than once that talking to an expert rivaled anything you could get from the computer.

"That quarrel, that type of quarrel, you'd likely use with something like this."

Nang swiveled to see the man point at an impressive black crossbow hanging high on the wall. "For example, that's an R29X, with a fully-integrated silent cocking system."

"I'm wondering if the killer used a crossbow because it is quiet," Piper said.

"Yep. Yep. It's quiet. But so is poison or a knife. I watch the TV cops." Ed pointed at another one. "That model's a beauty. Fast, almost thirty inches when fully drawn, six inches axle to axle and weighs less than seven pounds. Good grip, easy to maneuver in tight spaces, which is a boon to hunters. Gives great control. I know a lot of bow hunters who use something like that now rather than a traditional bow."

Nang thought that crossbow, and the few others he saw, looked more like guns. It had the appearance of a rifle, with a telescopic sight, handgrip, stock, trigger, a mechanism where the quarrel sat, barrel, not at all like the old crossbows from Robin Hood and other movies. High-tech, something a James Bond type might favor.

"That's not the fanciest or most expensive," Ed put in. "But it's the most popular model I have. There are some sporting goods stores around here that carry them, too, and other models. Are you going to check with them?"

"Maybe," Piper said. "Depends where the investigation takes us. I just need to get a basic understanding of the weapon. And I'd like a list of the customers you've sold them to."

"I have no problem putting together a list. Do you have to give me some sort of court order or search warrant?"

"If you want that."

"Nah, I'll go through my records tonight. Okay if I send it to you? Email? Fax?"

She nodded and passed him her business card.

He padded over to the wall, took down one of the fancier crossbows, brought it over and handed it to her. "Try it out, get a feel," he said.

Piper examined the crossbow, whistled softly. "Nothing like what my dad had when I was a kid."

"Effective hunting range is fifty, sixty yards. You can go well beyond that," Ed said. "I'd wager that even an eighty-yard shot would have enough power to kill medium or big game ... or a person. The big question is if you go past fifty yards do you have the precision to land the shot and penetrate vital organs. Sounds grisly, but I'd think your shooter was maybe thirty, thirty-five yards away. That's the sweet spot for most crossbow hunters, the thirties. They like that range not because the quarrel won't kill from a greater distance—it can—but because they want to make certain the quarrel will land right where they want it. The farther the distance, the greater the chance the quarrel will drift and you'll only wound the animal without killing it. An ethical hunter wouldn't want that."

"No one ethical killed the teenagers," Piper said.

Ed went on, as if he was excited to be questioned by the sheriff. "If you don't care about hitting a specific target, these modern babies can shoot a few hundred yards. If you do care about the target, better stick to fifty yards or less, that thirty-yard sweet spot." He rocked back. "Been of any help to you?"

"Definitely," Piper said. "I appreciate your time."

"I hope you catch him," Ed said. "Or her. Murder's nasty."

Nang believed Piper would catch him—or her. Piper was excellent at her job.

CHAPTER FIFTEEN

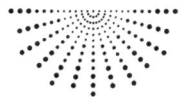

8 A.M. MONDAY, NOVEMBER 2ND

Handled any cases in Chicago with quarrels?" Dr. Annie Neufeld stared through plastic goggles. Her voice came out low and muffled because of her mask.

Basil shook his head. "Gunshots, mostly. Stabbings. People clubbed to death. Death is old hat. But this is new for me."

Basil had arrived for the autopsy an hour in advance. Oren had told him the coroner typically started ahead of time if her body was first up for the day, maybe not wanting an audience. Basil thought maybe she was just an early riser; he rarely slept past five.

He thought the sterile, antiseptic smell of the room unusual. Billie's corpse had been fresh when found, so it didn't yet have the stink of a decomposing body. She would smell soon enough, though, when Dr. Neufeld started cutting. Nothing pleasant about the air in a morgue or autopsy suite.

Dr. Neufeld started in on Billie Glempse, pulling the sheet back. The girl lay on her stomach, the quarrels still in place in her back and neck. Billie's natural hair was pale and wispy; the red wig had been bagged along with her steampunk costume.

"Sharp-force injuries," the doctor began. "Knives, scissors, wooden stakes, even icepicks like we had in July with that comic store owner, sometimes most of the blood loss, damage, is on the inside. These quarrels, same thing." She let out a breathy sigh and shook her head. "Poor kid. Before I retired from my pediatrics practice, I had patients her age. I checked my records yesterday. I saw this girl back when she was little, and then when she reached ten her dad decided she should go to his adult doctor, didn't need a 'kid doctor' anymore."

Basil watched her, fascinated and repulsed, admiring the coroner for her skills and willingness to do this work. He knew detectives in Chicago who were numb to this. Basil hadn't reached that numb point and prayed he never would.

"Poor kid," she repeated. "Position of the quarrels suggest the shooter was slightly above the victim, firing at a downward and left angle, which would be consistent if she was in the ditch and the shooter was on the roadway." She removed the first one and set it on a tray. "When I'm done you can take these and fingerprint and DNA them or whatever else you need to do."

Dr. Neufeld continued the examination. "Detective, I've handled some accidental deaths of hunting victims, one last year shot with an arrow. The thing with arrows, quarrels, some other sharp-force injuries, death rarely is instant. Neither of these hit her heart or spinal cord. Yes, they were killing shots, but they didn't kill right away. This girl laid in the ditch for a little while and bled out from her neck wound. The first quarrel pierced her lung, and that likely caused her to collapse, gasping for air. And I'd say that was the first wound, and this one in her neck, probably came second. But I won't promise you that's the case. The sequence of injuries like this are tough to lock down. My guess … and maybe my judgment is nudged by watching too many true-crime shows … is that she was trying to get away, caught the lung shot, and then as she fell forward, was hit in the neck. The angle of this quarrel hints at that. And it's the big culprit, nicked her left carotid. Unconsciousness would have been almost immediate, fortunately. She wouldn't have felt pain long."

"I suppose that's something," Basil agreed. He could see the scenario Dr. Neufeld painted, the girl fleeing and being cut down. It's precisely how he would have called it. Was the shooter in one of the vehicles the man on the bicycle had noted? Had that man spotted other cars he hadn't mentioned, something slipping his mind on Halloween because he was caught in the rush of the situation? Basil intended to visit Rhimer's car lot later tomorrow and prod his memory.

Dr. Neufeld had been saying something, part of it lost because he'd been focused on the possibilities of the murder.

"Pardon?"

"I asked how your kids are doing?"

Basil smiled. "I love them, they're doing great." They really were at the root of why he left Chicago and ended up in Spencer County. "They love the house, the yard, the neighborhood, don't seem to care that there isn't another black family nearby."

"I loved my practice," Dr. Neufeld returned. "I love kids. They're innocent souls, laugh a lot. I have two grandsons."

Basil had heard she'd been married years before and had an adult daughter living somewhere out of state.

"Esme's pregnant." Basil was surprised that came out, but the coroner was easy to talk to. "I haven't told anyone in the department yet. Esme hasn't even mentioned it at church."

"Congratulations." Dr. Neufeld continued to work, not looking up. "Boy or girl?"

Basil shrugged, then realized she couldn't see him. "Don't know. Doesn't matter. We decided we want to be surprised. The house has four bedrooms, so we figured we could have one more kid. Don't need to keep a guest room. Santa Claus isn't a place where Esme's relatives are likely to visit. We go down to see them in Nashville."

"You got a big yard?"

"Yeah, and Esme wants it fenced."

"Because she wants a dog."

"Perceptive," Basil replied.

"Kids need a dog or two."

"They want a pug, saw Paul Blackwell's dog."

"Wrinkles." Dr. Neufeld chuckled. "My wife has two cats. They're her cats. I am not fond of cats. I tolerate them, though. Someday I'll have a dog … when the cats are gone. But you got a yard, so you need a dog. Or two."

"A yard in a white-white-white neighborhood," he returned, watching her finish probing the wounds from the quarrels, make notes, and then roll the girl over. "Esme's mostly happy here, but she craves more diversity. This county is too damn white."

"Well, the county seems pretty damn straight, too."

"Former partner of mine moved down, needed a break from the city. He bought a bar in Fulda and is planning a grand opening. It'll be nice to have him around, a little less whiteness. Don't think he'll stick long, though."

"Too quiet here?" Dr. Neufeld looked up, then she gestured at Billie Glempse. "Can't call this quiet."

She finished with the girl in two hours, bagged the quarrels, and set them on the counter for Basil to take with him.

"The tox screens won't come back for four to six weeks," she said. "We won't know for a while if she was drinking or had drugs in her system. But it is the quarrels that killed her." She stepped back from the table. "You staying for Captain Hook? I do not anticipate being done much before noon."

"Wouldn't miss it," Basil said. "Catch lunch afterwards? My treat."

"Angelo's on Main. Italian, homey. You're a vegetarian, right?" Before he could answer with a "mostly" she went on: "Spinach ravioli, eggplant cutlets, and if you're not carb conscious, the fettuccini alfredo is truly divine."

Maurice's autopsy took longer than Billie's, with similar findings on the quarrels. The difference was Maurice's stomach held eight little sealed bags of powder. The coroner put them on a tray, and Basil growled.

"Drugs, certainly," Dr. Neufeld said. "Probably cocaine. If one of these had broken open, it would have killed him. Wouldn't have needed to shoot him in the back."

"It's my motive," Basil said. "It's why these kids were killed. Gotta find out if they were dealing or stealing and whose nasty path they walked across."

Dr. Neufeld covered Maurice's body and pulled off her goggles. Basil noted the little lines at the corners of her eyes and the dark circles.

"I've got to send all of this to the state's crime lab in Indy, pronto. I might even drive it there," Basil said.

The coroner shook her head. "Not necessary. There's a new state police lab here in Evansville, headed by a friend of mine, a man who used to run Kentucky's regional crime lab. I'll push for a fast turn-around. And as for the drugs, I know you have test kits back in Rockport, but I have one, too. I can get you an answer in a few minutes. I'm curious."

She plucked one of the baggies and they retreated to a nearby office, where she searched through a cabinet until she came away with a satchel.

"I insisted the morgue get one of these two years back. Not terribly expensive. They can help a medical examiner determine if more labs need to be run on a body."

She put her mask back on, made a tiny slit in the bag, inserted a strip, and put that in a vial she cracked open. "If the bag hadn't been in his stomach, I could've gotten away with just swabbing the outside of the plastic, pick up a trace that way. This one's a basic colorimetric test," she explained. "The state police lab has something more sophisticated you might want for the rest of it. But this will let us know what we're dealing with."

"I worked with a field test kit something like this in Chicago," Basil said. "We used it in concert with a smartphone app."

"Then I don't need to tell you that the color in the vial means it's meth." She frowned. "My guess would have been cocaine. I try to stay up on things, usually little baggies of cocaine or heroin that they swallow. Can't be right all the time, eh? I guess both can look like powdered sugar."

"Meth." Basil growled again. "Meth can look like a lot of things."

"I've some wipes in the cabinet. I'll test Captain Hook's skin, go back for Tink and check hers."

"I'll wait."

"And then we'll be off for Italian."

Basil was pretty sure he'd lost his appetite. He hated meth. The drug was complicated and he honestly would rather deal with heroin or cocaine. Street drugs … all of them were bad, but meth was the greater evil. He'd spent four-and-a-half-years as a patrolman, five years as a detective, and during those latter five years one with major accident investigation, four with Gangs and Narcotics. Worked a lot of drug cases; meth was the worst in his opinion. The sheriff's department, the Rockport police, and Santa Claus police knew meth was a problem in Spencer County. Rural, hard to find the little hidey-holes where it was manufactured. Same situation with a lot of rustic areas throughout the Midwest.

"Positive," Dr. Neufeld said, returning. "Traces of meth on the fingers of both of them, and on the girl's right forearm. They both came in contact with meth. Probably show up on the clothes, too."

"They were killed because of it," Basil said, voice low, eyes daggers. "Dealing or stealing."

"You're not going to lunch with me, are you?"

He shook his head.

"State police crime lab?"

"Yeah."

"I'll give you directions." She paused. "And take a raincheck for Angelo's."

CHAPTER SIXTEEN

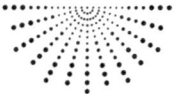

10 A.M.

P aul rolled back from his desk, reached down, and scratched Wrinkles behind the ears. The elderly black pug with a mostly white face stretched out on an ergonomic dog bed. He snorted contentedly at the attention and rolled over so Paul could tickle his belly.

"We've quite the case, old man. Awful and exciting and I don't know if we're going to solve it. Could be too cold."

The pug lolled out his tongue in reply.

When Paul applied for the Santa Claus police chief opening this past spring, he told the board he'd bring his dog to work on occasion, which had turned into most of the time. The board hadn't objected and hired him after they finished all the interviews. Basil Meredith had been among those who'd also applied, and Paul was surprised to beat out the decorated Chicago detective. He'd wondered if race played a part, but learned after settling in that Basil had been the board's second choice—and by only a narrow margin. Paul had won out because he'd served so many years with the Spencer County Sheriff's Department, was familiar with Indiana's laws, and knew every inch of Santa Claus and the county. With him, there was no learning curve.

"Want a treat, old man?"

Wrinkles wagged his curly tail and Paul dipped into his biscuit stash and passed one over, liver-flavored by its shape, a clear favorite. The pug became a pleasant, brief diversion from dealing with Teegan's House of Horrors. That's what he'd dubbed the case of the skeleton in the as-is old home Teegan had bought and moved into.

Dr. Neufeld texted him that she wouldn't get to the skeleton until tomorrow or the day after, that Piper's dead teenagers were fresher and took precedence. Further, she suspected she'd send Mr. Bones to the state lab in Evansville for an anthropologist to study, as her expertise involved bodies that had flesh attached. She'd found it odd that there were no clothing remnants with the skeleton.

He scooted forward, opened his laptop, and looked through the pictures he'd taken in Teegan's attic. He opened a second window and reread the notes he'd made while the coroner was on the scene, smiling when he recalled Dr. Neufeld cursing for having to climb a ladder and balance on the rafters to ogle the bones. She'd mentioned retiring a few times.

It looked like all the bones were there. But Paul's science background was limited to a high school biology course he took forty years ago. He figured some of the little finger and toe bones could have been absent and he wouldn't have noticed. Too, he hadn't counted the number of ribs. Dr. Neufeld said based on the pelvis she was certain it was male.

The age? She'd shrugged, then said: "An adult. Young bones are different."

"No young bones in this office, are there, old man?"

An anthropologist could likely pinpoint the age to within five years, she'd said, height to within an inch or so, and race. She'd thrown around words such as "long bones," "ossification centers," and "diaphysis." DNA samples would be pulled from the teeth and marrow and could help in identifying who the man had been; it would take a while to get those results.

There was nothing else in the trunk, and the coroner transported the bones in it, saying the trunk would also go to the state lab. The rest of the attic? Paul and two of his officers removed an old carton of wedding photos and a worn leather satchel containing yellowed papers that appeared to pertain to the land and house. One of his officers had taken photocopies of everything, returned the originals to Teegan, and now they were tracking down the names on the decades-old paperwork. Maybe someone listed would turn out to be Mr. Bones, or his killer.

How long ago had the man been murdered? Paul hoped the anthropologist could tell him.

How was he killed? Maybe the anthropologist could figure that out, too.

The house was old. If the slaying happened too long ago, the killer might be as dead as the victim and all their work pointless.

"Wrinkles, this is probably the oddest case I've ever worked. How about another treat?"

Paul had the names of everyone who'd owned the property, and an officer was contacting those still living or their descendants. The real estate agent had been helpful, but nervous, saying he'd met with an attorney this morning in case Teegan decided to sue. Paul remained pretty sure she wouldn't, Teegan not being the litigious type.

"She bought it 'as-is' with everything included," the realtor said. Paul had recorded the conversation. "I didn't know someone had been murdered there and the body hidden in the attic. It's not my fault or responsibility." The realtor had sold it for a woman living in Florida, Lucinda White-Barnes, the older sister of the previous owner. That owner, and his wife, had died a year ago in an auto accident. Lucinda said she understood that the house had been sitting empty "for quite some time" when Paul called her yesterday. Lucinda said she'd never been to the house or Spencer County. Paul had marked this as a dead end.

Paul and two of his officers spent hours in Teegan's attic yesterday afternoon and into the evening after the skeleton was removed, perched on the rafters while inventorying almost everything up there just in case there were clues. One hundred and fourteen boxes of various sizes, more than half of them filled with Christmas decorations. The amount of Halloween costumes for adults and children impressed him, along with a dozen boxes worth of Easter baskets, bonnets, bunny knickknacks, wind-up chicks, and decoupage eggs. Thanksgiving and Valentine's Day fit in one box each. He also noted a black manual typewriter, two rotary telephones, three cast iron frying pans, assorted toys, a tackle box, and a pair of broken fishing rods.

"I got why a lot of that stuff was up there. To tuck it out of the way until a holiday rolled in," Paul told Wrinkles. "Except for the cast iron frying pans. Why the hell would you stick those up there?" He paused, an idea flitting … had the victim been killed with one of the frying pans? He'd send an officer back for them. "Or a skeleton. Why stick a skeleton in the attic? Well, to hide it obviously. All those boxes … I bet it had been hidden for decades. Like how they stashed the Ark of the Covenant in *Raiders of the Lost Ark*." He looked at Wrinkles. "Yeah, I doubt you saw that movie. A big place full of boxes, you would never find the important one."

He wondered if the killer had trouble hauling a naked body up the ladder. Had the murder victim been heavy? Did more than one person lug the body? He leaned toward the latter, that more than one person was involved.

They'd dusted the bones—surprisingly finding some viable fingerprints, and fingerprinted various other items in the attic. No matches yet, other than Teegan and Zeke's prints.

They'd walked the rest of the house, too, finding nothing else pertinent to the skeleton.

Paul patted Wrinkles, the fur like velvet against his hand. "Heck of a puzzle, eh, old man?" The pug snorted and pawed at his pant leg. "No more treats. Piper is coming over for dinner tonight, so I know there'll be table scraps in your future."

He had ribeye steaks ready to grill, potato salad from the grocery store, snow peas, and a cherry pie. Just the two of them for a change. They'd likely talk about their respective murder cases, which while sounding a little morbid, would probably make for an enjoyable night. Maybe they could provide insight into each other's investigations. Paul looked forward to it; hadn't spent much time lately with Piper.

Seemed all her hours off were wrapped up in Nang.

Probably how it should be, Paul thought. He remembered being in love many years ago. He'd thought it had been a good, comfortable family—clever and beautiful wife, two young daughters—until something didn't work anymore. Wasn't her fault, not entirely. Seemed there weren't enough opportunities for her growing ambitions in this small county, and Owensboro across the river wasn't big enough either. She'd said she felt trapped here. He wasn't about to move, anchored to the sheriff's department. Maybe he shouldn't have been so stubborn. They drifted apart and she drifted away, and he raised the girls on his own.

"Everything turned out all right, didn't it, old man?" Wrinkles cocked his head from side to side in pug fashion. "How about just one more treat?"

CHAPTER SEVENTEEN

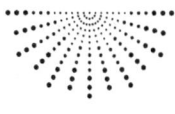

NOON

Search warrants made everything cold and formal, but Piper knew they were necessary, and these had been quick to obtain. The warrants would ensure that she could search Billie's room, legally collect all electronic devices, and included opening any locked or closed containers.

Why someone would kill two teenagers had vexed her to the point she took a sleeping pill last night.

A senseless and evil act to cut them down.

What could Billie and Maurice have done to provoke someone? Piper knew she and Basil would have to solve this to gain any peace… and she suspected Basil would connect whatever dots there were first; that was why she had hired the decorated detective.

"Sheriff, please come in." Sandra Glempse appeared exhausted. She wore blue sweatpants, an over-sized Colts t-shirt, and her Gucci sneakers. The diamond earrings and fancy watch seemed incongruous to the clothes. "I just fed the kids lunch, and they're in the backyard playing. I kept Grant home from school today. We told them about Billie, but they don't really understand." She pointed toward the kitchen, where a round table sat in front of sliding glass doors. Piper saw the children in a sandbox just beyond it. "Really, how can kids understand that their sister isn't ever coming back?"

"It will take time," Piper offered. She didn't know what else to say.

"I've lemonade. Do you like lemonade?"

Sandra closed the door behind Piper, latched it, and shuffled into the kitchen, retrieving a pitcher of lemonade and two superhero glasses.

Piper wanted to search the girl's room right away and grab her laptop, but she sat still. "I like lemonade."

Piper's phone chirped with an incoming text; she'd check it in a few minutes. She smelled jasmine, or something like it, noticed a thick off-white candle burning on the kitchen counter next to a pewter framed picture of Billie in a cheerleading uniform. A shrine. The girl was smiling, eyes bright. The photo was a good way to remember her. Again, Piper pictured Billie in the ditch.

"Is Mr. Glempse here?" Piper would talk to both of them.

"Bob?" Sandra filled The Incredible Hulk glass and nudged it toward Piper, sat, and filled Captain America for herself. "Bob went to work this morning. He needed to keep busy, keep his mind off Billie. I encouraged him, actually. Well, I basically told him he needed to leave. God, but he is heartbroken. I couldn't handle it. I couldn't take the brooding and crying. I think he blames me because of the steampunk fairy outfit. I really think he does. Thinks that led to her getting killed. She was a good kid, Billie. I told him he had to go to work. He *had* to." She rubbed at her eyes and took a swallow, making a face. "Not enough sugar. Sorry. I'll go—"

"No, it's fine. I like it tart." Piper took a long pull and forced herself to not pucker at the sourness. Not enough sugar? Likely not any.

"He's going to stop at the funeral home after work, make arrangements. The coroner hasn't released her yet, so we can't set a time for a service. I offered to help, pick out a casket and flowers and stuff, but he said he'd handle it. I really didn't want to help, you know. Billie was too young. I really really don't want to help bury her."

Sandra ran a finger around the top of the glass. Piper noticed that despite the woman's casual attire, she wore three rings set with large stones of assorted colors and a bracelet with red stones. Maybe she liked to decorate herself. Billie's Halloween outfit had been extravagantly decorated.

"Do you have kids, Sheriff?"

Piper shook her head. "Not married yet."

Sandra sighed. "Well, you don't have to be married to have kids. I like kids. Keeps you young, looking at the world through their eyes. A handful. Takes away most of your free time. They're worth it, though. Kids are great. I called Billie my bonus kid."

"I came here to—"

"How soon's your wedding?"

Piper wanted to look through the girl's room and tried not to display her impatience. "We're talking January. Early January."

"Wow." Sandra met her gaze. "A big wedding?"

"Probably not. We've just started planning it."

"You better plan quick. January will get here fast." A pause. "I don't think I put any sugar in this. I must have forgot."

Piper edged back from the table, glanced at the children building a crooked sandcastle. "I'm here to look through Billie's room, collect her laptop, iPad, things like that." She took the search warrant out of her pocket and handed it to Sandra.

"Second door on the left at the top of the stairs," Sandra said. "I have to stay here, keep an eye on Grant and Wendy. Is that okay? That I stay here?"

"Sure." Piper got up and walked to the stairs.

"You'll bring her laptop back, right? The iPad? When you're done? You won't keep them, will you? I don't think you should be able to just keep them. I'd like to pass them along to Grant so he can work on his ABCs, watch cat videos, have something of Billie's. I need my car back, too. I've got a rental coming this afternoon, but I want that ugly orange jeep back. I need a car. I think I'm going back to work tomorrow, keep my mind off stuff. I need to keep my brain busy. How soon can I get my jeep?"

Sandra continued to babble, opened the search warrant, and

started reading it aloud. Piper went up the stairs and into Billie's bedroom.

Nothing overly feminine, Piper thought. Not what she'd expected from a teenage girl's room. No hint of pink. No pom-poms sitting out. Beige walls with a wallpaper stripe of orange and yellow chrysanthemums above the wainscotting. Twin bed with an ivory comforter, a three-foot-tall stuffed koala leaning against the headboard, simple desk, dark brown leather beanbag chair by the window next to a low bookshelf filled with paperbacks and knickknacks—most of the figurines were koalas. She glanced at the books: Stephen King, Peter Straub, Nora Roberts, Danielle Steel—horror and romance, interesting mix. A framed poster on the wall had a trio of koalas with a logo for the Taronga Zoo in Sydney. Piper sat on the bed and stared at the poster. Had the girl visited the zoo? Or did she dream of it? Did it matter?

Piper felt empty. The energy she usually had for investigating any case had been siphoned away when she came in here, depression replacing it. Billie's room was a place of ghosts and memories now, the life the girl had brought to it, dissipated. Piper had been touched by each of the murder cases she'd handled since taking office in January. This one probably hit the hardest. Sixteen years old. Billie should have had a lot more than sixteen years.

It looked like the room had been a peaceful retreat for the teenager, muted colors and koalas, books. Piper imagined it had been a good spot for study, for reading, for chatting with friends via cell phones and Skype, posting tidbits on TikTok and Facebook, on which she'd been active.

She took out her phone and read the text from Basil.

"Traces of meth on Billie. Baggies of meth in Maurice's stomach. Meth is the motive. Talk this afternoon."

She shuddered and stood. Her search stopped right now.

Piper hurried down the stairs, waved goodbye to Sandra, and rushed to her Explorer. Warrants indeed made everything cold and formal. They were specific, limiting the scope of the search. She needed a new warrant now to expand the scope of her search, allowing for Thresher, and explaining the probable cause because of drugs. She'd get it to the prosecutor's office for review. She called ahead, so DA Scales would be waiting for her. In turn, Scales would present it to a judge on call, who would either approve it or turn it down. Scales texted her back minutes later that he'd alerted the judge. Fast-tracked. She'd have a mirror warrant for Maurice's house.

Computers, smart phones, fax machines simplified things, meaning this didn't need to be handled in person and warrants could be managed faster. Still had all the hoops to jump through, which to her often seemed unreasonable and unnecessary. But it was the courts system, and the system loved hoops.

Piper had stopped herself from telling Sandra: "I'll see you again in a little while." She knew not to tip off Sandra that the situation had changed and that the search would be more extensive.

Did Billie's parents know the girl was into drugs?

P iper was back at the Glempse house two hours later. She turned on her body cam and handed the new warrant to Sandra.

"I don't understand," Sandra said. She looked numb. "You already searched."

"Mrs. Glempse," Piper began, stepping to the side so Sandra could see Diego and Thresher on the walk. "Billie had drugs. Methamphetamines."

Sandra sucked in a breath so deep she gagged. "No. It's a mistake."

Piper waited a beat, then explained what Basil and the coroner found.

"A good girl," Sandra said after a few minutes, not budging from the doorway. She put her hands on the frame and spread her legs, making herself a barrier. "Billie was a good girl. She didn't do drugs. Meth? She wouldn't do meth. She didn't really drink, either. She went to parties, but she never came home drunk or smelling of alcohol. Billie did not do drugs. It is a mistake." She hit each word of the last sentence for emphasis. "I need to call Bob, talk to him. You can't come in. Not this time."

"Mrs. Glempse—"

"And you think you're bringing a dog here? To sniff for drugs? No. You can't do that. Billie didn't do drugs. You're not bringing a dog in here. Go away. I'd know if she did drugs. I pay attention to the kids. I paid attention to Billie. I'd know if she did drugs."

Piper let her ramble. She hadn't expected resistance.

"I'm an actuary," Sandra said, abruptly changing the conversation. Piper knew people switched topics to avoid talking about something unfortunate. "I minored in computer science and worked for insurance and consulting firms in my young years when I was bent on passing the actuarial exams. The exams are tough. Ball State. I became a fellow, a member of the Academy of Actuaries. I specialize in creating hybrid life insurance policies that include coverage for long-term care." She laughed softly, but there was no humor in it. "I had all these little companies coming to me to build the policies. See, long-term care policies have become way too expensive, and the claims are way higher than people expected. Companies try to put out life insurance policies where you can use some of the future death benefit to cover long-term care, which is the single biggest threat to most retirement plans."

Piper didn't really care what Sandra did for a living. It sounded boring as hell, numbers, life expectancy, insurance.

"Mrs. Glempse, we're coming in to search—"

"We took out life insurance policies on Grant and Wendy when they were born," she continued. "I insisted. They can cash them out when they're older if they want. We didn't have a policy for Billie. I suggested it. I should have insisted, but Bob thought it morbid, life insurance for a teenager. I'd insisted for Grant and Wendy, didn't really give Bob a choice there. I should have insisted for Billie, too. Billie was a good girl, Sheriff. She didn't do drugs." She finally released the doorframe and folded her arms. "It was Maurice, wasn't it? An older boy, wild boy. A bad influence. Why the hell did I buy her the damn skimpy outfit and let her go to that steampunk party with him?"

She never made it to the party, Piper thought.

"You're not coming in here. You're not bringing a dog into my house, Sheriff." Sandra glared defiantly. "Grant's allergic, and I won't have it. You're not bringing a dirty, stinky—"

"Thresher doesn't stink," Piper said. "And he *is* coming in. We're all coming in now."

CHAPTER EIGHTEEN

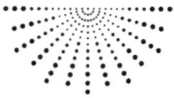

3:30 P.M.

I 've missed having a car, but I've been getting a lot of exercise," Zeke told Nang. "I think my leg muscles are getting impressive."

The pair had the 1974 Chevy Nova up on the rack, bolting parts onto the undercarriage, replacing sections that had rusted to ruin.

"I will reinforce here and here," Nang explained, "and weld this piece."

"I'll help."

"You certainly will," Nang returned.

Zeke's latest expenditure: polyurethane-based sealant, that would go on after the undercarriage was declared done. The car had cost him $300; the parts had set him back triple that so far. Nang had given him a list of additional material they would need to fully restore Serilda and Zeke expected to spend about four-to-five-thousand for everything.

'Seventy four was the final year for the Chevy X-Body, and if they got it gleaming, he should be able to sell it for at least thirty-five thousand ... provided he could bring himself to part with it. He hadn't told Nang, but he intended to share some of the profit. Nang had been doing most of the work.

He'd probably have it painted red. Zeke had researched Chevy Novas, and it appeared the restored red ones went for higher prices. The color made the car look fast.

"I can give you two more hours today," Nang said. "Then I will close the garage and go home."

"Wow. Thanks. You don't have to work nights anymore?"

"I have added three employees in the past two weeks and I have a new manager working today. She needs to handle everything on her own. Learn the business. I need to trust her and not hover." He waited a beat. "She can call me if there is trouble."

"That's Shelly Evans, right? I saw her through the window."

Nang nodded.

"I thought she managed the Rockport grocery store."

"She used to. Shelly lives in Fulda, three houses down. She answered my ad because she can walk to work and save gas money and wear on her car."

"You needed a manager? I thought that you handled—"

"I don't want to spend all of my time here. I used to be here every day, eighteen hours at a clip. All these new hires are letting me spread out the work and gives me an opportunity to enter cooking competitions and have more hours with Piper." He paused. "When Piper isn't working a big case like now. My business, it is good and growing, catering is up, I'm getting another mechanic. In the spring, if catering continues like this, I will look at opening a restaurant downtown."

"Downtown Rockport? Or Santa Claus?" Those were the only halfway good-sized communities in the county.

"Either one, depends on the building I find."

"You're serious," Zeke said. "You're really serious. No wonder you hired Shelly."

"I was able to match Shelly's previous salary and retain nearly the same profit margin. I am fortunate to have her. And, best of all, she is a fast study and a good cook."

Zeke wanted to ask what that salary was, but he stopped himself. A curious sort, he didn't really need to know. However, he thought he did need to know if the sheriff's department gossip was true.

"Heard you and my boss are getting married in January."

"That is the plan," Nang replied.

"Big wedding?"

Nang shrugged. "I hope enough people come to eat the grand cake I will make."

"You're not going to cater your own wedding, are you?"

Nang shrugged again. "I think just the cake. Maybe the guests won't need anything else to eat. If they are really hungry, they can eat two or three pieces. But maybe I will make spring rolls."

The two hours melted like warm butter, and Zeke's arms were stiff from holding them above his head for so long. He admired Nang for not showing a hint of fatigue. He took a deep breath, detecting over the scent of oil and automotive grease a touch of soy and maybe chicken cooking. The Quick Stop door must be open.

Zeke had skipped lunch and came here right after his shift ended at three. He'd order something from Nang's kitchen before he left; he hoped for some pork fried rice and a few egg rolls. An opportunity to find out if Shelly was indeed a good cook.

"I'm thinking of looking for a fixer-upper like Teegan did, get me a little house, though, nothing honking like hers. Get out of my dinky third-floor apartment. Fixing a house can't be that much more difficult than fixing a car, right? Probably easier. Hey, where are you and Piper going to live? Her house in Hatfield, probably, right? That's an awfully nice place. Big, only a few years old, killer huge garage. I've house sat for her a few times. Beautiful backyard. You'll probably live there, right?"

"We haven't talked about that yet."

"Oh."

Zeke watched Nang make adjustments and glance at the clock on the wall.

"I like her house," Nang said after a few minutes. "I like that it has a dog door, and I have a dog. She has a dog."

"A cat, too."

"Piper and I will decide after she finishes this double-murder case."

"Hey! I'm working a murder case right now, too," Zeke volunteered.

Nang cocked his head in question.

"Not officially, of course, dispatchers don't do that. But Teegan and I found a skeleton in her attic. You've probably heard all about that. I don't think there are any secrets in this county. It's too bad her new-old house isn't fifty yards farther east. Then it wouldn't be in the Santa Claus city limits. It would be a county case and Detective Meredith could handle it."

"Paul Blackwell is—"

"Oh, Paul can definitely solve it. He was the sheriff of Spencer County for a lot of years. But Basil is really sharp. *Really* sharp. You can see it in the way he studies the whiteboard back at the department. I overhear him talking with Piper. He's ... well, Paul can definitely solve the skeleton case, figure out who the bones used to be, who killed him. But Basil could do it faster, you know."

"What I know is that you underestimate Paul Blackwell." Nang never looked away from the undercarriage. "Paul Blackwell will put a name to the bones in Teegan's attic."

Zeke drifted back and forth on the balls of his feet. Nang was likely so supportive of Paul Blackwell because he was Piper's father and thereby would be his father-in-law. Sure, Paul had to have the cop chops or he wouldn't be in law enforcement for so long, right? He wouldn't have been re-elected as sheriff, and he wouldn't have been hired as the police chief of Santa Claus. But he was in his fifties, heading toward sixty, and his eyes weren't fresh anymore.

"Maybe he can," Zeke admitted. "Still ... Teegan's gonna mention the skeleton to Basil. He's pretty busy with the steampunk murders." Zeke paused. He was still morose over the deaths of two people he knew, but he liked the sound of steampunk murders, as if it could make a nifty title for a book or one of those Lifetime movies. "I suspect Basil isn't going to have time. But—"

Zeke drew out the "but" as if it had three syllables. "Teegan and I are going to investigate it ourselves. After all, working at a sheriff's department, being around all the crime reports, we've learned a lot.

Maybe we can discover who the victim is, and who killed him. I'm going over to Teegan's when I leave here. She gave me a key and said she set up her laptop for me. Maybe I'll poke around the attic some more. When she gets off work at eleven, I'll let her know what I've found. Maybe we can do a little more digging after that."

Zeke continued to ramble, not hiding his excitement of pursuing the skeleton. "And after we call it a night, I'll catch two or three hours of Zs. I have to be at work by seven, and it takes me longer to get there since I'm on my bike. I'll need a few extra minutes to stop and grab a donut or two because I haven't gone grocery shopping this week. I have to pace myself."

Nang eyed his handiwork, then stepped back, reached for a rag, and wiped the oil off his hands. "You will be driving Serilda next week, maybe by the weekend if I have more free time."

"Awesome."

"Put your bike in the back of my pickup and I'll take you to Teegan's. That will save you some time so you can get to your investigation faster." Nang grinned. "But I believe Paul Blackwell will find the killer first. Experience often trumps youth and enthusiasm."

"Yeah, well, maybe it does." Zeke wiped his hands and futilely rubbed at a spot of grease on his jeans. "Maybe, but me and Teegan, we're gonna give it a try anyway. I mean, I'll have to work it around my dispatcher job and some online courses I'm taking, but I'll manage. Who needs eight hours of sleep? And I'll take you up on that ride. Thanks, big time. Gonna grab me a couple of bags of ice for Teegan's cooler and get me some fried rice and eggrolls first."

"Make your order to go," Nang advised. "You'll have to dig fast into your case to beat Paul Blackwell."

CHAPTER NINETEEN

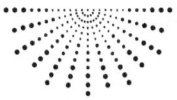

8 P.M.

Marmalade perched on the windowsill. The orange tabby's tail twitched, her gaze fixed on something outside. Camaro curled at Piper's feet, snoring. The old golden retriever had planted himself there soon after dinner and likely wouldn't move until Piper got up to refill her raspberry iced tea. A large glass of it dotted with water beads sat invitingly on the coffee table.

She'd inherited the dog and cat with the house; the third bedroom was theirs, decked out in pet beds, climbing trees, and bins of toys. Their previous owner, Mark the Shark, had spent money on the duo.

Resting next to her on the couch, muzzle on her leg so close to the laptop it fogged the screen, was a butt-ugly mutt. Tater was Nang's, and by extension, hers. He stayed here most of the time because the dog door made everything convenient and Nang was often here during his time off from the Quick Stop. Except tonight. He had paperwork to tackle for his business, and she had a double-murder to ponder and body cam footage to review.

She felt bad about cancelling dinner plans with her father, wanting to chat about their respective murder cases, but she had too much material to review. The steaks would keep, he'd said. They moved their dinner plans ahead two days.

Project Runway played on the television; it was an *avant garde* challenge. Nang liked reality cooking shows: *Diners, Drive-ins, and Dives* and *Beat Bobby Flay*. She skewed toward *Project Runway*, New York Fashion Week, and *Blue Bloods*, though she admitted to enjoying *Beat Bobby Flay* and would sometimes help Nang recreate dishes the competitors on the show made. Reality TV lacked plots, and so it could provide background noise while she worked.

Tater snorted. He was easily a hundred pounds, a mix of pointer, shepherd, and some kind of retriever. Piper suspected there was Great Dane in the recipe. His off-white fur was patchy, his legs bowed when he stood. He had one eye; the left had been removed while he was at the animal shelter, leaving a depression. To add to his singular appearance, Tater had a pronounced underbite, and the visible teeth were crooked. Fate had also handed him Cushings Disease, which meant a special diet, medication, and a shorter lifespan.

Initially Piper had been repulsed. Now, she thoroughly adored him. It helped that she thoroughly adored Nang.

She replayed the video from the Glempse home, Thresher going from room to room, to closets and cabinets, and to the garage. They'd found nothing but a lot of grief and anger.

Basil was going through Billie's laptop, iPad, and the cell phone they'd found earlier, downloading messages and friends lists, looking for a meth connection.

"I damn well want Billie's electronics back," Sandra growled, face red and eyes watery in the body cam footage playing. "Tomorrow. Bring them back tomorrow for Grant to use. I want my car back, too. You've no right to just come in here and make everything worse and take things. And to bring a damn dirty dog into my clean house. A dirty stinking mutt."

"A highly-trained Belgian Malinois," Piper said to Tater. "An expensive dog."

Plenty of grief and anger and not a hint of meth.

But they'd found traces on Billie and Maurice's skin ... and on the floorboards of the jeep … and in the grooves of the soles of the green sequined tennis shoes still at the lab in Evansville. Traces on the pantlegs of Maurice's Captain Hook costume, and in his boot treads. Nothing that had been visible, but touches the test kits picked up.

Tater sneezed, spraying droplets on her screen. Piper used her sleeve to wipe them off, stretched across the dog, and grabbed the iced tea. She took a long drink and held the sweetness in her mouth. The scent of it masked the pong of the big mutt. At her feet, Camaro shifted so he was on his back now, legs splayed. He wanted his belly rubbed, but Piper would get to that after she watched the next footage again.

She keyed the body cam recording from Maurice Langston's house. Basil was with her for this one, having come back from the autopsies. Diego and Thresher were along. The few neighbors not at work had come out of their houses to gape, taking out cell phones to record all the excitement. Piper suspected it was likely the first time the Spencer County Sheriff's Department had appeared in force in the neighborhood.

They found a lot of grief and anger at the Langston house, too.

Piper hit pause, studying Wallace poised at the front door. Disheveled, in worn blue jeans and a plaid sport shirt he hadn't buttoned, eyes red, dark circles underneath. He'd looked fatigued, but Basil had seen something more.

She hit play.

"You came in the other night," Wallace had said to Piper. "I let you in then. I'm not letting you in now. None of you. Not the dog. You can go away. Just leave me the hell alone."

Piper gave him the search warrant, made an attempt to be affable.

He crumpled the sheet without reading it and dropped the wad on the stoop. "Paper don't mean nothing. My house. It's all mine now with Maurice dead. And I say you're not coming in. Private property. I'm within my rights. I know my rights. Go the hell away."

Had Basil heard something in Wallace's voice beyond anger and grief? Something about his speech? Piper played the section again, finding a little fogginess in Wallace's words, like on the edge of drunkenness.

Basil had shifted behind Piper, as if he was going to press the matter of going inside. Piper didn't think she needed her detective's help to serve the warrant, determined to show herself in charge. She stepped so close to Wallace she shared his breath and smelled his sweat. The stink settled sour in her mouth.

"We *are* coming in," she'd said. "We are coming in now. You can step aside and cooperate, or you can be cuffed and have a ride down to the department where we will charge you with obstruction of justice."

"Charge away," Wallace sneered, suddenly reaching into his pocket. His demeanor instantly changed from ire to rage. "You're damn well not—"

"Gun," Piper said, drawing hers and taking a step back, bumping into Basil. "Drop it. Wally, drop it now!"

Watching the footage, Piper realized Wallace was on *something* to pull a gun on three people from the sheriff's department, and a dog. Drugs or alcohol had mixed with his anger and made him act stupid.

"Drop it!"

"Piss." Wallace dropped the gun and she holstered hers and grabbed her handcuffs, everything more difficult working with one hand. It was a heavily scratched Ruger that had clattered to the stoop.

"Hands up." Piper kicked the Ruger out of Wallace's reach. "Hands up now!"

"Piss on you." But he complied.

"Turn around."

He snarled, but did it, and she pulled his arms down and cuffed him, managing with one hand.

Basil patted Wallace down and put him in the back of his Explorer. Wallace cursed and spit.

Piper had waited for the detective to return, looking through the open door and seeing no change to the living room from her first visit.

"I didn't expect that," she'd said to Basil. "Wally wasn't like that the other night. Just sad, not belligerent. Maybe he had a gun then. I had no cause to think that, and no cause at the time to search for anything."

"Presence of the dog," Diego cut in. "Thresher changes a situation, especially if someone is guilty of something. A dog like this escalates things, can set someone off."

Piper knew that from working with dogs in the Middle East.

"And more than the dog," Diego added, "he just lost his brother. I read the file. Wally is on his own here. Grief can do things, you know."

"It wasn't the dog, Sheriff," Basil countered. "It was meth. I saw it in his face, his teeth, his eyes. The way he talked. Meth makes people act stupid, incapable of thinking straight. He's not as far gone as some I've encountered. You can smell it on him, too." He'd paused: "You've not been around it like I have. Tug could spot meth even better, faster than me. Been around it often enough, and it pops at you."

Piper had been around drugs in the Middle East—to an extent. A few of the men she'd been stationed with used, not often, and rarely in her presence. It was mostly marijuana and some cocaine. Some at Fort Campbell, too. Maybe she'd chosen not to look too closely then. She hadn't known how the soldiers got it, hadn't wanted to know. Maybe there'd also been some meth in her unit and she'd been oblivious. She'd had no interest in drugs then, and her interest now had been confined to studying it because Spencer County—and other rural counties in the Midwest—had a meth problem.

"I hate meth," Basil said. "Messy. Stupid."

Thresher barked and leaned forward.

"Masks, gloves, boots," Piper said.

"Maybe more than that," Basil returned. "If there's a lot in there, we're backing out, getting suits."

Minutes later, the dog went first.

There was no indication of drugs in the living room with its worn, plain furniture, the coffee table still cluttered with magazines and soda cans. The old television was on, playing a Netflix show about vampires. The trophies still stood to mark Maurice's accomplishments. The kitchen was sparse, dirty dishes cluttered the sink.

It smelled old, fusty, and there was the hint Wally had burned something again.

"Hello 1960," Diego said. "Very vintage. Mustard-colored appliances."

Thresher tugged Diego to the small table with a chipped Formica top.

"Serious bingo," Diego said.

The glass pipe was a five-inch-long cylinder with a bulbous end. There were black burn marks on the underside and a waxy, yellowish residue in the bulb, evidence meth had been smoked in it.

"Fresh. Told you he's high." Basil growled. "Puzzle pieces, Sheriff. Meth on the teenagers, meth here. We need to have a long talk with Wally Langston back at the department."

"A very long talk." Piper wondered if he'd been high the night she'd stopped to deliver the bad news about his brother, and she was too inexperienced to have realized it.

In Wallace's bedroom they found needles, crumpled foil, straws, pens missing the insides, and spoons ... all paraphernalia associated with meth use. A bag containing what Basil estimated at fifty grams of meth was hidden under a stack of t-shirts. A pouch with roughly forty grams of marijuana nested under a few pairs of sweatpants.

"You put meth in the crease in the foil," Basil explained to her. "You heat the foil to evaporate the meth, and inhale the smoke. The pens missing the ink cartridges inside, you use those for snorting it. Straws work, too. This fellow uses meth in all sorts of ways, smoking, inhaling, injecting. Lovely. He has enough to be a small-time dealer."

No paraphernalia in what had been Maurice's room, but Thresher was still agitated walking through it. The entire house bothered the dog. She recorded every inch of it on her body cam.

Piper wondered if the meth detected on Billie and Maurice had been picked up here. And the little bags Maurice had swallowed?

"No little bags," Piper said.

"No. No little bags empty or full."

They found no crossbow or quarrels, one box of ammo for the

Ruger, a wicked-looking hunting knife, dozens of old *Playboy* magazines, and nothing else of interest.

Piper fast-forwarded the footage to the holding cell at the department, where Wallace remained defiant.

"No comment. No comment. No comment, you pissers," he said. "I want a lawyer."

They'd talk to him again, with a lawyer present, sometime tomorrow. Then get him arraigned in court for obstruction and possession of controlled substances, gun charges, too. And they'd comb through his cell phone and the battered laptop found in the hall closet.

Piper closed the file, knowing she'd come back to it and watch one more time before turning in. She did a Google search on meth arrests and found a recent article that mentioned swallowed baggies.

MIDLAND, TEXAS: A young woman, mother of two, died Saturday after swallowing six grams of crystal methamphetamine contained in three baggies, Midland County Sheriff Department reported.

Brie Walker, twenty-one, allegedly ingested the meth Thursday night in what was an attempt to protect her husband during a routine traffic stop.

Francis Walker, twenty-six, is in federal custody awaiting charges. He told DEA agents that he passed the meth to his wife, and she swallowed it. He declined to say if he had instructed her to do so.

"Brie died protecting that scum," said Sonja Tipper, the woman's older sister. "Brie knew if Frankie got caught, he'd get tossed in jail and her two babies would be without a father. Meth is the devil."

Brie Walker was booked in the county jail Thursday night, after declaring she had no medical conditions and no narcotics or weapons on her.

"If she had told us she'd swallowed baggies of methamphetamine, we would have transported her to the hospital," a sheriff's spokesman reported. "If she simply said something, they could have pumped her stomach. She didn't have to die."

The spokesman went on to say: "She was behind bars roughly thirty-six hours and she was beginning to succumb to severe methamphetamine poisoning. A guard noticed something wrong, said that she was shaking, and escorted her to the jail's medical department for treatment. There, the nurse called for an ambulance to take Brie Walker to the hospital." The spokesman added: "She could not be saved."

Maurice hadn't been saved either.

Why had Maurice swallowed baggies of meth? Because he didn't want to be caught with them, Piper decided. Caught by whom? The soul who'd shot him with quarrels?

Piper closed the laptop and set it on the coffee table, leaned over without disturbing Tater, and scratched Camaro's belly.

"I'm with Basil," she told the dogs. "I hate meth. The drug is messy. These murders are messy. And we still have no idea who killed Tink and Captain Hook."

And why, she thought. They didn't have that, either. Not entirely. They had meth as the reason, but that wasn't enough. It didn't really answer the *why* of it.

CHAPTER TWENTY

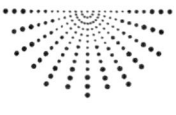

9 P.M.

There were ghosts in this house. Zeke swore he could feel them, circling, taking turns leaning over his shoulder as he sat at Teegan's kitchen table and used her laptop, all the paperwork from the sale and assorted file folders pulled from the attic within arm's reach.

People had died in this house, or while they owned this house, and that didn't include the bones retrieved from the attic. Maybe this place was not just haunted, it was cursed.

He'd been digging into genealogy sites, property records, old newspapers online ... anything he could think of, using the list of previous owners as a springboard. He'd watched Basil and Piper at the department, investigating various cases during the past several months. They had a dogged determination he admired and envied, and he desired to emulate that, hellbent on working his way into a law enforcement career. Maybe one day, if he stayed in the county, running for sheriff. Maybe if he moved away becoming a police chief. Top dog. Ambitious and driven, insatiably curious and keenly fixated —he knew he was all those things.

Zeke had downloaded all sorts of interesting tidbits that fueled his design to put a name to the bones and find the killer. He was going to beat Paul Blackwell; he was certain the police chief wouldn't think to use this route. He was Zeke the Geek, after all.

He was going to win.

Santa Claus was founded in 1849, eleven years before Teegan's house was built.

Reynolds Shepherd was the first occupant of this place, having purchased it for $2,200 from Meyer Weldon—who'd paid for the construction, then abandoned the notion of living here when his wife died in childbirth. Weldon moved to someplace in Tennessee with his (unnamed) baby boy.

Shepherd was a daguerreotypist, which Zeke had to further Google. Daguerreotype was the first widely available photography process that involved polishing a sheet of silver-plated copper, treating it with fumes that made the surface sensitive to light, and then exposing it in a camera. The resulting image was salted with mercury vapor, then rinsed and dried. Later, Shepherd became an ambrotypist, which was similar, but the photographs he produced would have sharper images. There were plenty of old photographs in the attic, maybe some of them had been taken by Shepherd.

"That's seriously dope," Zeke said, filing that curious fact away for trivia challenge night. He bet nobody who played at their monthly pizza gatherings would know what a daguerreotypist was. He thought he'd had them stumped in October with "Who is Stefani Germanot-ta?" Three people piped up right away with: Lady Gaga. Daguerreo-typist would stump them all.

Shepherd died in this house September 12th, 1894, an old man who succumbed to "natural causes" and was buried about three miles away in Buffaloville Cemetery. Zeke counted Shepherd one of the ghosts.

He pushed back from the table and rolled his shoulders. Between his dispatch job, working on his car, taking college courses, and digging into the mystery, he was close to exhausted. Zeke paced in the kitchen, thinking he should have done his digging at his apartment. He had a better laptop, though here he had access to the paper files from the attic. Besides, Teegan had given him a key.

The key was the problem.

Sitting in his pocket, it felt heavy. Teegan had passed it over so easily when he'd mentioned working on the Mr. Bones mystery. Told him to come over anytime to work, except for the hours she reserved for sleeping.

Teegan wasn't interested in him, romantically, was she? God no! he hoped. She was a year or two older than his mother. That would be creepy. Should he ask her? Should he say "you know, Tee, we're just friends, right?" Or should he not say anything?

Maybe he should give the key back, tell her he would do all future digging at his place, save himself the bike ride.

He settled back at the table and pulled up the next owner.

Leroy Johnson—purchased the house for $3,000 from Shepherd's widow, no mention where the widow moved after the sale. Johnson worked for an awning and tent maker and was paid $1.25 a day. Zeke couldn't imagine how Johnson had enough money to buy this place. Maybe he'd inherited money somewhere. Johnson, his wife, Evangelina—a member of the Women's Temperance Union—and two children (one of which was a White Ribbon Recruit of the Union) lived in the house until 1910, when they sold the property to Dr. Nathan Shepherd, who was no relation to the first Shepherd to live here.

Dr. Nathan Shepherd ran his small practice in an office where Teegan's three-car garage sat. He lived in the house with his brother, neither married during their years in Spencer County. The brother, Wilbur Shepherd, worked as a carpenter "assisting with the building of homes in Santa Claus." In 1917 when President Wilson's Selective Conscription took hold, Wilbur went off to war, dying in January, 1918. That same year, Dr. Shepherd's medical office was struck by lightning and burned to the ground. Dr. Shepherd left the area, selling the home for a mere $2,200. Zeke could not find where Dr. Shepherd moved, but he counted Wilbur as one of the house's ghosts.

Zeke's phone buzzed, incoming text. He glanced at it: Teegan. He waited a beat, then pulled it up.

"Any luck on Mr. Bones? I talked to Paul. He's got zippo right now."

"Still digging," Zeke texted back. "Interesting stuff on your house's history. I'll share it later."

He hit send. He really really hoped Teegan was thinking all of this platonic. He liked her. They had a lot in common—dispatchers, curiosity with criminal cases, a geek-factor. He shuddered. Friends, anything more than that would be beyond creepy. How could he make it clear to her they were just buddies? He didn't want to hurt her feelings. But he couldn't handle her wanting more than friendship from him.

"Next," Zeke said, directing his attention back to the search.

The next owner, **Cooper Anderson**, moved in during the end of April, 1918. No mention of his profession. His wife, Geraldine, son, Julian, and stepson, Arthur, died in October of that year to the Spanish Flu. Cooper died of the flu a month later. Four more ghosts. The house was willed to Cooper's sister, Olivia Anderson.

Olivia Anderson moved into the house in January, 1919, and married James Bullock in February of that year, becoming Olivia Bullock. Zeke saw a picture of them on a genealogy site.

"Bingo. Bingo. Bingo." Zeke had leafed through the small album of wedding photos from the attic that the police had returned. Said album sat on the kitchen table. Olivia and James Bullock matched the couple in the photos. "Bingo. Bingo. Bingo." He kept digging.

James Bullock was arrested in 1928 for bootlegging, manufacturing and distributing alcohol during Prohibition. Tacked to that were charges of tax evasion and cross-border smuggling. Olivia maintained the house during the years he was in jail, and gave birth to a boy two years into Bullock's incarceration. Zeke figured that might have been quite the scandal.

Bullock was released from jail in 1934, a year after Prohibition ended, on a rare pardon. He returned to the house, where Olivia was living with her son, David. Later that same year, James Bullock was reported missing. Zeke could not locate any mention of whether the man had been found, whether he'd died, or if he simply left because his wife had a child with an unnamed man.

"He could have been killed," Zeke said. "Murdered. The bones might be what is left of rumrunner James Bullock."

He eased back from the table, opened the cooler, and reached in for a Mountain Dew. If the bones were James' had his wife killed him? Had her lover? Little David would have been four and not likely the culprit.

Olivia never remarried, worked as a seamstress, was known for her lavish holiday décor—some of which likely filled Teegan's attic, and stayed in the house until she died in her sleep in an upstairs bedroom in 1999 at the age of one hundred. "Another ghost," Zeke muttered. The house passed to her son, David, who moved back to Spencer County from where he'd been living in upstate New York.

David Bullock, a jazz musician of moderate renown along the east coast, was sixty-nine when he retired from playing in New York club bands to live in this house in Santa Claus. News clippings showed him performing at events and festivals throughout Spencer County. He played violin, bass, clarinet, guitar, and piano. Quite the accomplished musician, there was no mention of him being a vocalist. Zeke found a list of works he'd composed, most of them jazz and blues pieces.

"That explains all the albums," Zeke said. And the instruments. It likely also explained who had owned the old poster Teegan had left on the table, with a note that she'd found it in the music room between some albums: an original folded concert poster from Woodstock, dated August, 1969, and signed by Arnold Skolnick, who Zeke Googled to discover was the artist for the poster. Unfolded, it was two feet by three feet, and a subsequent Google dive put its value at around $2,000 since there was no certificate of authenticity to verify the signature.

"David was probably the most interesting guy to live here," Zeke pronounced. In New York, he'd been a longtime member of a fraternal group, The Independent Order of Odd Fellows, holding the Royal Purple Degree and being elected Noble Grand in his lodge. He was spearheading the lodge's efforts to build an Odd Fellows museum, but the work never started, the lodge closed, and David took some of the

143

treasures to Spencer County, planning to donate them to a local lodge willing to take on a museum endeavor. Zeke read on: there was no local lodge, so at the age of seventy, David joined the Masonic Lodge in Spencer County, looking for a suitable replacement fellowship.

Zeke did some more searching and learned that the Odd Fellows and Masons had similarities, but were wholly different organizations. The Odd Fellows seemed to have a motto: Friendship, Love, and Truth. Aha! Another interesting bit for trivia night: several historical Odd Fellows were also Freemasons: Winston Churchill, Franklin Roosevelt, William McKinley, and Red Skelton. "And jazz musician David Bullock," Zeke said.

In 2019, at age eighty-nine, Bullock sold the house and its contents for fifty-one thousand dollars to Aaron and Rhonda White, and was moved into a "memory care" center in Evansville, dying a year later.

"No kids, apparently," Zeke said. "David Bullock wasn't married. Wonder where he was buried?" He paused and tipped his head back, staring at the ceiling. Married, you'd have someone to be buried next to when you were done dancing. He'd pursue Bullock's burial place later. Piper and Nang were getting married in a couple of months. He should be thinking about a wedding present. It would have to be inexpensive; Serilda and the college courses were drinking his money.

Aaron and Rhonda White, who owned several rental properties in Spencer County, had intended to repair and update Teegan's house, convert it into three apartments. Zeke found the proposed plan and zoning change paperwork. The remodeling never happened, the house sat vacant, the Whites died in a car accident across the river in Owensboro, victims of a drunk driver, and the property passed to Aaron White's sister in Florida.

The sister contacted the local realtor and told him to sell it "for whatever someone is willing to pay."

And that was Teegan's offer of thirty-thousand.

Unless some wandering murderer stuffed the body in the trunk and tugged it up into the attic when no one was home, Mr. Bones was killed by someone who had lived in this house, Zeke believed.

Maybe Mr. Bones ran rum, was the man who'd disappeared.

That possibility did the quickstep in Zeke's head; it seemed the most likely option. But he wouldn't limit himself to that; Basil and Piper wouldn't, they'd keep looking. He still had a lot of work to do: chat with older neighbors in the area about the previous owners of this place; find some nurses at the memory care center in Evansville who had taken care of David Bullock; call Aaron White's sister in Florida and any other relatives and friends of Aaron and Rhonda White that he could locate; and learn about the Whites' other rental properties and what had happened to those places.

It was a big list, and he wondered if he should meet with Paul Blackwell, spread out the work. No, he decided as soon as that idea surfaced. The Santa Claus police chief would likely take Zeke's research and tell him to butt out of the investigation.

"I've got some leads," he told Teegan when she came in the back door at 11:30. "I have tons of interesting shit on the past owners of this place." Should he say something to her now about him and her being just friends? Give her key back? Make sure she knew romance was not in their future?

She reached in the cooler for a Diet Dr. Pepper and joined him at the table. He thought she looked tired and could do with a good night's sleep. He'd not encourage her to help with more ferreting in what little was left of the night. He needed to ride home and catch some sleep. If he could sleep, as excited as he was with his discoveries. And she needed to know about the friends bit.

"The people who lived here before you," Zeke began, "make up an eclectic bunch. A physician, tent maker, bootlegger, seamstress, and a jazz musician with a Royal Purple Degree who had something in common with Winston Churchill. I saved all the stuff on a file called 'ghosts.'"

"Awesome," she yawned. "And now a sheriff's dispatcher with spiced plum hair calls this home." She hadn't opened the soda and apparently changed her mind about caffeine, pushing the can aside. "You think one of them in your file is the murderer?"

"I don't know yet," Zeke said.

"Got a clue who the bones belong to?"

"Maybe the bootlegger. Maybe."

"Someone killed him for running liquor?"

Zeke shook his head, then shrugged. "Prohibition was over when he would have died, after he got out of jail. But maybe someone had a vendetta from his bootlegging days."

"Exciting." Teegan raised an eyebrow that had a silver barbell piercing in it.

"A lot of maybes, Tee. But I am going to figure it out. It'll help when we can take a look at the report on the bones, get an approximate age on the guy."

"Speaking of guys and ages—"

Oh, no, Zeke thought. "Listen, Tee, you should know—"

"Basil wants me to meet a friend of his who's moved to the county," she plowed on, apparently oblivious to Zeke's "friendship" issue. "I dunno. I swore off men, dating, but he's forty, that's kinda close to my age, and Basil says he has a tattoo. I think I'll meet the guy for lunch at Nang's tomorrow, see what I think. He'd better be pretty special, or I'll just shake his hand and say 'have a nice day.' I'm pretty well entrenched in single life, and younger men are not my thing."

Zeke sighed. Safe. Teegan wasn't interested in him after all.

"Anyway, you don't need to know about my love life or lack thereof. About the bones ... the stuff you dug up, you going to pass it on to Paul?"

Zeke waited a moment before answering. "Sure," he said. "I'll let Paul Blackwell know what I've found." But not right away, he decided, not until either he got stuck and couldn't go any further ... or until he solved it, closed the case.

Zeke really wanted to win.

CHAPTER TWENTY-ONE

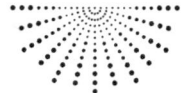

8 A.M. TUESDAY, NOVEMBER 3RD

T he field corn hadn't been harvested for silage yet. Piper stared at the yellow-brown stalks, tops cloaked by a layer of fog. The sky so overcast this morning, it looked like a dove-gray dome lidded everything.

Basil had gotten here first, and he stood by his Explorer on the side of the road waiting for her.

"The house is back in there." He pointed down an access road that bisected the field. It was the sort intended for use only by the farmer for his equipment, perhaps also serving as a driveway. A PRIVATE PROPERTY notice coupled with the lack of a street sign and the narrow road's rough condition should discourage someone from turning onto it, unless they had business with the landowner or intended to trespass.

"What did the drone catch?" Piper looked down the road, noting clumps of scrubby grass that grew in the center. The cool breeze that cut through the dried stalks conjured a haunted *shushing* sound and tinged the air with an acrid scent that added to the eeriness. It called up *Children of the Corn*, a movie she'd watched some years ago and found unsettling.

"The house is rundown, pretty sure it's wholly abandoned.

According to property records the man who owns the land moved to a condo in Santa Claus sixteen years ago. We gave him a search warrant for the house, though he said we were welcome to look anywhere on his property. He still farms the land, but said he's thinking about selling it and retiring, moving to Georgia."

"This isn't the only search warrant you have."

"No," Basil admitted. "I got six. One for this and five for some other abandoned properties along the road and around the curve. The judge signed off on all of it fast, says he hates meth, too."

"And you picked this one first, because—"

"Because Maurice would have passed by this access road between where Billie was found and where he went off the road. Dead middle of his route. And—" Basil again gestured to the distance, "there's a blue van parked outside the house. At least there was twenty minutes ago when the drone went over."

"You think it could be a meth house." Piper didn't pose it as a question.

"It's why I called you. Thought you might want to check it out with me."

Piper left her Explorer on the shoulder and got in Basil's. He drove down the access road slow, creeping quietly, not wanting to alert whoever might be in the house. The breeze gusted, eerily rattling the cornstalks.

"Ever see *Children of the Corn?*" she asked him.

"Esme reads him. I'm not a fan of King's books or movies. Too much squish," he replied. "We can call in Diego and Thresher if something looks promising. And I have hazmat suits in the back in case we find a lab."

"Wallace Langston's attorney is coming in at two, a little before the arraignment," she said. "Just so you're back by then. I want you in on it."

"Yeah. I wouldn't miss that."

Checking the access roads along Maurice's route Halloween night was necessary, Piper knew. Meth manufacturers loved rural places like Spencer County because they could set up operations in the middle of nowhere and not risk being noticed by neighbors. Rustic spots in the Midwest were prime—make the drug and transport it in all directions to larger cities, probably to Indianapolis, Evansville, Louisville, and the like from around here.

Hard to catch them because they could move their operations and didn't need much space to work. They could hide like the creepy children did in the King movie. Piper's dad had told her he'd only managed to shut down one meth lab in all his years with the sheriff's department. "The labs are so hidden you'd need a force of bloodhounds," he'd said. Thresher was the first drug-search dog the department had, and she counted him as good as a "force of bloodhounds" the way he'd been trained.

Piper hoped this particular access road would lead to something significant.

Basil hit a rut and the Explorer jumped. She held her sling close and stiffened at the jarring thump that sent a jolt of pain from her shoulder to her fingers. Soon, she could ditch the sling if she didn't do anything to screw it up. She really wanted both hands free to do her job.

The access road continued straight, narrowing and fading into nothingness in the stalks, but it also forked to the right, and Basil took this and drove a hundred yards down to a beat-to-hell house with a crumbling center chimney and a gable roof.

"A fixer-upper's dream," Piper said.

"Nightmare," Basil argued. "Unless you want an out-of-the-way place to make meth. Yeah, then you could call it a dream."

Definitely abandoned, the building had only a few intact windows, and looked like it had been some shade of navy in earlier years. Hints of paint clung stubbornly to weathered wood shake siding. A couple of shutters remained, crooked and broken. The roof sagged, the railing on what might have been an impressive front porch a few decades back leaned forward into scraggly evergreens that grew in profusion. The weeds were tall and thick, except for a worn-down path to the front steps; the place clearly had been visited. *Even with the surrounding field corn harvested, this wouldn't be easy to notice from the road because of the weeds and a few spindly pines,* Piper thought. At least not noticed in any detail.

"Abandoned sixteen years ago?" Piper said. "Looks more like it's been empty for sixty."

"You'd think when the owner moved to town, he would have knocked this down, planted it in corn," Basil said as he pulled up behind the van so it couldn't back out. He turned off the engine and turned on his body cam.

"Probably thought it was too expensive to tear down," Piper said. "Some farmers around here just let the land and the weather take the buildings they're done with. It's why you can drive along the county roads and see some modern homes built near big farmhouses that are left empty and rotting. People want something more modern and leave the old building to decay. There was probably a barn on this property, too, likely not as stubborn as this house."

The van was a Honda Odyssey, Piper guessed it about ten years old. The driver side window had been left open and dried leaf blades littered the seat, blown there from the field. The keys were in the ignition. She reached in and took them, making double-sure if the driver was in the house, he wasn't going anywhere.

"I think the van's been sitting here at least a little while," she observed. "We'll come back to it."

She studied the ground around the van, taking pictures of shoeprints, looked like a work boot. Only one set of clear prints, but there'd been a lot of rain, and that could have taken care of anything earlier. No motorcycle tracks, either, and she searched in a circle farther out thinking she might find something to match what she'd seen in the field near Maurice's body.

Basil went up the front porch steps first, hand on his gun. She thought he moved like a cat, careful where he stepped, quiet despite the porch steps looking like they'd cave if any weight was placed on them. She followed, finding the wood soft, like it held all the recent rain. The planks bowed under her feet.

She smelled the dried corn, the oldness of the wood, and a rottenness she couldn't place that pulsed from inside. Passing through the front door and crunching on the husks of dead insects, she revised her initial description of "fixer-upper." The house was unfixable.

The stench was stronger, a wall she had to push through.

And it was quiet.

There was a hole in the ceiling of the living room, and looking up through it, Piper saw a hole in the roof a level above. Rain had damaged everything. Mold bloomed in thick swaths on the walls and on some of the broken furniture. Broken glass from the windows and nails, probably from the walls, lay along the margins. A battered couch was reasonably intact, a blanket that looked newer than anything else draped over the back. A chair sat opposite the couch, and a beaten coffee table sat between them, remnants of drug use on its surface ... burn marks, powder, pieces of foil, a needle, a glass pipe, rolling papers. Maybe there was residue from meth, but the powder could be from other substances, heroin, cocaine.

Piper's eyes watered and she rubbed at them, saw that the stink bothered Basil, too.

"This smell," he said, "people who use this place can ignore it. They're intent on one thing."

Getting high, she thought. Chasing whatever piece of euphoria their drug of choice offered.

She glanced through a wide doorway into what had likely been a dining room. No furniture, more mold, faded wallpaper peeling, broken glass, and clear evidence termites had a party here. There were two more blankets, these folded and set away from the windows in front of a black radiator, perhaps in an effort to keep them dry. A pair of torn blue jeans lay in a corner, a John Deere t-shirt crumpled next to it.

Why would anyone squat in a place like this?

Because who would find you here, she answered herself.

Because you could do drugs or whatever else you wanted and not risk discovery.

Because this teetering, termite-ridden, stinking dump made you feel safe.

She winced.

"Place is empty," Basil said. "If someone was upstairs, we would have heard them."

The bathroom was the source of the reek. The plumbing no longer working, the squatters had continued to use the toilet and bathtub, both filled with human waste.

The kitchen's appliances were gone, the cabinets all rotted from the rain, one plaster wall so badly fissured she could see the home's wood lath nailed to the wall studs. A porcelain farmhouse sink defied destruction. Idly, Piper thought someone should come in and rescue it. There was a hole in the ceiling in this room, too.

Stairs led down into a basement, but neither she nor Basil ventured there—not enough steps remained to navigate it. Maybe they would send the drone down if Basil thought it necessary.

A glance out the back door, which was so swollen in the frame Piper had to throw her good shoulder at it to get it open, showed undisturbed weeds, the remnants of a shed, and cornstalks. No one had ventured out this door in a long time.

Upstairs revealed more ruin and mold and evidence of drug use, along with a plethora of empty bottles of alcohol, beer cans, and a few more blankets. A second bathroom, also well-used and fetid.

Piper itched and resisted scratching at herself. Her eyes continued to water.

What an awful place.

Would Basil find something similar among the other buildings he intended to search?

Did the farmer know what his old house was used for? And if he did, why not do something about it?

Because tearing down the place would cost too much, she thought again. She'd let him see the pictures, maybe that would get him to do something.

"My dad, when he was sheriff, said he didn't make many meth-related arrests, that it was basically a hidden crime."

Basil looked thoughtful. "Hidden here, in country places, maybe. Meth is more than a hundred years old, Sheriff, traces back to 1919 when ephedrine was used to synthesize it, and in World War II the

Japanese gave a form of meth to soldiers to increase their alertness. It was called Fly Away, or something like that. Fell out of focus and fashion, but Hell's Angels and other biker gangs trafficked in it, and criminal elements gave it a boost in the early eighties by pulling ephedrine from Sudafed and other drugs to manufacture it. No matter how it's made, it does the same thing, addicts you, damages your brain. You don't typically die of an overdose, but meth kills. It causes you to decay."

"You know a lot about it," Piper said.

"Because I hate it. I study the enemy, Sheriff." They returned to the porch. "Meth might have been manufactured here at one time. Doesn't look like it was recently. But it's clearly a place where people come for drinking and drugs. Looks like some of the remnants on the coffee table are recent."

"Like a kid's clubhouse." Piper's voice was flat.

"Yeah, a hangout. Except nothing good ever happens here."

"Billie and Maurice might have been here."

"True," Basil said. "If not the night they were killed, some other night. They might have been here. Them, their friends. Maybe got their drugs here, but not likely Halloween night. It's almost dead center of where they were each found. I'm thinking their demise started farther west. Maybe they were chased."

"Maybe Maurice stopped to let Billie out, thinking to keep her safe from whoever was after them."

"Captain Hook a knight in armor?" Basil shook his head. "Yeah. Okay. Maybe. I guess I could see that. It could explain why they weren't killed together. Maurice lets her out, thinks the killer will keep chasing him and ignore her. But the killer stops to get her first, then continues after Maurice. The idea plays."

They paced around the van. Piper leaned against the front window and took a close-up of the Vehicle Identification Number, got the registration out of the glovebox and took a picture of that, too.

"Tomas Waring," she said, "of Dale. A local man."

"Hopefully Mr. Waring just had trouble with his van and left it here. Hopefully we'll find him breathing," Basil said.

Piper keyed her radio, told Zeke to run the plates on the van and check for Tomas Waring, if he had any arrests or outstanding warrants, send a deputy to his house in an effort to find him.

"I'm going back to the department," she said. "I've a dozen things to do before two, including some paperwork I really can't ignore."

"I'll sweep through this house again, collect some things, samples, see if there was meth." He paused. "I'm sure there was meth. Take some fingerprints." He gave a sad laugh. "Maybe find Billie and Maurice in the mix. Maybe find a lot of other prints that will lead nowhere if the people aren't in the system."

He gestured to his Explorer. "I'll take you back to your car, first."

Piper shook her head. "I'll get Diego and Thresher out here. Take them down the other access roads with you, let me know what turns up." She walked past his Explorer, then stopped to look over her shoulder. "I appreciate the education you're giving me. I truly do."

"I'll give you a ride—"

"I want to walk, think. I can use the exercise."

"See you at two," Basil said.

Piper headed down the narrow road, stepping around ruts, looking for traces of a motorcycle track, and peering into the corn. She listened to the shushing sound brought by the wind, remembered the disturbing movie about the children, and thought for the hundredth time about Billie and Maurice.

CHAPTER TWENTY-TWO

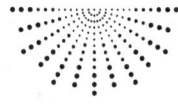

11 A.M.

Piper watched Zeke field a 9-1-1 call and dispatch a deputy and the volunteer fire department to Gentryville, flames seen coming from a garage. Quick, efficient, he clicked off the call and reached for a large mug of coffee.

Coffee.

She'd never seen Zeke drink coffee.

Piper stepped to the side of his desk and pointed at the mug.

"Dark Italian Roast," he said. "It was in the coffee maker. It's not awful. Especially when you add three things of creamer and a couple of sugars. Maybe I can acquire a taste for it, you think? I just about emptied the pot. I'd refill the machine, but I'm not sure what all the buttons are for."

She raised an eyebrow.

"Soda just isn't doing it today. Not enough jolt. I've been staying up too late, not sleeping well. Between thinking about Maurice and Billie —kids I knew, and working on the bones in Teegan's attic, I'm sort of fried." He paused. "But not so burnt I can't do my job here."

"Teegan's skeleton is my dad's case," Piper said. "Santa Claus' jurisdiction, and he hasn't asked for help." Her father hadn't even discussed the skeleton with her, and she planned to rectify that at dinner at his house tomorrow night. She was curious who had died in her second shift dispatcher's house. Teegan mentioned that Zeke had become obsessed by it.

"I'm just digging. Not hurting anything. Just digging."

They listened to radio chatter for a moment.

"I'm not using department resources," he added. "And I'm doing this on my own time."

"I'll put on some more coffee," Piper returned. She edged toward the breakroom, and then glanced over her shoulder. "I hope you solve it, Teegan's box of ones."

Minutes later she settled at her desk, opened her laptop, and held her nose over the coffee. She appreciated the smell and the heat and let both tease her. She held the strong, bitter taste on her tongue as she reviewed the body cam footage from Maurice and Billie's houses. How many times had she watched this?

Maybe too many, but something scratched at the back of her brain.

She replayed the video from Billie's house.

What bothered her?

If there was something there, Basil would have noticed it, right? Sherlock, his friend called him, a nickname from his days with the Chicago police. Sherlock hadn't spotted anything disquieting. Thresher hadn't keyed on anything. From room to room, to closets, to the halls, to the basement and garage. To the little Billie shrine with the cheerleading picture in the kitchen.

She replayed the video from Maurice's. The rundown house with its vintage furnishings and funky odor had yielded plenty of hits from Thresher. Room to room to a shed in the back, to the cars and the crawlspace. Trophies of Maurice's athletic accomplishments, a sense of abandonment, mother's ashes in an urn, drugs, girlie magazines.

Two starkly different houses, different parts of the county, different lives, yet the young occupants had a romantic relationship that ended tragically.

Something gnawed.

Piper closed the video and cross-checked friends Billie and Maurice texted and called, seeing if any of them had records or complaints in the system. Juvenile records wouldn't display, but it would indicate something was there. She'd already run checks on the teenagers she'd brought in for interviews. Basil had done the same.

Nothing. All of the pair's friends seemed clean. She suspected they weren't. She suspected some of them had secrets or were lying.

She spent more than an hour at it, and then watched the body cam video again. From rooms to closets. Trophies and a little shrine.

Considering it a dead end, she went for a coffee refill, studied the whiteboard with all of its photos and maps, finished some paperwork, and headed to the courthouse.

W allace and his attorney—Eleanor Greene of Rockport—sat in a conference room on the second floor. Wallace wore a brown suit, tan shirt, and a green tie with red stripes that Piper figured was for Christmas gatherings. She wondered who'd brought him the clothes, since he'd traveled from the jail to the courthouse … she'd check the visitor log. Maybe he'd given Eleanor access to his house.

He'd cleaned up a little, but he hadn't shaved, and he had a sour smell. The attorney should have suggested he shower before the arraignment. Wallace's eyes seemed sunken under the bright fluorescent fixtures, his teeth dingy; she realized his appearance signaled meth use, but she hadn't noticed it on their first meeting. She'd like to think it was the dim lighting in Wallace's house instead of her lack of experience.

Eleanor, who sat an arm's distance from her client, wore a pale gray pinstriped suit with a navy blouse and three strands of pearls. She had close-cropped white hair and no-rim glasses, designer briefcase, designer shoes. She looked as fashionable and expensively styled as some of the models on the *Project Runway* show Piper watched. She was probably taking the case pro-bono, as Piper was certain Wallace could not afford someone like this.

Basil entered, nodded to Piper and Eleanor, and placed his cell phone in the center of the table, making a show of recording the proceedings.

"All right, Wallace," Piper began, "you said you'd talk to us here."

"With my attorney," Wallace put in defiantly. "Miss Greene is my attorney. I want a deal. To talk to you, I want a deal."

Piper figured that was coming, and she and DA Scales had already discussed the possibilities. It was up to Scales if any agreement was made.

"My client has agreed to help, and to answer your questions, in exchange for you getting the charges dropped." Eleanor's voice was melodic and pitched like an alto clarinet. "Resisting arrest, possession of controlled substances, and a minor gun charge—for which he has a license, will be stricken."

Piper thought she heard a rumble from Basil. She glanced over; the detective busied his fingers with a pencil.

"To begin with," Piper opened, "ultimately any decisions on charges and plea agreements are up to the DA. I can't force his hand. However, I have a good working relationship with him. He tends to listen to the sheriff's department on recommendations."

"It's too much meth to strike it all," Basil said. "Five grams, that's what you usually find on someone who's just a user. You had fifty. That's a Level 2 felony, and you're looking at ten to thirty years in prison. I used to work in Chicago, and in Illinois there'd be no possibility of probation with a guilty verdict. Do you understand how serious this is?"

Wallace looked down, studying his fingernails.

Basil continued. "And the amount of cannabis you had, that's a dealer amount, too."

Piper knew meth was the more serious crime, that courts were more lenient with cannabis, and suspected DA Scales wouldn't be too worked up about the pot charge.

Eleanor tipped her chin. "My client will talk if we can come to some understanding and—"

"Understand this," Piper interrupted, her ire surfacing. "Wally, your brother was murdered. You should want to help us discover who killed him. We're not going to recommend to the DA that you get a deal *simply* for telling us what you know about your brother's murder."

"If we take you to trial," Basil added, "and the jury finds out that you got some sweet deal from the DA to cough up information on Maurice's murder, they will not look kindly on you. I'm sure Miss Greene will agree with me."

Eleanor crossed her arms, narrowed her gaze, and looked between Piper and Basil. "There is room for negotiation," she said.

Basil nodded. "Wally's dealer is the wiggle room."

Piper listened. Basil had worked narcotics in Chicago and had a world of experience with drugs and courts.

"We're very much interested in getting the name of Wally's dealer," Basil said.

"The bigger fish," Eleanor said dryly.

"Wally gives up his dealer, and we catch said questionable soul selling, then we'll talk to the DA about lessening some charges. And Wally has to agree to truthfully testify in any related trials. Look at it this way, Wally, the Spencer County Sheriff's Department is driving a bus. You can hop on the bus and take a seat, or you can be run over by it. What do you want to do?"

Basil sat back and waited.

Piper watched Wallace shift uncomfortably.

"I wasn't going to deal the stuff I had. All of that was my personal stash. Honest," Wallace said. "And pot should be legal here. It is in Illinois. Pot's no worse than beer, and that's legal."

Eleanor glared at Wallace, a signal to keep his mouth shut.

Pot was legal in a lot of states, Piper knew. But in Indiana recreational cannabis use was illegal, and the state had no provision for medical marijuana. The only thing that wouldn't get you arrested was hemp-derived CBD oil with less than .3 percent THC content. Indiana had some of the strictest cannabis laws in the country.

"Wally had more than thirty grams of marijuana," Basil said. "I say again, that's felony possession, and that's punishable by up to two and a half years in prison and a ten thousand dollar fine. That's nothing next to the methamphetamine charges. Are you ready to spend the next three decades in prison? Do you want the bus to run over you?"

Wallace paled at that.

Eleanor straightened and tapped a file folder. "Class A misdemeanor possession on the marijuana charge," she countered. "Six months. No fine. As for the meth—"

"That'll depend on the DA," Basil said. "And we won't make a recommendation until after we have the dealer." Basil glanced at his watch. "Arraignment starts in twenty minutes. You have—"

"Okay," Wallace said. "Okay." He slumped in the chair and rubbed at his eyes. "Okay. Okay. Okay. I just want you to find whoever killed my brother. None of this was his fault. He never used. Worse he ever did was drink Budweiser."

Piper texted DA Scales, and she held up the questions until he joined them.

"It was the girl," Wally said after everyone was in place at the table. "It was Billie. She knew I ... she knew I—"

"—used meth," Basil said.

"Yeah, Billie knew. Maurice probably told her. My dealer raised the prices. Not that meth is ever all that expensive. You used to be able to get a hit for five bucks. She raised it to twenty, and with paying bills, I wouldn't be able to get as much meth as I needed. Billie told me she could get it cheaper. I could buy it from her. She brought me the fifty-gram pouch to prove she could deliver. Hell, she didn't charge but a hundred bucks for it. I said sure, I'd buy from her. It was fine chalk, what she'd brought me. Real fine, hit all the right spots. I know she gave me such a great price because of Maurice. She was nuts about Maurice. I think she was trying to impress him by helping me."

"Go on, about Billie," Piper encouraged.

"I gave her another hundred, the night she and Maurice were going to that party. She said she'd get the meth on the way to the barn and bring it by after they were done dancing. Said she'd be my dealer from now on. Said she'd always give me a special rate because of Maurice."

Wallace rocked forward in the chair, fingers fidgeting. "Maurice, he argued with Billie, said it was risky. But she said … I remember exactly what she said … 'It'll be easy,' she said. 'Just like before. Nobody'll be there now. We can break in and load up.' That's what she said. It sounded good." He shook his head. "Real good. Too good. I knew that girl was trouble. Too good to be true. Maurice should've left her alone."

"Where was she going to get the meth?" Basil snapped the pencil and glared. "Who was she getting it from?"

"Th-that I don't know," Wallace returned nervously. "A place in the country. Middle of nowhere she'd called it. 'Out whoop-whoop.' Said that's why they had to take the jeep instead of Maurice's car. She said they needed the four-wheel-drive for out whoop-whoop."

"We want the name of your previous meth dealer," Piper said.

Wallace moaned, but nodded. The name he gave matched one of the partiers from the barn.

Basil scrolled through his phone. "That would be Betty Boop," he told Piper. "I have her address. She's a college sophomore. Zoology major."

Piper made a fist of her free hand. She'd interviewed Betty Boop—Vic Halliday—Sunday morning. The girl had admitted going to football games with Wallace to watch Maurice.

"And who supplies the marijuana?" Piper asked.

Wally gave it up. "Trent. Trenton Carlson."

"That's George Washington," Basil said, looking at Piper. "The son of Roger Carlson, the farmer who threw the steampunk Halloween party."

Piper and Basil left the courthouse and walked back to the sheriff's department.

"I'll do the paperwork on the warrant for the Carlson barn. And house, vehicles, and all the extras. For Victoria Halliday's apartment, electronics, car. Can't just arrest them on Wally's chatter, gotta have some proof. I'd like to catch them selling, but we'll see. Judge better be in a good mood with all these warrants I've been passing over."

"At least we got something from Wally," Piper said. "A lot more than we had."

Basil made a hissing sound. "We got that Billie was at the bottom of the Halloween mess. Her taking someone's meth stash led to her and Maurice's deaths. We shift all the focus to her and where the ugly orange jeep went on Halloween."

Where the jeep went ... it went to hell, Piper thought. The vehicle went to the "middle of nowhere," Billie crossed paths with a very bad soul who had a stash of methamphetamine, and then it all went to hell.

CHAPTER TWENTY-THREE

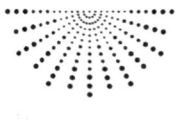

5 P.M.

C hicken rice paper rolls. Is that like spring rolls?" Chief
Deputy Oren Rosenberg folded his six-foot-four frame into
a chair at the back of Nang's Quick Stop. He had the build
of a linebacker, with curly steel-gray hair that he'd grown longer in
the back so it covered his collar. No trace of his sheriff's department
garb, he wore a pair of indigo blue jeans with a pressed crease down
the front, and a yellow and brown plaid flannel shirt. He pointed to
the menu above the counter. "Are there carrots in it?"

Nang finished a conversation with Shelly. "I'll take this," he told
her. "Oren is a friend." He came over to Oren's table. "They are basically the same as the spring rolls I usually have. But these use rice
paper—a translucent sheet of rice-flour dough, and they have slivered
carrots and shredded bok choy in them."

Oren rubbed at his chin. "I like your spring rolls. I'll try two of the
rice paper things. They're appetizer size, right?"

Nang nodded.

The fingers of Oren's right hand played with the edge of the placemat, folding it. "Your place always smells good, Nang. On vacation,
we stopped at this little Thai restaurant outside of Pigeon Forge. Wife
thought it looked pretty on the outside, and inside there was this huge

aquarium with two dozen big fantailed goldfish. I counted them, the goldfish, some as big as my hand. Lots of plants in the tank, too, and a plastic treasure chest that opened and closed and released a stream of bubbles. We sat right up against the tank so she could watch the fish. She didn't talk all the way through dinner, just watched the fish. Anyway, the place smelled … oh, I don't know … funky. Not like anything had spoiled, but like they used too much oil and grease, spices, whatever, and it had soaked into the carpet. It just smelled funky. Yours smells all the time like something good is cooking. Can't smell the gasoline from the pumps outside, either. And we could smell fish, the goldfish. There were a lot of them in the tank, and it didn't have a lid. I don't think we should have sat right up against the tank."

"Was the food bad?"

Oren shrugged. "I wouldn't call it bad, exactly. I had chicken and broccoli over noodles. It looked good, but it tasted … meh. I was hungry, so I ate it. Here? I've never had a bad meal. I think you've spoiled me for any other Asian cooking."

Nang smiled at that. "Everything here is good," he said. "My new manager Shelly—"

"—Evans from the grocery store? She works here now? I thought I recognized her when I came in."

"Yes. And she is an excellent cook."

The bell over the door rang and Millie stepped inside. She waved to Oren and hurried over, sat next to him, and put her hat on an empty chair. "I only have a half hour for dinner, Pops. I'm still on the three to eleven. Glad you called me, and nice to join you, but why aren't you still on vacation?"

Oren pointed to the menu again. "Two of those rice paper rolls," he repeated. "And what is shaking beef?"

"New on my menu," Nang said. "I dress the plums with sesame oil, sear the slices of top round, mix it with garlic, soy sauce, lime, shishito peppers, mint, rice vinegar, and shake it around in the wok. Hence, shaking beef. It is basically a stir-fry. I serve it over rice and baby romaine. It is very good."

"It sounds wonderful," Millie said. "I'll have an order of that, and hot tea."

"I'll try it," Oren said. "I want coffee. Black, the largest cup you have."

Nang washed his hands and retreated to the kitchen. Millie fixed Oren with a stare. "Grandpa, why are you back from vacation so early? Didn't like Tennessee? You've been talking about Pigeon Forge for—"

Oren's fingers worked faster on the placemat. "We stopped at a Thai restaurant near Pigeon Forge, close to our hotel. She didn't talk to me all through dinner. Hell, on the drive there I knew something was bothering her. She talked a little bit about craft shows and the magazines she liked, but most of the time she just looked out the window and didn't say anything. Didn't want the radio on either."

"Something's wrong," Millie said, leaning forward. "Is grandma sick?"

"She's not sick. Not physically, anyway." Oren stared down at the placement. "But there's something wrong. With me apparently."

"Pops, what—"

"Right after we ordered dessert, she said she wanted a divorce. Said this Pigeon Forge vacation was our last nice week together. That our marriage could end on a happy note. Happy like hell, eh?"

Millie's eyes grew wide and her voice louder. "What? Seriously? Not real, Pops. This isn't happening. She didn't—"

"I don't know why she didn't say something before we left. She never let on that there was a problem between us. Never. I told her I'd retire if that's what she wanted. She said 'hell no,' then I'd be around even more often. She used to ask me to retire, you know. Maybe if I would have retired a year ago, she wouldn't be doing this."

Nang brought the tea and coffee, retreated. Oren could tell he'd overheard them.

"She doesn't mean it, Pops. She's going through something. She's—"

"She's going through all our accounts to list what we have for the attorney to sort through. Said she contacted him several weeks ago when she'd made her mind up. She said there's some paperwork in a folder on top of the fridge I need to look through and sign. We didn't make it to Pigeon Forge, though she still wanted to go, wanted that last hurrah. We came back yesterday and I haven't looked in the folder yet. Why the hell couldn't she have said something before we left?"

Millie reached a hand over and grabbed Oren's wrist.

"I'll go talk to her, Pops, see what's going on. You and her ... you mean the world to me, and—"

"You can't talk to her, unless you use your cell phone. We got back yesterday," he repeated. "She called Indy and booked a flight to Birmingham. Her sister owns a townhouse there, and the side she'd been renting out opened up. Guess who's going to be staying in it? At least for a while, until she figures out what she wants to do. Her flight left at noon. She claims she'll be back in a few weeks to pack."

Nang brought their meals without saying anything and went back behind the counter. Oren listened, heard Nang tell Shelly he was going to stick around a little while longer.

Probably wants all the gossip on my sad life, Oren thought. He'd lost his father in September, and now he was losing his wife. He took a bite of the rice paper roll. It was so much better than what he'd had at the Thai place. Thai One On, that's what it had been called. He ate both rolls and started on the shaking beef, noticed Millie hadn't touched her plate.

"I'm sixty-six," he said between bites. "Sixty-six and I'm going to be alone."

"I'll talk to her."

"Fine, you talk to her. I tried to talk to her. On the ride back, all she talked about was how to divide up stuff and how she'd need to rent a U-Haul. Said she doesn't want the house or the furniture, except for the big clock and the walnut curio cabinet. Doesn't want the boat, doesn't want to stay in Spencer County. She talked about some article she'd read about 'gray divorce' when she started looking into separating."

"Gray divorce?" Millie stirred the beef with her fork.

"Gray divorce, like Bill and Melinda Gates," he said. "You divorce when you're gray."

"Pops—"

"After I sign the paper, two months or so later the court waves a magic wand and I'm single. Indiana is a no-fault state."

"Meaning either spouse can ask for a divorce for any reason," Millie supplied.

"You'll make a great lawyer," Oren said. "She says it's not going to be painful, that we'll compromise, that she won't ask for spousal support since she already has social security and a pension. But because she's not taking the house, she wants more than half of our investments." He ate several forkfuls of the beef before continuing. "Hell, she can have it all. Except my damn boat. Good thing she doesn't want my boat. Or doesn't want me to sell it and split the money. And the cats. She can't take my cats."

Millie looked like she was going to cry. "Maybe we can fix this, Pops. Maybe she just needs time away. Maybe her sister will talk some sense into her."

"Her sister talked her into moving to Birmingham. I wonder how long ago that conversation started. You know, up until mid-September she'd been asking me to retire. Said she wasn't happy, thought my retirement might make her happy. She said she saw a therapist on the side when I was on duty. Never told me she was doing that. Said the therapist helped her work through issues. Said in the end divorce would solve everything. I never knew she wasn't happy. Never ever knew."

"Then you need an attorney, Pops."

Oren shook his head. "I'm not going to contest anything, Millie." He ate a few more forkfuls of beef, washed it down with a big slug of coffee, worried at the placemat some more. "But I'll ask you to go through the papers with me."

"Of course." She motioned to Nang. "Can I get this to go?" To Oren: "I have to go back on patrol. But I'm coming over first thing in the morning. All right?"

He gave a single nod and reached for the bill.

Oren watched Millie leave, finished his meal, and noted that Nang observed him from behind the counter. Shelly busied herself by straightening the candy bars.

He stood, stretched, and walked up to pay the bill. "Don't marry Piper Blackwell," he told Nang. "Don't marry anybody. It's not worth it."

"I love her," Nang said, as he gave Oren his change. "My parents divorced, her parents divorced. Maybe we will divorce, too. But I hope not. I love her with everything." He had a sorrowful expression. "I am very sorry what you are going through Oren. I have no words other than that. Very sorry."

"Yeah, well, I'm sorry, too."

Oren shuffled to the parking lot and slid into his pickup. He grabbed the steering wheel so hard his knuckles turned bone white, and he sobbed. He'd lost his father; he was losing his wife. He felt like a rag rug that was unraveling.

CHAPTER TWENTY-FOUR

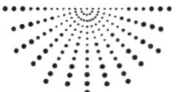

11 A.M. WEDNESDAY, NOVEMBER 4TH

Basil wanted to go through the jeep again while he waited on search warrants. He nudged Zeke and his laptop out the door and saw Piper sit at the dispatcher desk and reach for the headphones. The sheriff was filling in for Zeke so Basil could borrow him.

"Bring you something for lunch?" Basil asked her. "We'll probably stop at Shirl's when we're done."

"Dinner at my dad's tonight, so no lunch for me." Piper shook her head, then smiled. "Except ... I'll take a Shirl's milkshake."

"Been through the jeep twice," Basil told Zeke. "GPS, too. But I need to try something else. That's why I pulled you off the desk." The other abandoned houses he, Diego, and Thresher had searched yesterday yielded zilch, and Basil was determined to discover where Billie and Maurice had ventured the night they were killed. He hoped the jeep would somehow yield that.

"You got a search warrant for the vehicle, right?" Zeke asked. "I've been reading about the department and procedures and—"

"Of course." Basil tried not to sound condescending to a question the dispatcher should have known better than to have asked. "Most warrants cover ninety-six hours, and that's why I want this done now." He was still waiting on the warrant for the Carlson properties and Victoria Halliday's apartment; he'd nudge the judge this afternoon.

"So, it comes under your deadline, this search," Zeke said. "Got it."

Basil opened the jeep's front doors and pointed inside. "It's the GPS feature I'm not satisfied with. I've downloaded all the places it was asked to navigate, but there were no requests on Halloween and—"

"Any good GPS does that, holds that information," Zeke said, as he climbed in, placed the laptop on the passenger seat, and turned the ignition. "I'm going to download everything again, all right?"

"Sure." Basil watched him work, respectful of the nineteen-year-old's skill with tech.

"A typical GPS is all about history, doesn't actually record *where* the vehicle has been," Zeke continued. "If you ask it to navigate to Indy, it'll log that, and you'll have a record of that *request*. But if you end up in Pittsburgh instead, it won't capture that."

Basil leaned against the jeep and listened to Zeke rattle on about GPS systems.

"Anyway, that's a typical GPS feature, basic," Zeke said. "But this is a new car with Bluetooth, navigation, and it looks like it has an event data recorder."

"Which is?"

"A good event recorder is capable of logging where you traveled, who you called, and can even retrieve your texts. Oh, and if you're wearing your seatbelt. Now, it's not all Big Brother. A lot of the information your car tracks is optional. You can turn it off."

"Did the Glempses turn it off?"

Zeke puttered on his laptop. "I don't know yet. This isn't instantaneous, you know. I'm pretty good with this stuff, but not as fast as the computer whizzes on TV. Like the hacker on *The Equalizer*? I'm not that good or fast."

"That's fiction."

Zeke shrugged, then whispered. "I'm not that good *yet*."

Basil closed his eyes and thought back to the abandoned house he'd taken Sheriff Blackwell to yesterday. He'd collected prints, found some that matched two locals who had records of minor offenses such as disorderly conduct at a bar, shoplifting from the Dollar Store. No prints matched Billie or Maurice's.

Millie located the owner of the blue van—Tomas Waring—last night at a tavern in Dale a few doors down from Waring's house. He admitted to being at the abandoned farm property, but claims he did not go in. Waring said he was having engine trouble and turned off on the access road, hoping it would lead to a farmhouse where he could get help, that all he found was an empty rundown dump. Waring said the van died, leaving him stranded. He claimed he walked back to the road and hitchhiked home, and that he hadn't yet gotten around to arranging for a tow for the van.

Millie described him in detail in her report. Based on that, Basil figured Waring was a drug user who'd visited the house on purpose to get high with some friends, and that indeed his van was not working when he wanted to leave. People lied in Spencer County, just like they lied in Chicago. Drugs shattered lives here, and in the city. There was just a lot more of it in Chicago.

This was a better place for his kids, he knew. They liked it, weren't bored. Esme found it a quiet place to get a lot of writing done, and not a far drive to her parents. Basil found it a little dull, but he was managing to put up with it. Maybe he needed to pick up a hobby. He was entertaining the notion of radio-controlled planes; his neighbor was into them and was the president of the county's radio control club. Operating the sheriff department drone had sparked his interest.

Millie said the bar where she'd found Waring—The Red Baron—was decorated inside with Snoopy and Sopwith Camels. He knew the radio control club met there; maybe he could talk his neighbor into meeting at Tug's bar instead, closer to Santa Claus. Millie didn't arrest Waring ... nothing to charge him with, and she said he was amenable to answering her questions. Just probably didn't answer all of them truthfully. Didn't matter what Waring's story was, Basil decided. It had nothing to do with Billie and Maurice.

Zeke continued to prattle. "Even if a car has a telematics service, like General Motors' OnStar, it doesn't constantly track your location. And this jeep doesn't have OnStar."

"What does it have, then, that might help us?" Basil huffed in frustration.

"Well, like I said, a solid event recorder. This system maintains a log of the last few places the jeep went. I think it's a feature designed to help people who want to go back to someplace and can't remember how they got there. Know what I'm saying?"

Basil didn't answer, but he turned and leaned in the window so he could better watch Zeke.

"It's breadcrumbs, really. The navigation system in this car also tracks frequently traveled spots, marking it with a breadcrumb trail. I think it's a dealership-enabled feature, and either the Glempses didn't know about it or never bothered to turn it off. Good thing, dontcha think?"

"You're saying you can trace *exactly* where this Jjeep went on Halloween?"

Zeke closed his laptop, turned off the ignition, and gave Basil the keys.

"Indeed. Already done, actually." Zeke tapped his laptop. "I told you I'm good with tech. You're buying me lunch, right? Shirl's? The most awesome bacon-triple-cheeseburgers on the planet with a side of curly fries. Sheriff wants a big milkshake, remember?"

"Yes, I'm buying lunch. You get your heart attack on a bun with a side of clogged arteries, boss gets her sugar, and I get my breadcrumbs. Let's move."

CHAPTER TWENTY-FIVE

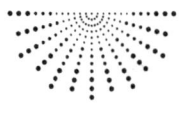

NOON

W hy are you there?" Oren stared at Piper sitting behind the dispatcher desk.

"Why are you here?" Piper returned. "You're supposed to be in Tennessee on vacation."

"Didn't Nang tell you? I figured Nang would have told you last night."

She shook her head. "I didn't see Nang last night."

"Good." He disappeared into the breakroom.

Piper guessed she'd have to puzzle out his return later; maybe he and his wife had a fight or a family emergency, though Millie would have mentioned the latter. Maybe she'd call Nang and ask. Had Oren been at the Quick Stop?

"Why are you on dispatch?" He emerged from the room with a cup of coffee.

"We're dealing with a double-murder, two teenagers."

"I heard."

"I sent Zeke with Basil. I have Diego and Thresher out in farm fields. Rocco and Cartwright are on patrol." She leaned back in the chair. "That leaves me here. I decided taking a turn on the desk would be good for me."

"Well, good for you." Oren strolled back into the breakroom and up to the whiteboard. "I guess I better get caught up."

Piper retrieved Basil's notes and interviews regarding the cars Rodney Rhimer had spotted on the county road near where Billie Glempse was found. She'd been through them twice before, but something itched at the back of her brain. She'd take another look.

One, a 1962 Rambler, owned by Darrel Polster of Grandview. Darrel, 72, and his wife, Lydia, 71, said they were driving around the county looking at fall colors and taking photographs. Lydia's work regularly appeared in national nature magazines and she took pictures at high school sporting events for the yearbook.

Lydia noted spotting Rhimer on his bicycle, that they knew him because they'd bought cars from him in the past. She and Darrel said they did not see anyone else out along the road.

"Honestly, I was more interested in the color on the trees," Lydia said. "I wanted to get some shots before the sun went down. The angle of the light made it look like the maples had been dipped in gold. I didn't even think to wave at Rodney. Besides, we needed to get back home to pass out candy. I got some great photos of trick-or-treaters."

Two, a 2001 Ford Explorer, owned by Elizabeth Schwartz of Santa Claus. Elizabeth, 28, said she was on this road because she hadn't been paying attention and missed her regular turn-off.

"I don't think I'd ever driven that road before. Potholes need fixing. I didn't notice anybody. Wait, there was a guy on a fancy bicycle peddling like crazy. Didn't see anybody else. I was looking for road signs, not people. I haven't lived here long, and I get lost. It's what I do. I get lost. I need to buy one of those GPS things. I would have bought one by now, but I'm going to get a new car, replace this piece of crap tank. New cars come with GPS. I was in a little bit of a hurry because I'd bought a bag of frozen chicken strips and ice cream. I didn't want the ice cream to melt. Did the guy on the bicycle do something wrong? Did you arrest him? Is he missing? Did he get hit? I didn't hit him. Oh, wait, I also saw either a dog or a coyote. It was too far away for me to tell what it was for sure. Maybe a farm dog. Is this about a missing dog? Or a dog that bit someone?" Elizabeth came up for air. "Did the guy on the bicycle get bit?"

Three, a 2012 Hyundai Sonata, owned by Brent Gardner. A freelance handyman from Fulda, Brent, 42, said he had finished a couple of all-afternoon jobs—cutting overgrown bushes and low-hanging tree branches from a strip of houses in a subdivision—and was heading for a quick fence repair at the end of the road, hoped to get it in before dark.

"I'd heard they found a body. Is that why you're asking me questions? A hunting accident? Like the guy who got shot last year?" Brent talked about the road, noticing the houses lacked Halloween decorations probably because they were too far apart to get trick-or-treaters. "Did some kid get killed? Hit by a car? I saw a guy on a bicycle. Was he hit? I've not been on that road much, haven't gotten a call out there for work in more than a year. Didn't see any other cars. Saw a bike. Saw lots of fall colors."

Piper called Gardner on her cell phone, kept her eyes on the board in case a 9-1-1 came in. He picked it up after a dozen rings and huffed a few times. She guessed she caught him in the middle of yard or repair work.

"Mr. Gardner?"

"Yep."

"This is Sheriff Blackwell."

"Sheriff? Is there some trouble? Is someone complaining about me?"

"I have a follow-up question about Halloween night."

"Okay. But I don't remember anything else than what I told the detective."

Piper glanced out the window, saw a man with drooping jeans and frizzy hair tromp past.

"You mentioned seeing a man on a bicycle."

"Yep. I told you about that. Pedaling pretty fast."

"You also mentioned seeing a bike. Did you mean a second bicycle?"

"No, bike. A yellow one. A dirt bike."

Piper's eyes widened.

"Tell me about this bike, Mr. Gardner. It could be important."

"Told you, I don't remember anything else than what I already said. Oh, I didn't say much about the bike. Just that I saw it."

And neither Basil nor she in reviewing the information had caught that he mentioned bicycle *and* bike, and that he meant two different things.

"This bike—"

"Well, yeah, it was a yellow bike, one of those smallish motorcycles, dirt bikes, they ride for off-roading. Guy was going fast, like he had to be somewhere in a hurry. I saw him following this ugly orange jeep."

"Tell me about the rider."

"Dark helmet. Maybe a guy. Maybe a gal. He was in a hurry. Or she was in a hurry. Don't know anything else."

"Thank you, Mr. Gardner."

Rodney Rhimer hadn't mentioned the dirt bike. Piper scowled. Apparently, Rodney Rhimer hadn't seen everything on the road that late afternoon.

Piper looked up when Zeke came in carrying two milkshakes.

"Chocolate and Strawberry," he said. "I could have told Basil that chocolate is your go-to, but I kept my mouth shut and let him buy one of each. He said you should take your pick and I could have the other. That's why I kept my mouth shut." He handed her the chocolate.

"Freeloading, Zeke?" Piper got up and gestured for him to take his post back.

"I wouldn't call it freeloading. I used my well-honed technical skills and got him the information he was looking for. He said he'd be back after he goes to the courthouse to check on two warrants."

Piper knew those involved Betty Boop and the Carlson property.

"Apparently, he's going to be looking for more warrants after that, since I figured out where the jeep went. Said he'll follow that trail later this afternoon and figure out what other warrants to ask for based on what he finds. Nineteen months, Sheriff, and I'll be old enough to be a deputy." Zeke smiled proudly and added: "Not free-loading, just taking a little well-deserved advantage." He slipped in behind the desk and took a big, noisy slurp of the strawberry milk-shake. "Delicious advantage."

"It's been quiet," she said. "I only got two calls while you were out. A guy in distress at the grocery store. Ambulance picked him up. A sideswiped car across from the park ... which didn't really need to come in on the emergency line. Rockport police sent a car."

"Awesome. If it stays quiet, I can dig into the bones and—"

Piper pointed to a six-inch high stack of file folders. "You can dig through those and enter them in the records management system. The bones are on your own time."

"Yes, Sheriff."

She grabbed the chocolate milkshake and poked her head into the breakroom. "Oren, if Basil manages to come back with search warrants, go with him."

Zeke took another noisy slurp. "I thought Oren was on vacation."

"Apparently not. I've got something to follow up. Call me if there's trouble." Piper stepped out onto the sidewalk and crossed the street. The chocolate was thick and sweet and made her teeth gently ache from the cold. It was in the mid-sixties today, a little above normal for November. She didn't bother with a jacket; she didn't have that far to go.

Rhimer's Reasonable Autos was about six blocks from the sheriff's department, and Piper decided to walk it rather than take her Explorer. She saw the man with the droopy jeans and frizzled hair sitting on a bench in front of the hardware store. He was reading a paperback, holding it close to his face. She'd noticed him around town in the past several days.

Piper's path took her past him. She paused at the bench. "Good afternoon," she said.

"It's a nice one for sure, Sheriff," the man returned. He had a smok-er's voice, and he briefly met her gaze then got back to his book, a Val McDermid mystery, the author's name three times the size of the title. His face was ruddy and wrinkled like a raisin, and he smelled of old sweat. "You tell your dad that Lefty Jay said 'hey,' okay?"

"Sure." She kept walking. Dinner at her dad's house tonight, she'd mention the man. She hoped he wasn't homeless; he had that look, old clothes, dirty hands. Spencer County didn't have much of a homeless problem … too small. A couple of the churches had accommodations.

She paused in front of the Dollar Store's window. It was plastered with advertising, all the sales for the week. She peered between the flyers and past the checkout counter. Dog toys, looked like they got some new ones in. She'd stop on her walk back and get something for Camaro and Tater, Wrinkles, too, since she'd see him tonight. Her cat wasn't much into toys, too serious, aloof, but she'd pick up some catnip.

Rockport's downtown had been pretty and vibrant more than a dozen years past. She used to come here with her mother and sister, visiting a fabric store, stopping to get a soda or ice cream, sometimes going to Margie's, which was a woman's clothing shop. The area dried up fairly quick, with people going across the river to Owensboro's big box stores. The massive Walmart had everything: clothes, car parts, groceries, toys, hair salon, eye doctor, insurance.

A few small, stubborn shops remained, and there was a rumor a used bookstore might take over a vacant building in the spring. The antiques place remained one of the happy holdouts; it had no set hours, open on the owner's whim. Even the exterior of the store looked like an antique, the paint chipped, only a hint that the green was once bright, the gold lettering muted now, the glass beveled. A selection of old toys, their color faded from the sun, sat in the window to the left of the door, which was fitted with brass hinges.

The window to the right had a portable Singer sewing machine up front, an old black model. Behind it, on a mannequin, was a wedding dress that had been there for a few years. Pretty, but too long in the sun. Piper wondered if it would survive a professional cleaning. Those dresses in the catalogues, beautiful as they were, cost hundreds and thousands, something she couldn't justify for one day. But this old dress presented an intriguing possibility. It didn't have a traditional veil. Instead, the faceless mannequin sported a wide-brimmed hat with silk flowers and a strip of lace. It would be something old and something new at the same time.

It might clean up just fine.

Piper picked up her pace, drained the last of the milkshake, found a bin to toss the cup into, and stopped at Rhimer's Reasonable Autos.

She drove by the place several times a week, but had never stopped here. The cars gleamed, the price tags bright white and large in each windshield, a mix of makes and models from recent to decades old. A red Buick Skylark was so shiny it looked electric. She hurried past them and saw Rodney finishing a phone call. He waved and met her on the lot.

"Can I help you, Sheriff? Looking for a car?"

"I have cars," she answered. Mark Thresher had willed her a garage full; she also had her little "suggestion of a car" as her father put it. "But I have questions."

"About Halloween night?" Rodney thrust his hands in his pockets. He wore a light blue suit with a white shirt and black tie, far different from his appearance on the county road. "Awful about the girl, about that football player. Figure out who did it?" He frowned and twisted his foot against the blacktop lot. "Of course, you haven't. Takes time, a murder investigation. Even on the TV shows. Hope you get the bastard and lock him up forever."

Piper nodded and turned on her body cam. "We want him too, Mr. Rhimer."

"Rodney."

"Rodney. Look, I know we asked about the cars you saw that night."

"I saw four. A pale blue Rambler, an ugly orange jeep—real recent model, a silver Hyundai Sonata, and a rusty Explorer that had to be twenty years old." He pulled his hands out of his pockets and waved at someone across the street. "But I told you that."

"What about a motorcycle? A dirt bike?"

He looked thoughtful a moment. "Motorcycle? Well, I did see a dirt bike, but you all just asked me about the cars I saw."

Piper felt punched in the stomach. They had asked him about cars, but why would he not mention the motorcycle?

"I don't sell motorcycles," Rodney said, as if answering her unspoken question. "They don't really register. They're not as interesting to me."

"Can you tell me anything about the motorcycle? Anything?" The dirt bike might not mean much, or it could be everything if the shooter was riding it.

Rodney stroked his chin and closed his eyes. "It was yellow, sunflower yellow, mustard yellow, but it had dirt splattered on it that dingied it up, like the fellow rode it through mud and let it dry on the fenders. Didn't take proper care of it. I'm guessing street legal because it had a license plate. Don't ask me for the number, the thing was going fast, following the pumpkin jeep, and like I said it was dirt-caked, even the plate. I think it was probably one of those dual-sports. A BMW or a Harley. Quite a few Harleys around here, popular and expensive. Wide tires, maybe knobbies. It was loud. Loud as hell. Maybe a 600 GS, but I couldn't say for sure. Like I said, it was going fast and I pay more attention to cars. I don't sell motorcycles, just cars. Sometimes pickups if they're cherry. Things with four wheels, that's my trade."

"What about the rider?"

Rodney blinked and rubbed at his eyes. "Oh, hell, I don't know. Ah, kinda skinny, man or woman, couldn't tell. Blue jean jacket, blue jeans, boots, I think. Black helmet, black gloves."

"Was the rider carrying anything?"

"Oh, I dunno … something on his back, over his shoulder, couldn't tell what it was. Hey, that's pretty good, ain't it, for not really noticing? That's pretty good. Hope I've helped."

"Indeed you did, Mr. Rhimer."

"Rodney."

CHAPTER TWENTY-SIX

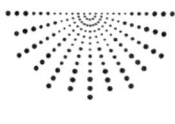

2 P.M.

B asil squeezed the steering wheel. He wanted to be in two
places at the same time.

Serving the no-knock warrant on the apartment Victoria
Halliday shared with her sister.

And serving this warrant on the Carlsons for their buildings, vehicles, and electronics.

He'd elected to pursue this one because he was angry at himself. He'd not acted on the pot he'd smelled Halloween night in the Carlson barn. At that time, he'd elected to do nothing other than break up the Hot and Steamy party because he and Millie were outnumbered one hundred to one, and the gathering, though loud, had been peaceful. It was all about the murder investigation then.

It still was, in a fashion, as Maurice and Billie had planned to go to that party, and the host's son was allegedly a marijuana dealer to Wallace Langston, brother of Maurice. There were connections.

Basil was more interested in Halliday's apartment, as she allegedly dealt meth, which he considered far worse than pot. More dangerous to deal with, he'd lectured Piper about protective clothing—if, indeed, there was meth present in the apartment or vehicles. Piper was serving the warrant there.

He hadn't needed to lecture; she was more than capable of handling it and knew how to use the test kits. Basil remained impressed by the young sheriff. He thought she had a fearlessness and resolve equal to his. He'd never seen her back down; she was well-suited to being in charge, able to manage a department far larger than Spencer County's. He wondered where a law enforcement career would take her years down the road. Despite his experience, he'd learned some things from her, especially her ability to notice details and act on them. She had impressive instincts.

Though he'd wanted to handle both of them, the warrants needed to be served at the same time in case Trenton Carlson and Victoria Halliday knew each other—probably were friends, as Betty Boop and George Washington were both at the party. Basil didn't want Trenton calling Victoria to alert her, or the other way around, so he was missing what he considered the more crucial warrant. Couldn't be in two places at the same time.

Or four places; he'd really wanted to be tackling everything related to this investigation.

He also wanted to follow the breadcrumbs Zeke discovered through the jeep's GPS, and based on that figure out what properties to seek additional search warrants for. He was determined to trace the route of the pumpkin jeep. Though he would need to do that at either dawn or dusk, if Google was right.

And he needed to be in the office filing the paperwork for those additional warrants, and hoping the judge wasn't tired of all the requests.

Five places.

Zeke and Diego had searched DMV records trying to identify people who owned yellow motorcycles. Basil wanted to be in on that, too. The only hit had been a canary yellow 2021 Indian Challenger, a touring bike that did not fit the description.

"A damn dirt bike."

Piper had radioed Basil about her conversation with Rodney Rhimer and the revelation about the dirt bike. It was one of the puzzle pieces settling into place, as there were tracks in the field where

Maurice had been killed. Basil recalled talking with Rhimer twice about the cars the man had seen during his bicycle ride on the county road Halloween. Basil had asked him about *cars*. Next time, next case or investigation, he would say *vehicles*.

"What damn dirt bike?" Oren was in the passenger seat. Basil had picked him up when he'd returned to the department with the signed warrants.

Basil glanced in the rearview mirror, saw Diego in the car behind him, Cartwright and Thresher with him. Two cars, four deputies, and one dog, all sent to search the Carlson properties. They'd likely be here until well after the sun went down because of the size of the place. Thresher might also be needed at the Halliday apartment; Piper said she would radio if she wanted the dog.

It would get too dark to chase the jeep's breadcrumbs today. First thing in the morning for that.

In Chicago there would have been plenty of officers dispatched to pursue all of these things at once. Spencer County had limited personnel. His mouth crooked up on one side; maybe he liked that aspect of this job. Fewer officers to divide and conquer meant he was involved in more aspects of a case.

"What about a dirt bike?" Oren persisted.

"We need to find a mustard yellow one," Basil returned. "But that's not for this trip."

"This is all about the pot."

Basil nodded.

"It won't be an issue much longer."

"What do you mean?"

"Marijuana's legal in a lot of states."

"Illinois," Basil returned. "A lot of pot shops in Chicago."

Oren ticked off on his fingers: "Also Michigan, Alaska, California, Colorado, Maine, Massachusetts, Nevada, Oregon, Vermont, Washington state, and Washington D.C."

"And you keep track because—"

"I keep track of a lot of things. They get stuck in my brain." Oren stared straight ahead. "I read the bulletins that come through the

183

department. They all list the states where it is legal, along with legislation that keeps getting introduced in Indiana and keeps getting shot down." He let out a grating sigh. "But it's not going to be an issue regardless of what conservatives here want. Congress is thinking about decriminalizing it across the whole damn country. States would still have their say, but it's the camel's nose thing." He tapped the dash. "*Nisht gut.* I don't like it. I know, I know, I'm old, right? Pot's no worse than a beer or a cigarette, right? What's the harm in it? I'm old. I don't think it's a good idea. Maybe I'm *too* old to be doing this job. You're young, from a big city, a state where it's legal. I get it, you don't mind pot. But I'm old and I don't like it."

"Well, I'm not old, and I don't like it either," Basil returned. "I don't want it legal here, not the recreational kind. I'll never be convinced that it's harmless. I read an article on my phone today that said pregnant women who smoke pot can birth babies with developmental problems. But meth is far worse, and that is what our two murders are wrapped around." He glanced at Oren. "Why did you come back from vacation early?"

Oren tapped the dash faster. "Because my wife doesn't want to be with me anymore. Because I didn't want to have a last 'good time' with her at Pigeon Forge. Because I don't need to be sitting home alone right now." He paused. "If the murders are keyed to meth, why are we going after a supposed pot dealer? Why aren't we serving the meth warrant? Why is our one-armed sheriff doing that?" Much softer: "She's forty-two years younger than me. Younger than you, too. Besides, you covered narcotics in Chicago."

Basil gripped the wheel tighter and didn't answer for a few moments. He turned down the access road that led to the Dutch knuckle barn and drove past it, seeing the farmhouse sitting in the middle of a park-like grove of trees.

"The meth warrant Sheriff Blackwell is serving isn't the dealer tied to the murders. I'm pretty confident of that. It doesn't fit because Betty Boop was at the party, and I'm real damn sure she doesn't know how to use a crossbow. We haven't found *that* meth dealer yet, but I know he or she is in the county. We learned about Betty Boop and her alleged meth operation, and so we have to act on her, shut her down. Maybe there's a connection."

"Betty Boop?"

"Long story."

"I saw your notes. I get that the murdered kids ripped off a meth house. I go away for a few days and—"

Basil pulled in front of the white saltbox, turned off the ignition, and turned on his body cam. He checked the warrant one more time, force of habit.

"In the morning, I'm going to follow some breadcrumbs and hope I can locate *that* meth house," Basil said. "Get a hint of it, get some warrants. Have to get the warrants to make it all legal. Shut it down. I'd like to be doing that right now."

"But we're a small department," Oren said.

"Yeah, and I can't be in five places at the same time."

"Roger Carlson's a good man," Oren said, as he got out of the car and followed Basil to the front stoop. "He has nothing to do with marijuana, cannabis, pot, weed, whatever the hell you want to call it. He's clean. We're not going to find anything here. All we'll do is piss him off. He hires a lot of local kids for farm work. Contributes to an FFA scholarship for high school seniors. He's good for the county."

"And throws young people a Halloween party where there was pot," Basil said, his voice flat. "Maybe there were other things there, too."

"This is a wasted trip," Oren warned. "We should be chasing the meth. Roger Carlson *really* is a good man."

"Fine," Basil returned. "He might be Spencer County Man of the Year. But his son apparently sells pot."

Diego, Cartwright, and Thresher waited by the second Explorer. The dog was anxious, muscles quivering, clearly wanting to be given a task.

The saltbox was white with black shutters, and it looked like the metal roof was new. The plantings around the front were trimmed, a mix of boxwoods and decorative grasses, the beds were filled with colorful landscape glass.

The air smelled good here, clean and laced with scents of the plantings. There was a dry odor from the remains of the cornstalks, coupled with a freshness Basil couldn't quite define, but could appreciate. No hint of car exhaust, so very different from Chicago. He took it deep into his lungs and checked his watch; Piper should be serving her warrant about now.

"Is this a no-knock?" Oren asked.

Basil shook his head. "I only asked for a no-knock on the Halliday apartment."

"Because you think meth is a worse threat."

"Because I *know* meth is the worse threat. I watched it destroy people." Basil knocked loudly on the door. He hadn't noticed anyone out in the fields or around the property. Carlson's corn had been harvested; maybe he was taking some time off. There were two vehicles at the side of the house, a Toyota Prius and a big Ford pickup with overlarge wheels, so he suspected someone was home. According to DMV records, Trenton owned a white Mazda Miata convertible, and unless it was in one of the barns on the property—the house having no garage—he was not here.

After a few more knocks, a woman came to the door. Basil guessed she was late forties, slim and tidy, light brown hair graying in places and tied back in a loose ponytail. She wore jeans, a red sweatshirt, and had an apron tied at her waist, smears of what was probably chocolate on it.

"Goodness! What on this God's earth are you all doing on my porch?" She looked around Basil. "Oren, what's going on?"

Basil handed her the warrant. "Mrs. Carlson, we're serving—"

"A search warrant? You're giving me no such thing." She refused to take it, wiped her hands on the apron, and looked over her shoulder. "Roger! Roger, get out here now. The sheriff's here." She glared at Basil. "You're not searching our house without—"

"It covers all your buildings, Mrs. Carlson. Vehicles, electronics, and—"

Roger appeared behind her, also in an apron similarly streaked with chocolate. Basil smelled something delicious baking. Roger took the warrant, plucked reading glasses out of his pocket, put them on, and his lips worked as he read.

"Amy's right, Oren, Detective, you've no cause to come searching our property. This is ridiculous. Marijuana? Drug paraphernalia? What the flaming hell? Is this because you *thought* you smelled pot at the Halloween party? You didn't find any then, did you? You didn't look. Well, you're not looking now. You're not doing anything right now. You're going to wait until I get my attorney out here."

"We're not waiting, Mr. Carlson." Basil kept his tone even, and his irritation in check. Again, he mulled over what he could have done differently at the barn party. "We're serving this warrant now. Step aside. And where's Trenton? We want to talk to your son."

"Trent has classes all afternoon," Amy said, backing out of the doorway. "Owensboro Community Tech."

"Oren?" Roger Carlson appealed. "Oren, this is ridiculous. You have no right—"

"Read the warrant, Roger. We'll make this as fast and painless as possible." Oren tipped his hat to the Carlsons.

"We'll start with the house," Basil said. "You can stay. Just don't get in our way."

"Damn straight, I'll stay," Carlson spat. Gone was all trace of the genial man Basil had met Halloween night. "And I'm calling my attorney." He pulled his cell phone out of his pocket and punched a number. Basil wondered why a farmer would need an attorney's number on speed dial. After a moment it appeared Carlson was being held up by a secretary.

Basil motioned Diego and Thresher in. "Keep an eye on Mr. and Mrs. Carlson," he said to Cartwright. "And watch out for Trenton, the son, in case he shows up."

Thresher discovered a sandwich bag of marijuana in the night-stand in Trenton's room—a personal quantity, not close to what a dealer would have. The only other marijuana in the house was in the kitchen, where the Carlsons were baking; it was the first place Thresher keyed on.

"It should be legal," Amy said. "Just mellows dessert, mellows you.

It's none of your business what we do in our home." She looked to Roger. "Have you gotten ahold of Harlan?"

Roger shook his head. "In court."

Basil figured the attorney was Harlan Cook, sometimes referred to as Harlan *Crook* by the department because he had a knack for reducing or voiding the sentences of county residents charged with DUI and assorted alcohol-related offenses. Sheriff Blackwell seemed to like the man; he'd handled the estate of Mark Thresher to the benefit of Piper Blackwell and the entire department. Basil cast a glance at the Belgian Malinois, one of those benefits. The dog was happy it had succeeded at a task and had been rewarded.

"You're not arresting us because we put a little weed in the brownies," Amy said. She'd puffed herself up and was wringing her hands in her apron. "I'm sure we're not the only ones in Spencer County who—"

She continued to vent. Basil noticed that Oren had been surprised by the baking revelation, and likely by the belligerence of someone he'd labeled a "really good man." Then again, Basil figured he'd offer up a substantial helping of belligerence himself if someone served a search warrant at his house.

"I'm not saying whether we're arresting you, Mrs. Carlson," Basil said. "We need to finish our search." He noticed Roger Carlson was working his phone and had backed into a corner. Basil suspected he was texting his son, warning him, maybe still trying to get ahold of the attorney. The phones could be confiscated as part of the electronics component of the warrant.

"We could sue you," Amy said, still wringing her hands, her apron twisted into a tight knot. "This is clearly an invasion of privacy. You're stomping on our rights."

"We're not stomping on anything," Oren said.

The search led throughout the afternoon to the shed and other outbuildings, the Dutch knuckle where the party was held—and where Thresher keyed on several areas; a few small bags of pot and an envelope of rolling papers were recovered in the loft. Basil noticed that the dog was enjoying the activity.

Then they searched an old weathered barn with a partially caved-in roof at the back edge of the property. A mirror of the one the party had been in, close to falling in, decades older and abandoned.

Except it wasn't empty.

Thresher howled with excitement.

"I take it back," Oren said, stepping to Basil's shoulder, "about Roger Carlson being a good man."

In the center stretched a grow tent, roughly ten feet wide and twenty feet long. Portable heaters had thick electric cords snaking out of a new-looking bank of outlets. Dried and drying plants hung from the rafters along the sides. A long workbench and table, covered with a makeshift hard vinyl roof to keep out any rain, was littered with scales, bags, a laptop, all the tools needed to package for distribution. The laptop might hold harvest and customer records.

Basil whistled low. Spencer County was not boring.

He made a slow circuit, following the dog, making sure his body cam caught the details, and recording the disgruntled comments of the Carlsons. He'd come back in a little while and take close ups with the department camera. He hadn't expected this. He figured that Wallace Langston had spoken truthfully about getting marijuana from Trenton, but he'd guessed Trenton a middleman, buying from a bigger supplier, and parceling it out to customers. He hadn't thought Trenton would also be that bigger supplier.

It was a good-sized operation, the plants in the middle in five-gallon buckets, appearing well-tended. Looking up at the rafters, the number of plants drying there, he thought the Carlsons also had growing operations somewhere else.

He pointed to the plants in the rafters. "Where is the rest of your growing plot? This greenhouse setup isn't big enough to produce all of that."

Oren made a huffing noise. "It's the cornfields, Detective. Isn't that right, Roger? You take the plants out of the barn when they are established, big enough, plant them alongside the corn and nobody driving by notices. When the marijuana plants get taller than the corn, you tie the tops down so they're still hidden. A state trooper friend of mine in

Henderson showed me that trick years back, when pot was the number one cash crop in that part of Kentucky. Bet you're real careful which detasselrs you put in that field."

Roger didn't reply.

Diego walked Thresher through the barn a second time, the dog still agitated, busy, stopping and signaling everywhere. "There are a few more outbuildings," Diego said. "I'll take him there."

"Take him everywhere," Basil said. "Every inch of this land. Record everything. Take him twice."

"This isn't Roger's," Amy said as Diego left with the dog. "It's not mine either. Not mine or Roger's." Basil continued his circuit. "We let Trenton have this barn. This is all his. We didn't know anything about this. We don't pay attention to—"

"You're not throwing our son under any bus," Roger cut back. "And you're not saying anything else until we get our attorney out here."

"You can meet with your attorney at the jail," Basil said. He shifted his gaze back and forth between the Carlsons and stalked toward them. "You have the right to remain silent." He continued reading them their rights, which he would repeat back at the department. The charges would be numerous: possession, manufacture, and distribution of marijuana. The DA likely would also go after them for violating the state's stamp tax. How much prison time and fines would depend on the amount of marijuana on the property. Clearly, there was more than ten pounds. Another look at the rafters, more than a hundred pounds. Maybe *hundreds* of pounds all told. Ten pounds or more made it a level-five felony, punishable with up to six years in prison and a ten thousand dollar fine.

Mrs. Carlson could claim all of this was her son's, but that wouldn't fly. Roger and she knew all about it, were baking brownies with it. All three of them would be facing prison time. Definitely no more Halloween parties at this place for a good while.

"Weed should be legal," Amy said. "It doesn't hurt anyone. No worse than beer."

"That might be," Basil returned. "But it *is* illegal right now."

"Do not pass Go. Do not collect two hundred dollars," Oren said softly as he watched Basil cuff the Carlsons and load them into the back of the Explorer.

Basil approached Oren. "I'm going to collect all the electronics, do another sweep of the place, get better photographs. It's not just a seasonal operation with this grow tent. Though their operation is curtailed in colder weather." He drew his lips together and shook his head in dismay. "I'll call the DA. He'll probably want to come out before we pack up all the pot. And I have to find Trenton, whether he comes home or I pull him out of class." He knew Trenton was in his second year of a two-year degree in cyber security. The laptop might be difficult to get into, but Zeke would probably manage.

It might cost Basil another triple cheeseburger.

CHAPTER TWENTY-SEVEN

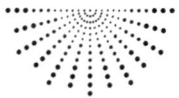

6 P.M.

I also got them on dealing meth *and* possession with intent to deliver," Piper said. "While we were at the apartment, a man came by to pick up his 'regular order of glass.' Otherwise, I was just going to get them on possession and manufacture. Glass is another name for—"

"I know most of the nicknames for meth," Paul returned. "And I know you have to basically catch someone in the act to get them on a dealing charge."

"Yeah. The buyer coming by sealed that. Happy and sad day at the same time." She took a sip of wine, strawberry zinfandel, one of her dad's favorites. Then she speared a piece of ribeye and chewed it slowly. He'd grilled it with garlic and rosemary, and she thought it delicious. "Happy for the drug bust, sad that it was operating in my county. Doubly sad that two young, smart women will end up doing time. Potentially, a long stretch of time."

"Not so smart," Paul corrected. "Not so smart if they got caught. You know, I read an article in one of those online newspapers a week or so back that said Indiana is one of the biggest producers of meth because so much of our state is rural."

"A lot of cornfields." Piper felt Wrinkles rub against her leg and settle between her feet. The dog busily chewed on the stuffed squirrel she'd bought at the Dollar Store. He had it sodden, and the wet seeped through her pantleg. A moment later, she smelled a powerful dog fart and made a face.

"I see that scowl. Don't like the steak?"

"I love the steak, Dad. I need to come for dinner more often."

"You need to accept my invitations more often," Paul shot back. "You're welcome to bring Nang, you know. You should have brought him tonight. I enjoy his company, and he usually brings something to eat."

"He's working late, problems with the electric, and he doesn't want the refrigerators and freezers to shut down. He's added some employees, and he's looking into opening a restaurant in Rockport or Santa Claus. He'll have an empire. Now if he can only get the electric fixed." She grimaced as the dog released another blast. What was the old pug getting fed? Her dad wasn't reacting to the stink; maybe he was inured to it.

"Rockport could use a good restaurant."

"How is the investigation going into the skeleton from Teegan's attic? I've been so busy with my own murders I haven't had a chance to talk to her about it."

Paul took a heaping forkful of potato, seemed to study it, then ate it. "Heck of a case, really. A damn cold case. No telling how long that skeleton has been up in that attic. Could've been decades. Probably decades. Annie—Dr. Neufeld—passed the bones over to the state crime lab today, said there's no visible cause of death, though there was evidence he'd broken a bone and it had healed. She gave them a thorough going over, guessed the man ... she said it was a man ... was likely in his fifties or maybe early sixties. They're checking dental records, so far nothing. And they're pulling DNA to compare with some national databases and genealogy sites, which could take a while. I'm looking at records of previous house owners and their extended families, checking for missing persons."

"It's going to take a chunk of time, huh?"

"It could take a long while. But it is interesting."

"Zeke, my dispatcher, has made a hobby of it."

Paul gave a good-natured laugh. "There are worse things a young man could do with his spare time."

Piper thought about Maurice Langston. "A lot worse," she agreed.

"So, enough about the dead man in Teegan's House of Horrors," Paul said. "Tell me about the arrests you made today, those young women. Your first meth lab bust." Paul turned his attention to cutting his steak. She knew it was his habit to slice most of it into bite-sized pieces before eating any of it. "I only busted one, about seven years back, in an old trailer at the north end of the county. Not that I didn't try to find them. They're practically invisible. Made a few possession arrests, though, every year it seemed."

"This wasn't much of a lab that we found today. The equipment could have fit in a big backpack. Some flasks, coffee filters, burner, ephedrine and pseudoephedrine. They're refusing to say how they came by the pills. Or the fentanyl and oxy we found, too, probably stolen or forged prescriptions. Rockport PD is helping dig into it since the apartment is in the town limits. The place reeked of ammonia. We suited up before we went in. Both of the girls were conveniently there—and cooking a batch. They only had classes in the morning. I had visions of it being exciting and dramatic, needing to chase someone, throw them to the ground and handcuff them. Draw on them. But it was easy."

"Easy?"

"Too easy. Way too easy. Nothing exciting." Piper took another sip of wine. "We surprised the hell out of them, showing up at two in the afternoon. While we were there Victoria got a text, warning her we were coming. We confiscated the phone: it was a message from a friend saying that deputies were at his dad's place, searching all the buildings, that he was staying away. Good thing we showed up before she got the message and had time to get rid of everything."

"They didn't fight it?"

She shook her head. "No, they were frightened, but they didn't resist. Victoria said if news got out—which in this county it probably already has—she was going to lose her scholarship. Worried about their parents finding out, too. Victoria broke down crying about that. I felt a little sorry for her. It was a small operation she and her sister were running, but it was still an operation. We found a list of their usual clients, and Wallace Langston was on it, with dates, quantities. It looked like he bought often."

"Both of them college girls?"

"Yeah, Victoria is a sophomore, full ride on a zoology scholarship. And I bet she's right about her losing the scholarship over this. Her sister Danica is a senior going for a four-year RN degree. School's going to be curtailed for some time for both of them," Piper said. "How long? I don't know. It'll all go to trial. The DA texted me that he'll go heavy because it's meth. I don't think they can get off without doing at least a few years. The evidence is too strong, and I have body cam video. The records of their clients, icing. They kept meticulous track of sales, quantities, money brought in, and money spent on supplies and equipment. Apparently, they were making some serious cash for as small a business as they had."

She paused the conversation and dug into the steak, alternating bites with the sweet potato and snow peas. It had been an easy bust, and she was honestly disappointed it hadn't been more challenging. "Basil and Oren had the bigger task today. More exciting."

"Oren's back? I thought he was on vacation."

"Not anymore. He's not saying why. Maybe he didn't like Tennessee."

"They bust a meth lab this afternoon, too? Him and Basil?"

Piper took another sip of wine. She'd decided it was a little too sweet for her, but it worked okay with this meal. She had a few bottles of semi-sweet vintages she and Nang had bought at one of the local wineries. Next dinner with her dad, she'd bring one of those.

"Marijuana greenhouse. A good-sized operation. Basil and Oren, Diego, Thresher, they're still out there. Basil figured he wouldn't get home until eight or nine. The DA's with them. It looks like it has been going on for a half-dozen years."

"Some of that would have been on my watch," Paul said. "And I didn't catch it."

"We only caught it by chance," Piper was quick to put in, not wanting her dad to think he'd been derelict. "Evidently, the son started it the summer before his sophomore year in high school, and the parents embraced it and helped in the cultivation. Turned it into a thriving family business. Can't give you their names, and I haven't seen any of the reports. Can't talk about it until the arrest reports are filed and on the blotter. I only told you about my meth bust because it's all logged in, public now."

"I know. The pot is an ongoing investigation. It'll hit the grapevine soon enough. And I'm pretty sure I know who it is. I can piece things together too, you know. Carlson's spread. Has to be since you were out there to break up his big Halloween party."

"Basil broke up that party."

"I stand corrected."

"I can't confirm that, about the Carlsons."

"Of course not. Ongoing investigation."

"Anyway, Basil and Oren wouldn't have discovered all the pot if it wasn't for the murders, investigating them," Piper said. She realized that was true. If Maurice and Billie had not been expected at the Hot and Steamy party, if Basil hadn't ventured to the barn and smelled pot, and if Wallace Langston hadn't named Trenton Carlson as his dealer, the operation would have remained secret. "It was a lot of marijuana. It'll hit the state newspapers when it comes out."

"Pot and meth in one day." Paul whistled. "Pot will be legal here someday. Meth, never. Wonder just how much meth production is in the county."

Piper wondered that, too. She'd asked the sisters when they had started making methamphetamines and whether they knew other manufacturers. Victoria had answered: "Lawyer."

The girls had sat side by side on a small couch in the living room. The couch was high-backed, leather, looked new. *All the furnishings were nice, probably paid for with the money from the meth,* Piper thought. Maybe it covered some of their school expenses, too.

There were pictures artistically grouped on one wall, and Piper had studied them. Victoria and Danica looked so similar in some they could have passed for twins. But that wasn't the case now. Victoria looked wholesome, toned. Danica looked hollow.

The nursing student had a pasty complexion, and was either fiddling with her fingers—short nails, chipped paint on them, or picking at her hair. Her eyes seemed unfocused, circles dark underneath, and she was skinny. Not thin, *skinny*, trending toward skeletal, her bones looking sharp, knobby elbows, wrists, jaw, the flesh was pulled tight over them.

Unless Danica had some sort of serious illness, Piper figured she used some of the meth the pair manufactured. Why would a nursing student use methamphetamines? They'd know better, right? They'd know the consequences.

Basil had told her it was the euphoria that hooked people.

Was the high worth the awful consequences?

Basil also had said, once hooked, there was little hope. Piper figured he had that attitude because of the things he'd seen in the big, bad city. Extremely addictive, it siphoned dopamine from the user's brain, making its victim lose the ability to experience pleasurable feelings. Meth became the only way to feel good. Binge and crash and taking more and more until it used the victim up, he'd said. One of the most difficult addictions to treat, she knew.

Maybe he was right, about little hope. Danica looked ... tragic.

"Quarter for your thoughts," Paul said.

"Victoria said, 'lawyer.' But Danica, she started talking. I'd read them their rights, and she talked. I had to separate them because Victoria kicked her, trying to get her to shut up."

"What did Danica say?"

"That they'd watched *Breaking Bad* when they were in high school, binged it, and figured they were smarter than the characters on the show, that they had the science chops and could make meth and pull in a lot of money. She said they figured out how to sell, where to find buyers, said Victoria kept the records because she was good at numbers. Danica would have kept talking if Victoria hadn't screamed at her to stop."

"Probably better for her that she did shut up," Paul observed.

"Sounds like she sufficiently incriminated herself, though." He finished his meal and nudged the plate back. "Did she say how long they'd been cooking?"

Piper shook her head. "The records went back two years. Wallace Langston was one of their first customers. Interesting to see how they'd been raising their prices every three months."

Piper saw why Wallace had been intrigued by Billie Glempse's claim to get him meth much cheaper and in greater quantities.

"Heartbreaking, you know, if you think about it." Piper speared the last snow pea. It was cold, but still tasty and crisp. She used to eat them raw out of the garden when she was a kid. Maybe she should plant her own garden in the spring. She had a big backyard and ought to do something with the land. Nang would likely be on board, maybe could use the produce for his restaurant.

"Heartbreaking because the girls are so young?"

Piper nodded. "I'm two years older than Danica. Only two years. That girl has so much life ahead of her, and she's going to do some time in prison. And it's going to color the rest of her life, slow her nursing degree, maybe completely derail it. Heartbreaking. But maybe she can break her addiction that way. And Victoria ... a sophomore in college with a full scholarship? Did she just throw it away? What will that do to the rest of her life?"

"Life is temporary," Paul said flatly. "Life is temporary." He stood and gathered the plates. "I still have some of the cherry pie left. Help me finish it."

"Whipped cream?"

"Certainly."

He loaded the dishwasher while Piper tried to push Danica's sallow face out of her mind.

"I think I'll plant a garden in the spring," she said to change the subject. "Snow peas, green beans, the fancy French kind Nang likes to cook with." She paused, trying to remember the term. "*Hercots Verts*, they're called, long and thin."

Like Danica.

"Shit."

"What?" Paul came back with a half-eaten pie and small plates.

"Nothing," Piper said.

He shook the whipped cream can and squirted an ample amount on Piper's piece. "I still have a little garden, you know."

"A garden would be good for me. I definitely have room for one."

"You and Nang are going to live there, right? In your house? Beautiful house. Nice property. Scuttle is you're setting a wedding date. Pity I have to hear that as gossip."

Piper closed her eyes and felt Wrinkles stir between her feet. A heartbeat later the pug farted again.

"I could be an idiot," she said. "A big idiot."

Paul raised an eyebrow and added whipped cream to his pie.

"I like being sheriff. I want to stay in this job. But there's this little itch at the back of my brain that says the world is big and there are a lot of possibilities. I love law enforcement, a lot, have ever since my MP training at Fort Campbell. Maybe that's your influence on me. So … I really do want to stay in this job, but the world is big. And I'm getting married. I could be an idiot."

"An idiot for wanting to stay the sheriff of Spencer County?"

She opened her eyes wider and shrugged.

"And why does that make you an idiot? And what does it have to do with you marrying Nang?"

"I didn't want to fall in love."

"But you did."

"But that wasn't my plan." She stared at her piece of cherry pie. It looked inviting, and she'd have to cut her calories tomorrow to compensate. "I like being a sheriff. Haven't hit the year mark yet and already I'm thinking I'll run for reelection. Maybe I'll win. Maybe I won't. If I don't win, what will I do with myself?"

Paul didn't answer that.

"What if I want to go back to the Army?" she continued. "What if I want to move out of Spencer County? Live somewhere else? Pursue law enforcement somewhere else? I can't see myself doing anything other than being some sort of cop." She took in a deep breath, the lingering scents from dinner pulling to the bottom of her lungs. "Will marrying Nang so cement me to this county that I can't consider other options? Am I trapping myself? Am I an idiot?"

"I cemented myself to this county a long time ago," Paul said. He took a big bite of pie, and smiled. "Your mom wanted something bigger and flashier than this place. Not even Owensboro across the river was enough. But in the end, I realized it was just me that she didn't want." He took another bite. "Do you really love him?"

"Yeah. I can't imagine not being with him. And it wasn't my plan."

"Plans can change."

"Apparently."

"Maybe he wants to be cemented to this county," Paul said. "Or maybe he just wants to be cemented to you. I think that both of you are strong-willed souls, enterprising. Maybe he's the one who will want to move out of Spencer County, looking for something flashier. Who knows?" Softer, but so she could still hear him: "And, really, why think about it?"

"I haven't even known him a year." Piper waited for her dad to say something else. Instead, he just kept eating the pie. "We're talking January 2nd, the anniversary of the day we met."

"Ah, your mind is all awhirl because of pre-marriage jitters. That's what this is all about." Paul finished his piece. "January. Sounds romantic. And cold." He eyed the last piece of pie sitting in the tin, contemplating it. "Church wedding, I hope."

Piper nodded. "I want a church wedding."

"Fancy dress."

"I've been looking at the dress in the window of the antique shop."

"I'd get to walk you down the aisle, right?"

"Absolutely."

"Then you're not an idiot," Paul pronounced.

"I just worry that I'm rushing into things."

"You've always rushed into things."

It was true, she realized. She'd rushed into running for sheriff at her dad's suggestion when she left the Army to take care of him during his second bout with cancer. She'd rushed into active shooter situations during her tours in the Middle East. She'd rushed into a relationship with Nang.

Rushed into a lot of things. Maybe because she'd seen many times that life is short, temporary.

"I'm not an idiot," she said.

"Of course, you're not. I can find a nice little band for the reception," Paul volunteered. "Country, bluegrass."

"I almost forgot. I saw an older man downtown, said his name was Lefty Jay. He asked me to tell you 'Hey.' Friend of yours?"

Paul leaned back in the chair, eyes wide.

"Dad?"

"Lefty Jay. One of the first arrests I ever made with the sheriff's department. Convicted of shooting his brother. They owned a grocery store, a small one, in Dale. Got into an argument, and he shot his brother in the head. He got sent away for life. What the hell is he doing out? Sent away for life."

Life is temporary, Piper recalled her father saying.

Tug had mentioned that too.

CHAPTER TWENTY-EIGHT

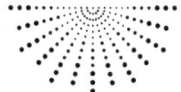

5 A.M. THURSDAY, NOVEMBER 5TH

Piper met Basil and Tug outside The Thirsty Turtle. Sunrise was about two hours away. She yawned, clutched a thermos of coffee, and leaned against the passenger door of a blue Volkswagen ID.4 SUV. A dog barked in the distance, staccato, sounding angry.

Piper stared into the dark across the street, no lights on in any of the houses along the road, the slight breeze pleasantly cool and just strong enough to flutter the leaves on the big oak that clung to the edge of the blacktop parking lot. The yellow security light over the bar's front door cast the tree into a creature of shifting shadows.

"Not a scratch, Sherlock." Tug handed the keys to Basil. Tug was shirtless, muscles evident, wearing a pair of knee-length gray shorts and thick-soled flipflops.

"That's my intent. We'll have it back to you before noon."

"With a full tank of gas."

Basil took the driver's side, and Piper slid into the passenger seat after setting the rifles in the back of the SUV. She placed the thermos between her feet. "Thanks, Tug. We didn't want to wait until tomorrow to do this. We would have rented something but—"

"—no used car lot is open this damn early. Not in Hooterville. And

Sherlock didn't think far enough ahead to rent one last night. Pre-planning was never his strong suit." Tug smiled as he nodded to Basil, his former partner in Drugs and Narcotics. "I'm going back to bed, where any sensible soul in the sticks ought to be." To Piper: "Good hunting, Sheriff Blackwell. I hope you bag what you're looking for."

"Comfortable," Piper pronounced the seat. But the car held a funky odor, and she wrinkled her nose.

"It can go off-road, that's why we're borrowing it. My car is not made for that. Neither are any of yours. We'll probably have to drive into a field or two. And, yeah, Tug was right. I should have thought of this earlier."

"You were busy at the Carlson farm until late."

He laughed. "Right under our noses, a big pot operation. If it hadn't been for the murders, or that Halloween party, we wouldn't have found it."

"Nice of Tug to loan us this."

"He thinks he owes me," Basil replied. "In Chicago, the department had several cars you could check out for undercover work, some equipped with audio and video in case you got a talkative perp in your backseat and wanted to record the session for posterity." Basil grinned. "Don't have that luxury here. I should have thought about a rental yesterday. Tug's right, sometimes I do not excel at pre-planning."

"You planned enough to get out before the sun came up."

"Google is my friend. Dawn and dusk for deer hunting."

They couldn't use one of the department's Explorers. That shouted "sheriff," and they couldn't have that this morning, not while trying to be stealthy. The SUV looked like a deer could be strapped to the roof or squeezed into the back.

Piper was dressed appropriately—a camouflage-design sweatshirt with a Screaming Eagles 101st patch on the right shoulder, brown sweatpants, and work boots. Basil wore khaki jeans and a camouflage jacket that Piper had borrowed from her father last night. Both had orange vests over the top, Piper a pair of binoculars around her neck. From a distance it would be passable hunting attire—though someone might question how Piper could manage a rifle with one arm in a sling.

Tug had taken a picture of Basil when they'd arrived, "for chuckles and eye rolls 'cause none of our old friends are going to believe you wore something that Hooterville chic."

"Do you smell that ... that—" Piper asked after the Turtle disappeared in the rearview mirror. She couldn't put a name to the odor, something acrid and oddly cloying. She cracked the window to bring in fresh air.

"Incense," Basil said. "Tug likes to burn it, seeps into the car upholstery. And I do not like this particular scent. He buys these little cones and burns them in the car ashtray. Always had one going in our ride in Chicago. Always. Always. Always. I was never a fan of it, but it didn't bother me enough to gripe about it. He said it covered up the exhaust perfume the city wore and the stink of the perps we hauled. Some of the guys we put in the backseat were pretty ripe. And the occasional puke puddle made it worse."

"No real car exhaust around here." Piper was, however, familiar with the occasional putrid backseat accident.

"Habits are hard to break, Sheriff. Tug is going to keep burning his incense until he checks into a nursing home." Basil pointed to the glovebox. "Open that. You got me curious about the fragrance."

"Dragon's Fire," Piper said, looking inside. "The package says imported from India. He's got two boxes."

"Ugh. I'm going to get him some sandalwood and lavender for Christmas. Something that smells better."

They drove past Nang's Quick Stop. It would open in an hour. Piper knew Nang was toying with the idea of going 24/7, but she didn't think the area got enough traffic to warrant it. Still, he seemed to know what he was doing, growing the business, more employees, full-service garage, eyes toward opening a restaurant in Rockport or Santa Claus. Ambitious. Driven.

They took 70 toward Chrisney, passing only two cars on the road.

"When's Tug opening his bar? I guess I should have asked him."

"Right before Thanksgiving," Basil responded. "Or earlier if he gets everything the way he wants it. He's had the place professionally cleaned and has a crew coming Monday to side the exterior green."

"Like a turtle."

"He's ordered a neon sign and beer glasses with turtles on them. And he's been acquiring stock, big variety of micro-brews. I told him not to overbuy. Fulda's tiny."

"There are even smaller communities in the county."

"And most of them seem to have at least one tavern. What is it about specks on the map and dive bars?" He paused. "Esme proofed his menu and played with it on a paint program, got it all fine and fancy and fitting on one sheet, front and back. Tug wants it simple. He's having them printed and laminated."

"I hope he's successful."

"I just hope it keeps him busy for a while, and keeps his daughter safe." Basil tapped the steering wheel. "He's one of my best friends, like a brother, Sheriff Blackwell. But he's built for the city. A big city. If it weren't for his daughter, he'd still be downtown. And be happier."

She thought about Billie Glempse. Piper didn't think there was anything Billie's dad could have done to keep her safe.

"We're traveling the route the pumpkin jeep took Halloween night. Hoping to find something, specifically where Steampunkerbell picked up that meth. Zeke managed to get the vehicle's path from some sort of internal GPS the car had, and it looks like the girl … or someone … had plugged in an address ten days ago that matched one of the Halloween stops."

Piper thought that might fit, as Billie Glempse had previously provided Wallace Langston with one big bag of meth and said she was getting him more before the Hot and Steamy party. Maybe she'd ventured to the place the week before for her first meth grab and had returned Halloween, encountering someone who'd objected to her plan and sent her fleeing.

"I looked up the address in our county directory last night," Basil said. "No name attached to it, but it is a valid address. Then I looked in earlier directories and found a name in a book seventy years back, Henry Thomas Vincent. Glad you keep these old books around. A farmer, Vincent died in 1960, and the property passed to a son who lives in Michigan."

"Maybe the residence is abandoned, like the one we went through Tuesday," Piper said. "It could be a place to cook or deal meth. Who knows what we'll find? An adventure."

"Adventure? Needle in a cornfield. We're looking for the equivalent of a path to Mount Doom somewhere in Mordor," Basil said.

"Didn't know you read fantasies."

"A classic," he returned. "I read the trilogy more than a dozen years ago. They're Esme's. Kept the books. I figure the kids will eventually read them."

They turned north through Chrisney, passing the Baptist church and a short strip of sad, empty buildings that used to be a downtown; she spotted two businesses that might still be in operation. The darkness coupled with the dilapidated structures made the place look depressing. It had a population of 470, but twenty years ago it was nearly one hundred higher. The little town was slowly folding in on itself. Piper had been reading up on the county's history, all its little places.

Chrisney had been busy in the late 1800s when it was founded as Spring Station and a railroad came through it. The tracks hadn't been used in a long while. At one time it had a post office. The library and elementary school remained, the latter having a reputation for providing a good curriculum.

The houses came cheap. Teegan had told her she looked at a saltbox at the southern edge only ten miles from the sheriff's department. Piper reminded herself she needed to get over to see Teegan's "House of Horrors" as her father called it. "BFH," Zeke had labeled it. Or maybe he'd said "FBH."

North of the town they turned east and hit the small county roads, Piper discovering that one in particular seriously needed potholes fixed. She'd contact the county board.

They drove around for half an hour, ticking off spots on the map Basil had marked, and seeing a few trucks and SUVs pulled off on shoulders by fields—deer hunters. The sky lightening, Piper noted farmhouses and plowed fields, scattered battered barns that looked like a strong wind could take them down. The old barns were striking in a way, subject matter for paintings and photographs. She wondered if Lydia Polster had captured any of them.

Basil turned south on a county road so narrow she wasn't sure it could accommodate two vehicles side-by-side. It would intersect with the road where they found Billie Glempse. He stopped a mile short of that spot and headed east.

"Here's the address from the GPS," Basil said, gingerly steering the Volkswagen down an even narrower farm service road so overgrown with weeds it was practically invisible. "Wouldn't know this road—what used to be a road—was here without Zeke."

The SUV lurched and Piper clamped her feet tight on the thermos.

"Not a scratch," she remembered Tug saying. How about with an intact undercarriage?

Basil seemed to discover every deep rut and sizeable rock in the borrowed SUV's path.

"It doesn't look like there is anything here except dry cornstalks and thistles," Basil grumbled.

It was light enough now that Piper saw stands of trees ahead, a suggestion that a house was nearby. Farmers often planted rows of trees around a house and outbuildings to serve as wind blocks and separate that part of their property from the fields.

She pointed at the tree line.

"Yeah, I see it." He cut the lights and edged the SUV closer. "Current landowner is Garret Henry Vincent of Lansing, Michigan. Tried to call him last night, no answer, but I left messages. According to county records he moved out of Spencer County forty years ago, kept this land and a few more patches to the south, rents all of them for farming, and not all to the same individual. I figure he's at least in his seventies."

Piper reached down and retrieved her thermos, poured half a cup, drank it in one swallow, appreciating the warmth and rush of caffeine, and screwed the lid back on. "I'd offer you some, but—"

"Sometimes caffeine tempts me," Basil admitted. "I remember the good jolt."

"But not today?"

He shook his head. "That orange jeep came here." Basil took out a pen flashlight and double-checked that on his map. "Billie and Maurice were here on Halloween." He took the SUV a little closer, stopping about thirty yards from a row of tall white pines.

"Maybe there's an old farmhouse or a barn somewhere behind those trees." Piper released her seatbelt and got out, reached in the back for a rifle, and slung it over her good shoulder. The air was much fresher than the Dragon's Fire-scented interior, though there was some dust. She gulped it in to clear her lungs of the incense reek. "Time to pretend we're hunting deer."

No hunting licenses, they couldn't legally shoot one. A part of her was anxious; her first undercover operation in Spencer County. Basil had suggested not wearing their uniforms, in case someone was watching; he didn't want to tip off their quarry and give them a chance to destroy any drugs. He'd said in Chicago he and Tug had posed as electricians, pizza delivery men, gang members, and trash collectors to pursue cases.

They could legally be here, on private property, because they were investigating a crime. Piper was familiar with the open-fields rule. A "warrantless search of the area outside a property owner's curtilage" was fair game. Said search could not include a house or any other structure … for those they would need a warrant. But they had to find the structures first, and enough cause to get a judge to sign off on a search warrant for them. DA Scales was aware what they were doing and would help fast-track the paperwork. They just had to find motorcycle tracks showing knobby tires, tracks that matched the jeep, physical evidence Billie and Maurice had been here—

"—something," Piper whispered. "Find something."

But when she and Basil stepped beyond the trees, they found nothing standing.

There'd been a house, Piper saw remnants from the foundation.

"Shit and two is four," she said.

"What?" Basil asked.

"It's a cribbage thing," Piper replied. "Means we got nothing."

"The pumpkin jeep came here," Basil said. "That's something."

They made like they were looking for deer tracks, when they were actually looking for tire marks. But the ground was too overgrown and pebbly to yield anything useful.

Piper walked the perimeter of where the house had been, the foundation a mix of stones and cinderblocks. Bits of gravel crunched under her boots. The place had boasted a reasonable footprint. She noted broken glass and wood planks hiding amid the weeds. A doll's head, the hair and one eye gone, a small rusted wagon without wheels. There wasn't enough wood to suggest the house had just collapsed; someone had torn it down and hauled the remains away. They just hadn't managed to haul quite everything. It all smelled old and musty.

She circled out farther and saw Basil heading toward a second stand of white pines. It was a serious bolt of luck that had landed him in her office when she'd posted the detective opening. To find someone with his experience and credentials was amazing. He moved here because he'd tired of Chicago's gun violence and wanted to keep his kids safe. Too many kids struck down by stray bullets, he'd said, the last straw being a little boy killed on the sidewalk two blocks from the Meredith home. Twenty-five shootings in downtown Chicago this past weekend, four of those fatal, claimed an online newspaper yesterday. There was violence in tiny Spencer County, too, as evidenced by Billie and Maurice. But it wasn't on that big-city scale.

Police work would definitely be more exciting in a place like Cook County and Chicago; Piper saw the allure. Wasn't something that fit her, though. Maybe she was cemented to a rural life.

"Cement," she said, seeing a large broken slab of it beyond the remnants of the house foundation, not quite big enough for a barn, too large for a garage, scraggly bushes bordered one side. Probably the base of a storage building. Some farms had aluminum storage buildings for their cars and equipment, putting it close enough to the house to be convenient. There didn't seem to be any detritus left of whatever had been built on this slab.

She raised her binoculars and scanned the area. The sun peeked just above the horizon, tinting the broken cornstalks yellow-gold. The last of the early-morning gray was burning off. She saw three deer, one a buck with a half-dozen points. Beautiful creatures, would they make it through this hunting season? Piper remembered her first hunting trip with her father. She was eight, too young for a gun, but she liked walking in the woods with him. He shot a buck and was pleased with his trophy, until she'd said: "Daddy, please put it back. Let it go." Her father had been stunned, cried, and didn't take her hunting again until she was in high school.

Piper had killed people on downrange assignments in the Middle East, but she couldn't bring herself to kill a deer. The buck raised its head and looked her way, stood immobile, the two does with it interested in something on the ground.

Minutes later and yards away she found something interesting on the ground, too. She padded toward it, bending over and letting her binoculars dangle while she reached for her cell phone and took a picture of a broken wand covered in green sequins and miniature clock gears. Steampunkerbell must have dropped it.

Piper straightened and continued scanning with the binoculars outward from the wand, trying to see where Billie had traveled.

"Gotcha," she breathed. She radioed Basil, not wanting to raise her voice to call him … just in case there was someone else on the property who could hear her.

"Find something?" he radioed back.

"I found a reason to pester the judge for another search warrant. Join me, but be quiet."

They stood about twenty yards from a weed-covered mound of earth behind where the farmhouse had been.

"I said we were looking for a path to Mount Doom, not a hobbit hole," Basil said, his voice low.

"It's a root cellar." The mound was about six feet at its highest point and tapered to nothing roughly ten feet on either side of a worn-looking wood door. So many tall weeds, it had been effectively camouflaged, but there was a path worn to it. The face of the cellar was mortared stone.

"Root cellar."

"A farm thing," Piper explained. "That one's old. You don't usually see them anymore. Underground, or partially underground, they were used for storing fruits and vegetables, mostly root crops, how the name came about. Can preserve stuff for weeks, maybe months. Doomsday preppers and subsistence farmers, organic farmers, still use them. But they mostly went out of fashion with refrigerators."

"And you know this because you took the same farm history course as Millie?" Basil crooked an eyebrow.

They turned their backs to the cellar and walked away from it, as if uninterested, past the broken wand and back toward the stand of trees.

"Not a course. 4-H Club. Lots of farming in 4-H. Did you know that the first refrigerator for home use was invented in Indiana, Fort Wayne, during World War I? A lot of people didn't start putting them in their homes until the thirties and forties, and so there are a lot of old root cellars around here. The farmer who lived here decades ago would have used that mound before Amana came along."

"Someone's using it now," Basil said.

Basil raised his rifle, aiming toward the deer trio that had not moved on. He fired at the ground, missing the buck and sending all three racing away. He fired a second shot at the ground.

"That was for the benefit of whoever might be watching us. Let 'em think we're hunters." His voice remained low. "Did you notice the wood strip above the door to that root cellar?"

Piper stared at the spot where the deer had been. "There's a small surveillance camera, like the kind you put on your front stoop."

"Indeed. And why would you put a surveillance camera on a root cellar door on a piece of property where nobody lives? There's also a big shiny bolt and padlock on that door. Wonder if that lock was put on there after Billie's visit."

They walked back to Tug's car.

"No signs of another vehicle," Basil said. "No motorcycle. Maybe tracks, but we'd have to look a lot harder to find them. I don't think anyone is in that root cellar at the moment. Doesn't mean they couldn't watch the feed remotely. Maybe they watched us poke around."

"Maybe we passed for deer hunters."

"If we're lucky," Basil said.

"Let's call the DA and get that search warrant. Come back with Diego and Thresher, Oren."

"And suits," Basil added. "If there's meth, I want suits."

"I want whoever killed Tink."

CHAPTER TWENTY-NINE

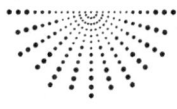

7 A.M.

Z eke felt quanked. It was a word he'd picked up one trivia night and committed to memory, dated back to the 1800s, meant overpowered by fatigue. Without the "ed" it meant a harsh croaking cry of a bird; earliest use of that found in a novel by Sylvester Judd, who died in 1853. But Zeke was experiencing the "ed" form of it.

He hadn't been getting much sleep. He'd managed less than four hours early this morning. He was definitely quanked.

He had been drinking boatloads of Mountain Dew to compensate.

Zeke felt a little jittery from the cold caffeine as he pulled up a link Basil had sent him called "Modern Meth." No 9-1-1 calls yet, and he wasn't in the mood to start inputting the piddly amount of incident reports nested in his basket.

Basil and Piper had ventured out a few hours ago looking for a meth house. In less than two years he'd be old enough to apply for a deputy position, and he could be doing that sort of work, out in a field, skulking around, a stakeout, undercover.

He justified taking time for this research as preparation for the job. He started reading the article:

"Methamphetamine, more commonly called meth, usually is found as a white, shiny powder or as crystal chunks. It is bitter-tasting, and it will dissolve quickly in water or alcohol." Zeke had a few friends into pot; he could smell it on their clothes when they came to trivia night at the pizza place. He'd tried pot once, but didn't get any "high" from it, and all it had done was make his mouth feel like he'd eaten hot ashes. Maybe he didn't do it right, but he decided not to try again; money was better spent on collectible card games. He didn't think he knew anyone into meth or anything stronger. And yet, he thought, some of the young people at Carlson's Halloween party were. So maybe he did know people—he vaguely knew Wallace Langston, Maurice's older brother, and he apparently was enamored with meth.

"Also found in orange, pink, brown, yellow-gray, and blue, like in the television series *Breaking Bad*," he continued to read. "It can be smoked, snorted, injected, or in its pill form swallowed." Zeke had made it through two episodes of *Breaking Bad* before he'd bailed on the series, couldn't find a likable character.

It had a variety of nicknames: beanies, chalk, chicken feed, redneck cocaine, tick tick, glass, hot ice, quartz, stove top; the list went on for a long paragraph.

A part of Zeke liked that Spencer County had some of the big-city problems he associated with New York, Chicago, and Los Angeles—drugs. It had murders too, not many, but enough to keep the department's deputies busy. Zeke was damn sure he was going to be one of those deputies. He knew he was capable of it right now, but the state was firm on its age twenty-one requirement. Piper Blackwell took office when she was twenty-three. He loved working for her. But if she tired of being sheriff before the next election rolled around, he'd be of legal age to run. She'd been elected the youngest sheriff in the county, probably in all of the state. He'd be even younger, make a mark on Indiana history.

He heard Oren shuffling papers in the breakroom, probably going over all the notes from the murder investigation. The chief deputy had come in before Zeke started his shift this morning. He usually engaged Oren, but held back today; the man did not look within a mile of happy. Something bad must have happened during his vacation, maybe a relative died, and though Zeke was a curious sort, he worried that coming right out and asking Oren might be the equivalent of poking a grizzly.

Back to the article: "Methamphetamine can come in large rock-like pieces. Powder can flake off these rocks, looking like shards of glass, which is responsible for some of the drug's slang terms."

"I get the glass," Zeke said. "But tick tick and redneck cocaine?"

He skimmed the rest of it, picking up a few tidbits that interested him:

A legal form of methamphetamine, Desoxyn, was sometimes prescribed to treat ADHD.

Ephedrine, pseudoephedrine, anhydrous ammonia, lithium, lye, antifreeze, drain cleaners, battery acid, lighter fluid, and freon were among components used in the manufacture.

"Geeze, why the hell would you swallow something that could have antifreeze in it? That's a special sort of stupid."

Meth users developed a tolerance quickly, needing increasingly larger amounts. He wondered if Wallace Langston had worked up a tolerance. Had Maurice used it too? Was that why Maurice had never tried making something of himself with college football?

Chronic use can lead to hallucinations and paranoia. Zeke shivered at that. The world was twisted enough without adding more curves to it.

Law officers in Thailand seized crystal meth with a street value of $30 million, found in punching bags bound for Australia. Authorities were suspicious of the shipment because boxing equipment is not in high demand for export. The Australian Border Force reported that there is a big market for meth; countrymen consume nearly a dozen tons of methamphetamine yearly.

"Holy shit," Zeke said. "Almost twelve tons?" The report did not say how many tons were consumed in the States, though he suspected it was even more than that.

A man in Australia slammed his vehicle into a parked police car. Close to $150 million worth of methamphetamines was found in his trunk. Yep. Special sort of stupid.

In the US, an east coast man sued a police department for desecrating his daughter's ashes after they pulled him over for speeding and confiscated a small urn, believing it contained meth. Some of the girl's ashes were spilled as they tried to test it.

Zeke wondered if Piper and Basil would find a meth house out along some county road, the spot where Billie and Maurice got in trouble. If they were successful, he figured it was because of his help. He'd essentially cracked the jeep's code and traced its course on Halloween.

Maybe, if Piper didn't run for reelection, he'd campaign on eliminating drug production in Spencer County and boosting the tech capabilities of the department.

"And maybe I am way too full of myself," he said.

"What did you say?" Oren was in the breakroom door, mug of coffee in hand. "Were you talking to me?"

"I said I need to log these incident reports into the system. I flipped through them. All pretty minor stuff." Zeke really wanted to add: "Why aren't you on vacation?" But he kept it in. Couldn't be as important as meth houses and putting a name to the bones in Teegan's attic, which he intended to delve into after filing the reports. He had a new idea on solving that case.

Not a single 9-1-1 call yet this morning. No radio chatter he needed to keep track of. If his luck held, he'd zip through the incident reports and get to the bones before Piper and Basil came back and gave him something else to do.

Then three calls came in a row.

He dispatched fire trucks to December Drive, smoke coming from upstairs windows of a house; a Rockport police unit to the Dollar Store for a shoplifter; and a sheriff's car out to an overturned car in the ditch by the monastery. There'd been a few accidents on that road in the past two weeks, and he radioed the responding deputy to check if any road signs were down.

He retrieved another Mountain Dew, grabbed the top incident report, and stared.

"Oren! Hey, Oren. You better look at this." Zeke waved the report.

"What's up?"

Zeke flapped the paper faster. "Theft report. Looked minor. A farmer on County Road 700, north of Santa Claus. He'd put in some winter wheat. He reported the theft of liquid fertilizer late yesterday."

Oren raised an eyebrow.

"Liquid fertilizer. Anhydrous ammonia. Report says two guys on motorcycles drained several gallons from his tank. He caught them in the act when he was putting a tractor away. They sped off."

"Fine." Oren's droll voice showed his disinterest. "We'll get someone out to talk to him and—"

"No, this is a big deal," Zeke insisted. Flustered, he glared at the chief deputy. "One of the guys was on a big yellow dirt bike. I should call the sheriff. She and Basil are on some sneaky surveillance thing. Not even using a department car. She's got her phone, though, and a radio."

"I know where they are," Oren said. "They're looking—"

"—for a big yellow dirt bike among other things."

"Dirt bike?" He still seemed uninterested.

"Those murders? Billie and Maurice? They might have been killed by a guy on a yellow dirt bike."

Oren snatched the theft report out of Zeke's fingers, thumped down his coffee, whirled, and headed out the door.

Zeke input the rest of the theft reports, answered one more 9-1-1 call, and opened a new browsing screen.

He Googled "human skeleton for sale."

He'd been thinking about the rest of the things in the attic, namely the boxes upon boxes upon boxes of holiday decorations. What if Mr. Bones had been a Halloween display, and not a murder victim? What if whoever owned the house at the time managed to get a real skeleton to set out in the front yard? To that end, he'd been chatting with the oldest neighbors along the street, picking their brains about the house's seasonal décor. So far, no one remembered a skeleton. But also so far, no one had a good recollection of what the place looked like all decorated ... other than "gaudy at Christmas."

He had emails out to surviving relatives of previous owners, and the caretakers at the memory center where jazz musician David Bullock had lived. He hoped maybe someone in that mix might know about Mr. Bones, because he'd been coming up with zilch and zip on the murder angle. Apparently, Paul Blackwell had zilch and zip, too. And the coroner had passed off the skeleton to the state crime lab, which hadn't come through with anything yet, either.

The skeleton had once belonged to someone. Had been someone.

His search revealed a lot of sites where he could purchase imitation human skeletons, some for a mere $200, others that had been replicated from an actual body for $1,600, high enough quality for medical schools.

Zeke also discovered *real* bones for sale, a site called Banard's Bone Room ... human and animal bones, fossils, and replicas. The creepy site even had an entire section on human skulls, with a bunch of photographs of the inventory. Following another link, he saw three whole skeletons also available, on discount, ranging from $5,800 to $6,000. He clicked on one: male, from India, thirty-two teeth, slight crack on the right scapula, dark glue on some joints, appeared to have been killed by a blow to the head. Whoa. He had a gruesome thought: had that man's relatives stripped the skin off and sold the bones? And if so, what sort of markup did the Bone Room claim?

He dug through all the corners of the site and a few others, learning it was legal to possess and sell human bones, import and export them ... except the latter was banned in some states, including Georgia, Tennessee, and Louisiana. The Native American Graves Protection and Repatriation Act excluded some remains, as did certain archaeology cases.

It made him wonder: what if a previous homeowner had bought Mr. Bones from something like that internet site?

Could a shifty funeral home have sold the skeleton?

"What if and what if?" Zeke mused. And if a purchase was the case, could he prove that?

It would take a lot more digging and at least several more Mountain Dews to figure it all out.

CHAPTER THIRTY

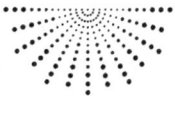

9 A.M.

Piper wanted more than the meth lab or whatever else might be hiding in the root cellar. She wanted whoever rode the yellow dirt bike—the possible killer of Billie and Maurice. She thought there was a likelihood that person would show up in the Vincent field.

That chance was worth taking, even if it could mean a long day of nothing. Or seventy-two hours of nothing; the search warrant for the root cellar was good for that long.

Still in her camouflage sweatshirt and orange vest, though it was well past optimum time to hunt deer, she walked parallel north of the overgrown access road, rifle slung over her good shoulder, coffee thermos hanging from a hook on her belt, the air cool, but dusty. The hope was if anyone saw her, they'd think her a persistent, lone hunter.

Heavy cloud cover, the sky looking pewter, she navigated the plowed rows and dried, broken cornstalks, somehow managing to keep her balance and cursing the sling. Nothing flat about a seemingly flat field.

Two more weeks or so and this damn sling will be gone. If I don't do something to screw it up.

The remnants of the farmhouse's foundation were a farther slog than she'd thought, and she was winded by the time she caught a glimpse of the root cellar's mound. Piper came up behind it, out of the view of the surveillance camera. She dropped flat and radioed Basil, keeping her voice lower than she suspected necessary. He waited with Diego and Thresher in a department Explorer, down the road and parked behind someone's battered barn. If motorcycles came from the north, Basil would spot them. South? Oren and Rocco were in an Explorer behind another not-so battered barn.

"No cars. No motorcycles that I can see. The place is empty." She radioed Basil and Oren as she rolled behind thistles where she could see the tamped-down path that led to the root cellar. "I've a good position. Lots of cover." She didn't add *and I'm uncomfortable as hell.* Hard, pebbly, dusty, itchy. Basil had told her one of the challenges of extended surveillance in Chicago had been staying awake. She was way too uncomfortable to drift off. And she had coffee.

Basil had intended to fill this role, but Piper claimed it. Her arm limited her; she was better off keeping watch rather than charging in if that opportunity presented. She'd had many surveillance assignments in the Middle East, crawling across fields and keeping her head down. Here, at least she didn't have to worry about detonating IEDs.

Oren had said it was a two-hundred-gallon wheeled tank the anhydrous ammonia had been siphoned from, and the farmer claimed it was not the first time it had happened. But it was the first time he'd reported it because on this occasion he saw the thieves—two men on motorcycles. Dusk, he was putting away a tractor for the season, and its headlights caught the thieves. The dirt bike all yellow and black like a big bumblebee. The other looked dark blue or black, and he thought it maybe a Harley by the *thrum* of it. He couldn't make out any of the riders' features, beyond one being slight and the other tall. It was a fast siphon and run. The farmer guessed by the size of the containers strapped on the back of the bikes they'd taken eight to ten gallons, a hardly noticeable drop given his tank's capacity. The other thefts had been more substantial.

Apparently, they'd cut a line and drained the stuff into their containers using a bicycle tube attached with duct tape. They had other containers with them, but the farmer had interrupted them midway. He repaired the damaged line and cleaned it using heavy gloves and a mask, and called in a theft report the following morning. The farmer said the thieves wore gloves and probably kept their helmets on to help protect them from fumes, likely aware of how dangerous the liquid gas was.

"He said this crap is volatile and explosive. And that after this latest theft he's decided to either get rid of the tank come spring or have it moved behind a barn where you can't see it from the road."

Oren reported that he'd retrieved the bicycle tube and duct tape, in case they could find fingerprints on it, but he was doubtful. Then he'd contacted other farmers in the county with anhydrous ammonia tanks to see if they'd been siphoned too and just never reported it. He'd thought a theft of so few gallons might not have been noticed or deemed not significant to worry about.

It worried Piper. If meth was getting made in the root cellar, using anhydrous ammonia—among other things—to cook it, she and her deputies would have to be particularly careful.

Time stretched, catching Piper with the eerie silence of the field. Not enough breeze to rustle the weeds or blow the dirt, the quiet unnerved her. She thought about Billie and Maurice, why they'd come here. Allegedly, Billie was getting meth for Maurice's brother and would make a little money for her effort, although she apparently charged far less than street value. Was it because she was so enamored by Maurice that Billie thought she was doing the family a favor? Was it to impress Maurice? Did she use herself? Did she need money? Piper doubted Billie lacked for money given the clothes hanging in the girl's bedroom closet and the jewelry stash on her dresser ... or maybe those were all gifted and she lacked her own funds. Had Billie thought stealing meth and reselling it would gain her enough money for the expensive fashion school she wanted to attend?

Did Billie use? she wondered again. Did Maurice?

Tox screens wouldn't be back for at least another week, and they would tell if the teenagers had meth or other drugs in their systems. Was Billie stealing the meth primarily for herself and Maurice?

Piper moved several inches to the right to keep her legs from stiffening. She reached into her pocket and pulled out her silenced cell phone, saw that she'd missed texts from Nang, her dad, and a few spam messages about car warranties. How did those companies get her number? She'd answer Nang and her dad later, needed to keep her focus on the root cellar.

Wallace Langston had said his meth dealers were the Halliday sisters in Rockport, the pair she'd arrested in their apartment yesterday. He'd said Billie had another source, and apparently by evidence of the dropped Steampunkerbell wand, this root cellar was it. How did Billie know of this place? Had she bought from here before?

Had friends told her? And, if so, which friends?

A customer had come to the door of the sisters' apartment when Piper was there. It wouldn't be so easy to come to the door of this root cellar to buy. It was essentially hidden, and the road to get here was nearly invisible and treacherous for anything not four-wheel-drive. But the pumpkin jeep certainly could handle the hint of a road.

Piper guessed meth wasn't dealt directly out of the cellar because of the terrain the buyers would have to cross. Probably it was made or stored here, then sold somewhere else through some nasty little network. Because of its location, the root cellar lay hidden like Superman's Fortress of Solitude. It was luck her department had discovered it, a trail of breadcrumbs from dead teenagers to a Halloween barn party to drug users and dealers to the GPS system of an ugly Halloween melon-colored jeep.

How had Billie found this place? The question soared again.

The jeep had been here the week before Halloween and then the night of the Hot and Steamy party. Had Billie driven it here even before those times? She'd check with Zeke in the morning to see if he had traced the vehicle's path farther back.

How many times had the girl come here?

What had happened Halloween night that led to Billie and Maurice's deaths? She'd dwelled on those questions over the past few days, and in the silence of the field various scenarios played in the back of her mind.

Four hours and a thermos of coffee later, Piper risked a bathroom break and returned to her post. She'd been chatting occasionally with Basil, and turning down his offers to switch places with her.

"Stubborn," he said.

"Determined," she corrected.

"Bored," Diego put in. "And so is Thresher. I'm taking him for another walk."

Oren radioed that he had a short list of farmers who suspected they'd had their fertilizer tanks tapped in the past year. They were in the northern part of the county, right in the area of the Vincent field.

Piper's legs felt stiff. Checking her phone; it was fifty-nine degrees, quite a drop from the practically warm temperature on Halloween. The forecast claimed it would drop to the high thirties this evening. She thought she should have worn two pairs of sweatpants or maybe even long underwear.

She thought about the wedding dress in the window of the antique shop. It looked like it might fit her; she could have it professionally cleaned and add sequins. The pictures in the magazines Candy had given her flitted into her thoughts—lacy and beautiful and too expensive to justify for one day, no matter how big of a deal the day was. A bluegrass band? There was one in Owensboro she really liked. Nang was a fan of country music.

What would the cake look like? Nang wanted to make something worthy of one of those baking competition shows he watched. She hoped he could enter the one he'd submitted to.

She thought about Camaro and Marmalade, about Tater and Wrinkles, and her house in Hatfield. It was big enough to add Nang. She didn't want to live in his trailer, and she didn't want to look for another place. The house had been willed to her by Mark Thresher, and that meant a lot. She didn't want to leave it.

She thought about her dad and the bones in Teegan's attic.

Her mind roamed. Then there were the riders on the motorcycles at the fertilizer tank. She and Basil had been looking for the yellow dirt bike. But it appeared there were two people involved in the operation, a dark blue or black motorcycle, too. Maybe there were more than that.

How had Billie Glempse come to this root cellar?

And why the hell didn't she just go to the Halloween party and avoid this place? Then she might still be breathing.

Three hours later, Basil radioed her. If he was again suggesting they switch places, she would take him up on it this time.

"Bumblebee just passed us, going south."

Piper heard the thrum of an engine, growing louder. Noisier than the vintage motorcycles in her garage at home. Annoyingly loud.

"Yellow and black dirt bike, a big one, Sheriff, and we'll hold until he's off and in. Let me know." Her detective meant when the rider was off the bike and into the root cellar. They needed to catch him away from the bike so he couldn't race away over the field.

"He's here," Piper said, certain they could also hear the engine through her radio.

She held her breath and parted the thistles just enough so she could see it. Loud, probably without a muffler, finally the rider turned it off. It was a chunky bike with big, wide tires that should carry it over any terrain in the county. A BMW by the shape of the logo, and it looked like the plates were purposefully obscured. Mostly yellow, but with black trim that evoked a bee image. The dirt bike seemed almost too large for the rider, who was dressed in jeans, a gray leather jacket, and a black helmet. Short, slight, could be a man or woman carrying a canvas pack hooked over one shoulder.

The rider got off and removed his helmet.

Piper took pictures with her cell phone and sent them to Teegan, hoping the dispatcher could start running facial recognition software. She exhaled and keyed the radio to Basil, whispering: "Older man, off the bike, pulling something out of his pocket. Keys. Pistol in his belt. He's going in the root cellar. Roll now."

The rider had surprised her. She'd expected someone younger, but this man looked to be in his late fifties or early sixties, with tanned, weathered skin and short white hair, a big gold hoop in his left ear.

"On our way," Basil returned.

"Following," Oren chimed in.

Two Explorers, four deputies, herself, and a dog. Overkill for one man, but she was erring well on that proverbial side of caution. *Only one man.* But maybe he was the soul who had killed Billie and Maurice.

And that made him a dangerous man.

CHAPTER THIRTY-ONE

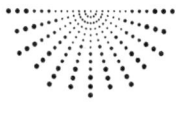

4 P.M.

Piper wanted to yell "Hands up!" the moment he got off the bike.

It was her gut reaction and probably how they would have handled it in the movies. But she had two cars of deputies coming, and a highly-trained Belgian Malinois. Not a time to go it alone. She'd wait.

Even if all of this effort was only for one man.

She set down the rifle; it had been for show and too awkward to manage with one good arm. She crept through the thistles, the dry parts scratching her face, turned on her body cam, and drew her pistol. She heard the two Explorers approach, tires crunching over rocks and chunks of wood. Stealth hadn't been an option given the terrain and the root cellar's surveillance camera.

Too, her quarry had left the door open. He'd likely see anyone coming.

The Explorers pulled side-by-side behind the dirt bike, and Rocco, Diego, and Thresher jumped out.

"Spencer County Sheriff's Department," Piper called as she came around the side of the mound and peered in through the doorway. She guessed it to be a dozen feet wide, with shelves on either side leaving a wide corridor in the middle. The air oozing out of the root cellar had a musty funk. The inside was a mass of shadows, one shifting and moving farther back—her quarry. "Toss out your gun. Come out, hands up."

At the same time, Basil and Oren headed toward the cellar, guns leading, in bulletproof vests and helmets. The four deputies and Piper swarmed the earthen mound in the Vincent field.

Overkill for just one man.

"Come out now!" Piper called. She saw the man edging even farther away, noticed the floor of the root cellar sloped down. The only light was behind her, what came in through the doorway; her eyes picked through the bands of gray and black inside, unable to discern how deep the place went into the earth.

He fiddled with something on a shelf.

She could just shoot him; her gut said she should. But she had no legal cause for that. No proof he'd killed Billie and Maurice. Her gut told her he had, though. She briefly wondered if she should listen to it.

"Throw out your weapon!" she hollered.

Difficult to distinguish things in the cellar, nothing but a jumble of shelves stuffed with various shapes. But his shape was darker, and it moved again; she wasn't going to let him get farther away. She edged in, and by the swish of fabric knew two deputies were squeezing in behind her. Then she saw the man's arm twitch and he tossed the gun; it landed at her feet.

"There you go, Sheriff," the man growled.

"Hands raised, come toward me now!" she said.

"All right. All right," came the reply. "Hold your chickens. I'm coming out." It was a damaged voice, uneven and with a deep rasp to it. "I suppose you want this one, too."

A second gun followed.

"I've one more. Here, you can have them all." The third gun thudded somewhere in the darkness.

"I don't like this." Diego was directly behind her. "Sheriff, I don't—"

Then Piper saw the man reach for something, maybe a rifle, and move fast. Her finger squeezed the trigger. Past time to follow her gut.

She hit him in the chest. He flinched, but he didn't go down.

"Look out, Sheriff, he's got—" Diego bumped into her; she felt his breath on her neck. "He's got—"

Piper fired again.

At the same time a crossbow bolt shot from the dark, narrowly missing her. It struck Diego instead. She turned her head and saw Diego go down. Basil stepped up, straddling Diego, and fired.

"Oren, pull him out of here!" Basil shouted. "He's hit in the throat."

"I've got Diego," Oren called.

Piper heard a shushing sound and knew her chief deputy was pulling Diego out of the way.

She moved forward. Basil closed, too, and she heard Oren call for an ambulance.

Everything blurred and happened at once.

Basil fired, but the target leaped to the side, winged.

Shadows and shapes, Oren's frantic voice from behind her. Rocco shouting something. Her head pounded with worry for Diego. If she'd listened to her gut right away, Diego wouldn't be down.

Thresher raced forward without being commanded, all seventy pounds of him hurtling at the man and knocking him down.

Piper wouldn't fire now and risk hitting the dog.

Hard to see, so dark, but a little light spilled in through the open door behind them. She slid in farther, closer to the man and Thresher, listening to the dog growl, hearing Oren from somewhere outside, a muted shout: "Ambulance coming!"

Basil was at her shoulder.

Lights sprang on; Rocco must have found a switch. It was harsh and yet inadequate, a string of bare bulbs dangling from the ceiling.

She saw the downed man bleeding from leg and arm wounds—either from the dog or because Basil and she had managed to hit him.

Piper pointed her pistol at him, her eyes daggers. He punched the dog. She rammed her foot down on his right outstretched arm, his flailing hand inches from the crossbow he'd dropped. Blood ran from his bicep. "Don't move, you son of a bitch!"

He screamed and thrashed, despite her admonition. Her heart

hammered in her ears, so loud she barely heard Basil tell Rocco to help Oren. "We have this," she was pretty sure Basil said.

Piper vaguely registered how sleek the crossbow looked, flat black, military grade, like the fanciest one that had been on display at the archery store where she and Nang had stopped.

"Don't move!" Her breath came ragged; the air was so dank and fusty in here.

He kicked out, difficult because of the dog, but he was able to hook her leg and topple her into a shelf filled with laboratory equipment. Glass shifted and dropped, breaking. She righted herself and slammed her foot down again. A combat veteran, Piper had been in skirmishes in the Middle East where she'd outmaneuvered her opponents without firing a shot. She kicked him, frustration and anger winning, the toe of her boot impacting with his side, discovering he wore some sort of protective vest, probably why her first shots did nothing.

He writhed beneath Thresher; the dog bit down on the man's left arm and he screamed again. He braced his heels and pushed up, trying unsuccessfully to dislodge the dog.

Piper dropped, pinning his right arm under her knees and holding the gun to his chest, above the lip of his vest. The man was small and had decades on her, but he was desperate and strong and tried to throw her off. The dog still growled and held his squirming prey. Spittle flew from the man's lips and his eyes locked onto hers—pale ice blue like the undead in *Game of Thrones*. She shivered and pressed the barrel of the gun in to make sure he felt it. The dog clamped again on his left arm. Basil loomed over them and reached down.

"Thresher, release," Piper said. "*Ertrag. Ertrag!* Thresher—"

The dog growled fiercely, but relented and released the man.

"We have him," Basil called out to Oren. "He's not going anywhere."

"Ambulance is close," came the reply.

Basil turned the man over as Piper rose and holstered her pistol. With her good hand muscling the man's right arm behind him. Basil retrieved his cuffs and clicked them tight, tugging the suspect to his feet.

"We have to get out of here," Piper said.

"As fast as possible," Basil answered, roughly pushing the struggling man down the corridor and out the door.

Piper paused to grab the crossbow and take a quick look around so her body cam could record the inside of the cellar, then she followed, anxious to see Diego.

She gulped in the fresh air and stared at the figures a few yards from the cellar entrance. Diego lay on his back, Oren's jacket draped over his chest. Oren remained on his knees next to him, hand around the quarrel in Diego's throat, keeping pressure on the wound. Blood seeped out through Oren's fingers.

Piper couldn't tell if Diego was breathing, the bulky jacket concealing whether his chest rose and fell. But as she stepped close, she saw his eyes blinking and mouth working. Thresher sat at attention next to him.

Her heart felt like a boat anchor. A lot of blood. It looked bad. Her fault. If she'd followed her gut and drew on the man the moment he got off the bike, took him down before the others got here, Diego wouldn't be wounded. Why had she waited? Why had she thought with her head and not her heart?

Her father had told her she rushed into things, impulsive ... the military, running for sheriff, Nang. Why couldn't she have rushed into this?

Oren looked up at her. "I'm thinking about the way in here. It's big and boxy, an ambulance, but it doesn't have four-wheel drive. It's going to have trouble. We need to take him out to the road to meet the ambulance. We don't have a backboard. Our first aid equipment isn't enough to handle this."

Piper saw Basil push the prisoner at Rocco. "Watch him. Do not put him in a car." Then he spun and headed to the nearest Explorer and opened the back.

Piper tugged at her sling.

"No," Oren cautioned. "You're not supposed to—"

"Diego's not supposed to die," Piper cut back. She got the sling off, dropped it, and opened and closed the fingers of her left hand, gingerly moved her arm. Then she went to Diego's feet, spread his legs and stepped between them, bent and grabbed him behind the knees.

"Seat's folded down," Basil reported. "I'll get his shoulders."

Oren hooked his hands into Diego's belt.

"Ready? One, two, up." Basil walked backward in little stutter steps, clearly mindful of the broken ground. Piper's left arm felt warm, maybe a warning. *But maybe it had healed just enough,* she thought, to handle this. She carefully helped load Diego into the hatch. Oren climbed in, resumed putting pressure on the wound. The chief deputy's hands were covered with blood.

She wanted to go with them, get her deputy to the paramedics. But she had to stay here and manage the scene.

Basil took the driver's seat. "It's going to be bumpy," he called to Oren.

Oren said something in return, but it was lost in the Explorer starting and wheels churning as it backed up and turned around, noisily crunching over rocks and chunks of wood, juddering down the ruts and rises of what used to be a farm access road.

"Thresher!" Piper whistled for the dog, who looked like he was going to follow the Explorer. He slowly joined her and sat straight, muscles in his legs quivering.

Piper's left arm felt on fire. She held it to her side, turned, and saw Rocco holding the prisoner against the driver's door of her Explorer. The man glared, eyes unblinking, shifting back and forth on the balls of his feet. On the ground outside the root cellar door lay his crossbow near a patch of dark-stained ground—Diego's blood. She'd set the weapon there in her haste to check on her wounded deputy.

"Sheriff, I didn't get a good look. What's in there?" Rocco gestured with his head toward the mound.

"Nothing good. A whole lot of nothing good." She'd not gotten a *thorough* look at the inside of the root cellar, just half-glimpsed things while she'd focused on their quarry. It appeared that the cellar descended quite a way underground, the string of lights dipping into a sloping tunnel and revealing the place was much bigger than the mound suggested. Shelves on both walls were filled with laboratory equipment, beyond beakers and test tubes, all manner of things she couldn't put names to and hadn't taken enough time to study. There were jugs, bins, and bags upon bags, some looking like powdered sugar stacked in a grocery store.

If that was methamphetamines, there was a lot of it.

"There's nothing good in there, Rocco."

She wanted to go back in for a better look.

But not until Basil and Oren came back. And not until she talked to this man.

Piper whirled, strode toward Rocco and the prisoner. She stared into his ice-blue eyes, smelled his sour sweat and almost gagged on it.

"Name," she demanded.

He cocked his head and smiled thinly. One of his front teeth was capped with gold.

Rocco tapped the man's pockets looking for an ID. "No wallet."

Piper remembered the gray backpack he'd had when he arrived. He must have dropped it in the cellar; maybe there was a wallet there, a driver's license. They'd check the VIN number on the dirt bike, and run the license plate, at least learn who it belonged to, maybe get an ID that way. "What's your name?"

He smiled wider and shook his head.

"You have the right to remain silent," she said. Piper would repeat the Miranda warning back at the station, though it would take a while before they'd get there.

"Anything I say can and will be used against me in a court of law," the man interrupted. "I have the right to an attorney. An attorney can be appointed if I cannot afford one." He rolled his shoulders. "I can afford one."

He had a record to be that familiar with the Miranda. Or he'd watched *Law & Order* so often it had become ingrained. She figured it was the former and so they'd find out who he was with fingerprints.

"I'll check his bike," Rocco said. "See if he's got a wallet there. And I can look—"

"Got a search warrant?" The man's voice sounded like gravel

bumped around in his throat. "You can't look anywhere without one. Private property. Shouldn't've even poked your nose in my bunker. Can't use anything in there against me without a warrant."

Piper was certain he'd had significant run-ins with the law; they'd find him in some database. Her left arm throbbed. How badly had she screwed it up?

Didn't matter.

Diego mattered. And finding justice for Billie and Maurice mattered.

She kept her focus on the man in front of her, but she couldn't *not* think about Diego. If she'd followed her instincts and tried to take the guy down right away, not wait for her deputies, things would have turned out differently. He never would have had the chance to shoot Diego with a crossbow bolt. Of course, some part of her mind told her things could have turned out worse. She didn't know right away that he had on a protective vest, that if she'd shot him squarely it wouldn't have taken him down; he'd have had time to draw on her, shoot her, shoot at the others pulling up in the Explorers.

Scenarios played out in fast-forward in her mind, but in all of them Diego would not have gotten hurt.

Please, God, please let him make it.

"Nothing on the bike," Rocco said. "I'll check in the—"

"No, don't go in the cellar," Piper interrupted. "We need gear for that."

"And a search warrant," the man snarled. "I told you that you can't look anywhere without a—"

"I have a damn search warrant," she spat. Piper thought she caught a response on his face, eyes widening ever-so-slightly. "I can search any damn place and any damn thing I want on this property."

She stepped closer. "Who is your partner?" Or partners. Maybe there were several people involved. While she hadn't gotten a great look at what was inside, she could tell it was significant with all the equipment and myriad filled bags. Rural Spencer County had a big drug manufacturing problem. She doubted that just one man was behind it.

"Partner?" He cocked his head and she noticed a thick scar on the side of his neck, ropy and running from his ear down under the lip of his protective vest. A smudge on his neck might be a tattoo, a poorly-done one. A prison tat?

"Partner," Piper repeated. "The guy on the other motorcycle. The big black motorcycle. The two of you were caught stealing liquid fertilizer for your operation. Who is your partner? Where is your partner?"

"I have the right to remain silent. I'm going to exercise that." He drew his lips tight to emphasize his point.

"Should I put him in the back of—"

"No, Rocco, we keep him out here," Piper said. Then she turned on her radio. "Teegan, contact the Santa Claus Fire Department and have them send out a type-four truck. I think that would be Blitzen. See if we can keep it out here for most of the night."

She needed to call the state police and the FBI, too. Whatever had been going on in the root cellar in Vincent's field was beyond the scope of the Spencer County Sheriff's Department.

CHAPTER THIRTY-TWO

5 P.M.

The fire truck made a *clunking thunking* racket lumbering down the hint of a road. The Santa Claus Fire Department had named all of its vehicles, and as Piper expected, they sent Blitzen, a bright red tanker that carried up to three thousand gallons of water for scenes with no access to a hydrant.

The glow of the glossy paint would appear to lose its luster with the sun setting in less than an hour. Piper needed to get external lights out here and a generator so everyone could work. The bare bulbs dangling from the ceiling in the root cellar would not be good enough.

"I think Diego'll be okay," Oren told Piper as he skirted Blitzen. He and Basil had returned minutes ago. "Actually, I *hope* he'll be okay. The ride to meet the ambulance was rough and didn't do him any favors." The chief deputy's hands were still bloodied, more blood on his shirt and pants. "The paramedics said it missed his carotid. Still—"

"He lost a lot of blood," Piper finished.

"Yes."

Basil talked to the firemen, who had taken down their hose and aimed it at the prisoner. She couldn't overhear the conversation.

"He has to be washed off," Piper explained to Oren. "That's why I called for a truck. He might have meth on him, and we don't want it in a car. I think we will get washed down too just to be safe. If there was meth swirling in there, if it got on us, it can be explosive." She paused: "I don't want it in the vehicles." Softer: "I don't want it anywhere." She nodded to the Explorer Basil and Oren used to take Diego to the road. "That'll be washed down, too."

"You read that somewhere." Oren watched them spray the cursing man. "About washing people down."

She nodded. "I took a crash course on methamphetamines. Since Halloween, I've read a ton of articles on the big law enforcement sites, watched videos of police raiding a trailer park where meth was made. They brought in a fire truck and washed things down, including the people."

"Damn root cellar," Oren said, smiling to see the prisoner thoroughly soaked and looking angry. "Who would have thought to put a meth lab in a root cellar? Damn good hiding place out here. Hard to spot, hard to get to. Basically invisible. Fluke you found it. Impressive work."

Was Oren's voice tinged with respect? Piper wasn't sure. Maybe disbelief. She still had a measure of disbelief that this had been operating in her county.

"We wouldn't have found it without Zeke's help. And we wouldn't have known to look without Billie and Maurice getting murdered."

"I'm still trying to catch up on the case," Oren admitted. "A lot of notes to go through, body cam footage. I go away for a couple of days and you land two murders and find major pot and meth dealers." He tipped his head back and shook it. "In this county. In this little county. I knew we had some sort of a meth problem. Not a secret. That goes back to when Paul was sheriff. Before him, too, probably. All the little rural places have a meth problem, because they're little and rural. Iowa. I watched a documentary called *Meth Queen*, or something like that. She operated for a lot of years out of a small town in Iowa. I just didn't know it was this bad here."

"Neither did I." Piper watched as a fireman put a blanket around the prisoner. No doubt he was cold. She wasn't looking forward to getting sprayed. "Helluva lot of drugs in there." She pointed to the root cellar. "I know it's not powdered sugar on those shelves."

"Feds coming?"

Piper nodded. She'd called them. "State police, too."

"Probably smart to let them handle it." He twisted his foot against the ground. "Might want to contact the DEA."

Piper didn't want to pass it off to the other agencies. The Spencer County Sheriff's Department had found this. But it was the right call.

"Happy to have you back to help with all of this," she told Oren. "I'm curious. Why did you cut your vacation short?"

"I didn't like the climate in Tennessee."

Piper motioned for Basil to join them. Rocco kept watch on the prisoner and engaged the three firemen in chatter about drugs. She caught him say: "Can't really say much, open case."

"The state police have a special unit coming out of Indianapolis, should be here in two- and-a-half hours," she said. "I don't know what they'll bring. So, we'll have to set up lights. Millie is hauling in two floods and a generator."

"They're coming in tonight?" Rocco called, letting her know he'd been listening.

"State's not waiting for tomorrow. Two FBI field agents from the Louisville office will be here in an hour or two." Softer: "Hate to turn this over."

"We'll work with them," Basil said. "Keep our hand in somehow. It's not like on TV, where the local cops play tug-o-war with the higher powers to keep a case. My experience has been the Feds work with you, respect you."

"I hope that's true." Piper pointed with her right arm. Her left felt like a molten concrete block hanging from her shoulder and she thought about putting the sling back on. Had she screwed her arm up? Had she made the injury worse? The sling lay on the ground, stained with Diego's blood; she decided against retrieving it. She pointed again. "That man has the deaths of two teenagers to answer for. The Feds can get him on whatever drug charges they want. We want him for murder."

237

In her mind there was no other murder suspect. Yellow dirt bike, crossbow, he was the guy; they'd hand the DA enough evidence to prosecute. It wouldn't be enough of a conclusion, though. She couldn't rest until she had all the pieces … why did he kill Billie and Maurice? How had Billie found this place? How long had this been operating?

She looked away from the firemen and stared at the opening to the root cellar. The string of bare bulbs cast a haunting glow.

"Meth labs blow up," Basil said flatly, as if anticipating what she intended to do. "All the chemicals they use, the way everything is stored. That hobbit hole has the potential to go boom. And you don't want to be in it if that happens."

"Agreed." She waited a beat. "But I want a better look inside anyway. I'm going to take the chance. I'll be quick about it." True to her father's words, she did rush into things. Impulsive. Driven. She'd just rush cautiously right now.

"Agreed," Basil echoed. "Suits in the back of my car."

Oren wandered over to help Rocco deal with their prisoner.

The white suits covered every inch and made Piper feel claustrophobic.

"I'd like to take a gander, too, Sheriff." This from Rocco. "Oren can watch—"

"We only have two suits," Piper said. Besides, she didn't want to jeopardize anyone else. She'd already jeopardized Diego.

It would be prudent for all of them to stay outside the root cellar and wait for the state police and FBI and whatever sort of special equipment they would bring. Let them do all the delving.

She was too curious to wait.

Didn't get enough of a look-see during her brief foray in there.

Although she had body cam footage, she craved an up-close exploration. "You can look at the pics later, Rocco. And keep Thresher with you. Don't need him to sniff for drugs. We damn well know there are drugs in there. Don't have a suit for the dog." But maybe she could get one.

"Yeah, there's a shit-ton of drugs. It's just a matter of how much of a shit-ton is in that hobbit hole," Basil said. In addition to their body cams, the detective took the department's camera and some evidence bags.

Piper brought a high-powered flashlight, and she turned it on the moment she stepped past the door, shining the beam along the floor and ceiling, seeing a snaking electric cable from the lights. "Leeching power from somewhere. Didn't see any generator outside. We'll figure that out later."

She likened herself to a cave spelunker in some horror flick, *The Descent, Journey to the Center of the Earth, Sanctum,* she'd watched all of those. The monsters in this place, however, were real and rode dirt bikes and pedaled methamphetamines. And murdered teenagers.

The beam hit each shelf, the lab equipment first, Basil taking close-ups. Piper thought there were as many beakers, tubes, plates, and other odds and ends arrayed here as could be found in a school chemistry laboratory. Stacks of flat bags, no doubt intended for the product, lined the floor, along with an electronic scale, goggles, plastic gloves, tubing. An open box with quarrels in it sat next to two boxes of ammunition. She spotted the gray backpack the man had brought in here. They'd take it on the way out. Maybe it held a cell phone and wallet; her warrant covered all of it. No doubt the Feds would want the backpack, but she'd take a look first.

The shelves on the opposite wall made Piper think again of the baking section of a big grocery store—stacks of powdered sugar, pounds upon pounds upon pounds of it. Except she knew it wasn't powdered sugar. And there was a scary amount of it.

Basil pointed to the crystallized version, stored in smaller bags. He continued to take pictures. She noticed he didn't touch anything. She didn't either, careful not to brush up against the shelves, behind which were old bricks and stones mortared together to form the walls. The root cellar had been sturdily built, and maybe it had also served as a safe spot for severe weather like tornados, a bunker.

Where was the money? She figured there'd be stacks of it on a shelf. This much drugs, there had to be a lot of money.

Piper edged in deeper, past more shelves where gallon jugs held unknown liquids. Maybe water, maybe the liquid fertilizer that had been taken from county farmers. Aa couple of large plastic containers appeared empty but fit the description the farmer gave Oren.

Roughly twenty-feet in, she gestured with the light. The brick and stone walls gave way to dirt, and here the floor sloped down at a much steeper angle. Along the righthand side steps had been hewn into the dirt.

"Newer," Basil said, his voice sounding far away because of the head coverings. "I'm guessing dug out by our mystery man outside, him and his cohorts."

"We'll ask him, but I doubt he'll say anything. He can recite the Miranda, though." She thought about his voice, how it sounded damaged and forced, pictured the thick scar that trailed down his neck. Perhaps the wound he'd suffered had affected his speech. "Word for word, the Miranda."

"Maybe he watches *Law & Order*."

They saw more shelves, with even more bags of powder and crystals. Large bags had been filled to bursting with hundreds of tiny meth bags like the ones the coroner found in Maurice's stomach.

Deeper still and the corridor opened into a chamber roughly a dozen feet in diameter. More bare-bulb lights hung from the low ceiling here. A vent helped bring air in from outside.

Basil hummed. "Didn't expect this."

Against the back wall stood a single bed with pillows and a patchwork quilt, the wedding ring pattern like someone's grandmother might have made. Piper noted it was handstitched and likely an antique. Underneath the cot peeked a long gray footlocker which she really wanted to open, but mustered enough willpower to leave alone.

"A few changes of clothes in it probably. More likely money," Basil said. He'd obviously noticed her interest in the footlocker. "Haven't seen money anywhere else, and drugs are always about the money." He whistled. "But with the serious amount of shit this guy was producing, I'd guess he has an off-shore account somewhere."

Other furnishings included a card table with three folding chairs, a lantern on top of it, and a small case with poker chips and cards. Against another wall leaned a metal-topped table with an electronic scale, beakers, and a wheeled cart. A portable toilet stood in the corner.

"Maybe they do their meth cooking here," Piper said. "On that table."

"Probably." Basil pointed to scorch marks on the metal surface. "Definitely."

"Bet they had trouble squeezing this down here." Piper sidled next to a wide padded recliner, a pole lamp behind it, and nearby, a mini-fridge like college students kept in their dorm rooms. She opened it, even though she'd told herself she wasn't going to touch anything. It held a feast: a few pounds of hard salami, provolone cheese, blueberry yogurt, a package of baby carrots, and eight bottles of Blue Moon Belgian White Ale.

It appeared someone had made this their second home for a few days and nights.

"The sisters running meth out of their apartment," Piper began. "All of their equipment, the drugs, would have fit on one of those shelves. That was nothing. That was like our county fair compared to Disney World."

"Sheriff, this is as large an operation as any Tug and I took down in Chicago. Probably larger." Basil continued to take pictures. "We should leave."

"Absolutely," Piper agreed. "Nang and my dad would probably be upset if I blew up."

"Yeah, Esme would be pretty pissed if I died and left her to deal with three kids on her own."

"What?"

Basil replied: "She's pregnant. I haven't said much. She wants to reveal the news after the doc says whether we're having a boy or girl. Though we're thinking of telling the doc to surprise us."

"Congratulations."

She saw Basil grin through the visor in the suit. "I like kids."

"And I'd like knowing how the hell this meth operation was going on in our county. And for how long."

"Root cellar in the middle of an abandoned yard. Well camouflaged. A road that a regular vehicle can't drive down. That's how the hell it was going on. On that bright side, we got a lot of meth off the streets. This goes way beyond Spencer County. This much meth ... it's going to other states ... Illinois, Ohio, Kentucky, Michigan, maybe farther. Probably farther. If it hadn't been for Tinker Bell—"

"Yeah, if it hadn't been for Billie dying in that ditch on Halloween." She glanced at the ground next to the recliner, seeing a thick puzzle book like they sold at the Dollar Store. This whole thing was one big puzzle. "Don't like that I had to call the Feds."

"Big operation," Basil said, following. "You didn't have a choice. And I don't mind that they handle the meth. I hate meth."

Piper grabbed the laptop and gray backpack on the way out.

"Feds are going to want that." Basil passed over the evidence bags.

Piper nodded. "I'm sure they are, but we're taking a look first. It's covered in the search warrant."

Once outside, Piper gave them to Oren to take back to the department. She noticed he and Rocco were thoroughly wet.

"I'm staying until the FBI and state police get here," she said. "Probably staying and watching them. I expect a long night." It was getting dark, twilight taking a firm grip. She hoped Millie would get here soon with the big lights and generator. "I'm going to get washed down, call Nang, and get him to bring me a change of clothes." She rubbed at her lip. "And maybe some dinner."

"You'll have to meet him out at the road," Oren said. "I think I knocked a few fillings loose driving here." He nodded toward the prisoner. "Want me to take him back?"

"Please," Piper said. "Read him his rights again. He knows them, but we'll do it all by the book. Call the DA and tell him what's going on. Scales might want to come out and take a look. Get Zeke have a go at the laptop after you fingerprint it. I want the drive copied. I'll get him some overtime. Go through the backpack, inventory and print everything. Hopefully you can figure out who the hell he is." And from there they could discover who worked with him, the man on the black motorcycle. Or partners ... there were three folding chairs at the table in the cellar. She tapped her foot, glanced at the ground before meeting Oren's gaze again. "And check on Diego. Let me know how he's doing."

Then Oren, Rocco, Thresher, and the prisoner were gone. Blitzen and the two firemen stayed, a precaution in case the hobbit hole exploded.

"I'm staying too," Basil told her. "I just texted Esme. She's bringing me a change of clothes and a thermos of decaf. I'll meet her at the road."

"Then I'll get Nang to bring enough dinner for us, and the firemen too."

Nang brought more than enough dinner for everyone and joined them for spring rolls, fried rice, and his special poached chicken salad —a bowl sans chicken for Basil—with bean sprouts, roasted nuts, fish sauce, lime juice, and chili dressing. Red velvet cupcakes served as dessert.

For Piper, who changed into jeans and a thermal shirt courtesy of Nang, the delicious meal was the best note sounding on a long day.

CHAPTER THIRTY-THREE

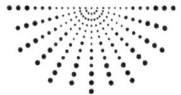

10 A.M., FRIDAY NOV 6TH

Z eke poked his head in her office. "You doing okay, Sheriff?"

"Fine."

"Good." He looked anxious, and he edged into the doorway and leaned forward on the balls of his feet. Hands on the doorframe, he bounced. "I got something. I got something. I really got—"

"What?"

He bounced again and talked fast. "Look, I stayed up late last night. I know all of you did, too, on the big drug thing. I was working on the bones in Teegan's attic. Couldn't help myself. Couldn't let it rest, you know. I was getting close. Very close. Actually, I just got an email that settles it. I solved the case!"

Piper cocked her head, waiting for him to continue. She settled in behind her desk and watched him bounce once more.

"I solved it!" Zeke beamed. Piper had never seen him smile so big. "I called Chief Blackwell, your dad. Told him I solved it. Not sure he believes me, but he's coming over here after I get off my shift. That's when I'm going to do the big reveal. I'm not saying anything else until then. You wanna sit in on that? You should sit in on—"

"Of course, I will. Not my murder case, but I'm terribly interested."

"Great." He disappeared back to the dispatch desk just as a call came in.

"9-1-1," Piper heard him say. "What is the nature of your emergency?"

Piper had just come from the clinic with a new prescription "as needed for pain" and a warning not to lift anything heavier than twenty pounds. The bottle read: "may cause drowsiness," so she put it in her desk drawer and wrapped the fingers of both hands around a big mug of Dark Italian Roast.

She was tired enough, having stayed at the root cellar until almost two. Even though her arm dully ached, she couldn't afford to take anything that would make her nod off. But coffee … she would take that.

The Dark Italian tasted delightfully strong. She savored it and suspected it would be the first of several mugs today.

X-rays showed that she did not make her arm worse by helping lift Diego, who was recovering in the hospital. The titanium rod still in place, her bone was fusing, but wouldn't be wholly healed for at least another few weeks. She no longer had to wear a sling, if she remained careful. Ahead of schedule, the doctor said, attributing her fast mending to her youth and stubbornness.

She listened to Zeke dispatch an ambulance to the Rockport grocery store, where a woman had collapsed in the parking lot.

"You said you wanted to talk, Sheriff. I figured I'd come to you this time."

Piper nodded and gestured Spencer County District Attorney DA Scales in.

He sat across from her, folded his coat and rested it in his lap. He was dressed in a dark suit, white shirt, and a maroon tie with tiny biplanes on it; court attire.

"Simon Payne," Piper said.

"I take it you're referring to the man you locked up and not the British basketball player," Scales said.

"He wouldn't give us his name yesterday, but his prints were on file. Last-known permanent address goes back a dozen years to Paducah, Kentucky. The house at that address hasn't existed for a decade. A gas leak and explosion that also took out two neighboring buildings. I'm thinking it was something other than gas."

"Meth."

"Coffee?"

"No thanks."

"Just turned fifty-three. I pegged him some years older than that. He looks craggy like Sam Elliott, the actor in a lot of Westerns."

"Elliott's pushing eighty. It's the mileage," Scales said. "I saw Payne up-close a little while ago, and it looks like there's a lot of mileage on his skinny frame." He tipped his head toward the bouquet on her desk —red carnations, yellow daisies, purple Monte Casino Asters, and green button poms. "Smells nice. I should send my wife some flowers."

Nang had them delivered. The card read: *For my warrior princess. Congrats on the big drug bust.*

"Eight years in the Army put some of that mileage on him," Piper continued. "Part of Operation Desert Storm. Picked up a handful of medals, then started picking up a record for mostly minor things, burglary, obstructing justice, battery from a bar fight. Spent eighteen months in a prison in Texas, got out in 2009, moved to Paducah, and a few years after that disappeared."

"Until you found him yesterday." Scales leaned back in the chair. "Probably started small, grew his business. Got it big enough that somewhere in there he fell in with a cartel or major trafficking cell."

"Feds estimate more than a ton of meth spread throughout the cellar, worth at least sixty million dollars. Shit. Right? Big enough that we're going to land in the national news." She let out a long breath. "The DEA is sending a team, should be here in a few hours, flying into Indy, driving down. They'll verify the weight and value and poke around. Take all of it away."

Piper stared at her reflection in the coffee, thought she should have taken the time to put on a little makeup. "One of the Feds thinks the operation has been running for quite a few years and that Payne's likely moved several billions in meth. They told me that Payne might have been flying the drugs out. They found a strip nearby in the field that could have served as a runway for a small plane. That quantity in the cellar? They figure he was due to ship any day."

"I suspect he didn't supply anyone locally," Scales said, staring at her flowers, as if he was pointedly avoiding her gaze. Piper figured he was going to tell her something she didn't want to hear. "An operation like that couldn't afford to do business in the county, wouldn't want anyone from around here to know about it."

"But Billie, our Steampunkerbell, found out." Piper took a big gulp of the coffee.

"Payne killed her and Maurice to keep them from telling anyone else. And, even more reason ... he killed them because they stole from him. Steal from a man like that—"

"I've still got a lot of work to do on this."

"No, you don't. Not your problem anymore." Scales finally looked away from the flowers.

Piper bristled and squeezed the mug. She definitely had not wanted to hear that. And she was not stepping away from this case.

"Relax."

Not relaxing, she thought.

"Seriously, Sheriff, it isn't your problem. It's between me and the Feds to figure out all the charges against Payne, prosecuting every-thing. It doesn't look like there is an overlap between the drug-running and murder charges, so we *could* each try our respective cases. No chance for double jeopardy."

"He has to answer for Billie and Maurice." Piper didn't blink, felt her face coloring with ire.

"Sure. I get you. The murder charges go to court. That's why I will push for taking a different route, *not* divvying it up. We're meeting late this afternoon. We'll compare what we think each of us can get in terms of sentencing. Me on the murders, them on the drugs. Nothing concurrent; murder isn't concurrent. Whoever has the potential for the bigger sentence should take the case, with everyone working together for the greater good. Try him in one place for everything."

"That much meth, possession with intent to distribute. Carries a

charge of ten years to life. That much meth, they'll go for decades."
Piper frowned. "The Feds will end up taking it."

"Lots of drugs. Lots and lots of meth. Hell, yeah, that was a lot of meth," Scales said. "But I doubt the Feds take it. Our two murders would put him away for longer. Dead teenagers? Forever. He'll never breathe free air again. Really, I think he'll end up getting tried for murder *and* the drugs right here, in the courthouse across the street. It's not your problem anymore. Should make you happy."

"Nothing with this case makes me happy." She eased her grip on the mug. "I'm glad we caught him. But there's no happy ending to this."

Scales nodded. "I think the Feds will keep a hand in just long enough to get some information out of Payne, use him to nab the other manufacturers and dealers involved. I guarantee there were others in this operation. They think it might stretch to California or Mexico. In fact, we're not arraigning Payne until Monday because he has some high-powered attorney coming in from California who will pair with a local counsel."

"Others involved." Piper's voice was flat. "That's the reason this department still has a lot of work to do on this, because of the others involved." She noticed Basil in the doorway, hoped he'd been there long enough to hear Scales' explanation about charging Payne.

"The Feds will—"

"—probably not be interested in how Billie and Maurice came to be at the root cellar in the Vincent field, or them stealing a few bags of meth. The Feds don't care about two dead teenagers. They care about the drug trafficking, the whole massive operation. But I care about the two teenagers who were expected at a Halloween party and who were murdered. I care about a mystery man on a black motorcycle who was seen with Payne stealing liquid fertilizer." Much softer: "And I care that all of this was going on in my county."

Scales held up his arms as if in surrender. "When I was a kid, I had this dog."

"You told me you had a lot of dogs when you were a kid."

"Well, Happy Higgins was maybe the most memorable. Big jowls, a bulldog with brown and white spots and crooked teeth. I loved that dog. When he got ahold of something, a rope, stick, my socks, anything, he wouldn't let go. You could tug and tug, and that dog wouldn't give it up, couldn't pry the treasure out of his mouth."

He stood and slipped into his coat. "You remind me of that dog, Sheriff."

After he left, Basil came in. "I'd take that as a compliment."

"That I was compared to a long-dead bulldog?" Piper gave a half-smile. "Anything on the cell phone? Prints?"

Payne's cell phone had been in the backpack, along with four granola bars, an Agatha Christie paperback, *Why Didn't They Ask Evans?*, and a roll of twenties amounting to $400. Ten times that much was in the footlocker under the bed in the root cellar. But there was a lot more somewhere else, given the amount of drugs Payne had been manufacturing and shipping. Maybe an off-shore account; they'd found no bank accounts in the US under Payne's name.

"Burner phone," Basil said.

"I figured as much."

"Recent. It was activated yesterday morning. He made eight calls to three separate numbers in Southern California, no names attached."

"More burners." Piper frowned.

"Plus, three calls to two separate numbers in Kentucky, Owensboro area code." He rolled his shoulders and bent to sniff her flowers. "Those are also burners, no one registered to them. But one of those phones is still active, or was when I tried it several minutes ago."

"Someone answered?"

Basil nodded. "Yeah. A woman's voice, I think. But I couldn't be sure. A lot of background noise, music playing. I got a 'hello, hello,' then a pause, a click, and a dial tone. Tried again, and it just rang. A third try and not even that. Dead."

"Great."

"Tells us someone right across the river from our little spot on the map is involved in the big methamphetamine cache."

Piper felt her heart speed. "Can we get a trace on it, somehow figure out where—"

"Nope."

"Maybe the Feds."

"Probably not. These people are serious pros. Burners they keep for maybe a day, or maybe for only a handful of phone calls."

"Feds found a box of unopened burner phones in the root cellar," Piper said.

"Ever see a show called *The Wire?*"

Piper shook her head.

"Great show, especially the early seasons. The last season, it was about the cell phones. Cop show. You should watch it."

Piper would put it on her list.

"I'm going to spend the afternoon going through the files that were on Payne's laptop, see if I can find some sort of ledger, dig into the websites he'd visited. Maybe we can get something to lead us to the people in Owensboro, maybe find breadcrumbs that will connect to a tall guy on a black motorcycle. I don't know. But I'm going to try," Basil said.

"Oren is taking another look at the kids on our list from the Halloween party, reinterviewing some of them, looking for a connection between Billie Glempse and the Vincent field." Piper drained the rest of her coffee. "I've got Rocco stationed at the root cellar, watching the Feds, recording everything."

"Millie?"

Piper ran her thumbs around the lip of the mug. "She's taking law courses, volunteered to talk to Wallace Langston, see if she can get anything else out of him about Maurice and Billie. Fresh face, fresh voice. Maybe she can shake something lose. I want his lawyer there so nothing comes back to bite us."

She stood and picked up her mug. Time for a refill. "Me? I'm going through body cam footage again. Again. Again. From the Glempse house, from the Langston place, from the Halloween party, your raid on the pot farm, our delve into the root cellar. All of it. Again. Again. There's something still not right. After all of that, I'm going to visit Diego on my way home." She'd check with the hospital and see if she could bring Thresher. The deputy would like seeing the Belgian Malinois, effectively his partner.

She'd also scheduled video chats with experts in Chicago and New York, and had sent them snippets of the body cam footage. That would take some time, those conversations. And then there was the trip to the grocery store before day's end for cat and dog food, sandwich fixings, cereal, and frozen pizzas.

"Sounds like you're going to drink a lot of coffee today, Sheriff."

"Indeed, Detective."

Piper got another mug of Dark Italian and started with the Glempse video. She'd just finished the one from the Langston house and called up Basil's footage from the Hot and Steamy party when Teegan breezed in carrying a big, flattish box.

"You know Zeke figured out who the skeleton is in my attic. Well, the skeleton's at the lab in Evansville, but he was in my attic. My attic. My skeleton. He's doing his big reveal when he's done with his shift. Says I have to wait to find out until then. What the heck, right? It's my skeleton? See if I invite him over again for sub sandwiches."

"I'm anxious to hear what Zeke discovered." Piper truly was. Had he actually cracked the case, when her father with all his years of experience in law enforcement had not yet come up with anything?

"You, I'm inviting over for sub sandwiches. Actually, I could cook for you. I have appliances now. You should come see my new-old house."

"I would like that," Piper returned. "After I'm done working overtime on this murder case."

Teegan held the box above Piper's desk, looking for a place to set it. At the same time, she raised her right leg behind her, hooked the door with her foot, and gave it a kick to shut it.

"For you," Teegan said, grinning broadly and jiggling the box. It did not look terribly heavy. "I cleaned the dust and mouse turds off."

Piper closed her laptop and moved it to the side so Teegan could deposit the box.

The box had been white at one time and now had brown splotches here and there and what looked like mold on one side. It had been fastened shut with a liberal amount of duct tape that looked incongruously new.

"Open it," Teegan urged. "Go on."

Piper wanted to tell her to go away, that she was busy—because she was busy. Teegan had another hour to go before Zeke finished his shift and she started hers. Another hour before Zeke's big reveal about the bones. Teegan could occupy herself in the breakroom with coffee and—

"Go on, Sheriff, open it."

Piper decided to comply. She slipped a pocketknife out of her desk drawer, sliced the duct tape on three sides, pushed off the top, and peeled back the blue tissue paper.

"See, I know you've been looking at bridal magazines, but I figure those dresses are way expensive and that you might rather spend your money on some nice reception and honeymoon. This dress is old, a tad over a hundred years. So, you'd have something old and new at the same time. New because it would be new to you."

"It's a wedding dress."

"Well, duh. And even if I were to someday get married, I could never wear it. I'd never be that little. And if I was that little, I wouldn't wear something that frilly." Teegan plopped down in the chair across from the desk. "It was in my attic. One of the treasures from my fixer-upper. A lot of clothes up there, Halloween costumes mostly. But this wasn't a Halloween costume." She dug in her backpack and pulled out a photo album. "This was worn by Olivia Bullock. And sometime after the wedding it was cleaned and put in that box and stored in my attic. It's a miracle it didn't yellow and get funky."

"Bone white." Piper lifted the dress out of the box.

It was breathtaking. Heavy white satin, lace, ribbon, chiffon ruching.

"You might need to have it adjusted a little, might want to have it cleaned again. Hell, I don't even know if it's your style or if you want—"

"Thank you, Teegan. I love it." Piper did. So many little pearl beads. As fine and fancy as any of the ones she liked in the magazines—the ones that cost hundreds and thousands of dollars. "Honestly, I'm not sure what to say. I can't accept something like this. It is—"

"Of course, you can accept it. I don't know anyone else planning to get married." Teegan paused: "And who's little. Do you think you'll—"

"Wear it? Absolutely."

"Then don't let Nang see it. Supposedly that's bad luck."

Piper thought she was going to cry and so immediately thought about Billie and Maurice, the girl's funeral tomorrow, the man with the ice-blue undead eyes, and all the meth. The cascade of unfortunate images worked well to keep the happy tears in.

"Olivia—"

"—Bullock." Teegan handed over the photo album. "She was originally Olivia Anderson until 1919 when she married James Bullock. They lived in my fixer-upper. Zeke calls it my BFH. Your dad has been calling it my House of Horrors."

"Nothing horrible about this," Piper said, still admiring the dress. "It's perfect."

"Not quite," Teegan said, rising and opening the office door. "I heard you want a lot of sequins. No sequins on that dress."

Piper decided she didn't need sequins after all. She refolded the dress and put it back in the box. "Thank you. Now I have to…"

"Yeah, yeah, just wanted to drop that off," Teegan interrupted. "I'll see you later."

Piper nodded, focusing on her need to find the tall man on a black motorcycle.

And she needed to go through all of the body cam footage a few more times. Something in the video did not sit right with her soul.

CHAPTER THIRTY-FOUR

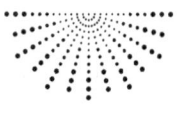

3 P.M.

Z eke kept the breakroom door open so Teegan, seated at the dispatcher desk, could hear his presentation. He knew she was pissed because he wouldn't tell her first about Mr. Bones.

"It's *my* skeleton," she'd argued.

Zeke told her he only wanted to go through his explanation once. Besides, he'd put in all the work, he deserved to revel in the big reveal with an audience.

He'd hoped to use the whiteboard, but it was covered with notes and photographs from the Halloween murders. He found a piece of pale blue posterboard and a big marker, and was satisfied it would work.

As his audience filed into the room—Sheriff Blackwell, Chief Deputy Oren Rosenberg, Basil Meredith, Paul Blackwell, and two Santa Claus police officers who were working on the case—he wrote names on the posterboard in big block letters.

- MEYER WELDON
- REYNOLDS SHEPHERD
- LEROY JOHNSON

- **Dr. Nathan Shepherd**
- **Cooper Anderson & family**
- **Olivia Anderson & James Bullock**
- **David Bullock**
- **Aaron & Rhonda White**
- **Teegan**

"These are all the people who owned the house," Zeke said. "One of them was responsible for putting the skeleton of a man inside a chest and sticking it up in the attic. Excluding Teegan, of course. She did not do it."

"I know all of that." This came from Paul Blackwell.

"Yeah, well, I know *which one of them* put the bones up there. And I know who the bones used to be." Zeke smiled smugly. He could just come out and give them a name, but he'd spent so much time researching, and he'd gotten so little sleep since his investigation started, that he wanted to enjoy this, draw it out as long as practical.

"So, get to it," Paul said. He looked at his watch.

Piper shot her dad a withering look. "I want to hear how Zeke worked this case."

Zeke beamed and pointed to the first name on the list. "Meyer Weldon built the house, but never lived in it. He sold it to the daguerreotypist turned ambrotypist Reynolds Shepherd, who died in the house. He was the first of Teegan's ghosts."

"The house ain't haunted," one of the Santa Claus cops said. The other next to him snickered.

Zeke cleared his throat, pissed that they weren't taking him seriously. "Leroy Johnson, a tent-maker, owned it next. Dr. Nathan Shepherd, no relation to the first Shepherd, bought it and later moved out and sold it to Cooper Anderson, who died in the house of the Spanish Flu ... as did his wife and two kids. Actually, they caught it first and Cooper died after them."

Paul folded his arms and tapped his foot, impatient.

"Cooper, before he gasped his last, willed it to Olivia Anderson. But she didn't stay an Anderson long. Olivia married James Bullock, and this is where I started closing in on the bones. First, I thought the skeleton was James Bullock's. He was a bootlegger and spent time in jail. When he got out, he disappeared."

"Is the skeleton Bullock's?" This from Oren.

Zeke shook his head. "No, whatever happened to James Bullock is a mystery. And I intend to tackle that one next, after I get caught up on my online college courses."

"Get on with it," Paul nudged. "Some of us have to get back to work." He took a noisy slurp of coffee.

"Olivia Anderson-to-Bullock willed the house to her son David Bullock, who was *not* James Bullock's son because he was conceived while James was in prison. Juicy, huh? Especially for back then. Anyway, David was a Mason, a Noble Grand Odd Fellow, a jazz man of some renown, and a composer. He died in an Evansville memory care center in 2020, *after* he sold the house to Aaron and Rhonda White, who died in a car accident before they could convert the property into apartments. The house was willed to Aaron's sister in Florida, who no doubt didn't want to move up here and miss all that sunshine and sea breezes. She sold it via a realtor to Teegan, and took less than what it was worth because just to unload it." He let out a deep breath.

"And—" Paul prompted, tapping his foot again.

"Jazz musician David Bullock was the one who put the skeleton in the chest and dragged it up into the attic when he moved from New York to Spencer County." He circled David's name on the posterboard.

"How do you figure that?" Paul leaned forward in his seat. His expression was a mix of surprise and irritation.

"I did a lot of digging to get this far," Zeke explained. "It took a lot of time to make the David Bullock connection to the bones, including several calls to a nurse at the care center who spent hours with David, even some off-duty days. They shared a mutual love of music, and she got him to start playing the piano again. She accompanied him on the flute. The Evansville paper did an article on them in late 2019. I downloaded a copy and can get it to you."

"Did they also share a love of skeletons and murder?" Oren asked jokingly.

"I don't see where this is going," Paul said.

Piper shot her dad another look.

Zeke scowled. "Ah, come on, this is my thing, let me—"

"—explain," Piper finished. "Of course, we'll let you explain. I'm interested. I want to see how you got to this part and solved it."

"He hasn't solved anything," Paul whispered just loud enough for Zeke to hear.

Zeke took them through all the steps of his investigation, computer searches, phone calls, county records ... all of which a citizen could do without the aid of a badge. Sure, he could've just given them the answer. But he wanted Piper to know how he'd worked the case, like this was his job interview, even though he couldn't yet be a deputy because of his age.

"My arrow pointed to David Bullock because after all my digging I went back up into Teegan's attic and took another look around. At everything. Decorations. I'd never seen so many Christmas decorations in one place, outside of the Christmas store in Santa Claus."

"Halloween decorations, too," Teegan stood in the doorway. "Easter, Valentine's Day. But the skeleton was real, not a Halloween decoration."

"And costumes. A lot of costumes. Mostly kid Halloween costumes," Zeke said. He saw Teegan tip her head toward the desk, listening for any calls. He decided to speed it up so she could hear the end before someone dialed 9-1-1 and chased her back to work. "Some of the costumes were for adults and were elaborate, well-made, expensive material."

Zeke drew another circle around David Bullock. "They looked like the stuff you'd wear in a theatrical production. Or that you'd wear in a play performed at an Odd Fellows ceremony."

He noticed that Paul looked more interested now.

"David Bullock was helping set up an Odd Fellows museum in New York, but it fell through. I don't know why, and I didn't bother to pursue that part of it, as it wasn't pertinent to my investigation." He figured that last bit made him sound official. "But David brought a lot of the things that were marked for the museum to his home in Spencer County. He intended to join a local Odd Fellows group and donate the stuff to them."

"There isn't one," Oren put in. "A local Odd Fellows group."

"Correct. He joined the Masons instead. I guess he just liked being part of one of those fraternal orders. He let the Odd Fellows stuff gather dust in the attic. The costumes, and some other Odd Fellow memorabilia that were under them." Zeke stepped forward and put his right hand in his pocket, pulling out a folded piece of paper. "Including the skeleton. The Odd Fellows talk about mortality in some of their ceremonies, and some Odd Fellows halls have real skeletons on display to remind the members of their mortality."

"The skeleton in my attic—" Teegan began.

"—was once a gentleman named Dwight Brue," Zeke finished. He opened the paper. "Dwight Thomas Brue, 64, of Bayside Terrace, New York, died peacefully in his sleep Wednesday, January 7th, 1935. He'd been treated months earlier for a heart attack, so the coroner listed heart attack as the cause of death. Brue was born in Eckert, Colorado, to Arlo and Eve Clark Brue, and he graduated from Huron College in Huron, South Dakota, with a degree in mathematics. He moved to New York City in 1915 and taught math at various high schools until he left education to become a successful entrepreneur. He designed and patented a few inventions, which he sold to a Fortune 500 company and gave him enough cash to buy a big brownstone in an upscale neighborhood, where he enjoyed the view until his death. Brue was a kindhearted, fun-loving man who was active in the Odd Fellows, attaining the rank of Noble Grand."

Zeke folded the paper. "It goes on. It's a rather long obituary. Anyway, he donated his body to science, and once the doctors were done with it, the bones were bleached, put together, and given to the Odd Fellows. Brue's will dictated that his skeleton should be displayed at a local hall. I contacted some of the New York lodges and found the one he'd belonged to. Though closed, it kept meticulous paperwork that wasn't too difficult to access. Brue's skeleton was handed over to

David Bullock for his museum when that lodge shuttered. Oh, and about a year before Brue's death, he fell and broke his leg and fractured his jaw. Dr. Neufeld told me the skeleton showed evidence of having had a broken right leg that had healed and had a cracked jaw. Bingo. Brue's got some relatives in Colorado, descendants of his brothers. If you need to check DNA on the bones, you can go that route. I've gone about as far as I can without having a badge."

"So, it wasn't a murder," Teegan said. Zeke thought she sounded a little disappointed. "The guy wasn't killed in my house."

"Oh, you had plenty of people die in your BFH of natural causes," Zeke returned. "But not this one."

"Well done." Piper stood and started clapping.

CHAPTER THIRTY-FIVE

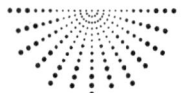

10 A.M., SATURDAY NOV 7TH

I t's different when a young person dies," Piper contended. "My opinion. My experience."

She stood with her back against the Explorer on a narrow road that wound like a twisty ribbon through the cemetery. Nearby, a crowd had gathered on the lawn for Billie Glempse's funeral.

"Disagree," Basil said next to her. "My experience. My opinion. I think dead is dead. Young, old. Doesn't matter how many years you have on the earth. Everyone ends up dead. It just matters what you do with the living years." A pause: "And whether your survivors decide to turn you to ash or buy you a plot in a cemetery or give your bones to the Odd Fellows."

"You're in a cheery mood."

"Pretty much matches yours, Sheriff."

"I think death for the young is different. All of this is different." Piper waved a hand to indicate the mourners. "The visitations and funerals. Who attends, who can't because they're already below ground or too infirm. I attended Mark Thresher's—Mark the Shark's —funeral, and only a handful of people came. He was in his nineties, and all of his contemporaries were gone. It seems the longer a person lives, the lower the attendance at things like this."

"I'd say you haven't been to enough funerals to make that general-ization."

"I've been to too many funerals in the past year, lost some friends who were in the Army. It just stings and stinks at the same time. Young friends. It's different."

"Okay. I get you. Yeah, this part of it is different, the ceremony of death. Unless you're talking about someone important or well known in the community, you're right. In general, the younger the victim, the larger the crowd. Gotta be about two hundred here."

"A lot of these same folks were at the visitation last night." Piper had attended that, too. She'd gotten there when it started, sat at the back, and intently watched each person file in and out of the chapel. She wasn't sure what she was looking for, and she hadn't found anything worth noting. Then she'd gone home and watched the body cam footage again, the images permanent in her head.

Nothing stood out about the people here this morning, except for their grief.

Mourners of all ages spread across a lawn covered in brown leaves, gathered in little clumps, voices buzzing. The teenagers and friends who knew Billie made up the bulk of the attendees. Dressed casually, many in blue jeans, some wearing school jackets and football sweat-shirts, they made a colorful splash among the dark garb of the adult mourners. One carried a cheerleader pom-pom, which she placed on the casket next to a massive spray of flowers. Piper picked up pieces of their conversations.

"Do you remember that night Billie was the top of the cheer pyramid?"

"How about when she forgot her locker number twice in the same week?"

"She was nuts about Maurice, wasn't she? Too old for her."

"Do you think she felt it? Dying? Do you think she went fast?"

"I wonder if she's in heaven, or if she went to hell 'cause she cheated on the big math test. I almost turned her in. She told me she bought the answers."

"Do you think they'll replace her on the cheer squad, or leave it one short?"

Billie's parents and relatives sat at the front of the crowd in folding chairs, all somberly attired—black suits, black dresses, black coats, black hats and shoes. Heads down. Quiet.

She assumed the remaining adults, dressed primarily in gray, black, and dark blue were friends of the parents, or were perhaps neighbors and business associates. Billie's great-grandmother wore a sad expression in contrast with her paisley coat that stood out in the sea of solid colors. She leaned on twin canes and stood in front of a wheelchair.

The multitude of flower arrangements represented about half of what had been at the visitation; she could smell them from yards away. So many flowers for the dead. *Flowers should be for the living*, she thought, picturing the bouquet from Nang on her desk.

There were no flowers for Maurice Langston. Maurice had been cremated, at his brother's request. Neither Piper nor authorities in Florida had been able to find Wallace and Maurice's father, who may or may not be "somewhere in or around Orlando or Daytona."

Wallace Langston intended to put his brother's ashes on the shelf next to their mother's urn. But it might be quite a while, since Wallace would serve time on drug charges. Who knew what was going to happen to the house in the meantime? She also wondered who would take charge of the ashes until Wallace was free. The funeral home? She'd look into it, take them herself, keep them safe until Wallace got out.

Piper watched the wind tease the clothes and hair of the people gathered. The teenage girls wrapped their jackets tight. She heard a few of them crying.

Piper felt like crying.

She'd never met Billie Glempse, but all of this made her sad. The murders, the drugs, it had sucked all the happy out of Spencer County and directed her thoughts to the many unfortu-nate things that had happened in her own life. Her dad's health struggles, Mark the Shark murdered, her military friends killed while on a weekend away at Jerusalem Ridge, Diego in a hospital bed.

The throng quieted.

The minister's voice carried, stirring Piper's melancholy. He talked about Billie's accomplishments in her sixteen years, how much she meant to people, her love of koalas and cheerleading, and that she was in heaven now, fashion-designing for the angels.

Piper thought the sermons different, too. The older the person who died, the more material the minister had to work with. Billie's obituary in the paper had been brief. Maurice Langston had only a two-sentence death notice.

If heaven existed, maybe Billie and Maurice were together again, dancing like they should have at the Halloween party. Tinker Bell and Captain Hook forever twirling, all the green sequins shimmering like stars.

"There's Dr. Frank N. Furter," Basil said, pointing to a teenager in a cluster, a head taller than his companions.

"From the party."

"Yeah. I bet a lot of these kids were at the party, just can't recognize all of them. Costumes were impressive and concealing. But I'm pretty sure that's Freddie Krueger standing next to Mary Poppins. And I think those two are Bullwinkle and a Roman Centurion."

"There's a brunch at the church," Piper said. "I think I've seen enough between the visitation and this. I'll pass on the brunch, but I'm sending Oren. I didn't see a big black motorcycle in the parking lot last night. Or here."

"But maybe at the brunch?"

Piper shrugged. "I had a dream last night that the rider would show up, pay his respects."

"We have more than a hundred names of people in this county, Owensboro, and Evansville, Vanderburgh County, who are registered with black or blue motorcycles and dirt bikes. Going to take a while to see if we can come up with a link from a bike to the fertilizer theft. And it's a big 'if,' since we don't have a visual of the rider's face. And his partner, Simon Payne, isn't talking. Besides, the bike could well have been stolen, making it damn near impossible to find Payne's partner. It could have been repainted."

"Payne isn't talking *yet*. But maybe at the brunch Oren will find a black motorcycle," Piper said. "Probably not, still worth a try. And at the very least, the chief deputy should get a good meal."

Basil tipped his head back and closed his eyes briefly. "You know, Sheriff, the Feds will pursue the drugs, the people involved. They'll probably find the guy and the motorcycle you're obsessing about, find a lot of people connected to the meth ring. Put a lot of people away."

Piper thrust her hands in her pockets and stared at a group of teenagers. "I suspect they will. They'll get Simon Payne to give up the names of his associates in exchange for something, maybe for better prison accommodations. Scales tells me Payne will never get out. So, yeah, eventually they'll probably find the man on the black motorcycle, but—"

"But you don't want to wait for them to do it."

"Call me Happy Higgins," she said with a half-smile. "I can't let go of it. And we're close, Detective."

"We're close because you have a bulldog grip."

"I figure the brunch will wrap up by two. I have some paperwork that will keep me busy until then."

"There'll be more paperwork after we stop at the Glempse house," Basil said.

"We should get it all wrapped up in time for an early dinner." She looked away from the assembly. "I'm going to the Quick Stop tonight, meeting my dad there. Nang's cooking. Would you, Esme, and the kids like to join us? My treat. A break from this …. A break from all of this."

"I'll check with her. But I think yes. Some spring rolls might make this day seem less bitter."

CHAPTER THIRTY-SIX

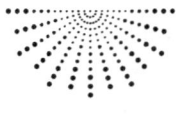

3 P.M.

Piper and Basil sat out front of the Glempse house until three. That was when the last of the cars pulled away. They turned on their body cams and walked up the front steps.

Sandra Glempse, still in her designer black dress, opened the door. "Sheriff, Detective. I saw you at the funeral. Thank you for—"

"May we come in?" Piper asked.

Sandra looked over her shoulder. "Bob, the sheriff is here. Bob! Maybe she has news about Billie's killer."

Piper watched him come down the stairs. He'd changed into blue jeans and a casual sweater. His eyes were red with dark circles beneath them; the visage of sorrow.

"I've not met you," Robert said to Basil, as he gestured them into the living room.

"Detective Basil Meredith," Piper introduced them and watch them shake hands. "We have a few questions, Mr. Glempse, Mrs.—"

"We just buried Billie," Robert said. "Unless you have news about the scum who killed my daughter, now is not the time to—"

"We gave you time to bury your daughter," Basil cut in. "We didn't have to do that."

Robert's mouth dropped open. "I suppose if you have to bother us."

"I hope this won't take long," Sandra said. "I have to pick up the children from the sitter's."

"It won't take long," Piper replied. She and Basil took the high-backed chairs, leaving the couch to Robert and Sandra.

"Would you like coffee? Lemonade?" Sandra asked.

Piper shook her head. She recalled the sugarless lemonade she'd had here days ago.

"It was a nice service, don't you think?" Robert asked. "A lot of Billie's friends were there. All of our neighbors."

Piper looked past him and noted the Billie shrine still in the kitchen, a few more mementos added to it. A candle burned.

"A nice service," Piper agreed.

"So, what do you need? What can you tell us about that piece of—"

"Robert—" Sandra cautioned.

"Sorry. I'm glad you caught the man who killed my Billie," Robert continued. "I heard it on the radio this morning. He should get the death penalty. Indiana doesn't have that, but it should. He should die. What can you tell us about him? About how you caught him?"

Sandra patted his arm. "I'm sure she'll tell us."

"He should fry. But nothing done to him will make it better," Robert said. "It won't bring my Billie back."

"How did you catch the man?" Sandra asked. "How did you find him? And a crossbow. Why a crossbow? Is he talking? Confessed?"

"Silent. A crossbow is silent. You don't need a license to buy one, like you do a gun." Piper shifted her gaze to Sandra, noticed that her sapphire earrings matched a heart-shaped pin on the collar of her dress. Tasteful jewelry, the stones beautifully cut to look like teardrops. "Billie led us to her killer. We followed the course she took Halloween night, out to a root cellar hidden in Vincent's field."

"A farm field?" Robert leaned forward. "You caught my daughter's killer on a farm?"

"That part of the field was rented by Wesley Johnson. And we just confirmed today that Johnson is your older brother, Mrs. Glempse.

Your husband had mentioned Billie's great-grandmother lived in Owensboro, her Uncle Wes, too."

"Small world," Sandra said, her voice soft. "I haven't seen Wes since—"

"—two days ago," Piper finished.

Sandra puffed up, anger suddenly lighting her eyes. "You should leave now, Sheriff Blackwell. I don't want you in our—"

"Wesley lives near the downtown area, in a big apartment over a pharmacy." Basil took a turn. "It's only two blocks from where you work part-time for an accounting firm."

Sandra glared. "My family is none of your business, Sheriff—"

Basil went on: "Billie's killer made calls to two different cell phones in Owensboro the day we arrested him. Burners. Difficult to track, but not impossible. We have another warrant, Mrs. Glempse. Are we going to find one of those burners in this house?"

Robert Glempse stood, mouth soundlessly working, looking indecisive about who he should yell at and what he should do. He wrung his hands and glanced between his wife and Piper. Then he peered over his shoulder to Billie's shrine on the counter.

Sandra Glempse squeezed her hands into fists. "You will leave now, both of you. Or I will call—"

"The Rockport Police?" Basil asked.

"Or the FBI?" Piper added, hoping Sandra wasn't intending to call an attorney just yet. "There are several FBI agents in town. You'll probably have a chance to meet all of them."

Robert found his voice. "What the hell is this about? What are you talking about? Implying? What do you—"

"Mr. Glempse, your wife, and probably her brother Wesley Johnson ... does he have a big black motorcycle by the way?" She noticed one of the family photos on a side table showed Sandra and a tall man standing in front of a black motorcycle with blue trim.

Robert nodded.

Piper stood and pulled her handcuffs. "Your wife is involved with selling methamphetamines. A multi-million-dollar operation, part of which was operating out of Vincent's field."

"Th-th-that's not possible." Robert's hands trembled and his jaw clenched. He fought for breath. "You've made a mistake. You're awful people. Mistaken. Lying."

"Now we have to figure out if you're involved as well," Basil said to Robert.

"A mistake. A horrible mistake. I could sue you," Robert said. "I *will* sue."

Piper continued to stare at Sandra. "Billie was out in Vincent's field Halloween night, on her way to the steampunk party. She and Maurice had stopped at the cellar to grab a bag of meth or two for Maurice's brother. She'd done it at least once before. But this time Simon Payne saw them."

"No." Sandra placed her hands on her stomach and cast her eyes down. She rocked forward and Piper thought the woman would throw up.

Robert continued to stammer and sob.

"We figure Billie had either been with you on one of your trips there, Mrs. Glempse, or overheard you talking with Payne and your brother." Piper hadn't wanted to be right, but the pieces had fallen into place with the family photograph, and with the framed art on the walls. "You bought the jeep, Mrs. Glempse, because you needed a vehicle that could ride over the rough ground out to the cellar. You'd broke the axle of your Mustang convertible trying to drive it on that access road."

Sandra cried, no sound coming out, just tears pouring and bleeding black streaks of mascara down her cheeks. Robert's lips moved, mumbling, sobbing louder. His frame shook like he'd plunged into ice water.

"It was lucrative, doing business with Payne," Piper went on. "Your designer clothes and shoes. Your beautiful jewelry. That's why I had to watch the footage of my walk-through of your house. Over and over and over. Something didn't sit right, and it took too long for me to figure it out. Your clothes, shoes, jewelry, they're expensive. Your tennis shoes that you wore Halloween? Google says they cost six hundred dollars. What woman spends that kind of money on casual tennis shoes? Robert's clothes don't carry designer labels. We've been through your closets, remember. Billie had some Versace dresses on her rack. The girl had diamond earrings, too. Expensive stuff you bought your bonus kid. Her steampunk Tinker Bell outfit was pricey as far as Halloween costumes go. I know actuaries make a lot of money, but you're part-time. These riches are well above a part-time actuary paygrade."

"Versace?" Robert whispered. "Versace? I don't understand what that—"

Piper crossed her arms. "All of that is more than you can afford working part-time, Sandra. And more than you can afford on Robert's ninety-two thousand a year salary."

Robert fell back onto the couch and shivered. "You're wrong," he sobbed. "You're making this up. I'll sue. I'll—"

"He's not in on it is he?" Piper asked, gesturing to Robert. "Sandra, you kept him clueless. Somehow he didn't know."

A silence swelled in the living room, eerie and odd. Finally, Sandra broke it.

"No, he didn't know. He works too damn many hours, is away too many hours to know." Her voice was a whisper. "He doesn't know any of it. Clothes ... how could you have noticed, Sheriff? How would someone like you recognize their worth? How could you have thought I was getting money other than working for an accountant?"

"I probably wouldn't have made the connection on the clothes alone," Piper admitted, inwardly thanking her love of *Project Runway* and New York Fashion Week. "It was the art. When I stopped here Halloween night, I admired some of the pieces. Robert said the décor was all your doing." She pointed to a colorful, somber painting that hung across from the dining room table. "That's an original Frida Kahlo."

"Who?" This from a still-sobbing Robert.

"Frida Kahlo, a famous artist who lived a relatively short life. I talked to experts at the Art Institute of Chicago and the Metropolitan Museum of Art in New York yesterday. They said it looks original, like the one auctioned a year-and-a half ago for twenty-eight million, though they would have to see it in person to be certain, to validate it. You don't strike me as someone who is into reproductions, Mrs. Glempse. It was bought by a proxy of S. E. Johnson." A pause: "Before you married Robert Glempse, your last name was Johnson. Sandra Elizabeth Johnson."

"Millions," Robert said. "We don't have art worth millions. We don't have anything worth millions. Sandra told me she found those pieces at Goodwill across the river. This is all a mistake."

Sandra sucked in a breath, looking wholly defeated. "I like art. Fine art. Originals." Her voice was so soft Piper barely heard her. "I like nice things."

Piper kept going. "You have other original pieces in your house, Mrs. Glempse, including a small Jackson Pollock in your bedroom. Another Kahlo hanging in the upstairs hall. More millions and millions. You put your wealth on the walls and in your jewelry box. Hiding an ill-gotten fortune in plain sight. Saves you from dealing with banks. I have no idea how you've managed to avoid detection, avoided paying taxes on all this stuff."

"She's good with numbers," Robert said gently. "She's brilliant."

"Hiding her wealth in plain sight," Piper repeated.

"How the hell could you—a pissant sheriff in a pissant county—notice the art? How the hell could you? Nobody else in this backwater place noticed, *could* notice." Sandra seethed and rubbed her stomach like it was a magic lamp. "There's nothing refined about you, nothing cultured. Hell, I read about you … high school diploma, and not close to the top of your class. Why you're—"

"What did you do for Payne and your brother Wesley?" Basil interrupted.

Piper knew Sandra wasn't one of the chemists, as they'd detected no methamphetamine anywhere in this house, and there would have been at least some trace if she'd cooked or handled the drug.

"What was your role?" Basil pressed.

Piper waited for either of them to ask for an attorney.

"Bookkeeping basically," Sandra answered, signaling her surrender. "Wes brought me into their circle. All I did was manage the accounts and track shipments, theirs and some others. For years. I never sold the stuff. Never. I never used the stuff. For years and years, I just did the numbers. I never touched the awful stuff. I took Billie with me one time. *One damn time.*"

"When was that?" Piper asked.

Sandra seemed not to have heard her. "And we didn't go *in* the cellar, just waited in the car while I passed the records on a jump drive to Wes. Payne didn't even come out that day to talk. Billie could not have known what was going on out there." She smoothed the fabric over her stomach and gulped in air. "One damn time. My brother and Payne, we used to meet at bars In Owensboro. Then Payne got skittish. Something shook him about a year ago. He started wanting to meet at the mound, nowhere public. I drove out there once in my Mustang, with Billie, and the road tore the hell out of my car. Bob believed I went up over a curb and Billie kept her mouth shut. I bought her nice earrings not to say anything. Bob didn't question me. Bob always believed me. I had to get the jeep. It could get out there. One damn time Billie was with me. Just once. Why the hell did she go back? She was a good girl, didn't do drugs. I'd know if she did drugs."

Sandra wailed. "When Payne called a few days ago, told me he killed Billie, I almost called you, almost turned him in. He said he didn't know she was my daughter. Just said he killed her because she stole, knew where the lab was. Killed the wild boy, too. I almost called you."

"But that would have implicated you," Piper said.

"Where can we find your brother, Mrs. Glempse?" Basil asked. "He's not at his apartment. Where does he like to go?"

Between sobs, she gave them a few addresses.

Piper remained silent on the ride back to the station. Basil drove, the Glempses secured in the backseat. She thought about the baby that would be born in prison, about Robert Glempse, who might not be charged with anything and might have to bring up three small children on his own.

Three marriages for Robert Glempse, three strikes. She prayed that he and the kids could get through this, that they could weather

FBI scrutiny, likely tax evasion charges, could handle all the gossip and pointed fingers from the neighbors who had respectfully attended Billie's funeral. She suspected the family would leave Spencer County as soon as possible.

Piper had the taste of sour lemonade in her mouth.

CHAPTER THIRTY-SEVEN

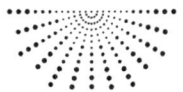

8 P.M., SATURDAY DEC 5TH

Millie glittered in a spangly maroon dress as she danced with a handsome man in a navy suit—Ethan Pendleton, a greeting card artist whom Piper had met only an hour ago.

Oren stood against the wall, intently watching the pair on the dance floor. Piper guessed from Oren's expression he did not approve of Millie's date. The chief deputy had finally told Piper about his pending divorce, and had suggested she not marry Nang. "It won't last," he'd said.

Zeke, Diego, Cartwright, and Paul Blackwell shared a table, all four volunteer designated drivers drinking Mountain Dew. Thresher lay under their table, warily watching everyone.

Teegan perched on a stool, Tug leaning over the bar in front of her, their faces inches apart, engrossed in a conversation hidden by the music of a bluegrass band. Teegan had served as Piper's maid of honor, and she looked radiant in a pale purple gown, sleeveless to show her tattoos in all their colorful glory.

The Thirsty Turtle had hung up a "closed" sign. It was invitation only for Piper and Nang's wedding reception.

Tug, Basil, and Esme had decorated ... streamers, fairy lights, silver garlands, and flowers everywhere. Each table had an impressive display of carnations and roses, bouquets for the living.

Esme and Basil glided onto the dance floor and pressed close, looking wholly elegant. The photographer snapped their picture, then stepped to the buffet counter and grabbed a plate. The Quick Stop had catered part of the reception: spring rolls, chicken pho, shrimp fried rice. The Turtle offered the rest: hot dogs with sauerkraut, hamburgers, onion rings.

The myriad scents of food and flowers hung suspended over the room.

An open bar, the glasses clinked in one toast after another, all of them directed Nang and Piper's way. Nang had won the Cake Bake the previous weekend in Louisville and insisted on picking up the tab for everything with his $10,000 winnings. He would travel to New York City late in May for the national championship. Piper planned to tag along.

He'd made their wedding cake, a big ivory and rose-hued castle with turrets and a drawbridge. Faintly, on the top tier, he'd placed a frosting star in the shape of a sheriff's badge.

The church wedding had been small, friends and family, planned hastily because Piper once again lived up to her impulsive nature.

"Why wait until January?" Piper had asked Nang after Sandra Glempse's arraignment. Bail had been denied. "Life is short. Why should we wait? I have a dress." They could still honeymoon in January, when she hit the one-year mark as sheriff and had some vacation time. A road trip, maybe Route 66, save a few days for New York City and Nang's next baking competition.

"No reason to wait," Nang had replied. "I have a cake recipe and a tux. We shouldn't wait. Life is short."

Life is temporary, she thought, Billie Glempse, Maurice Langston. At least she found them some measure of justice.

"Life ... I want to spend all of it with you," Nang added.

She danced with him, in the middle of the tavern, in the perfect dress Teegan had gifted her from the attic of the BFH. The tables had been pulled back against the walls to provide enough floorspace.

The band broke into "Lady."

Nang's eyes locked with hers. "You shine," he said.

THE END

ACKNOWLEDGMENTS

Piper Blackwell is a good sheriff because of Robert Scales, who provides expert advice on all of her legal issues; Mike Black, a fine writer and former police officer, who knows all the ins and outs of law enforcement; and Bill Gilsdorf, who helped shape her from the beginning and taught her how to properly wear a badge.

Thanks also to Vicki Steger, the best beta-reader ever.

The Kenosha Writers' Group for being an awesome sounding board—Steve Sullivan, Christine Verstraete, Steve Rouse, and Warren Langlois.

Brian Hopkins for providing the motorcycles.

And Echo Shea and Mindy Mymudes for their incredible promotions, friendship, support, and for loving dogs.

SPENCER COUNTY, INDIANA

It's a real place, about as far south in Indiana as you can go. The towns, roads, and some of the businesses I reference in this novel exist. There really is a Santa Claus—it's nestled between the Ohio River and Interstate 64. On my visit to the Christmas store there I picked up some walnut fudge and a Boston terrier ornament that I had personalized with Missy's name. Rockport is about twenty miles away from Santa Claus, and is where the real Sheriff's Department sits. I've fictionalized the county, taking considerable liberties. I used to live in Indiana—Evansville, during my newspaper reporter days. Spencer County isn't far from there. The place is a good home for Piper Blackwell and company. I also took some liberties with Jerusalem Ridge and Horse Branch, KY, real places thick with bluegrass music and mosquitoes and lacking cell phone service.

ABOUT THE AUTHOR

I write…a lot.

I write with dogs wrapped around my feet. I get to wear sandals or bedroom slippers to work, and old, comfortable clothes. When the weather is fine, I write on my back porch. I love summer. I started getting published when I was twelve, studied journalism at Northern Illinois University, and then went to work as a news reporter…eventually for Scripps Howard, where I managed their Western Kentucky bureau. Getting itchy feet, I moved to Wisconsin and worked for TSR, Inc., the then-producers of the Dungeons & Dragons game. I wrote Dragonlance tales for several years and reached the *USA Today's* Bestseller list with a few of them.

I've written forty-some novels (along with a couple of ghosted projects … shhh!), more than a hundred short stories, and I've edited more magazines and anthologies than I care to count. Right now, it's all about mysteries…thrillers, suspense, and uncozy-cozies.

I am a recipient of the Faust, the Grand Master Award from the International Association of Media Tie-In Writers. My novel, *The Bone Shroud*, won the 2019 Soon To Be Famous Illinois Author Project competition. And *The Love-Haight Case Files*, that I wrote with Donald J. Bingle, hit #1 on Amazon. That about sums up my writing accomplishments, more than enough to Snoopy dance about.

I attend game conventions–I am a geek about boardgames and RPGs, visit interesting and quirky museums, and at every reasonably good opportunity I toss tennis balls for my cadre of dogs. Writers and dogs go great together. Mine get me away from the keyboard and show me how very important it is to chase butterflies.

Visit me at www.jeanrabe.com.

www.ingramcontent.com/pod-product-compliance
Lightning Source LLC
Chambersburg PA
CBHW061944170626
46813CB00006B/2522